Summer Fridays

Also by Suzanne Rindell

• • •

The Two Mrs. Carlyles
Eagle & Crane
Three-Martini Lunch
The Other Typist

Summer Fridays

A Novel

Suzanne Rindell

DUTTON

DUTTON
An imprint of Penguin Random House LLC
penguinrandomhouse.com

LIBRARY OF CONGRESS CATALOGING-IN-PUBLICATION DATA
Names: Rindell, Suzanne, author.
Title: Summer Fridays: a novel / Suzanne Rindell.
Description: [New York]: Dutton, an imprint of Penguin Random House LLC, 2024.
Identifiers: LCCN 2023040182 (print) | LCCN 2023040183 (ebook) |
ISBN 9780593473917 (trade paperback) | ISBN 9780593473924 (ebook)
Subjects: LCGFT: Romance fiction. | Novels.
Classification: LCC PS3618.I538 S86 2024 (print) |
LCC PS3618.I538 (ebook) | DDC 813/.6—dc23/eng/20230908
LC record available at https://lccn.loc.gov/2023040182
LC ebook record available at https://lccn.loc.gov/2023040183

Printed in the United States of America
1st Printing

Title page art: Brooklyn Bridge © vectorcity / Shutterstock

BOOK DESIGN BY ALISON CNOCKAERT

Summer Fridays

New York City

• • •

2001

1.

When her eyes catch on the little clock on the far wall beyond her desk, she realizes it's already ten past noon.

She gets a sudden urge: she wants to take her bag lunch outside and eat it in the park. This seems wrong, to a certain extent—but then, everything seems wrong lately. Every time she scans the newspaper headlines or opens her email, she reads of another event canceled. It seems that no one feels right doing anything but staying home and feeling not right.

She glances at the clock again, and makes up her mind. She wants to be reminded of things that are simple: Trees. Sky. Birds. Squirrels. Bench. The way the park path bends around a big brownish-gray boulder. Things that haven't changed, in a time when it feels like everything will never be the same.

From her office, it is a short walk to the southwest corner of Central Park. There are fewer people out than there would normally be in mid-September. No drummer guy merrily tapping away on his plastic buckets, no flower guy with the blue roses, ink stains on his fingers. But there are still a couple of snack vendors hunched over the stainless steel carts that are their livelihood, looking guilty for selling hot dogs. A handful of people dressed in office attire, clutching giant pretzels and cans of diet soda. Even a few joggers intent on a return to normalcy.

She walks a little bit of the way into the park—just to the bend in the path she was longing to see—and finds a bench in the shade.

People pass by. A middle-aged woman pushing a stroller. A man walking a golden retriever with reddish-tinged fur. An off-duty doorman smoking a cigarette, sweating under his heavy uniform.

After a while, two girls come along and settle into the opposite end of the bench, a polite distance away from her. She takes out a book and pretends to read it, between bites of her lunch. Potato salad that she made herself—extra dill. She eats the salad out of a Tupperware bowl with a plastic spork from the office kitchen.

She listens to the girls talk. They are young. She is young, too—probably only a few years older than them—but somehow they are youthful in a way that makes her feel already slightly invisible.

So, just like that, he's back in touch? one of them asks the other.

Yes, the first girl replies. *He wrote a long email. I got it that night. It was really sincere, actually.*

He said the attacks made him think of you?

Well, yeah, I mean—in a roundabout way. He said it just put things in perspective. Made him think about what's important.

Ah. So: you, the friend says in an approving voice.

I guess so, the girl replies.

Will you get back together?

I don't know, the girl says. *We might.*

Hmm, the friend says.

After a pause, the girl adds, *The thing is . . . I was thinking of him, too, when it happened. I know his office isn't downtown and there shouldn't be any reason he would have been in the area, but I still just . . . found myself thinking of him. Wanting to know he was OK. And wanting to talk to him again, I guess.*

I guess it says something if you were both thinking of each other, the friend says.

Yeah, the girl agrees. *We'll see. I'm meeting him tonight for a drink.*

The friend giggles.

The girl doesn't laugh. She gives a furtive, self-conscious glance across the bench. *I kinda feel like a jerk, talking about my love life right now,* she confesses to her friend. *You know . . . with everything else going on in the city . . . in the world.*

Nah. What the hell else are we going to talk about? her friend points out. *The rest is too depressing.*

• • •

Eventually, the girls get up and walk on, leaving her alone on the bench again. The potato salad is all gone and she isn't pretending to read a book anymore. A glance at her watch tells her she ought to be heading back to her office.

On her walk back, she gets to thinking. She's overheard the same thing a few times now—it's in the air. People getting back in touch with old friends, old acquaintances, and old flames. *Are you OK?* they ask each other. *I was thinking of you. I hope you're OK. I wanted to hear your voice.*

At her desk, she replies to a few work emails, forwarding an early review of a novel to the book's author and cc'ing her boss, then responding to the marketing department, mostly to agree with the marketing director about which bits from the review make for the best pull quotes.

Then she sits for a moment, staring vacantly into the even, bluish-white glow of the computer screen, lost in thought again.

After a moment, she clicks on Internet Explorer and brings up the web portal for her personal email. She logs in, and clicks on the envelope icon to start a new email message. She doesn't type in the address, not yet. She clicks on the body of the email. *Start there,* she thinks.

The blank message glows brilliantly white and empty, its cursor blinking like a character tapping their foot in a cartoon.

She stares for a long time. Minutes pass. She isn't sure how many. The message remains empty. The cursor blinks in place, having never moved.

Finally, she closes the blank message, then the browser window altogether.

New York City

. . .

1999

2.

FRIDAY, MAY 28

The first surprise of the evening came when Charles didn't have an opinion about her dress.

Sawyer knew that plenty of men didn't have opinions about what their girlfriends wore, but Charles was not one of those men. He liked nice things. He respected style and admired design. Granted, he possessed a much wider array of in-depth opinions about men's fashion than he did about women's fashion—but either way, he had *opinions*.

Although Sawyer didn't necessarily agree with *all* of Charles's opinions, she appreciated that he always had one. A year earlier, when Charles first started as a junior associate at Wexler Gibbons, he'd been acutely sensitive to the fact that landing a spot at the prestigious corporate law firm had been like winning the lottery, and he'd wanted badly to make a good impression. He'd had plenty to say about what they *both* wore to company events. They'd made a ritual of it: Sawyer tried on the various possibilities and emerged from the bedroom in the back of their apartment to show him. Charles waited for her to ask what he thought, then proceeded to give her the carefully considered input of a true friend. Sawyer was grateful. Living in New York in your twenties meant trying to make your way in a mind-bogglingly expensive city while simultaneously paying off student loans. Looking the part on a budget required strategy, and having a huddle with your other half made it more fun.

So, when Sawyer pulled out the two dresses she was considering from their closet and held the hangers aloft to show Charles, she was thrown off to hear him say (after barely glancing at the dresses), "They both look nice."

She tried one on. Then, the other.

"Sure. Whichever you like; they both look great."

It was like a cliché scene in a movie: the husband's flat, comical indifference to his wife's appearance, the wife's alienated frown.

This isn't who we are, Sawyer's brain protested, with a hint of indignance. They'd gotten engaged less than a year ago; they were hardly an old married couple. Usually, getting dressed up for a night out was an occasion to flirt, a chance to hint that there might be sex later.

But having changed out of both dresses, Sawyer stood there in her underwear, frowning through the open bedroom door to where Charles sat in the other room. He didn't look up, not once. His attention was wholly trained on his company-issued laptop. The IBM ThinkPad was cracked open on the kitchen table, a heavy black clamshell with thuggish rectangular angles. Sawyer squinted, already knowing what she was likely to see—she could just barely make out a work-related legal document glowing on the screen.

She sighed and turned her attention back to the two discarded dresses now lying on top of the bed. One was powder blue, with cap sleeves. The other was black, with spaghetti straps that sat tautly on Sawyer's prominent collarbones. One was Jackie, the other was Marilyn. If Charles had actually looked at either dress when she'd tried them on for him, Sawyer knew he would have picked the Jackie.

Sawyer studied the two choices. Then, casting another frowning glance at Charles, she picked up the black dress with a hint of defiance and slipped it over her head. It had a slinky weight to it, and splashed down over the curves of her body like water. She took a moment to examine herself in the mirror, smoothing the fabric over her waist and hips and fiddling with the straps, wondering if she was actually brave enough to wear it.

The phone rang, its shrill cry seemingly able to snap Charles to attention when moments ago Sawyer had failed to coax more than a glance. He jumped up and grabbed the receiver from the kitchen wall.

"Hey—our car is downstairs," he said. "Ready?"

"Just need to slip on shoes, throw a few things into my bag. Is it cold out?"

"Nah. It's pretty much summer now. But who knows, bring a coat; it might get cold later."

• • •

Whenever they were invited to a company event, Charles insisted they skip the train, and not just take a cab, but splurge on a car service. Tonight, he'd used the one they usually reserved for picking up her parents at the airport, the one with the phone number that ended in all sixes—hopefully that wasn't an omen of anything in particular.

The car smelled of air freshener; the drive downtown was quiet. Sawyer gazed out the window, hypnotized by the city streets whizzing by. And then they were there, squeezing between the narrow streets of the old Dutch version of New York and being dropped off at Cipriani, the neoclassical columns of the restaurant brilliantly bathed in a regal gold-and-purple-colored series of floodlights that seemed to have been selected especially for the evening.

They stepped out, climbed the stairs, and went inside.

It was immediately obvious: the whole place had been shut down, reconfigured, and was now decked out for the Wexler Gibbons corporate dinner. In fact, it was less like a "dinner" and more like a gala of some sort. A band played in one corner. Hors d'oeuvres circulated on silver trays. There were items up for bid via a silent auction, raising money for children's literacy. Campaign posters sporting blown-up photographs of adorable children holding books and pencils proudly announced that the firm gave millions annually to a well-known national foundation.

The building itself dripped with old-money intimidation: more neoclassical arches and columns, echoing marble, and an ornate, gold-laid coffered ceiling crowned with a Wedgwood dome at the center of it all.

"Wow," Sawyer said, immediately wishing that she'd opted for the powder-blue dress. They'd checked their coats. There was no going back now.

"I think we're over here," Charles said, steering Sawyer to one of countless tables wrapped with a white linen cloth tied with a purple satin bow. It was surrounded by a milling cluster of Wexler Gibbons's younger, ambitious-looking employees. Charles hovered, squinting at the place cards.

No one was sitting yet. After a moment, Sawyer became dimly aware that Charles merely wanted to verify his position in the room. And verify who would be sitting near him. Sawyer followed his gaze.

The place card next to his read "*Kendra Larson.*"

• • •

The name "Kendra" put Sawyer in mind of a Ken doll—which was rather fitting, actually, because there was something Barbie-like about Kendra's beauty that was simultaneously athletic and masculine. She was tanner and blonder than a New Yorker had any right to be, with broad shoulders and a strong jawline, and she carried herself like a beach volleyball player.

When Kendra took her place at the table next to Charles, she introduced her boyfriend. Sawyer caught the name over Charles's shoulder—*Nick Something-or-Other*—and once everyone had been introduced, Charles and Kendra turned toward each other and more or less didn't turn back for the rest of the night.

It was the second surprise of the evening. Charles knew that company dinners made Sawyer feel like a fish out of water, and he'd always been good about including her. When business talk left Sawyer on the outside, Charles worked a few of their stories as a couple into the conversation—usually a humorous anecdote that he and Sawyer could tell together. Conversation inevitably turned back to business, but by then at least Sawyer didn't feel faceless. After, Charles always tenderly kissed Sawyer's hand during the car ride home and thanked her for coming.

But that night, Sawyer found herself staring at the back of Charles's head and straining to hear. At one point, she made a feint to pivot and make new friends by engaging the man sitting to her left instead, but he was already deep in conversation and facing away from her, too. So her options boiled down to choosing between the backs of two heads: the unfamiliar cowlick versus the cowlick she knew. At least straining to hear her fiancé's conversation felt less like eavesdropping on strangers.

Or did it?

Charles and Kendra spoke with a surprisingly giddy intensity. They talked over each other like old friends and laughed at each other's jokes—a number of which were decidedly inside jokes, leaving Sawyer to smile blankly while waiting for their laughter to peter out. She was able to gather that they had been assigned to the same team handling a big case—a huge merger between two big telecommunications companies. Charles had mentioned his excitement about being assigned to the case to Sawyer before, but had stopped short of naming the names of the players involved. *I don't know if I should be talking about this so much*, he'd said. *I forget; you work in publishing.*

Yeah, Sawyer had joked cynically. *I can see how editorial assistants who work at small literary imprints for twenty-seven K a year pose a real threat to Wexler Gibbons's security.*

No, but really, he'd insisted. *One of the telecommunications companies has a serious media branch.*

That had been a month and a half ago. Since then, Charles had not only left shoptalk at the office . . . he'd left himself physically there, for daily hours that stretched longer and longer. While she didn't love his being at work all the time, Sawyer hadn't given it too much thought; after all, you were supposed to prove yourself during your twenties—weren't you?

But now, as Charles leaned toward Kendra and said in a low voice, "Oh my God, I've been dying to step outside for a smoke—you?" Sawyer felt herself bristle.

Kendra gave a sly, conspiratorial smile and nodded. Then her eyes grazed over Charles's shoulder and fastened on Sawyer.

"Sawyer—go for a smoke with us?" Kendra asked, friendly, chipper.

"Nah, Sawyer hates being around cigarette smoke," Charles answered for her. "She graciously puts up with my occasional cravings." He looked at Sawyer. "Is it OK? I promise I'll stand upwind, air out my jacket, pop a mint."

Kendra laughed. "Do you want me to make Charles take a quick jog around the World Trade Center after, Sawyer?" she joked.

Kendra had struck the perfect tone of light, breezy . . . inoffensive. Sawyer forced a polite smile.

"Not sure you can 'make' Charles do anything," she replied, equally light, breezy. "But maybe I've just never tried."

"Sounds like you're underutilizing the whole point of a boyfriend," Kendra said with a wink, as though she and Sawyer were suddenly on the same team.

"Hey!" Charles protested, grinning.

"It'll only get worse after you're married," the man at Sawyer's elbow with the cowlick piped up to point out.

"That's right—dead man walking!" another guy teased.

The table laughed.

Charles shook his head affectionately. He turned to give Sawyer a peck on the cheek.

"Promise I won't come back all smoky," he said in parting.

Then Kendra and Charles were up from their chairs and absorbed in more chatter as they made their way toward the front exit that let out onto Wall Street. Sawyer sat, watching them go. She realized her brow was furrowed. She forced it to relax.

She turned back to the table, lost in thought, resisting the impulse to reach a hand to her mouth and gnaw at her nails. Across the space of two now empty seats, Kendra's boyfriend sat drinking what appeared to be a glass of whiskey, poured neat.

She studied him for a moment.

His suit was every bit as nice as those worn by the corporate lawyers who surrounded them, but he wore it with less care, a few buttons undone. Sawyer had noticed earlier that, as she had strained to listen to Charles and Kendra's conversation and interject polite commentary, Kendra's boyfriend hadn't even bothered. Instead, he'd sat there in his chair, staring antisocially into the distance with the kind of cool, condescending indifference typically perfected by rebellious teenagers. That kind of attitude normally annoyed Sawyer, so she was surprised to realize she found him very good-looking.

She cleared her throat, feeling oddly nervous.

"Nick—was it?" she greeted him, smiling awkwardly.

He took a swig of the amber liquid in his glass and held the sip in his mouth for a moment, tasting it as he turned to look at her with a bored expression. He swallowed, and wiped his lips with a wry, cowboy demeanor.

"They didn't need to go outside to smoke," he replied.

"Beg pardon?"

"You can smoke in here," he said. "It's a restaurant, not an office. See?"

Sawyer followed his pointing finger to where a cluster of people stood smoking at the bar.

"Everyone keeps talking about the smoking ban that's been proposed here in New York." He shook his head. "It's never going to happen."

Sawyer blinked, baffled. "Well . . . I don't know. I don't smoke."

"My point is, they didn't need to go outside to smoke."

Sawyer understood his implication. She wasn't sure what to say. "You could have said you wanted a cigarette, too, and joined them."

"No dice. She knows I don't like to be around them. Like you."

"You don't smoke?"

He shook his head again, but this time looked away. "I know someone with respiratory problems," he said.

His tone warned Sawyer off from asking whom he meant, or more about the details. She thought for a minute.

"I'm sorry," she finally replied.

This caused him to turn and study Sawyer's face as if seeing her for the first time. Sawyer felt her cheeks involuntarily burning. She fidgeted.

"Charles mentioned that he and Kendra got assigned to a pretty big case. He said it was super competitive."

Nick only continued to look at her, clearly unwilling to pretend interest in the case, much less the fact that Charles and Kendra had been assigned to it.

"I'm in publishing," Sawyer blurted out, feeling an inexplicable pressure to keep the conversation going. "Well—that makes it sound like I'm important. What I mean to say is, I have an entry-level editorial job. But I guess I still find it pretty exciting that I get to read some interesting new books that aren't out yet."

Nick remained quiet. He tilted his head and looked at her with stoic bemusement, almost as though Sawyer were a space alien speaking a different language.

"What . . . uh, what do you do?" she finally asked, thinking a point-blank question might help poke the conversation along, or at least break his stare.

"Ad agency," he replied, after a long pause. He drained the last swallow of whiskey in his glass. "Junior accounts manager."

"Oh."

The monosyllable was out of Sawyer's mouth before she could stop it. She hadn't meant to sound disappointed. She wasn't sure exactly why, but for some reason she had gotten it in her head that he might be an artist of some sort. Something about the attitude and rumpled suit. But now it made more sense why—rumpled or not—it was still an expensive suit.

A look of irritation registered on his face as he detected her disappointment.

"Yep," he continued, as though reading her thoughts. "That's me—yet another sellout writing slogan copy for diet cola and hemorrhoid cream on Madison Avenue."

"I didn't mean to suggest—"

"What's your name again?" he asked, cutting her off.

"Sawyer."

He took this in, bobbed his head. Sawyer recognized instantly: he was not nodding in approval. He pursed his lips sarcastically.

"'Sawyer'? Were your parents, like, Mark Twain fans or something?"

Sawyer cast her eyes down and didn't reply.

"Wait—I'm right?! Are you kidding me?" Nick said.

He laughed. There was something mean laced into it, and Sawyer stiffened. She declined to join in, hoping he'd have a moment of self-awareness about what a jerk he was being.

But Nick proved impervious.

"What, were they teachers or professors or something? I can see it now: A pair of early American lit lovers, family vacations on Walden Pond. Moleskine journals in your stockings for Christmas. The kind of people who always assured you it was perfectly fine to take out student loans and major in English."

Sawyer willed her expression to stone.

"God—I'm right again! Wow."

As he continued to laugh, Sawyer began to suspect that he was the kind of guy who had been called a jerk more than once in his life, and instead of allowing himself to be shamed for it, he wore it like a badge of honor. A swaggering smart-ass, too cynical for apologies.

She decided to ignore him.

He picked up on her disdain.

"All right, all right," he said, winding down his laughter. He sighed and glanced around the room. "Well, since it appears our waiter has forsaken us, I'm off to the bar."

"Yeah, you seem like you could use *more* whiskey," Sawyer muttered sarcastically under her breath—but not quietly enough. Nick offered a bitter grin.

"It's twenty-five-year-old Scotch, actually," he corrected, with a condescending wink. "And, an open bar." He got to his feet, adding as though to gloat, "Cheers. Sorry about your name."

Sawyer watched him stride away, fuming. It was clear from the way he said it, he didn't mean *sorry I was rude about your name.* He meant exactly what he'd said—*sorry ABOUT your name.*

Asshole.

• • •

Charles and Kendra came back in time to hear a speech given by one of the firm's senior partners. The conclusion of the speech was met with an uproar of applause. Then, entrées were cleared, and dessert came out. Sawyer joylessly poked a spoon at the molten lava cake and the miniature football-shaped pill of vanilla ice cream, watching hot and cold ooze together. She had given up on trying to listen to Charles and Kendra's conversation, let alone join in.

Every molecule in her body was vibrating with irritation and awareness—awareness of swaggering, cantankerous Nick, sitting two bodies away from her, and his smug rudeness. Awareness of Kendra's laugh, a breathy, tittering sound that rose and fell like a musical scale, floating over the top of Charles's head. And awareness of *Charles* . . . particularly of his turned back.

When it was finally time to retrieve their coats from the coat check and leave, Sawyer was grateful to stand up and walk away from their table, and to be free of the enormous, echoing museum of a restaurant altogether. She was relieved to climb into a cab and hear Charles speak their address.

Hurtling toward home with Charles beside her, she felt her irritation melting away and her body loosening back up. It was just a lousy work dinner; Charles was expected to socialize with his team. She allowed her head to rest on his shoulder, where it was only occasionally jostled as the driver gunned it over the bumpy, potholed streets that led uptown. She smiled when Charles reached for her hand, and waited for him to kiss it, their usual ritual.

But after a moment she realized the kiss wasn't coming. Charles was staring out the cab window, intensely preoccupied with his own thoughts. Finally, he squeezed Sawyer's hand and cleared his throat.

"Kendra was able to get an inside scoop," he said. "It's looking like they want to push this merger through by September."

Sawyer picked her head up off Charles's shoulder, confused. She frowned. "Well, that seems like plenty of time, doesn't it? It's still May. We've only just hit Memorial Day weekend."

"Well . . . I guess that's my point," Charles replied. "It's looking like I have to go into the office this weekend, and to be frank, it's going to be an intense summer. I won't be able to take any time off."

"Oh," Sawyer murmured, her mind quietly reordering the information.

Charles squeezed her hand again. "If I pay my dues now, we'll be set later."

She was quiet.

"I'm only doing this because I want us to have a good life together, you know that," Charles urged in a kind voice, gently jiggling her hand for emphasis. "It's for our future."

Sawyer understood that the words coming out of Charles's mouth were right. She wanted to be supportive.

"It's just that . . . well, I'll miss having you around," Sawyer relented. She sighed, and allowed her head to rest again on Charles's shoulder. Her nose picked up the scent of tar, tobacco, and chalky smoke embedded in his clothes. She set her mind on ignoring it.

Was Sawyer expecting him to say something in return?

She hadn't thought so. But as Charles patted her hand, his touch felt strangely distant as he replied, "I know."

She waited for him to add *I'll miss you, too.* Or something about the trips they might plan in the future. But all he said was—"This case is such an amazing opportunity. We might have to go to Chicago for a week or two, though."

Sawyer understood instantly: by "we," he didn't mean him and Sawyer.

He meant him and Kendra.

3.

FRIDAY, JUNE 4

In some ways, it felt like summer had turned up like an unexpected houseguest. Winter had lingered in New York like a bad hangover that year. Balding patches of snow crusted with black city dirt held fast to the shadier, narrower streets of Greenwich Village, all the way through the first week of May. Tiny buds appeared on the trees in Central Park, but remained shut tight against several spells of icy drizzle. The light, too, had clung to its wintery hue, leaning in against the brick buildings and wrought iron fire escapes in a shadowless, bluish haze. But then the seasons had lurched forward all at once, and the cool, reluctant spring had slid into an abruptly balmy summer. The light turned pink; the trees rained blossoms. And just as quickly as the light had turned pink, it turned golden. A canopy of lush, swampy green foliage covered the streets, and the air turned sultry and filled with mosquitoes.

Summertime in New York.

Now, on the first Friday after Memorial Day, Sawyer could feel the office around her mentally bedding down for the drowsy naptime state that the entire publishing industry was about to enter for the rest of the summer. It wasn't as if business itself would grind to a halt. New beach reads would still come out and line the bookstore shelves like clockwork, every Tuesday. And work would still get done, of course—but mostly by the small army of interns and editorial assistants grinding away at the millstone of entry-level labor. Big decisions were put on hold until the right people came back from Europe or Bermuda . . . or Vermont, or Maine. As it was, even those who remained in town for the workweek were really only expected to work four days, as Memorial Day also marked the beginning of summer Fridays.

Summer Fridays more or less meant that, every Friday at noon, the city experienced a mass exodus to the Hamptons. The older, more established New Yorkers went by car and helicopter, while the younger, hungrier set climbed aboard the Jitney. The city felt distinctly empty, the streets utterly deserted. Grocery stores, movie theaters, and sometimes even entire subway cars turned into echoing, cavernous spaces, filled only with the brisk chill of fanatical air-conditioning. The few neighborhoods that still buzzed with activity were the touristy spots, like Times Square and the old seaport, where anyone who actually lived in New York never went anyway.

Summer in the city could get a little lonely sometimes. And *hot*—the subway grates sending up heat so intense it made the air above them shimmer in mirage-like waves, the MTA buses kicking out black exhaust. With Charles busy at work, there would be nothing to break it up—no mini-vacations, no little weekend adventures to Fire Island or the Jersey Shore, or even day trips to Jones Beach. Sawyer knew she was probably destined to spend most of the summer rattling around the muggy urban landscape, alone. Under ordinary circumstances, she would have roped her best friend, Autumn, into hanging out . . . but suffering from a mixture of wanderlust and indecision about grad school, Autumn had signed up to teach English in Japan. The Japanese school term ran through July, and Autumn planned to spend the entire month of August seeing more of the country.

Sawyer stared at the calendar pinned to the fabric wall of her cubicle and sighed. After a moment, she snapped out of it and scolded herself. There were still things to look forward to—after all, she and Charles were getting married in October, and there was a wedding to plan. Although . . . for better or worse, Sawyer had less on her to-do list than your average bride. The dynamic had shifted after Charles's parents insisted on paying for the wedding, and Charles's mother, Kathy, had enthusiastically begun performing the work of ten wedding planners, leaving little to Sawyer. Still, Sawyer reminded herself, it was the summer before her wedding! And Charles's big case might lead to a promotion.

When noon rolled around, Sawyer's coworkers began to take off for the day, gathering their things and dashing for the elevator with a stealthy giddiness, like bank robbers hopping into the getaway car.

"*Psst!* Happy Friday!" Sawyer's coworker Kaylee whispered to her from the next cubicle, once their boss had left.

Sawyer and Kaylee were editorial assistants; both of them had been assigned to Johanna Bailey, a senior executive editor who had been with the imprint for twenty years and who pronounced it "*Jo-HAWN-nah.*" Though she had never said so outright, Johanna had the kind of sophisticated yet stern air that suggested she would find an assistant clocking out before her appalling. Sawyer knew Kaylee had been counting the minutes.

"Have fun, Kaye," Sawyer said.

Kaylee shouldered her bag with a smile and a wave.

Eventually, Sawyer gathered her own things to go. She hummed a few bars of "Summertime," stubbornly forcing herself to adopt a holiday mood, in spite of the fact that she was headed home to an empty apartment.

"Home" was a fourth-floor brownstone walk-up on the Upper West Side. When she and Charles first found the place, Sawyer had loved the historical aura of the building, the oddly narrow yet open railroad layout, and the creaky wood floors. They'd had fun settling into the place, awkwardly wrangling their hand-me-down furniture up the narrow hall stairs and cooking their first few dinners together—cozy makeshift meals served up on mismatched plates.

But now, as she rode the subway uptown, she tried to think of how she might occupy herself. There was always more reading to be done for her job. Sawyer was passionate about becoming a full-fledged editor . . . but even she knew she couldn't read the entire afternoon and evening away; there was such a thing as overkill, burnout. Vegging out in front of the TV held limited appeal—not because Sawyer had any moral or cultural snobbery about watching television, but rather because she and Charles hadn't sprung for cable. If there was nothing good playing on the five basic channels, Sawyer wound up doing what plenty of other New Yorkers did: turning to NY1 and letting the TV play in the background, until the segments looped back around after the thirty-minute mark, giving her déjà vu. There weren't many other options besides books, snacks, and TV. She hadn't built up much of a social life since moving to the city, mainly because she and Charles had been settling in, then getting engaged, and were always pinching pennies.

When she keyed into the front door, the apartment was hot and stuffy, having trapped the heat of the early morning and afternoon. Sawyer quickly scurried around, struggling with each window in turn until it budged from its ancient sash. Once the windows had all been thrown open and she had cranked on an electric fan, the phone began to ring.

She froze, thinking of who it could be.

"Hi, Kathy . . . !" she said, when she finally picked up.

"Oh! I didn't know you would be home. I thought I would just leave a message," Charles's mother responded, flustered but chipper.

"I have summer Fridays," Sawyer explained. "I'm home for the afternoon."

"Ooo—summer Fridays!" Kathy enthused. "Well, I won't keep you, but of course it's just a little something about the wedding planning . . ."

Sawyer listened as Kathy chattered away, a little awed, as always. From centerpieces to aisle runners to stemware to string quartets to the exact kind of vanilla used in the cake (only Tahitian would do) . . . no detail was too small for Kathy to scrutinize, plan, and arrange.

Sawyer genuinely liked her future mother-in-law . . . although it was true that Kathy had a way of bowling people over. Sawyer's own parents had been forced to take a back seat in the wedding planning—but with little complaint; they were professors who lived modestly, and were inherently a little skeptical of the "wedding industrial complex." They would have never planned the kind of ceremony Kathy was cooking up, and the amounts of money Kathy thought it was perfectly OK to drop on caterers and tea roses and live swans (live swans!) would have given them sticker shock—or even a literal stroke.

Truth be told, the money gave Sawyer a queasy stomach and sweaty palms, too. But Charles insisted that it was important to his parents. Besides, he persuaded Sawyer, who didn't love a big wedding? *Let's get married like we mean it,* he'd cajoled, grabbing her and tipping her into a corny dip, then kissing her until they both collapsed onto the rug, laughing.

So far, with Kathy making all the arrangements, it was shaping up to be the kind of wedding that took up an entire page of coverage in the Sunday *New York Times*, which had Sawyer biting her nails.

Sawyer had never wanted a big wedding.

But she also hadn't *not* wanted a big wedding.

She didn't know quite what she thought.

"So, what do you think?" Kathy asked now.

Sawyer snapped to attention. Kathy had just played a few samples of music from three different bands by holding the phone up to her home stereo speakers.

"Hmm . . . I'm not sure which one I like better," Sawyer answered truthfully of the bands. "We should ask Charles. He'll probably be fine with any of them, as long as they can play our song."

"Remind me—what's your song again?" Kathy asked.

"'Fly Me to the Moon,'" Sawyer replied.

"Aha!" Kathy said, satisfied. "I knew Charles was fond of that song, but I didn't realize you are, too. You're such a compatible couple!"

The main reason Charles liked "Fly Me to the Moon" was because it was a way to show off his singing voice at karaoke bars. He was far from a professional musician, but he'd perfected singing that one song in particular; he had it down pat. Sawyer suspected he'd performed it for a few other girlfriends before they met, but he'd sung it to her with such heart on their third date that she was happy to go along with it when he officially declared that it was "their" song. After all, when he sang it to her, it always made them both smile.

"I'm just glad you two appreciate the classics," Kathy said in approval. "Everyone likes Sinatra! I don't know where I'd even start if I had to find a band to play, I don't know, say . . . Ricky Martin!"

Kathy laughed, and Sawyer joined in with a chuckle, sympathetic that Kathy had likely dug deep to come up with what she believed was currently hip.

"So," Kathy continued, back to business. "These bands get booked up quickly and I think we should make a decision as soon as possible—when will Charles be home? I'd love to play them for him."

"Well . . ." Sawyer bit her lip. "To be honest, he's been pulling some pretty long hours lately . . ."

"Oh, of course," Kathy hurried to reply. "That big case! Ed and I are so proud of him. You must be, too!"

"I am," Sawyer agreed. It was true. Or—at least, it was what she believed was the correct way to feel. She just wished the situation didn't also make her feel a little like a housewife, always waiting for her husband to walk in the door in his suit and tie.

"How late is too late to have Charles call you back?" Sawyer asked, in an attempt to refocus her attention on the subject at hand.

"Oh, he'll be tired when he gets home, I'm sure. Tell you what I'll do," Kathy decided. "I'll go back to all three bands and tell them I need to hear their renditions of 'Fly Me to the Moon.' I'll see which one plays it best, and then I'll report back to you!"

Sawyer thanked her, genuinely meaning it and still feeling a little intimidated by the fact that Kathy was doing so much.

"As long as you're not putting yourself out . . ." Sawyer meekly tried to insist.

"Nonsense!" Kathy replied. "I'm having a ball with it. And I'm counting the days until you officially become our daughter!"

Sawyer blushed and grinned.

After they'd hung up, Sawyer felt freshly aware of the empty apartment. The thought of trying to fill up the rest of the afternoon and evening alone had her feeling lonely and agitated at the same time.

She and Charles had decided to cut corners when it came to cable TV, but they *had* sprung for dial-up. Sawyer went to the desk wedged in a small alcove in the kitchen near the open arch of the living room and powered on the computer. She opened AOL and listened to the familiar song of the computer logging on—the dial tone, the high-pitched squeal and twang, the rushing hiss and spit of the connection establishing itself.

"WELCOME! You've got mail!"

Sadly, it was all junk mail, but Sawyer clicked on the new-message icon and began composing an email to Autumn, unloading her thoughts and feelings about the summer ahead. Autumn always understood; they were the sort of friends who—ever since the moment they'd met, freshman year of college during orientation week—had always spoken their own private best-friend language.

She tried to picture her friend in Japan. Autumn had sent postcards of Kyoto—narrow historical streets lined with traditional teahouses. On the other hand, Autumn had described the internet café she frequented as "super trendy and futuristic."

Sawyer wrote the email and sent it, vaguely wondering when Autumn would check her inbox next.

She logged off and sighed. Charles had been getting home later and later each night. Seven o'clock had turned into eight . . . and then nine. Then nine thirty. Then, closer to ten.

For an hour or so, Sawyer puttered. She tidied the apartment and folded laundry. She dutifully studied some bridal magazines Kathy had sent. Then—when all the white dresses began to blur together and look the same—she put on some music, and got out some manuscripts she needed to read for work. Eventually, the late summer dusk glowed blue in the windows.

She was idly contemplating dinner, flipping through a Spanish cookbook she had bought mainly for its beautiful photographs of the Spanish countryside, when the phone rang and made her jump.

"Hello?"

"Sawyer!"

"Autumn?" Sawyer blinked with total surprise. "What time is it there?"

"Eight a.m. *Tomorrow*, of course," Autumn replied. "What would you like to know about the future?"

Sawyer laughed at the joke, then sighed. "I'd settle for what time to expect my future husband home this evening."

"Yeah, sounded like that in your email."

"That bad?"

"You sound a little, I don't know . . . lost."

"This call must be costing a fortune," Sawyer said, worried.

"Nah, we'll talk until my phone card runs out."

"Doesn't your mom buy you those to phone home?"

"*And* for emergencies."

Sawyer felt bad. "Oh, no. I'm not an emergency! I'm just . . . ugh. I don't know what I am."

"Well, for starters, you're my best friend," Autumn reminded her. "Now: spill. Is the wedding part of it? I know you didn't think Charles and his family were going to be in such a rush."

Sawyer bit her lip; it was a little bit true. She'd always assumed they'd have a long engagement, not less than a year.

"Maybe . . . but I feel like I should be flattered that Charles is in a rush? And glad that he isn't one of those guys who act like a woman is supposed to drag a man down the aisle, kicking and screaming. It's a little romantic, even. Right?"

"Sure," Autumn agreed. Then, after a brief pause: "If that's what *you* want."

Sawyer closed her eyes and thought for a moment. She had a flash of Charles doing that corny dip. *Let's get married like we mean it.*

"Yeah," she said to Autumn over the phone. "It's what I want."

Autumn was quiet for a moment.

"Why?" Sawyer asked. "Does it not sound like what I want?"

"Hmm, I guess it's just that, between the two of you, it's easier to tell what Charles wants."

Now it was Sawyer's turn to be quiet.

"I don't mean anything bad by it!" Autumn rushed to qualify. "Only that Charles has always been . . . well, Charles. And you're more go-with-the-flow. In college, you were like this whimsical, arty book nerd, and he was, like, *the man with a plan*. It was cute to see how you balanced each other out. Opposites, but totally united as a team. Remember how we used to call you guys 'Mom and Dad' as a joke?"

Sawyer smiled faintly at the memory. It was true; back in college, she and Charles always showed up to everything as a couple. When they didn't agree on something, people used to affectionately tease, *Ooo, Mom and Dad are fighting!* But they were never "fighting." Not really. As a freshman, Sawyer had immediately gravitated to Charles, the older upperclassman already applying to law school, and the two of them had formed a couple so naturally, it was hard to pinpoint the exact moment they'd become official; it was as if they had always been together. That she and Charles planned to stay together was one of the few sources of consistency in an otherwise mercurial collegiate scene. Sawyer might worry about her grades, her parents' approval, the relative future employment opportunities for English majors . . . but her worries were Charles's worries, and vice versa. They were solid, steady.

Autumn interrupted Sawyer's reverie, clearing her throat and adding, "I guess I'm just saying . . . I hope it's still an *equal* balance."

Sawyer paused, and seriously mulled this. She'd never really second-guessed how much of the plan was *Charles's* plan, versus theirs together. She'd finished her undergrad as he had graduated law school; they'd both been excited about the move to New York. While it was true that she hadn't expected to plan a wedding *so* soon, or spend *so* much time home alone as Charles's career took off, she hoped she hadn't given Autumn a negative impression of the relationship itself.

"Look," Autumn continued. "It's just an observation. Mainly, I called because I love you! I was worried that you sounded lonely."

"I probably just have to get used to the whole adult-jobs-mean-we're-busy thing."

Sawyer grinned, then added, "And, of course, I'll *never* get used to not having my best friend around."

"Don't," Autumn agreed.

They talked for a little while longer, until the connection abruptly dropped just as Autumn was recounting a story about a cool lantern festival and how she'd met a quirky French guy who was in Kyoto teaching French but how she didn't speak French and he didn't speak English and they'd spent the evening comically trying to communicate in Japanese. Sawyer wished she'd gotten to hear the rest of the story. But she was grateful to have heard Autumn's voice, period.

She went back to skimming the cookbook, and more puttering. The light in the windows turned navy . . . then black.

• • •

Finally, Sawyer heard the sound of Charles's key in the front door. She glanced at the clock: 9:52.

"Hey."

"Hey."

"Are you hungry?" she asked. "I made some gazpacho."

Charles smiled at her in puzzlement. "You make gazpacho?"

Sawyer grinned. "Did you know? There are two great things about gazpacho. One: the ingredients are super cheap. And two: you don't have to warm it up to serve it. If that's not shabby chic, I don't know what is."

"We're doing 'shabby chic' now?"

Sawyer shrugged. "It has a better ring to it than 'federal student loan chic.'"

Charles laughed, then turned to go get undressed in the bedroom. Sawyer followed him. She perched on the bed as he sat down to take off his pants.

"I could get it out of the fridge, fix a nice bowl with a dollop of sour cream in it and some toast. It came out pretty decent."

"Oh—no, thanks," Charles replied. "They feed us when we work late."

By now he was down to his undershirt and boxers. He got up to toss his socks into the hamper and hang his tie back on the tie rack nailed to the back of the closet door. Sawyer picked up his pants and dress shirt from the bed.

"Dry cleaner?" she asked.

Charles nodded appreciatively. He shook himself and let out a comical grunt of desperate relief. "God, I can't tell you how good it is to finally be home with my fiancée!"

He crossed back to the bed and gave Sawyer a kiss.

"Makes it all worth it," he added, grinning.

Sawyer kissed him back.

Why had she let his late hours get to her? Clearly, the overtime was for her . . . for both of them.

"Your mom called," Sawyer remembered. "It was about the bands she's considering booking for the reception. She even played samples of their demo CDs over the phone. I told her they all sounded good to me. And that you probably just wanted one that can play 'Fly Me to the Moon.'"

"Perfect," Charles approved.

Sawyer hesitated. "Do you ever feel a little funny?" she asked. "That we're not doing more . . . you know, more of the planning? I mean, your mom is pretty much handling everything."

And choosing everything, Sawyer also thought, but didn't add.

Charles shrugged. "It makes her happy. Besides, we couldn't hire a better wedding planner if we tried."

"We can't afford to hire *any* wedding planner."

"Well, *exactly*!" Charles quipped. He laughed. "It was so hot and gross on the subway today. I'm going to jump in the shower and then probably hit the hay."

"OK."

Charles disappeared into the bathroom, but left the door open. Sawyer listened to the squeak of the taps being turned, the pitter-patter of the shower sputtering to life. She turned back to the shirt and pants draped over her arm, and frisked the pockets in preparation for drop-off at the dry cleaner.

Her hand was met by some loose change and a crinkled slip of paper, all of which she extracted and dumped on the dresser for Charles to go through later. She turned to get some wire hangers but paused, glancing again at the slip of paper. She picked it up and unfurled it, curious. It was a receipt.

A dine-in receipt for a restaurant called "Golden Dragon Palace."

She absent-mindedly dropped Charles's pants and dress shirt back on the bed and wandered through the open door of the bathroom, still staring at the receipt clutched in her hand.

"Hey," she called to him through the drawn shower curtain, over the white noise of running water. "Did you get Chinese today?"

"Uh—yeah," Charles answered from the other side of the curtain. "I popped out for lunch today."

"By yourself?"

"No, I went with Kendra—I owed her a lunch."

"Oh. That's nice. I . . . I thought you said you guys were so busy you never got to leave for lunch."

"Yeah, most days that's the way it is," Charles replied. "But we had some unexpected downtime while the other team was reviewing our notes, and we snuck out."

"Oh." Sawyer was quiet for a moment, deep in a state of consternation. She shook herself. The last thing she wanted to be was an uptight, irrational ball-and-chain. "Well, that's cool," she said, slightly impressed by her own ability to muster such a breezy tone.

She wandered back out of the bathroom, and went to add the receipt back to the pile of coins on the dresser. But before she laid it down, she took one last look. She wasn't sure why, or what she was looking for—was she curious to know more about Kendra? Whether or not Kendra liked pot stickers, or moo shu pork? She couldn't say what she was hoping to decode.

Her eyes ran over the receipt. It listed all of Charles's favorite dishes. Either Kendra didn't have much of an opinion on Chinese food, or else she shared Charles's taste exactly. Sawyer *did* notice they'd ordered two Tsingtao beers, and then another two . . . which was a bit bold for a work lunch. But even this wasn't proof of anything at all, really. Sawyer sighed, suddenly tired. She moved to set the receipt down.

Then, the very second she placed the receipt back on the dresser, she saw it—

A time stamp.

9:28 p.m.

Sawyer stood staring at the numbers, their slightly blurry shapes printed in purplish carbon-copy ink. She felt a strangely hot sensation, like a bee had just stung her in the face. What if Charles hadn't been working late—or, at least, not *as* late as he claimed—but when he'd left the office, instead of coming home to spend time with Sawyer, he'd opted to go get beers and Chinese food with Kendra? Why had he said it was lunch?

Sawyer took one last lingering look at the receipt. The time stamp could be wrong, of course. But Sawyer felt a twinge at the back of her brain, suggesting that wasn't the case.

They didn't need to go outside to smoke, that guy, Nick, had insisted at the Wexler Gibbons dinner.

She frowned, then left the receipt on the dresser and went back to prepping Charles's shirt and trousers for the dry cleaner, listening to the sound of the water still running in the shower.

THURSDAY, JUNE 10

If Sawyer had one thing in plentiful supply that summer, it was "alone time."

Even before the summer rolled around, Sawyer spent her lunch hours alone. It wasn't that Sawyer necessarily *wanted* to eat alone; it had to do with the daily schedule. In addition to being a stickler about the pronunciation of her name, Johanna was also a stickler about the phones being manned at all times. She lived in horror of the idea that a single call for her desk might roll to voicemail, or worse yet, roll down to the publisher's central receptionist.

Most days, Johanna was scheduled to have lunch with a literary agent or a fellow publishing executive . . . or occasionally, an author. A little after the clock struck noon, she would typically tie a Hermès scarf about her neck, tuck her handbag under her arm, and sail out the door, calling over her shoulder (somewhat erroneously), *Be back soon, girls.* As a faint cloud of Chanel No. 5 settled in Johanna's wake, Kaylee—who held three months' seniority over Sawyer and was assigned to the first lunch shift—would quickly gather her things and dash out to catch up with a gaggle of other editorial assistants headed to lunch, while Sawyer would remain behind to answer Johanna's phone. Around 1:30 p.m., Kaylee would return to cover the phones, and Sawyer would be free to take her lunch from 1:30 to 2:30 p.m.

By then, though, there would be no one to take lunch *with*.

When Sawyer first started at the company, she'd hoped to make friends—she'd always imagined publishing to be a very social industry. But she felt completely cast adrift, especially during her lunch hour. The publishing house was located in the East Fifties. Midtown was all concrete and narrow sidewalks, cabs honking, everyone walking fast, no place for dawdling or a leisurely bag lunch.

Then, a few months into the job, she turned a corner and happened upon something she never in a million years expected to see in Midtown Manhattan: rushing water, and an oasis of green. She stared into the peaceful space wedged amid a cluster of high-rise buildings, utterly baffled. She thought it was some fancy restaurant's patio, but a sign announced the name, "*Greenacre Park*." The benches, the tables and chairs, were open to the public.

She started bringing her brown-bag lunch to the park, where she would sit at a little café table overlooking the waterfall that rushed over the vaguely Japanese-style geometric blocks of granite, a fountain of green ivy cascading lushly beside it. She often brought along a manuscript from the office. There, in the park, working didn't feel like work; she *enjoyed* reading and coming up with editorial notes—a reminder of why she'd wanted so badly to work in publishing in the first place. She was starting to feel like she had what it took to be a top editor—someone who read carefully and whose mind automatically flexed like a muscle, gravitating naturally to all the places that could use a little tightening and brightening, and knowing where to suggest cuts.

Discovering the park had transformed her otherwise lonely lunch hour into a peaceful, productive part of her day.

And then there were days when, instead of a manuscript from the office, she started bringing a notebook of her own. She'd always liked to write, though she had never called herself "a writer." Calling yourself a writer required a kind of hubris Sawyer found embarrassing. The people her own age who called themselves writers usually weren't; most were pompous young men who dreamed of fame and fortune. They did a lot of posturing, but very little actual *writing*.

Over the course of that first year in New York, Sawyer had begun to finish full drafts of stories and poems. She was surprised when she finished not only first drafts but second drafts. Before she knew it, she began to finish third drafts . . . and then drafts that felt so finished she didn't know what else she could possibly do with them.

Except, she *did* know. The next logical step for a writer was to submit her work for publication. The thought thrilled Sawyer—but also terrified her a little. Earlier that spring, in a fit of sudden bravery, she'd mailed a handful of her best poems to some of the literary journals she revered, knowing it was a long shot. New, online literary "e-zines" had started to become a thing. They were less of a long shot, but a number of them were becoming rather well regarded, putting their poets up for Pushcarts and The Best American Poetry series. Sawyer picked her two favorites and also mailed off a pair of "e-submissions."

Then the fit of bravery passed. Her submissions were out in the world, but she didn't expect anything to really come of them. She almost forgot she'd sent them anywhere at all (which spared her the rush of embarrassment to imagine an editor might be *actually reading* them).

So, when Sawyer arrived home that Thursday, she wasn't thinking of her poems as she opened the apartment windows, then plopped down in the chair at the little computer desk in the kitchen. She waited through the snowy hiss and squelch of the dial-up for a familiar sound—

"WELCOME! You've got mail!"

She smiled, assuming Autumn had replied to her latest email.

But when she clicked on her inbox, she discovered a surprise: there, in the top line, a reply to a batch of poems she had submitted . . . and best of all, the editor of the e-zine was writing to say that they would love to add one of her poems to the online edition they were about to post, and also enter it into consideration for their prestigious end-of-year printed edition.

Sawyer read the email once, then twice, then made an involuntary noise that sounded like a crow cawing and clapped a hand over her mouth.

She got up from the computer desk and went to the fridge, unsure if she was looking to celebrate or tranquilize herself. She found a bottle of white wine that she and Charles had opened a few nights ago and forgotten about . . . She pulled out the cork and sniffed, then poured herself a glass. The evening was muggy and the wine was icy cold from having been pushed to the back of the fridge.

When she sat back down at the computer desk, she reread the e-zine editor's acceptance letter one more time, and thought about emailing Autumn to share the news. But when she clicked over to her inbox, she noticed a second email waiting there. She blinked, baffled, and squinted more closely at the sender's name.

Nikolai70@aol.com

She didn't know any Nikolai70@aol.com.

The subject line read: "My Apologies."

Frowning, she clicked on it.

To: Adventures_of_Tom@aol.com
From: Nikolai70@aol.com

Hi Sawyer.

I wanted to say I'm sorry if I was a dick to you at the Wexler Gibbons thing. I didn't mean to pick on your name. I'm not always good with people. I can be insensitive, or so I'm told. I kind of have a biting sense of humor, too. It gets me into trouble. Anyway, I promise it was nothing personal. You seem perfectly nice and it's been on my mind that maybe I offended you. That was not my intent.

Sorry again,
Nick

Sawyer stared at the email in shock. She was still baffled—no longer baffled about who the sender was, but rather, utterly surprised that he had sent it.

How had he even gotten her email address?

She seriously doubted he'd asked Kendra to ask Charles for her address. In fact, something in her gut told her Kendra and Charles were oblivious to the contentious exchange she'd had with Nick, let alone the fact that he'd sent an email to tell her he was sorry.

So, Nick had looked her up somehow. Which must have taken at least a little effort. She'd never mentioned her last name to Nick at the Wexler Gibbons dinner. Her screen name, Adventures_of_Tom@aol.com, was a roundabout jokey reference to her first name, easy for friends to remember but probably not easy for a stranger to pull out of thin air.

Sawyer stared at the screen. She tried to make up her mind whether to respond.

The angel sitting on her right shoulder felt touched that Nick had decided to apologize—maybe even strangely flattered in a way . . . but the devil sitting on her other shoulder needled her with his pitchfork to give Nick a little bit of what he'd dished out at the Wexler Gibbons dinner back to him.

She clicked on the reply button. A new window popped open, the message screen white and blank, the cursor blinking. Waiting. She thought for a moment.

An idea came to her, and she clicked back to his message, copied it, and pasted it into her reply window. Then she got to work, her fingers dancing lightly over the keyboard. When she was done, she reread her reply:

To: Nikolai70@aol.com
From: Adventures_of_Tom@aol.com

Hi Nick,

I've inserted my editorial comments below, in parentheses, and free of charge:

I wanted to say I'm sorry if I was a dick to you at the Wexler Gibbons thing. **(Reconsider use of "if")** I didn't mean to pick on your name. **(Fact check: You absolutely meant to pick on my name)** I'm not always good with people. **(This checks out)** I can be insensitive, or so I'm told. **(Cut—redundant)** I kind of have a biting sense of humor, too. **("Humor" implies wit, amusement, making people laugh . . . word choice does not seem to apply to what you are calling "humor")** It gets me into trouble. Anyway, I promise it was nothing personal. **(Erroneous use of expression "nothing personal"—you mocked my name and made assumptions about my personal background)** You seem perfectly nice and it's been on my mind that maybe I offended you. That was not my intent. **(Ambiguous ending—What WAS your intent?)**

Sorry again,
Nick

This concludes your free editorial consult. You're welcome.

Sawyer.

Sawyer looked the message over, wondering if she should actually send it. She wasn't used to being so acerbic and in-your-face. He might be offended.

After a moment, Sawyer convinced herself: Why should it be her problem if Nick was offended? He started it. And young women were always tiptoeing around men. He was probably expecting her to thank him for the apology. And as far as she could tell, he could use a little pushback.

She took a breath, and moved her mouse to click send.

WHOOSH!

* * *

Sawyer assumed it would be easy to keep her mind occupied with the good news about her poem . . . but as the minutes ticked by, she found her thoughts returning to Nick's email . . . and her reply. The exchange danced in her brain.

After an hour of debating her own regret, Sawyer decided to log back on and reread what she'd written. She returned to the computer desk and waited for the dial-up to connect. Once it did, she was surprised to be greeted yet again by the same sound she'd heard earlier—"*You've got mail!*"

She clicked on her inbox, and there it was:

Nikolai70@aol.com. RE: My Apologies

A hot flush crept into her cheeks. She tried to ignore it. She clicked on the email and opened it.

> To: Adventures_of_Tom@aol.com
> From: Nikolai70@aol.com
>
> Hi Sawyer.
>
> Good to know you got my email. Thank you for your free editorial consult. I guess you DID give me fair

warning at the dinner that you work in publishing. I have other friends who work in publishing; from what I hear, given the pay scale in your field, "free editorial consult" might be somewhat redundant, so maybe that's an edit you can use on your edits. But what do I know, I'm just the guy who sold his soul to work in that field of lesser literary masterpieces, otherwise known as advertising, where the object is to sell something with as few words as possible, and preferably with a photo of a hot girl or a chimp in a tuxedo. It ain't Chekhov, but we do try to dot our "i"s and cross our "t"s from time to time.

I really am sorry that I was rude to you.

—Nick

Sawyer blinked at the glowing computer screen, unsure how to make heads or tails of what she'd just read. Was he putting her down again? Or putting himself down? Or . . . both?

In the next second, Sawyer had clicked on reply.

To: Nikolai70@aol.com
From: Adventures_of_Tom@aol.com

Dear Nick,

Your publishing friends speak the truth. While it is currently 1999, publishing salaries are stuck in 1959. But if this is your punch line of sorts, we need to revisit that "definition of humor" thing again.

As for your commentary about your own profession—I only met you once, and this is the second time you have dubbed yourself a "sellout" for working in advertising. If you don't like it, why don't you just quit?

—Sawyer

Sawyer clicked send.

Ordinarily, when she was done checking and sending emails, she logged off. But this time she got up to pour the remainder of the wine from the fridge in her glass, then sat back down at the computer desk. And there it was again—"*You've got mail!*"

She clicked on Nikolai70@aol.com without a second's hesitation, now deeply curious about his response.

To: Adventures_of_Tom@aol.com
From: Nikolai70@aol.com

Can't quit. But that's another story.

—N

Sawyer clicked reply.

To: Nikolai70@aol.com
From: Adventures_of_Tom@aol.com

Funny thing about people who work in publishing—we happen to like stories. Lay it on me.

—S

She waited. After five minutes, her inbox lit up with a new email again.

> To: Adventures_of_Tom@aol.com
> From: Nikolai70@aol.com
>
> Nah, we'll save it for another time. It's great that you love your work. What is your favorite part?—N

Sawyer grinned and replied immediately.

> To: Nikolai70@aol.com
> From: Adventures_of_Tom@aol.com
>
> Lunch.
>
> —S

She waited. And waited.

Then, suddenly a box popped up on her screen—AOL Instant Messenger. Sawyer jumped.

> **Nikolai70:** No, seriously.
>
> **Nikolai70:** Or is this your attempt to school me further on the subject of humor?

Sawyer blinked, feeling a little naked, almost as if Nick had come into her apartment unannounced. She thought about what to do. She wasn't one for instant messaging—it seemed like that was for people who spent their time in chat rooms. She took a deep breath, braced herself, and placed her slightly trembling hands over the computer keys.

Adventures_of_Tom: No—seriously!

Adventures_of_Tom: Lunch.

Nikolai70: So you're a slacker in wolf's clothing?

Nikolai70: Hey, no judgment from me. Lunch has been my favorite part of the day ever since they started serving tater tots in the school cafeteria in the third grade, whereupon it narrowly beat out my other favorite, recess.

Adventures_of_Tom: "Whereupon"?

Nikolai70: Yes. I believe that is an accurate use of the term.

Adventures_of_Tom: It's very formal.

Nikolai70: I told you—lunch is my manifesto. Lunch, and general slack-ery.

Adventures_of_Tom: Oh, man. You're going to hate the real reason that lunch is my favorite, then.

Nikolai70: Don't tell me!—"You get your best work done on your lunch hour." Barf.

Adventures_of_Tom: But I do!

Nikolai70: You're right, that violates every tenet of my manifesto. You're beyond saving if you sit at your desk. Nothing sadder than a chick sitting at her desk during lunch eating a yogurt.

Adventures_of_Tom: Do people still say "chick" these days?

Adventures_of_Tom: And while we're on the subject, do people still say "barf"?

Nikolai70: I do. I say both.

Adventures_of_Tom: Well, to answer your question, I do NOT sit at my desk.

Nikolai70: There is hope for you yet.

Adventures_of_Tom: But I do go to the same place every day. I found this tiny but really amazing place—Greenacre Park. Do you know it?

Nikolai70: Nope.

Adventures_of_Tom: Oh, it's crazy! It's smack in the middle of Midtown, this little green oasis with a waterfall and café tables.

Nikolai70: New York has a lot of cool surprises. I'm from here, but you still find unexpected stuff to inspire you, all the time.

Adventures_of_Tom: Stuff inspires you?

Nikolai70: Yeah, you know. To write the perfect one-word slogan to pair with a giant photo of a chimp in a tuxedo.

Adventures_of_Tom: Don't sprain yourself.

Nikolai70: I don't. Like I said: Chimp in a tuxedo. That does all the heavy lifting.

Adventures_of_Tom: Anyway. I like it there. In the park. And because I take my lunch late (the other editorial assistant goes first) the park is always empty when I go.

Nikolai70: That sounds a little sad.

Adventures_of_Tom: I don't ALWAYS do work. Sometimes I just write.

Nikolai70: Write?

Adventures_of_Tom: My own things. I like to write.

Nikolai70: Hmm. So you're a writer.

Adventures_of_Tom: I like to write. I don't know if that makes me a writer.

Nikolai70: OK, I concede. You're a cut above the yogurt-at-their-desks girls.

Adventures_of_Tom: I'm glad my existence meets with your approval.

Nikolai70: I'm sensing some sarcasm, but I'm gonna move past that.

Nikolai70: What have you written?

Adventures_of_Tom: Ha ha. Nothing you would know.

Nikolai70: I won't take that personally.

Nikolai70: But my friend the chimp might. He'll have you know, he's very well read and up on all his literary fiction. Like I said: Tuxedo. Classy.

Adventures_of_Tom: Well

Sawyer stopped typing abruptly, and her pinky accidentally hit enter as she froze. Why was she telling him all this? About the park. About her writing.

Was it the wine? Or the fact that talking over the internet didn't feel quite real? She couldn't figure it out.

And she couldn't figure out why she wanted to tell him even more.

The computer pinged with a new message.

Nikolai70: "Well"—what?

Adventures_of_Tom: Sorry

Adventures_of_Tom: Actually, I got my first acceptance from a literary magazine today.

Adventures_of_Tom: Well, it's an online e-zine. But it's pretty cool. My poem's not up yet, but here's a link to the site—www.DeckleEdgeOnline.org

Nikolai70: Congratulations. That's big.

Adventures_of_Tom: Thank you.

Sawyer stopped typing again. She immediately felt a small twinge of regret. Her cheeks grew warm with embarrassment. The computer pinged again.

Nikolai70: Hey, I have to run.

Nikolai70: But congrats again.

Nikolai70: And I'm glad I didn't offend you.

Sawyer smiled.

Adventures_of_Tom: Short memory. You DID offend me.

Nikolai70: Oh, yeah—that's right. I did. I meant I'm glad you've forgiven me.

Adventures_of_Tom: Did I?

Nikolai70: If you didn't, I'll get the chimp in a tuxedo on the case. That'll do it.

Adventures_of_Tom: I'm sure.

Nikolai70: No one says no to a chimp in a tuxedo. I'm telling you.

Nikolai70: OK, but for real, gotta go. Nice talking to you.

Sawyer scrambled for something to say back—something nice. But before she could type anything at all, he was already gone, logged off.

She sat there, staring at the screen, still surprised by the interaction.

She scrolled and skimmed back over the messages they had exchanged. He was still kind of a cocky jerk, but he wasn't all bad. She sighed, alone again, and closed the AIM window.

Then she glanced at the time and blinked in surprise. The evening had flown by, which felt strange—Sawyer had grown so accustomed to watching the clock and wondering when Charles might come home.

• • •

A short while later, Sawyer heard Charles's key turn in the lock. She glanced at the time again—force of habit. 8:58 p.m. That wasn't so bad. And, he was balancing a six-pack of cold beers atop a box of hot pizza. Sawyer recognized the logo from the devilishly delicious-yet-greasy pizza joint on the corner by the subway. He threw his keys on the entry table and grinned.

"I thought since it was looking like I'd be home in time for Thursday-night TV, we could do pizza and beer on the couch."

Sawyer smiled.

"Sounds perfect."

He stripped down to his undershirt and boxers, tossed his clothes over a chair, and flicked on the TV. Sawyer ducked into the kitchen, grabbed two plates and a roll of paper towels, and brought them over to the coffee table.

The show started. It was a rerun of *Frasier* that Sawyer had already seen, but Charles hadn't, and Sawyer was content to enjoy it together. The pizza was hot and delicious; they folded each slice in half and reddish-orange pepperoni oil dripped from the corners. During commercials, their hands were too greasy to hit mute on the remote, but they tried to talk over them.

"Any wedding updates from my mom?" Charles asked.

"Not today," Sawyer answered.

"Hey—how's Autumn doing in Japan?"

"She's good. She made a French friend."

"In Japan?"

Sawyer nodded. Charles laughed as though to say, *That Autumn, what a nut,* but didn't ask anything further. The commercial ended and the show came back on.

Later, after *Frasier* ceded to *Will & Grace,* and eventually to *ER,* Sawyer glanced over to where Charles sat, now reclined on the couch, his expression tired and zombie-like. She couldn't help but wonder if they should have spent some of their time actually talking to each other.

Or doing something else.

They hadn't had sex in a while.

They'd always found time in the past—even when Charles was in law school and had to cram all night for a test, Sawyer had put on a pot of coffee and stayed up with him and they'd found ways to fit in "study breaks" (*I've never seen someone take the "flash" in "flashcards" so literally,* Charles had once joked with a smile). They'd been together since college, when Sawyer was just nineteen—so she knew it wasn't always glamor and fireworks; sometimes it was beer and laundry day. But they were comfortably affectionate. They'd always made time.

Her mind flicked back to the Chinese restaurant receipt she'd found. As hard as she'd tried, she hadn't been able to get it out of her head.

• • •

When they got into bed an hour later, Charles rolled over on his side and immediately began snoring. It always took Sawyer a little longer to drop off. She stared up at the ceiling, thinking. Tomorrow would mark another summer Friday. She pondered what she could do to fill up the time.

It dawned on Sawyer: she hadn't told Charles her news about having her poem accepted to the online literary magazine.

The only person she'd told was Nick—Nick, the guy who had so rudely snubbed her at the Wexler Gibbons dinner.

How strange that was.

5.

MONDAY, JUNE 14

"Sawyer? Would you mind stepping into my office, please?"

Sawyer looked up from the TIP sheet she was preparing for Thursday's internal launch of new titles, surprised. Johanna rarely called anyone into her office. In fact, most days Johanna even kept the door shut—which lent the office an air of off-limits mystery. But upon being summoned, Sawyer immediately grabbed a pen and yellow legal pad from her desk drawer and scurried through the door, curious to know what this might be about.

Once inside, Sawyer stole little glances around the room. In some ways, Johanna's office was similar to other editors' offices, in that the bookshelves were stacked with copious copies of novels Johanna had edited, and her walls were adorned with blown-up covers of some of her favorites. But Johanna's office was unique in its aura of Old World elegance. She came from old money, and had swapped out the modern, brightly colored furniture that was standard-issue at the publishing house for tasteful antiques. Even the gray indoor/outdoor office carpeting was covered by a lush Persian rug. Framed photographs of Johanna in formal attire, posing with her authors at the PEN Gala and the National Book Awards, lined the credenza, the same spot in other editors' offices where they tended to display photos of their spouses and kids and dogs. Johanna had worked in publishing a long time, and—you had to hand it to her—in her younger days, she had carved a path for herself during a time when women weren't really welcome in the field. Johanna had stuck to her guns, nurtured her list over time; her authors won Pulitzers.

Most editors' offices possessed a slight air of clutter (as soon as they managed to clear out an avalanche of superfluous copies of manuscripts, galleys, and finished copies, twice as many came flooding in), but Johanna's clutter was mixed with a treasure trove of antique knickknacks—first editions, tortoiseshell paperweights, ivory-handled magnifying glasses. There was a lot to look at, and without meaning to, Sawyer let her eyes wander, staring in a daze.

"Sawyer?" Johanna said, impatient.

Sawyer snapped to attention and tried to look composed.

"Yes."

Sawyer gripped the yellow legal pad and pen, poised to take notes.

"Do you know why I called you in here today?"

Sawyer blinked and shook her head.

"Do you recognize this?" Johanna slid a manuscript across her desk.

Sawyer picked up the title page. It was familiar.

"Oh, yes!" she said. "That was in the slush pile—I think I pulled that, maybe, three months ago? Usually you know by skimming over the first ten pages that it's a no-go. But that manuscript . . . I couldn't put it down. In fact, I read the whole thing in two sittings! Her query letter said she based it on her family's own immigration story, coming from India to Queens. The family felt so *real*. Oh, and the writing voice! It was so fresh, so lush and vivid . . ."

Sawyer halted. She realized she was gushing, and Johanna's expression was steely, inscrutable. Sawyer had passed the manuscript along to Johanna, with a recommendation to consider it.

"Gosh, I hope I didn't waste your time. I really felt it was a standout, the best thing I've ever seen in the slush." She hesitated. "But . . . maybe I had . . . 'slush goggles'? You know . . . like, beer goggles?"

Johanna's expression was still stoic, but she arched an eyebrow at the reference.

Sawyer willed herself to shut up.

Johanna waited a moment, as if to make certain Sawyer was quite finished babbling.

"Well, I called you in here to give you some good news. I signed the author."

Sawyer blinked.

"Oh. You *liked* it."

"Yes. I finally got a chance to read the manuscript last week, and I reached out to the author. She was unrepresented, so I put her in touch with Celine, and between the three of us we were able to put together a deal for the book that I believe is good for all parties involved."

Celine was Johanna's favorite literary agent to work with.

"Wow. That's amazing. And really nice of you to set her up with Celine. I guess I've never really seen how an unsolicited submission works, deal-wise."

"Yes, well, it happens so rarely, there's no real set way. But I think best form is to recommend an agent and go from there. It's a bit backward, in terms of a manuscript's usual sequence, but a good writer will want a good agent in her life, anyway. And the idea of talking directly to a writer about money is just abhorrent."

Sawyer listened to all this, thinking what a strange system publishing was. She'd been to some work meetings wherein they talked about nothing *but* authors, sales, and money . . . so the fact that it was taboo to ever talk about money *to* an author struck her as somewhat ironic.

"Anyway," Johanna continued. "We're going to announce the deal next week, so I wanted you to be in the know."

"Oh, thank you," was all Sawyer could muster. She waited, hoping there was more. But Johanna simply raked the manuscript back across the desk, then lifted it and tapped the edges into neat alignment.

"I'll let you get back to organizing the TIP data for Thursday's launch."

"OK, thanks," Sawyer repeated.

She got to her feet and saw herself back out.

Once at her desk, she sat down and stared at her computer screen, not really seeing anything on it, still in a daze. She realized she'd kind of been hoping that Johanna might say, *Good eye, keep up the good work.* Or something to that effect. And she was a little surprised that Johanna hadn't mentioned anything sooner . . . that she hadn't told Sawyer she was reading the manuscript Sawyer had recommended, hadn't told her when she decided she liked it, hadn't told her anything was afoot last week when Johanna must have reached out to the author and started putting the deal together.

But on the whole, Sawyer was elated that the book was going to be published—she felt it truly deserved it. And even if Johanna hadn't given her a pat on the back, Sawyer felt a tickle of pride to think she'd had some small role in its discovery. The fact that the book was good in Johanna's eyes was proof that Sawyer's taste was pointing her in the right direction . . . and that Sawyer might make a good editor herself someday.

• • •

Sawyer was still pleased about her slush-pile victory when she got off work. As she came up the stairs from the hot, steamy subway, she made up her mind to stop at the wine shop—the nice one that obviously targeted people on their way to dinner parties and also sold cheese and flowers. She felt like a celebration, however small. She picked out an ice-cold sauvignon blanc, a tiny triangular wedge of goat's milk Gouda, and a small bouquet of pale pink peonies.

Once home, Sawyer went to the record player and put on her favorite—a Van Morrison album that had once belonged to her father, until she'd discovered it as a teenager and borrowed it so many times the record had haphazardly become hers. She stood listening to the first strains of music with a smile, then cut the stems of the flowers and put them in a vase that was actually a pencil cup. She put the wedge of Gouda on a plate along with some crackers, and poured herself a glass of the cold, crisp sauvignon blanc.

Then she sat down and tried to think of what else to do. Eventually, she moved her celebratory bounty two feet from the kitchen table to the computer desk, even moving the flowers into her eyeline so she might still smile at them. She powered up the computer, clicked on the AOL icon.

This time, when she logged on, the tinny male voice only said, "*WELCOME!*"

No mail.

At first, she couldn't quite put a finger on why the inbox felt so empty to her. She hadn't been expecting to hear back about any of her other poetry or short-story submissions. But she *had* sort of, if only in the back of her mind, been expecting to hear from . . .

She thought for a moment, then popped open a new email window.

> To: Nikolai70@aol.com
> From: Adventures_of_Tom@aol.com
>
> How's the chimp? Seems like the tuxedo is a pretty big part of his identity. I worry that it factors heavily into his self-worth; does he sleep in it?—S

Sawyer was pretty sure she'd lost her mind, but after gazing at the screen for a minute, she shrugged, rolled her eyes at herself, and clicked send.

She sat back and took a sip of her wine, then nibbled at a bit of cheese, ignoring the crackers she'd taken great pains to rummage through the cabinet and produce as a concession to decorum (were people allowed to just make themselves a plate of nothing but cheese?).

She refreshed her inbox.

Nothing.

Then the computer sounded with a trill and the Instant Messenger box popped open on the screen, making Sawyer jump and catching her off guard every bit as much as the previous time.

Nikolai70: You're just like all the other girls.

Sawyer read the message, furrowed her brow, and read it again.

Adventures_of_Tom: What do you mean?

Nikolai70: You act like you want to be my friend. But really you just want to get the skinny on whether the chimp already has a girlfriend or not.

Sawyer's lips involuntarily twisted into a smile.

Adventures_of_Tom: You saw right through me. In my defense, you said yourself that no one can resist a chimp in a tuxedo.

Nikolai70: I know, and it's true. I can't blame you.

Nikolai70: I had a friend just like him in high school. Human. Not chimp. Although, now that I think about it, there WAS something simian about the guy. Big ears.

Adventures_of_Tom: But not so big they repelled the ladies.

Nikolai70: The ladies only had eyes for the earring. They thought it made him look like Johnny Depp. Or Christian Slater. Or something.

Adventures_of_Tom: I see. The rebel-without-an-intact-earlobe type.

Nikolai70: Girls would always buddy up to me . . . and then drop in a question about whether he'd already asked a girl to prom.

Sawyer mulled this for a moment. It didn't quite sit right. Nick was far too good-looking, far too full of exactly the kind of egotistical swagger that high school girls adored. She had trouble picturing him as the dowdy sidekick. She wanted to call bullshit on him, but . . . if she did, she'd be complimenting him in a roundabout way.

The computer pinged again.

Nikolai70: Anyway, it's always been him or the chimp, everybody's favorite.

Adventures_of_Tom: "Always a bridesmaid, never a bride." Or, in your case—"Always a homosapien, never homoerectus."

Nikolai70: Nice joke. I wouldn't have pegged you for blue humor.

Adventures_of_Tom: Well—"when in Rome." I hear you guys in the ad business are experts in innuendo.

Nikolai70: It IS an art form.

Adventures_of_Tom: So, you DO like your work, after all.

Nikolai70: I didn't say that.

Adventures_of_Tom: I'm sure you've done SOMETHING in the course of your job that you found cool.

Nikolai70: Is that a question?

Adventures_of_Tom: Yes.

Nikolai70: Clearly you want to tell me about the cool thing you did at work today.

Adventures_of_Tom: What do you mean?

Nikolai70: I just find that people tend to ask the questions that they really want other people to ask them.

Adventures_of_Tom: I was actually interested and sincere.

Nikolai70: I've got nothing interesting to tell.

Nikolai70: So tell me about the cool thing you did at work today.

Adventures_of_Tom: Well

Adventures_of_Tom: I found an unsolicited manuscript in the slush pile, and now it's going to be published.

Nikolai70: That is cool.

Adventures_of_Tom: Yeah. I mean, I think this author's work is so good she would have gotten discovered sooner or later, but . . . I don't know. It feels good to have maybe played some small part in getting her book to its well-deserved destination.

Nikolai70: It doesn't sound like a "small part." What you did is huge.

Adventures_of_Tom: Well . . . I don't know about "huge."

Nikolai70: Don't edit me. I stand by my word choice. Her life is about to change. And tell me you DON'T think some other editorial assistant dickhead would have probably passed right over this manuscript.

Adventures_of_Tom: Hey! My coworkers are awesome.

Nikolai70: Tell me that manuscript wouldn't have gotten passed right over by someone else.

Adventures_of_Tom: Maybe. Maybe not. I don't know.

Nikolai70: It would have. And here's why: It takes a special kind of person to find the gems in the slush pile. You have to be a real dyed-in-the-wool optimist, but you also have to be really smart. And most people tend to be only one or the other.

Adventures_of_Tom: I guess . . . "thank you"?

Nikolai70: No problem. And you can remove those scare quotes. I complimented you. I meant it. And it's OK to say thanks.

Adventures_of_Tom: Thank you.

Nikolai70: Even if I was a jackass and made fun of your name.

Adventures_of_Tom: Oh, that reminds me—what's up with "Nikolai"?

Nikolai70: You can remove the scare quotes there, too. It's not irony; it's my name.

Adventures_of_Tom: Nick is short for Nikolai?

Nikolai70: In my case, yes.

Adventures_of_Tom: Is that Eastern European? (Forgive me if that's an ignorant question)

Nikolai70: Russian. My mom was a chemist who defected from the USSR when she found out she was having me.

Adventures_of_Tom: Wow.

Adventures_of_Tom: She sounds impressive.

Nikolai70: She's had to deal with a lot in her life.

Adventures_of_Tom: There's a novel there.

Nikolai70: No thanks.

Sawyer paused and lifted her fingers off the keyboard for a moment. The subject felt sensitive, and she wondered if she might be trespassing. Could you tell that through a computer?

But she also didn't want to end the conversation, especially if she *had* overstepped. She tried to think of a polite direction to steer the conversation.

Adventures_of_Tom: Do you prefer for people to call you Nick or Nikolai?

Nikolai70: No one calls me Nikolai. Not even my mom—real Russians prefer nicknames anyway. Half my friends don't even know Nick is short for Nikolai.

Adventures_of_Tom: Oh.

Adventures_of_Tom: So then . . . if I may ask . . . why do you use it as your email address? That doesn't confuse your friends?

Nikolai70: We don't email each other. If I want to talk to them I see them. Or I call them. I don't go online much.

Adventures_of_Tom: You're online now.

Nikolai70: I am.

The apartment was still hot from the long summer day, but Sawyer thought she felt a little extra warmth creep into her cheeks. He said he didn't go online much . . . but both times she'd emailed him, he'd gotten back to her so quickly, even popping up on AOL Instant Messenger. So, was he lying? Or was he letting her know his chats with her were an exception?

But then her computer pinged with a new message, and the mystery was dispelled.

> **Nikolai70:** Look. I'll cut to the chase here about something that's been on my mind. It's pretty clear your fiancé and my girlfriend are having an affair, no?

A minute passed as Sawyer sat staring at the screen. It was as if she believed that, as long as she kept her suspicions from attaching themselves to *actual words*—as long as she kept them from becoming *language*—then she could keep them from being real. It was almost like a witch using words to cast a spell, but in reverse.

But now Nick had gone and dropped it all into one little tidy sentence. And it was still there—that grenade of a sentence—glowing on the screen. As she reread it over again, a new message nudged her from her trance.

> **Nikolai70:** Sawyer? Are you there?

She knew she should answer him. Did she think Charles and Kendra were having an affair?

> **Adventures_of_Tom:** I don't know.
>
> **Nikolai70:** I was thinking we could meet up and talk about it.
>
> **Adventures_of_Tom:** Meet up?
>
> **Nikolai70:** Yeah. Call me old fashioned. Feels like the kind of thing I don't want to talk about over a computer.

Adventures_of_Tom: Sure. I guess that makes sense.

Nikolai70: Well, we know they work late. And we both have summer Fridays—right?

Adventures_of_Tom: Yes

Nikolai70: So, let's meet then. This Friday, the Yale Club, around 2pm, since we both work in Midtown?

Adventures_of_Tom: You belong to the Yale Club?

Nikolai70: Yeah, why?

Adventures_of_Tom: I don't know. I guess I didn't picture that.

Nikolai70: I'll try to pretend like you didn't just say you didn't picture me going to an Ivy League School.

Adventures_of_Tom: That's not what I meant

Nikolai70: Actually, I gotta log off and take care of something, but we're good to meet on Friday, yeah?

Adventures_of_Tom: Yes

Nikolai70: Cool. See you then.

Nikolai70: Gotta go, bye for now.

Adventures_of_Tom: Bye

Sawyer had barely finished typing "Bye" and hit enter when in the next second, Nick had logged off.

She sat there, still staring at the computer, in a daze.

They didn't have to go outside to smoke, Nick had said at the dinner. She'd let his comment slip to the back of her brain, like the receipt. She'd been having fun chatting online.

But now she knew: she wasn't the only one who thought Charles was having an affair.

And she had agreed to meet Nick in person. On Friday.

6.

During the rest of the week, Sawyer tried to untangle her feelings, with little luck. The days passed in a blur, until Thursday—when the internal launch of new titles broke up the grind a bit at work.

Sawyer liked launch days. It was when everyone who worked at the imprint met in the publishing house's big boardroom. Sometimes snacks were brought in—bagels, Danish, cheese, crackers, grapes, cookies. The room buzzed with excitement as everyone got settled. Witty banter bounced back and forth among the more senior employees, until the head of the imprint called the room to order.

Then, the presentations started. Editors took turns introducing their upcoming novels, giving enticing summaries of the books' plots and telling the room a little bit about the authors, and sometimes mentioning the books' foreign rights sales, if they already existed.

When an editor was *really* in love with a book, they told the story of how they'd encountered and fallen in love with the manuscript, and why. It was transporting, like hearing about a romance. And then, if it was done in time, there was something magical about a cover reveal. Sawyer loved seeing how the art department had translated the manuscript into an image. It was a transformative moment, the moment when a book went from being a mere stack of white pages or a word-processing document—to something you could picture on a bookstore shelf. Sawyer always felt a tingle of excitement when new covers were revealed.

That Thursday's meeting served as a much-needed distraction for Sawyer. Johanna presented the TIP sheet and other materials Sawyer and Kaylee had worked all week to prepare, and the presentation went well. The book in question laid bare the emotional inner lives of characters who lived in a small blue-collar factory town in remote Maine. The book cover that the art department had come up with was striking—a juxtaposition of beautiful rural New England as contrasted with the brick smokestacks of an old factory, depicted in the American realist style of an Edward Hopper painting.

Johanna did not mention her latest acquisition—the unsolicited manuscript that Sawyer had pulled from the slush pile—but this wouldn't have been the time for that. Eventually, that book would be allotted its own presentation in yet another launch meeting. It would get talked up and get its own cover reveal.

Sawyer couldn't wait.

• • •

After the launch, the rest of the workday went by quickly. Johanna was happy with how her presentation had gone, so at quarter to five, she told Sawyer and Kaylee they could pack up a little early for the day and go home.

Sawyer took the subway home, thankful for both the early reprieve and—after waiting on a particularly gross, sauna-like subway platform—the train car's vigorous air-conditioning. Once back at her apartment, she fell into what had become her regular routine: throwing all the windows open, switching on the oscillating fan, and settling into the computer desk to check her email.

"You've got mail!"

It was from the online literary e-zine.

Sawyer clicked on it, quickly scanned the message, and . . . realized it was a notification from the editor letting her know that her poem had gone live.

Congratulations! he'd written. *We are so proud to share your work.*

Sawyer clicked on the link he'd pasted into the email, a nervous flutter in her stomach.

A browser screen flashed open and loaded the e-zine's landing page. *THE DECKLE EDGE*, it read in a pleasing font, above an image of original artwork by one of the visual contributors. Below that was the issue's table of contents . . . and there it was: Sawyer's name, and the title of her poem. She clicked on it, and the site jumped to her poem's page.

She stared at it in disbelief, admiring the layout. There was nothing too amateur, nothing too bright and internet-y. No newfangled fonts in fluorescent green or royal blue. Instead, a classic, dignified black font on a pale taupe background. Her poem was centered to the left with another image of original art from the issue's visual contributor to the right of it. It looked really nice—something she could be proud of.

She'd put something out there! She could only cross her fingers and hope that it was worthy. She reminded herself that she was safe from the judgment of anyone she knew, because she hadn't told anyone.

Then she remembered: She'd told Nick. She'd even sent him the link. But that was before her poem was up. It was silly to think he might remember and go online and look at it—wasn't it?

She felt her cheeks burning to picture it.

She tried to push the sudden rush of self-consciousness aside as she clicked through the rest of the issue, reading the other contributors' work. This occupied the better part of an hour. She studied the others, trying to learn from their poems and stories, and feeling honored to have her poem in their company.

Finally, she closed the browser window, then her email inbox. But the very second she logged off, the phone rang, making her jump. Its shrill, tinny bell cut through the air like a knife. She grabbed for it.

"Hello?"

"Sawyer! I've been trying to get through for ages—your line has been giving me a busy signal for an hour!"

"Hey, Mom. I was logged on to the internet."

"You were on the internet? During that *whole time*?" her mother questioned in disbelief. "What were you doing?"

Sawyer squirmed.

"I was reading something."

"What were you reading?"

"A literary magazine," Sawyer answered. She considered telling her mother about her poem.

PROS:

- Her mother was an English professor.
- The whole family shared a very genuine love of literature.
- Her mother was an excellent critic.

CONS:

- Her mother was less than enthusiastic about the fact that Sawyer had chosen trade publishing over academia. What would her mother think of dabbling in creative writing?
- Her mother was an excellent critic.

"A literary magazine? *On the internet?*" her mother echoed now, as though the idea of something literary on the internet was impossible.

Sawyer quickly made up her mind to keep the news about her poem to herself.

"Hey, Mom—I forgot to ask: How was the conference?"

"Oh! It was lovely! I gave my paper and the Q & A after went great. And I wish they had it in Florida more often—your father and I felt like we were on vacation."

"Did you guys get to the beach?"

"We sure did. I might even have a tan somewhere under this sunburn."

Sawyer laughed.

She listened as her mother chatted about the academic conference that Carol had just attended with Sawyer's father.

Her parents were both professors at a small conservative college in Oregon, where Sawyer had grown up. They both taught and loved literature; Nick had been right about that part. But Sawyer's father, Dennis, was an "early modernist"—in other words, he taught Shakespeare—while her mother was the one who adored American literature, and had chosen Sawyer's name.

Carol had had her heart set on a university life for her daughter, in part because Carol's own entry into academia had been hard-won. She hadn't considered the path open to her, marrying Dennis while they were still undergrads, and tagging along as "the wife" when he went to grad school. She'd typed and proofread his dissertation, even written a significant portion of his footnotes. By the time Dennis had landed a tenure-track position in Eugene and Sawyer had been born . . . Carol had realized that she wanted her own academic career. She worked part-time on her master's, then a PhD. After that, she toiled as an adjunct and a lecturer until she could finally throw her hat in the ring as a full-time faculty member at her husband's university. Carol knew that's how people thought of it: her *husband's* university. It didn't matter that Carol had become the more active scholar. It didn't matter that, in recent years, Carol had published more, had gone to more conferences, had given more papers than her husband had. Some faculty members would forever regard her as a "spouse hire."

When it came to Sawyer, Carol saw an opportunity for her daughter to enjoy the obstacle-free version of her own life.

Sawyer could tell her mother was still hoping Sawyer would come to her senses and apply to go to graduate school after all. A year after

Sawyer and Charles made the move to New York, Carol was still dropping little comments into their conversations—comments like: *It's never too late!* Or else: *There may be some grad programs that might even find your recent work experience in trade publishing very interesting.*

It sometimes made their conversations tense.

"How are the wedding plans coming along?" Carol asked, once they'd finished catching up about the conference.

"Good," Sawyer answered. She told her mother about Kathy's latest plan—an impromptu bridal shower in September. The two moms were coming into town for Sawyer's second-to-last dress fitting. Kathy wanted to do brunch at Bergdorf's, followed by a Broadway musical, then some party favors and gift opening in Kathy's hotel suite.

"Just so long as the musical isn't *Cats*." Sawyer's mom laughed.

"Understood," Sawyer agreed.

"I'll give Kathy a call and ask if there's anything I can do to help with the planning," Carol offered.

When Sawyer had allowed Kathy to take the reins, Carol hadn't been offended. She'd understood it as being what Charles and Sawyer wanted. It wasn't her area of expertise, anyway. Running a grad program, chairing a committee, or planning an academic conference, yes. Planning a society-page wedding in Manhattan . . . not so much. She'd made it clear she wanted to help, but not get in the way.

Sawyer sometimes wondered, though, how her mother truly felt about the engagement itself. Carol had never said anything specifically, but Sawyer suspected she wasn't crazy about the idea of her daughter getting married so young. The world had afforded Sawyer's generation of young women more choices—and here Sawyer was, voluntarily choosing the old-fashioned path Carol felt had once held her back. Another nail in the coffin that was Carol's hopes for Sawyer to eventually go to grad school and become a professor.

And while Sawyer's parents liked Charles—or at least genuinely seemed to welcome him into the family—Sawyer knew her mother also had some opinions about what it was to be the wife of a corporate lawyer. Carol was outspoken about her disapproval in an abstract sense, as though she wasn't criticizing Charles and Sawyer per se, but faceless versions of a young corporate lawyer making his way up the ladder, and the young wife willing to shelve her ambitions for his.

It wasn't mean-spirited, but it was . . . *opinionated.*

Sawyer loved her mother dearly; her mom was the smartest human she knew. But sometimes she wished it was easier to tell her things.

"How is Charles doing?" Carol asked now, over the phone.

"He's good . . ." Sawyer replied.

Her mind went immediately to the merger, to his long hours, to what Nick had said. Suddenly, she wanted nothing more than for her mother to reassure her that the receipt from the Chinese restaurant didn't mean anything.

Carol seemed to pick up on her daughter's hesitation.

"Charles is OK?" Carol echoed Sawyer's words back to her. "And everything's good?"

Sawyer bit her lip.

"Yeah, of course," she said, forcing a smile into her voice. "We're just, you know, *so* busy. He probably won't be home until pretty late tonight."

"And . . . are *you* OK?" her mother added, gently.

Sawyer felt a pang of embarrassment. She shook herself and brightened. "I'm good," she insisted.

There was a pause. Sawyer knew her mother was debating whether or not to let it go.

"They must really like him at Wexler Gibbons to have picked him to be part of such a big case," Carol said finally, attempting a positive note. "I imagine it's very competitive among their junior associates."

"It is," Sawyer agreed. "I'm proud of him."

"Well," Carol continued, shifting back into pedantic, professor-mom mode. "I suppose this is all part and parcel of marrying a lawyer, especially one who is just starting out, and as ambitious as Charles."

Sawyer thought she could hear just the slightest hint of *I told you so* in her mother's voice. She bristled.

"Yes," Sawyer agreed, firmly closing the topic to further discussion. "It is."

After they hung up, Sawyer made a mental list of all the things she hadn't told her mother about:

- Her loneliness.
- Her poem.
- The manuscript she'd found in the slush pile.
- The fact that she'd begun to wonder if the long hours Charles worked were about more than just being a junior associate at a major New York law firm.

There was no one to talk to about that last part.

Except . . . that wasn't true. There *was* one person, and Sawyer had agreed to meet him on Friday—the very next day—at 2 p.m.

Sawyer sat there, still recovering from the aftermath that was talking to her beloved mother, wondering how to feel about her impending meeting with Nick. She supposed she ought to feel some relief in being able to discuss her suspicions about Charles with someone.

Mostly, she just felt nervous.

7.

FRIDAY, JUNE 18

In addition to getting home later and later, Charles had also started leaving the apartment earlier.

He'd recently developed the habit of getting up early and going to the gym before heading in to the office. It took the edge off sitting down at work all day, he said. And it allowed him to shower and shave and arrive at the office fresh.

It was vaguely amusing to Sawyer at first; Charles used to make fun of the protein-shake-guzzling guys who went to the gym religiously. Now, in a surreal twist, Sawyer regularly woke up to the sound of the blender running in the kitchen, while the windows were still dark and the sun had yet to fully rise. It seemed like Charles never missed a day, and had begun to accumulate copious amounts of gym clothes, gym shoes . . . a ridiculously expensive gym bag.

And so, that morning, Sawyer woke up twice. Once, when Charles left for the gym, and then the second time, when the summer sunshine began to fill the windows with the honeyed light of a much more reasonable hour. She got up and dressed for work, oddly self-conscious that she was going to meet Nick later that day.

She surveyed her clothes. She had to wear something nice enough for the Yale Club, which she knew had a dress code. What exactly *was* the correct level of formality best suited to meeting someone at a social club in order to discuss the possibility that your partners might be having an affair?

She opted for a sundress—one that was forgiving in the heat, but could be dressed up to defend against both the rigors of decorum *and* central air-conditioning with the right cardigan and ballet flats. Once showered, dressed, brushed, and glossed, she set off, unsure what the day might bring.

• • •

There was a distinctly “Friday” mood at work.

Johanna was there, but left by 10:30 a.m. She owned a house in the Hamptons (in “Bridge,” as she referred to it) and was an avid gardener. She tied her Hermès around her neck (every day a different one, it seemed), announced something about it being time to dig up the spring bulbs that had finished flowering, then breezed past Sawyer and Kaylee to the elevator, where she vanished for the day.

Sawyer tried to picture Johanna gardening, sweating, kneeling in a flower bed, fending off mosquitoes, dirt under her nails. It was slightly impossible. Sawyer mentally added a costume—Ralph Lauren jodhpurs, Chanel sunglasses, and these Gucci-logo gardening gloves Sawyer and Autumn had once mocked when they'd dared each other to ring the bell and go inside the Gucci boutique on Madison Avenue. That made it somewhat easier to picture, but it was still a stretch.

Free of Johanna's watchful eye, Kaylee departed for the day soon after.

“I don't think the phone will ring,” Kaylee said as she hastily packed up her things in a well-advised attempt to hurry over to the Plaza in time for the next Jitney departure, before the noon rush set in.

Sawyer understood. Translation: *Will you watch the phone?*

“I'll be here for a while anyway,” Sawyer assured her. “Don't worry about it.”

"Thanks! You're the best!"

In a flash, the building had emptied out, and Sawyer was at her desk alone. She'd planned to stay until it was time to walk over to the Yale Club and meet Nick, but had forgotten how abandoned and eerie the office could feel on a summer Friday afternoon. Luckily, she had something she liked working on. Johanna had asked Sawyer to do an editorial pass on Sawyer's "diamond in the slush," aka, the unsolicited manuscript they'd recently acquired.

She sat there, reading and marking up the manuscript while abstractly listening to the creak and groan of the elevator shaft, the mechanical thump of the central air kicking on and off. Her stomach growled. Stupidly, she'd also forgotten to pack a lunch—normally she left the office early enough to eat at home on summer Fridays. She went to the kitchenette on their office floor and rummaged through the fridge, finding a yogurt set to expire the next day. It was completely out of character for Sawyer to plunder food, but she hoped that between the expiration date and the fact that the yogurt's original owner was probably somewhere eating a lobster roll, she might be doing them (and the yogurt) a favor.

She went back to her desk and settled in, spooning bites into her mouth as she continued to read. But as compelling as the manuscript was, her eyes kept drifting to the time, and her thoughts kept drifting to her impending rendezvous. She was surprised that Nick had picked the Yale Club as a place to meet. New York was big on social clubs, but Sawyer had never much liked them. They struck her as stuffy, elitist.

For some reason, Sawyer had assumed Nick was like her: not a social-club type of person. He'd struck her as an outsider, the kind of guy who went against the grain by nature. But she had to remind herself that she didn't really know Nick, and he was also the cocky, expensive-suit-wearing, junior advertising executive who had been rude to her at the Wexler Gibbons dinner.

As Sawyer scraped the last bits of yogurt from the container and licked her spoon clean, she suddenly froze. Nick's words came back to her: *Nothing sadder than a chick sitting at her desk during lunch eating a yogurt.* She couldn't help but laugh aloud. She looked around to see if anyone had heard her . . . then remembered she was alone, and laughed aloud again.

• • •

When the hour finally approached two o'clock, Sawyer left the office on foot.

At Grand Central, she entered the food hall and crossed through the terminal and out the other side—partly to cool off a little, and partly because she simply loved historical New York. The Main Concourse, with its gilded clock, marble staircases, and grand arched ceiling painted with a sky full of constellations, always took her breath away.

Once back out on the street, she was a stone's throw from the Yale Club. She spotted the giant white-and-blue "*Y*" banner fluttering in the crosstown breeze. She made her way toward the navy awning and pushed through a brass revolving door. Inside, she was immediately met with a very imposing yet dignified sign atop a brass pole that read "*GUESTS MUST BE ACCOMPANIED BY A MEMBER.*"

She spotted Nick sitting in an armchair in the lobby, reading what appeared to be a copy of *Rolling Stone*, and made a beeline. It wasn't until she was standing directly in front of him that Nick looked up and blinked in recognition.

"Oh, hey."

He stared openly for a brief moment. Sawyer felt his eyes taking in the sight of her, from head to toe. Her skin prickled, and she became suddenly and very acutely aware of how opposite she and Kendra were in terms of appearance. Sawyer was slight and dark, with big eyes and neatly trimmed bangs that she considered vaguely arty; when people gave her compliments, they usually made Audrey Hepburn comparisons.

Finally, he cleared his throat, then closed the magazine and stood.

Sawyer wasn't sure how to greet him. After their online chats, a handshake now seemed too formal.

"Should we, uh . . . ?" Sawyer said, holding her arms open.

He flinched with surprise (or was it a wince?) but quickly cleared his throat again nonchalantly. "Sure. Why not?"

They embraced. Stiffly, awkwardly.

He was tall, Sawyer realized. He also smelled like fresh laundry—which seemed at odds with the impossibly humid day. It occurred to her that he might have chosen the club on purpose in order to get there early and change into a fresh shirt prior to meeting her. But why go to the trouble? This was not a date.

After the awkward greeting, Nick showed her the way to an elevator.

"The roof gets a nice breeze," he said. "That work for you?"

"Sure," Sawyer replied. "Anything's fine."

• • •

Whereas other social clubs were often full of dark wooden paneling and stone fireplaces, the Yale Club was quite bright and new-looking, everything in shades of white, pale blue, and cream, and decorated in the neoclassical style reminiscent of the White House. Sawyer suspected Nick had led her off the elevator a floor early so they might walk through some of the more impressive lounges and public rooms.

Finally, they reached the rooftop terrace, which indeed delivered on the promise of a pleasant breeze. It was as if the air molecules were suddenly freer up there. Sawyer felt stray wisps of her hair lifting from her shoulders, moving drowsily around her head.

As they sat down, a waiter came over to take a drink order, then hurried away again.

"Wow," Sawyer said, admiring the view.

A sea of buildings surrounded them, vibrating with the muffled, echoing sounds of the streets far down below.

"It's funny how, up close, concrete and glass can be so depressing," she continued. "But when you see them like this—like a *landscape*—it suddenly seems pretty . . . all those different shades of concrete turn into a mountain range, all that blue and black glass turns into a sparkling, bottomless body of water."

Nick looked at her. He studied her face, then looked at the view.

"There's that instinct for poetry, I guess," he said.

"Oh—no . . . I wasn't . . . I mean," Sawyer stammered, blushing. "You're the one who took me up here. You don't like the view?"

He shrugged. "I'm a simple guy. What I like is being outside on a summer day anyplace you can go and not sweat your balls off."

"Oh."

He looked at her again with that direct gaze. "Your words just made the view more interesting and beautiful than it ever occurred to me it was."

Sawyer felt a blush creeping back into her cheeks again.

"Were you waiting long?" she asked politely, squirming under his direct gaze.

"Nah."

"I saw that you were reading *Rolling Stone*. Did your company do one of the ads in the issue?"

Nick arched an eyebrow at her.

"I *do* know how to read," he joked. "Although I know magazines about pop culture hardly qualify as literary material."

"That's not what I was getting at. I just thought . . ." Sawyer began, but trailed off. She thought, *This is going badly. Already.*

The waiter returned with their drinks—a beer for Nick and a glass of white wine for Sawyer, both glasses beaded with condensation. He set them down and disappeared.

Sawyer took a breath and tried again.

"I'm sorry," she said. "I think I'm nervous. It feels weird meeting you like this."

Nick looked at her. He picked up his beer and took a long, deep sip, then set it back down again.

"You make it sound like *we're* the ones having an affair," he said.

Sawyer blanched. She still couldn't wrap her mind around it . . . or perhaps, her heart.

"Do you really think they're having an affair?" she asked. "Like, definitely?"

Nick cocked his head. "What do you think?"

"I don't know," she confessed. "I guess there have been a few things to make me . . . well, *wonder.*"

He didn't speak. She felt the pressure to keep talking.

"I guess I didn't want to jump to any conclusions. To tell the truth, you're the first person I've talked to about this. I haven't even told my best friend, Autumn. I mean, part of that might be because she's off in Japan teaching English, but also . . . I just haven't told her . . ."

She knew she was rambling and stopped. He still didn't speak.

More timidly, she asked, "What . . . what made *you* think something might be going on?"

Nick took another long sip, then wiped the corners of his mouth.

"The night of the Wexler Gibbons dinner. It just seemed so obvious," he answered, blasé. "And then a couple of days later, when I put it together that he was the same guy as her quote, unquote 'workout partner' at the gym she was always raving about . . . I was like, well, *that's* sketchy as hell."

Sawyer's blood ran cold.

"They . . . they work out together?" she asked, still blinking in surprise.

Nick nodded. "Pretty sure it's an everyday thing."

Sawyer thought back to all the mornings she'd woken up to the sound of the blender, the rustlings of Charles packing up his gym bag, and felt her stomach twist itself into a knot.

“Still,” she insisted, trying to keep a level head. “It’s not like they’re having sex at five a.m. in the gym.”

“No,” Nick agreed dryly. “They’re probably having sex in the middle of the afternoon during a quote, unquote ‘working weekend.’ ”

Sawyer recoiled as though Nick had said something obscene and offensive . . . which he *had*.

He saw her expression and shrugged.

“Hey—you asked what I thought. That’s my gut,” he said.

They both sat there in silence for a moment.

“Anyway—what about you?” he prompted in return. “You said you’d noticed a few things that made you ‘wonder.’ What did you pick up on?”

Sawyer thought back over her recent interactions with Charles.

“Chinese food . . .” she murmured.

“Come again?”

“Chinese food,” she repeated, and proceeded to tell Nick the story of the receipt she’d found, how they’d had four beers, and how it was time-stamped 9:28 p.m. . . . despite the fact that Charles had told her it had been lunch. As she spoke, she noticed Nick physically recoiling—much as she had moments earlier.

“I’m sorry, Nick,” she said. “It . . . it could be nothing.”

He stiffened. A veil dropped over his expression.

“Nah,” he said, his voice suddenly callous. “Don’t feel sorry for *me*.” He paused, then added, “Feel sorry for yourself.”

His tone was rude—disdainful, even. Like how he’d acted toward her on the night of the Wexler Gibbons dinner.

“What do you mean?” Sawyer pushed.

Nick shrugged. “If Kendra’s got something going on with Charles, then it’s pretty simple for me.”

“It’s ‘simple’?”

“Sure. If that’s the case, then it’s time for me to break it off and move on.”

Sawyer shook her head at him, incredulous. "Sorry—stupid question here: Do you actually *like* Kendra?"

The question didn't faze him. He shrugged. "You've seen Kendra," he answered, matter-of-fact.

"So . . . she's hot, but *replaceable*?"

"Or maybe I am. She likes attention—she needs a lot of it from guys, but she's not interested in getting that deep."

"Then . . . why be with her?"

At this, he laughed. It sounded a little like a scoff. "You've seen Kendra," he repeated.

Sawyer frowned.

"Look—I wouldn't be with her if I didn't *like* her. Like most guys, I think Kendra is pretty spectacular. Plus, she's uncomplicated. Any time I've taken a step back, she's always . . . you know—made it worth my while to stick around."

Sawyer rolled her eyes.

"Not sure I want to hear about this," she said.

"Girls never do."

"What are we doing here, then? Why ask me to meet?"

"Two reasons."

She waited.

"First, I work on a system of risk and reward," he answered. "And right now I'm simply doing my due diligence."

It was her turn to scoff.

"You're doing your 'due diligence' on . . . the risks involved in loving Kendra?"

Nick gave a casual nod. "On the risks involved in maintaining a boyfriend role in relation to her," he corrected slightly.

"Don't you think that sounds a little"—she struggled for the right word—"I don't know . . . um, clinical? Detached?"

Another shrug. His propensity to shrug in response to her every question was beginning to annoy her.

"What about love?" Sawyer asked.

"Love is a feeling."

"Yeah . . ." Sawyer replied. "And?"

"And feelings are not my thing," Nick said, tossing back another sip of beer. The glass was almost empty now.

"You don't have feelings?" she asked, unable to help the sarcastic tone creeping into her voice.

"Sure, I have feelings," Nick replied. "But feelings are irrational stuff, so I don't factor them into my math."

"Your math?"

"The math I do when I make decisions."

"It's impressive you can keep your feelings completely out of it," Sawyer said, with another eye roll.

"Well, I keep things separate—the rational versus the irrational. The tangible versus the intangible. I just remind myself: feelings aren't real."

"Aren't real?"

"Nope. They're a distorted reality. They come and go. Hence, not real."

"Wow, I guess you've got it all figured out, then," Sawyer said.

"You're being condescending now," Nick replied. "But I got what works for me."

Sawyer relented. She was quiet a moment. She lifted the wineglass to her lips and took a deep sip of her own. She remembered something.

"You said there were *two* reasons you wanted to meet and discuss Charles and Kendra," she said. "What was the other reason?"

"Oh—that," Nick replied. "The other reason is . . . I don't know. You seem nice."

"I seem nice?"

"Yeah: nice. You belong in the category of 'really genuine person.'"

Sawyer didn't respond, unsure what to make of this.

"There's something about you. You're a real rarity."

Despite her irritation, Sawyer felt a flicker of flattery. But in the next second, Nick's words snapped her out of it.

"Your problem is that you don't stick to the pure math."

"My *problem*?" Sawyer said, dumbfounded.

"Yeah. You're one of *those* chicks. I bet you make it all complicated," Nick continued. "You think feelings *matter*. So, for you, one plus one equals three. Or maybe one plus one equals twenty-seven billion. I don't know—whatever you decide those feelings are worth. Which, PS, probably changes day by day."

Sawyer blinked at Nick, tongue-tied and thoroughly insulted.

"That's why I say, don't feel sorry for me; feel sorry for yourself," Nick concluded. "Like I said, your kind of math makes the world complicated for you."

Sawyer's jaw had dropped again, but she made no attempt to hide it.

"Who's being condescending *now*?" she volleyed back at him. "You don't know the first thing about me."

A sly smile played on Nick's lips, infuriating her. He looked smug.

"I'm pretty sure I know a few things," he said.

Sawyer was irritated by the way he made things sound patronizing and flirtatious at the same time.

"I seriously doubt it," she said with a snort. "Anyway—who are you to judge? From where I'm standing, it sounds like all you've figured out is how to keep your distance from someone you might love, out of fear of getting hurt."

Nick rolled his eyes. "Please. Your judgment of me is based on an assumption that I want the same things you do."

"Oh yeah?" Sawyer said. "What do I want?"

He held her gaze for a moment, then cocked his head and nodded at the engagement ring on Sawyer's finger.

"When's the wedding?" he asked.

Sawyer detected a taunting tone in his voice. She frowned.

"October," she replied.

"Congratulations."

She only gave him a cold look.

He smirked, and continued. "And you've booked the—let me guess . . ." He paused and pretended to look her over appraisingly. "The Boathouse? The Pierre?"

Still frowning, Sawyer crossed her arms. "The Plaza."

Nick fixed her with a smug, self-satisfied look, and didn't reply.

Sawyer glared at him, feeling the hot flames of indignance burning under her skin.

"Look," she said, trying to calm down and take a different tack. "I'm really not one of those girls. I wouldn't care if we got married in a barn."

"But you're not getting married in a barn," Nick challenged.

"OK, fine," Sawyer conceded. "But to me, it's not about the wedding, it's about . . . well, the marriage. The commitment. The *love*."

Nick leaned closer to her and pointed, as though he had just won the argument. "And *that's* why I say don't feel sorry for me—feel sorry for yourself," he said, wearing a maddeningly bemused smile.

Sawyer stared, cut to the core, incensed.

"If Kendra and Charles are having an affair," Nick continued, "I already know what I'll do." He gave one of his maddening shrugs. "I've been single before. There *are* perks."

She declined to comment. He continued.

"*You'll* be the one who has to decide to call off an entire wedding, an entire marriage—as you say." He paused, as if taking into account an afterthought, then added, "Or, not."

She took a moment and gathered herself. Finally, she cleared her throat, ready to put him in his place once and for all. But just as she opened her mouth to dish out her reply, a knock sounded on the glass that separated the club restaurant from the outdoor terrace.

Nick turned to look, and the smile dropped from his face. Two young men about their age smiled through the glass at Nick. He nodded at them, then glanced at Sawyer, suddenly jumpy.

"Couple of guys I work with," he explained in a low voice to her.

They waved to Nick from inside the restaurant, then hurried over to the door in order to come around.

"Hey—Nick!" the guys called as they approached.

Nick stood up and turned to greet them, taking several steps across the terrace to intercept them.

"Hey! What're you doing here? I thought all you guys on Kirkham's team went in on a summer place in Montauk," Nick called.

"Yeah, but Jeff and I have some time to kill while we wait for our ladies to get off work," said the taller of the two guys. "He thought we should wait and all drive up together."

The one evidently named Jeff shrugged.

"What's the point of going to a beach house if we don't bring along the girls in bikinis?" he said rhetorically.

"Fair enough," Nick replied.

"Have a drink with us?" the tall one invited.

"Sure," Nick replied affably. "I was just about to see my friend out. You guys start without me. I'll be right up."

The two guys blinked in Sawyer's direction, as if seeing her for the first time.

"See you inside?" Nick nudged them.

"Yeah—sounds good," the tall one agreed.

They turned and went back through the open door.

• • •

Nick saw Sawyer back down the elevator, to the lobby. She felt oddly rushed out—like he'd been embarrassed to be seen with her, or else was eager to ditch her.

"Sorry this was so brief," he said, as though reading her mind.

"Hah. I'm sorry it wasn't *briefer*," Sawyer retorted.

Nick raised his eyebrows.

"I've offended you again," he remarked. After a pause, he added, "I told you, I'm not good with people. I can't help it; it's the way I am. I try—I really do. But even on my best behavior, I'm always blunt, frank."

"Maybe what you are is opinionated and superior," Sawyer countered.

He smiled. "I'd love to stay and argue—I actually really would. I *like* talking to you. But we'll have to pick this up another time."

"Whatever."

Sawyer rolled her eyes at him, and turned to go. Over her shoulder, she called a chilly "bye." There was no second hug.

• • •

She decided to skip the subway. It was a long walk home to the Upper West Side, but Sawyer was agitated and suddenly felt she had energy to burn.

The idea of Nick pitying her was an irritating thorn, burrowing deeper and deeper under her skin. She was annoyed at herself for having been so open over email, and during their online chat sessions. She'd told him about her slush-pile discovery, her poem—*what an idiot!* Sawyer took it as further proof that her loneliness was making her strange, that the growing distance between her and Charles was making her do strange things.

She walked along Fifth Avenue. The bells were ironically ringing for someone's wedding as she passed St. Patrick's Cathedral. She glanced up the stone steps to where the large doors stood slightly ajar but couldn't make out anything in the gloom of the cathedral's interior, contrasted by the bright summer day. She had decided she would make her way north on Fifth and then walk most of the rest of the way through Central Park. It was only a little after 3 p.m., after all, and not the worst way to spend a summer Friday. She was counting on the park to calm her down and allow her to better parse her thoughts.

At first, all her anger was directed at Nick. Who did that guy think he was?

But then . . . as she walked along, her irritation at Nick receded, and other, bigger feelings began to come into focus.

Pretty sure it's an everyday thing, Nick had said, about Charles and Kendra working out together at the gym. Sawyer thought it through carefully. If true, it meant that every morning, when Charles rose and hurried out the door to go to the gym, he was also hurrying to meet Kendra there.

He had never once mentioned this fact to Sawyer, not even in passing.

If it was true.

8.

In the days that followed, Sawyer continued to wake up to the sounds of Charles getting up early to go to the gym.

"Do you ever work out with anybody?" she casually asked one evening, as they brushed their teeth for bed after he'd gotten home after another long day at the office.

Charles shrugged. "No one in particular," he answered, his mouth ringed with frothy white toothpaste foam. He spat, rinsed, and wiped his mouth. "Why?"

"I don't know," Sawyer said. "The reason you picked that gym is because it's so close to your office. I just thought you probably run into coworkers there."

"Sure. I see coworkers there sometimes," he replied. "And in line at Starbucks afterward. Inevitable. We basically all spend every waking moment within one city block of the office at this point."

Sawyer noted: he sounded indifferent and tired. Not at all defensive. She reminded herself that just because Charles went to the gym and Kendra went to the gym, it didn't mean they went *together*. Nick could be wrong, filling in a bunch of blanks without any real proof.

She felt reassured by this thought as she crawled into bed. Charles got in beside her. He put an arm around her and, along with it, a sense of warm comfort.

But the next morning, as Sawyer listened to the growl and whine of the blender, she caught herself frowning and chewing her lip, lost in thought again. She sighed, and for the rest of the week, threw herself back into her work, her writing.

* * *

Friday rolled around—another *summer* Friday. Another free afternoon. Sawyer wondered how she would fill it up.

At least her morning spent at work promised to be interesting; Johanna had sent out an early a.m. email letting the office know that one of her authors would be dropping in for a short, friendly meet and greet. When Sawyer read the name of who would be coming in, she gasped in excitement. It was Preeti Chaudhari, the author of the unsolicited manuscript she'd pulled from the slush pile. Sawyer had spent the last week rereading the manuscript and making editorial notes that she'd already handed over to Johanna.

It had been a pleasure to read the novel again. She'd put all her energy into the notes, and was excited for what would come next for the author. She couldn't wait to meet her.

"Sawyer," Johanna said as she emerged from her office. "We ought to have something to welcome Preeti. She'll be here around ten thirty. See if you can run out and buy a box of pastries and some fresh-pressed juice from that boulangerie around the corner?"

She laid three twenty-dollar bills on Sawyer's desk, then dusted her fingertips together, as though touching money with her bare hands was distasteful.

"Sure."

Sawyer glanced at the clock—ten thirty was in twelve minutes. She hurried off and practically sprinted to the boulangerie.

When she got back, she spotted Johanna talking and laughing with a tall, angular woman with dramatic cheekbones and her dark hair swept back into a graceful chignon. Sawyer recognized that Johanna was making her usual circuit around the office, introducing Preeti to the various people involved in the publication of Preeti's novel—whether it be art or sales or marketing. At present, they'd worked their way over to the art department and had stopped at the cubicle that belonged to Ellie, the graphic designer who had created the covers for Johanna's last five books.

Excited to finally meet the author whose manuscript she had so admired, Sawyer set the pastries and juice down on her desk and bounded over, a wide smile on her face.

"Hi—Ms. Chaudhari?" she said, after waiting for Johanna to finish what she was saying with regard to her early thoughts about the tone of the cover.

The woman turned around, surprised, but with a pleasant smile.

"Please; Preeti is fine," she said.

"Hi, I'm Sawyer. I'm so happy to finally meet you."

Sawyer held out her hand. Preeti took it with a cool, elegant handshake that matched her composed, unhurried prose style. Preeti smiled . . . but it soon dawned on Sawyer that there was no glimmer of recognition in it. The name, "Sawyer," did not ring any bells for this woman. She had never heard of Sawyer.

"Did you get the juice and pastries?" Johanna asked.

"Oh—yes. I did. They're on my desk."

"Wonderful. Can you bring them into the small conference room? And make a pot of tea? I think Preeti and I will sit and chat in there." She turned to Preeti. "You said you prefer tea to coffee, right?"

Preeti nodded, and Johanna continued with the tour, clearly on a mission to introduce Preeti to as many of the imprint's relevant personnel as possible before they all started leaving the office for summer Friday.

It's so lovely that we were able to coordinate this last-minute drop-in visit, Sawyer dimly heard Johanna say as they walked away.

I'm glad, too, Preeti replied. *I'm visiting my family—they still live in Queens, in the house I grew up in, much like the one described in my book, actually . . .*

Their voices fell to a low din as they moved away from Sawyer, deeper into the sea of cubicles. Sawyer watched them go, a little stunned. One thing was abundantly clear: Johanna hadn't bothered to mention that Sawyer was the one who had first pulled Preeti's book from the slush.

Sawyer set the juice and pastries up in the small conference room, then made a pot of tea and set out a tea service in the room, too.

Was she crazy to have wished Johanna had mentioned her by name? Maybe what Sawyer had done wasn't terribly monumental in the larger scheme of things—she'd recommended something she liked to her boss. It was *Johanna* who'd offered Preeti a book deal, and made it all happen. Johanna had that in her power. Sawyer was the lowest order of gatekeeper; Johanna was the one who had changed Preeti's life.

Still, Sawyer felt a tickle of malcontent at her invisibility. She'd gotten it in her head that she was part of a team. That when it was time for her to move up from editorial assistant to assistant editor, one of the shining moments to recommend her for the promotion would be that she could say, *I worked with Johanna Bailey's author Preeti Chaudhari.*

It was strange; having fallen in love with Preeti's manuscript, Sawyer felt like she *knew* Preeti. Meanwhile, it was unlikely that Preeti would ever be able to pick Sawyer out of a lineup.

* * *

Johanna and Preeti emerged from the small conference room just before noon. Johanna walked Preeti to the elevator, bid her goodbye, then turned back to where Sawyer and Kaylee sat.

"Look at the time!" she exclaimed pleasantly. "You're both free to go for the day, if you wish. Go enjoy your summer Friday."

She hummed and returned to her office.

Irritated, Sawyer decided to pack up and leave before Johanna changed her mind and remembered to order one of them to clean up the conference room.

"I'm outta here. Have a good weekend, Kaye," she called to Kaylee, who gave her a sympathetic look. They hadn't discussed it, but Kaylee seemed to understand that Sawyer had harbored the hope that Johanna might include her more in Preeti's book deal.

* * *

Sawyer was still mulling what had happened at work as she rode the subway home.

When she got to her apartment, she began to execute her regular routine out of habit, opening the windows, stripping off her work clothes, pouring herself an ice-cold glass of water from the pitcher she kept in the refrigerator, and automatically firing up the desktop computer that sat on the little desk in the kitchen.

She wasn't really expecting any email messages, so she was surprised when she heard the suave male voice shout, "*You've got mail!*" and saw that there was not just one but two messages waiting for her in her inbox.

More surprising still was the sender: Nikolai70@aol.com.

What more did the two of them possibly have to say to each other?

Sawyer's eyes moved to the subject lines, and she found a second surprise. They were labeled "READ ME FIRST" and "READ ME SECOND."

She stared cautiously for a few seconds, then gave in to curiosity and clicked on "READ ME FIRST."

To: Adventures_of_Tom@aol.com
From: Nikolai70@aol.com

Hi Sawyer.

Today is Friday. I'm guessing (and by "guessing," I mean making a highly intelligent conjecture, having gathered a reasonable amount of data) that you left your office, came home, and are now looking at your email, with no plans to do anything, other than stay in and probably read books for the rest of the afternoon.

I would like to suggest you meet me for a libation at The Watering Hole, which is not just a euphemism but the name of an actual establishment, perfect for city-bound folks like us on a summer Friday, as it is both dark and cool and free of judgment as to why one might be stuck in the city and drinking on a Friday afternoon.

Meet me. Hester and Essex on the Lower East Side.

—Nick

Sawyer sat blinking at the email, her face twisted in a skeptical expression, her lips puckered to one side, brow furrowed, one eyebrow raised.

She had no intention of trekking over to the Lower East Side to meet Nick for another drink.

Still leery, she clicked on the email titled "READ ME SECOND."

To: Adventures_of_Tom@aol.com
From: Nikolai70@aol.com

Hi Sawyer, me again.

I'm making another highly intelligent conjecture that, having read my previous email, you are presently making that face that you make when you are skeptical and resistant to something someone is saying (the one where you twist your lips and raise one eyebrow and a little crinkle appears on the bridge of your nose).

I further conjecture that you are saying to yourself: "No way am I going down to the Lower East Side to meet Nick for a drink."

But I think you should reconsider.

You said your best friend is out of town. So I'm betting you're free.

Think about it. Your hot apartment. Or coming out for a drink. Not a lot to lose.

I'll be here. The Watering Hole. Hester and Essex.

When you're done rolling your eyes.

—N

Sawyer was indeed rolling her eyes.

And when she stopped, she realized she was angry. Angry and irritated. Angry and irritated and not in the mood to sit still. She'd been about to tell him off at the Yale Club when they'd been interrupted. If Nick wanted to pick up where they left off, fine—he would be sorry; she had no plans to hold back this time.

She went to her closet and dug out something to wear. Not something that looked like she'd made any effort, but rather, something comfortable. Something she could be herself in. The day was still scorching hot. She pulled out a pair of black denim shorts and a spaghetti-strap tank top, then looked in the mirror. It seemed like everyone bemoaned grunge fashion nowadays, but Sawyer still liked it; her dark hair and heavy bangs easily assimilated to the aesthetic. She grabbed a black-and-white-plaid flannel and tied it around her waist, then pulled on a pair of black Doc Martens.

Nick might be annoying, but he was right in one regard: Sawyer really only had two choices. Stay home in her stuffy apartment and be annoyed at him . . . or tell him to his face that she was annoyed with him. And it was simply too hot to sit around angry and all alone.

• • •

Just as their names might suggest, the Upper West Side and the Lower East Side were at opposite ends of Manhattan, and Sawyer's route was not a straight shot. It required a bit of effort and an inconvenient train change.

When she arrived at the Watering Hole, she pushed through the door and stood in the entrance a moment, frozen, her eyes straining to adjust from the brilliant sunshine outside to the near-total darkness inside.

A man hovered behind the bar, presumably tending it. His leathery face signaled older age, yet there was something youthful and puckish about him. His hair was salt-and-pepper, but longer on top, and spiked up like a gentler version of a Mohawk. He wore a weathered army surplus T-shirt and was leaning over the counter on his elbows, reading a paperback novel. Two patrons sat at the bar, both grizzled older men gripping the drinks in front of them with both hands, vacant expressions on their faces. One appeared to be on the verge of nodding off.

Nick was nowhere to be found.

I'll be here, he'd written. Maybe he was just playing a joke on her.

Sawyer considered doing an about-face and leaving, when the bartender caught sight of her. He stood up at attention, and shoved the paperback into the back pocket of his jeans. Then he whistled and waved her in.

"Welcome! C'mon over! What can I get you?"

Sawyer approached the bar, uncertain whether she truly intended to stay.

"Um . . ."

"Don't know how to make an 'Um,'" the bartender joked good-naturedly. "How about something else?" He waved his hand again, gesturing for Sawyer to sit down.

She gave in, and sat.

"Well, what do you recommend?" she asked, half-joking, half-serious.

The bartender looked her over. "A Sea Breeze," he finally diagnosed. "A lady like you should have a nice tall Sea Breeze on a hot day like this."

There was something kind about how welcoming he was, how happy to see her.

"All right," she agreed.

"One Sea Breeze, coming right up!" He grinned and set about making the drink. He had a distinctly wiry energy about him that struck her as being both urban and feral at the same time. His left earlobe was missing a noticeable chunk, reminding her of an alley cat.

When the drink was ready, he set it before her and waited for Sawyer to try it, watching. She warily poked the maraschino cherry safely down under the tinkling ice (she was of the firm belief that maraschinos were freakishly unnatural) and took a taste of the drink. It was pleasant—grapefruit and cranberry, and what tasted like a stiff pour of vodka.

"Lovely," she said. "You're right—perfect for a day like today. Thank you."

The bartender grinned again. He did a fanciful little bow.

Then the door opened, and a silhouette appeared, a flat black shape chiseled out of the blindingly bright light that blasted in from the street.

When the door swung shut again, Nick materialized in the silhouette's place.

His eyes went straight to Sawyer, and a crooked smile appeared on his lips.

"Nicky!" the bartender greeted him.

"Hey—Vic!" Nick called back.

The bartender came around from behind the bar and the two men hugged. Sawyer watched, intrigued.

Vic returned to his post and Nick sat down next to Sawyer, elbowing her in greeting.

"I see you took care of my guest," Nick said to Vic.

"*Your* guest, eh?" Vic teased. "I didn't see you come in with her. Besides, she's too pretty to be *your* guest. Guest of the establishment, I say."

"What did he fix you?" Nick said, addressing Sawyer this time, and pointing to the drink sitting in front of her.

"A Sea Breeze," she replied.

Nick smirked. "Ah. Vic thinks you're classy," he said. "That's his classy-lady drink."

"Uh, I'm flattered—I guess?" Sawyer wanted to be annoyed—annoyed that Nick had heckled her into coming out to a hole-in-the-wall, and showed up late—but in spite of it all, a genuine laugh came out before she could stop it.

"You should be," Nick insisted. "Vic's been tending bar since he was a kid, barely tall enough to stand behind one. If there's one thing he knows, it's people."

"When I got here and you were nowhere to be found, I would have left . . . if Vic hadn't been so nice," Sawyer said.

"I'm glad you like him, and I'm glad you stayed."

He smiled, and Sawyer could feel him looking over her spaghetti-strap tank, shorts, the plaid flannel tied around her waist, her Docs. She looked him over in return—ripped jeans, a faded black T-shirt, his hair fashionably rumpled.

"Hey, Vic—can I get a cold one?" Nick called. He turned to Sawyer and dropped his voice. "The beers on tap are always piss-warm," he confided. "Also, it doesn't help that they taste like piss."

Vic spied Nick mumbling in Sawyer's ear and frowned.

"What kind of slander are you feeding my guest about this establishment?" Vic pretended to scold.

Sawyer suppressed an amused smile.

Behind the bar, Vic bent over and slid open the door to an ice chest. He rummaged around and pulled up a bottle, then pried off the cap and set the bottle of beer in front of Nick. Bits of ice chips slid down the sides of the bottle as Nick lifted it and took a sip.

"Let me show you around the place," Nick said, and proceeded to set off on a tour to jokingly highlight various features of the bar, waving for Sawyer to follow.

"Here we have the Watering Hole's Annual Pool Tournament Wall of Fame," he said, pointing to a wall full of framed photographs of guys holding up trophies. "Note the number of times Vic himself here has won the championship . . . nothing fixed or fishy about that . . . nope!"

Nick winked.

"'Fixed' would be me throwing a game!" Vic complained from behind the bar. "It's not my fault I've been granted wicked pool skills by the powers that be."

They exchanged a grin and Nick carried on. He pointed to a sagging leather couch pushed against one wall.

"And here we have the Lap of Luxury, aka, the sofa that one of the bar's previous owners abandoned here a couple of decades ago and nobody ever got around to throwing out. Note how the rips in the fine leather have been expertly repaired with silver duct tape." He turned and called over his shoulder. "How old would you say this sofa is, Vic?"

"Fuck if I know. Once it got old enough to order its own beer, I stopped checking ID," Vic retorted.

"Rumor has it, Sid Vicious once sat on this sofa, shortly before his untimely death," Nick said to Sawyer. "No direct cause-and-effect connection between the sofa and his death was found, of course. But if you wish to sit, be warned that you do so at your own risk to health and safety."

Sawyer smiled at Nick. He caught her gaze.

"What?" he prompted.

Sawyer shrugged.

"Nothing," she said.

He arched an eyebrow at her but continued the tour.

"And here we have the VIP in-house DJ," he said, flourishing an arm at the boxy glass jukebox. "Otherwise known as 'DJ Do It Yourself.'"

He peered down into the glass case and worked the handle to flip a few pages of the selection list. Then he rummaged his pocket for a handful of quarters, dropped a couple in, and punched in his selection.

To Sawyer's surprise, Van Morrison's "Sweet Thing" from the *Astral Weeks* album began to play. She blinked.

"This is my favorite song," she said.

Nick looked at her, his eyes searching her face in that way he had.

"Huh," he said.

He set his beer on the table of a booth, and they proceeded to slide into the wooden seats opposite each other.

Sawyer sat and listened to "Sweet Thing" play over the bar's scratchy speakers. She took a sip of her Sea Breeze and looked at Nick. Again, he caught her gaze.

"What?" he prompted a second time.

"I don't know," she said. "I came here ready to chew you out. But you seem more like . . . how you seem when we talk online. You're funny online."

"Don't worry, I'm sure I'll say something rude and unfunny to put you off again soon," he said. "We could get right to it and talk about religion or politics or something."

Sawyer laughed. "No, please."

Nick was quiet a moment. "Maybe it's the setting," he finally said. "It's easier to be funny here. I definitely prefer it to the Yale Club."

"You don't like the Yale Club?"

"Not really. Sorry about those guys showing up—I should've guessed that could happen. They're pretty obnoxious."

"Your coworkers are?"

"Pretty much. I tried to limit your exposure as best I could."

So, that's why he'd hurried her out the front door.

Nick paused, then added, "I forget that I kinda hate that place sometimes."

Sawyer frowned. "If you don't like it, why are you a member?"

He shrugged. "Truthfully?"

"'Blunt and frank'—you said that was your thing," Sawyer reminded him.

"It's a kind of currency, I suppose."

"What do you mean?" She frowned.

"To me, social clubs are just a bunch of horseshit. But they matter to other people. 'Yale' matters to other people. And if I'm going to sit down at the table of life and play poker, then I want a good hand of cards."

"I see," Sawyer said. "More of your 'math.'"

"Pretty much, yeah," Nick replied.

He paused.

"Anyway, I misdiagnosed you," he concluded.

"Beg pardon?" Sawyer asked, confused.

Nick shrugged. "I had you pegged for the kind of girl who would be most comfortable meeting at a fancy social club. But, I can see now, you're . . . different."

He gazed at her for a moment too long, and she grew uncomfortable.

"I guess when I picked the Yale Club, it was my version of making you a Sea Breeze," he joked, easing the moment.

"But I *like* this Sea Breeze!" Sawyer protested, holding up her glass.

Nick laughed. "Well, that just goes to show: Vic has been doing this a long time, and he knows better than I do how to size a person up."

"Still," Sawyer said, laughing. "I'm pretty sure in some roundabout way, you just said you thought I was a classy girl who would like the Yale Club but you were wrong."

She continued to laugh, but Nick turned serious. He put his hand over hers on the table. "Don't do that," he said.

Sawyer froze at his touch, mustering a confused smile.

"I didn't say that. I said you were something *different*," he said. "I happen to like what makes you different. I just didn't expect it."

They locked eyes again. Sawyer felt blood rushing to her ears.

Nick lifted his hand and withdrew it. "Sweet Thing" finished on the jukebox and "Brown Eyed Girl" started playing. Sawyer fidgeted. She took a heavy sip of her Sea Breeze, then cleared her throat.

"Do you and Kendra hang out here often?" she asked.

"She prefers the Yale Club," Nick answered.

Sawyer raised her eyebrows. They exchanged a knowing look.

"She came with me here exactly one time," Nick said.

"What drink did Vic make her?"

The smirk reappeared on Nick's face. He laughed a little, to himself.

"A beer on tap," he said.

It was an accidental punch line. They both laughed, a conspiratorial mixture of tickled and sheepish.

"Maybe it explains why she didn't come back," he admitted.

"Could be," Sawyer said.

Nick turned serious again. "Actually, how about we don't talk about them," he said.

Sawyer blinked.

"I mean, we'll tell each other if either of us finds some kind of . . . proof," he qualified. "But other than that, how about we don't talk about them."

"All right," Sawyer agreed.

It seemed respectful: she and Nick weren't going to sit around and complain about their partners. Then it occurred to her that Charles and Kendra were pretty much all she and Nick had in common.

"But . . ." Sawyer said. "Why invite me down here, then?"

"It's a beautiful Friday afternoon. What else were you going to do?"

"So this is . . . a *pity invite*? We're back to that?"

"No!" Nick protested. "What if . . . what if I just like talking to you, and thought you might be free?"

Sawyer mulled this over, a look of deep consternation on her face.

"Is that OK?" Nick prodded.

"Yeah," she said finally. "That might be OK. I'll let you know."

A long pause ensued. Then, Nick shrugged. "It's supposed to thunderstorm this afternoon. Want to go for a walk before it rains?"

"Sure."

Sawyer drained the rest of her Sea Breeze and groped in her purse for her wallet, but Nick waved her off.

"Hey, Vic—put it on my tab?"

"Don't think I didn't already, my friend," Vic called back. To Sawyer, he said, "Nice to meet you, m'lady. Your next one's on me, if you come back."

9.

Taking a walk turned out to be a terrible idea.

The mosquitoes were out, and the air was like soup, having already acquired that chokingly humid, pre-thunderstorm heaviness, with absolutely no hint of the cool relief that would come later.

Then, about ten minutes after Nick and Sawyer left the Watering Hole, the first raindrops began to fall—big, splotchy drops that made the sidewalks steam and filled the streets with a swampy, metallic scent tinged with diesel.

"Should we make a run for it back to the bar?" Sawyer said, laughing and holding her bag over her head as a makeshift umbrella, as the drops began to patter faster and faster.

Nick pointed to a gaggle of tourists clustered together in front of what looked to be an old brick walk-up. "What's that?" he said.

They got closer and discovered that it was a tour being conducted by the Lower East Side Tenement Museum. The tour guide, a slender mouse of a man in a beret, was ushering people through a door. He blinked into the rain and hurriedly gave Nick and Sawyer the OK to join the tour and pay afterward. Thanking him, they joined the ten or so bodies shuffling into the building.

Once inside, the tour guide began to tell the group about the history of the building. Sawyer was instantly fascinated. The structure was a time capsule of sorts . . . used as a tenement from the 1860s until 1935, when the then-owner simply evicted the tenants and boarded it up, leaving it sealed like a tomb until it was discovered by the present owners, who bought it and turned it into a museum dedicated to remembering how people used to live in New York's earlier days.

Sawyer and Nick followed the tour group up the rickety wooden stairs, to the apartments above, winding under the stamped-tin ceilings and along the narrow, smoke-stained halls, past a small closet containing a toilet—*Plumbing wasn't installed until 1901, at which point residents shared two toilets per floor,* the guide announced, to much chuckling and cringing from the group.

The guide led them into one of the tiny apartments, and began to describe who might have lived there, and what life was like back then. He demonstrated the use of cast-iron stoves, washboards, antique iceboxes. There wasn't much space in the claustrophobic apartments, three little rooms, including the kitchen; in some rooms it was possible to hold out your arms and touch the walls on opposite sides at the same time. It wasn't uncommon to raise six kids in an apartment like this, the guide said. It was mind-boggling to fathom.

"See?" Nick confided in a low voice to Sawyer. "Aren't you glad you came out? We're doing something cultural."

Sawyer smirked at him. "All right, this is pretty cool," she admitted. "And I'm a sucker for history."

"Shocker," Nick joked sarcastically, but not unkindly.

There was an intimate, cozy feeling to the tour that was heightened by the weather. Each time the group stopped and gathered around the guide, Sawyer could feel Nick standing behind her. She could feel his breath on the back of her neck, and a curious shiver despite the heat. Outside, as the storm ramped up, lightning flashed in the window, thunder rattled the panes, and the rain began to pour. People instinctively moved closer together in the already cramped space. The other tourists' eyes were bright and restless, like children trapped indoors during recess on a rainy day. There was a kind of alertness in the air, like the mishmash of people on the tour had just tumbled out of the dryer, all of them faintly crackling with static electricity.

Forty-five minutes later, the guide showed them the way out through a back alley that led past the former outhouses, which—according to the guide—served this whole block of tenements before indoor plumbing was added. More chuckles and groans. A few of the tourists rummaged in their pockets to tip the guide, *thank-you*s were murmured and acknowledged, and then everyone was released back into the streets of Manhattan. Nick and Sawyer paid for having joined the tour belatedly, as promised, and Nick added a bit extra, along with their thanks.

It was still raining.

"Hungry?" Nick asked.

"Starving," Sawyer replied.

• • •

They made a mad dash for it. Nick led the way.

"Look!" he shouted, pointing as they neared Katz's Delicatessen. "There's no line!"

They ducked inside.

Minutes later they sat down with two Reubens with extra pickles.

"Have you been here before?" Nick asked.

"No, but I've heard about this place," Sawyer answered.

"'Heard about it'?" Nick teased. "You mean you watched *When Harry Met Sally*."

"Fine. Maybe."

She took a huge bite out of her sandwich and chewed with dramatic, barbaric relish, then licked at a drip of pale orange Thousand Island at the corner of her mouth. Nick raised an eyebrow. Sawyer laughed.

"Don't worry, I'll refrain from reenacting *that* scene," she said.

"No. Please—by all means. Go for it."

Sawyer laughed. "That's right—you're the type who probably can't be embarrassed by anything."

"That's me," Nick announced with mock pride. "Utterly indecorous and completely lacking any sense of shame." He shrugged. "It's a gift."

Sawyer laughed and covered her mouth with a napkin. The pastrami *was* good. They chomped away casually, their elbows on the table, their fingers and lips shiny with grease under the fluorescent lights.

The rain continued to patter the street outside. The cabs and buses going by sprayed up water as they passed, making *WISHHH WISHHH* sounds.

"Had you ever been to that tenement museum before?" Sawyer asked.

Nick shook his head. "No. I wish I'd known it existed."

"I loved it," Sawyer admitted. "It stirred something up for me. Something about all those different lives, different stories . . ."

"Spoken like a writer," Nick commented.

Recalling how much she'd shared online, Sawyer felt a telltale warmth creep into her face. Her palms grew sweaty.

"Or just someone who works in publishing," she said.

"Or both," Nick insisted. "No need to deflect."

Sawyer squirmed a little.

"Well, anyway," she said. "Just thinking about all the stories of the people who must have lived in that building piqued my curiosity about the world again . . . I appreciate when that happens."

She paused and mused for a moment.

"Imagine, too . . . the bravery it took to come to America as an immigrant, starting your life over again," she murmured. "Feeling homesick and excited at the same time."

Nick snorted. "I don't have to imagine."

"Oh—that's right," Sawyer remembered. "Your mom?"

“Yeah,” Nick replied.

“Thinking you can’t ever go back must be extra tough. Does she still get homesick?”

He shrugged. “Probably. She’d never let on, though, not in front of me. But where my mom lives in Brighton Beach is a little like what the Lower East Side must have been, eighty years ago,” he said. “If you’re homesick and strategic enough, you can spend your whole life there, never hearing or speaking anything but Russian or Ukrainian.”

Sawyer listened and smiled, watching Nick’s face carefully. Just as it had been the last time his mother had come up, she detected a slight hint that he was reticent to talk about her. She wondered if she’d made a misstep. With Nick, everything felt oddly familiar, yet the simplest of questions sometimes felt *too* personal, and they suddenly transformed back into two strangers.

“Hey,” he said, abruptly looking at his watch and changing the subject. “It’s after six. I told my friend Ryan I would go hear his band play. The club does a lottery for time slots, and unfortunately for him, his band drew the opening slot. They’re on at seven, and he’s worried no one will turn up that early. Want to come? It’s not far from here.”

Sawyer hesitated, chewing her lip and thinking.

Nick frowned.

“Time to go back to the hot apartment and read? Sounds boring. And sweaty.”

“How do you know I don’t have air-conditioning?” she challenged.

“Because I know,” Nick insisted. “You don’t have air-conditioning.”

She sucked in a breath and pictured her stuffy apartment . . . and imagined herself there, watching the clock and waiting for Charles to come home.

“C’mon,” Nick cajoled. “Sea Breezes on me.”

He winked.

Sawyer attempted to suppress a grin, but lost.

* * *

The rain stopped, the temperature dropped ten degrees, and the city suddenly felt fresh and clean.

It was a short walk to the spot where Nick's friend's band was scheduled to play. The space itself was small; a long, narrow room with a bar at one end and a stage at the other. It appeared devoid of patrons but full of activity. A twenty-something bartender with the looks of a male model (or, at least, a male model with a wicked hangover) was busy inventorying and stocking the bar. A group of guys on the stage were diligently plugging in amps and testing the sound. They looked up as Nick and Sawyer crossed the room.

"Nick!"

"Hey, man—thanks for coming!"

"Yo, you playing tonight?"

"Nah, just here to listen tonight," Nick said to the guys, smiling. "Well, listen and drink."

"'Preciate it, man."

It seemed Nick knew everyone, and everyone knew him. He introduced Sawyer around. It was, of course, too many names for her to keep straight. But she smiled and nodded. They were friendly; it was clear that Nick was well-liked. He took her over to the bar and made yet another quick, jokey introduction (Sawyer tried to keep up, but between the barrage of names and the deafening blare of all the sound checks going on, it was tricky; the bartender's name was definitely either Jake or Blake). Nick ordered two Sea Breezes, heavy ice, no maraschinos.

"You gotta be kidding me," Jake or Blake said, rolling his eyes. "Sea Breezes?"

"Yup," Nick confirmed. "And keep 'em coming."

Jake or Blake laughed, clearly too fond of Nick to be convincingly annoyed. He reached under the bar and produced two pint glasses meant for beer, then proceeded to make two enormous Sea Breezes.

"You're lucky I have grapefruit tonight; not always the case," he said gruffly, but with a smile.

Nick pocketed some bar napkins, lifted the two pint glasses, and gestured at Sawyer. She followed him through the narrow club, past the stage to the far end of the room, and through a little door marked *"DO NOT OPEN—ALARM WILL SOUND."* Despite the warning on the door, no emergency alarm sounded. Instead, it let out onto a tiny outdoor space.

It was probably just a place for band members to hang out and smoke before and after going onstage, but it had the ramshackle charm of a slightly derelict, overgrown backyard. Uneven, broken bricks covered in moss paved the ground, which in itself was uneven and dipped down to a drainage grate in the middle. Snarls of overgrown ivy climbed every vertical surface—over the fence, up the wrought iron fire escapes, all the way up to the ancient power lines strung between buildings like Christmas lights. A jumble of milk crates and plastic patio furniture was pushed off to one side, along with an assortment of clutter: long-forgotten ashtrays and empty beer bottles swimming with rainwater and cigarette butts.

Nick handed the pint glasses brimming with pink-and-yellow Sea Breezes to Sawyer to hold, then righted a plastic table and two plastic chairs. He wiped them down with the bar napkins and finished with an invitational flourish.

Sawyer sat. Now that the rain had stopped, the evening had turned pleasant. The storm was pushing off to the east, and the sunset was creeping in under the cloud cover in the west. It flooded into the sky like light coming through a crack in a door, bouncing between the city and the cloud canopy, bathing everything in a radiant reddish-gold glow.

They sipped their Sea Breezes.

"So, that's why you were reading *Rolling Stone*," Sawyer said. "You're a musician."

"You make it sound so serious," Nick said. "I'm just a guy who works at an ad agency." He paused, and added, "Who sometimes checks out the album reviews in *Rolling Stone*."

"And plays in a band," Sawyer pointed out.

Nick gave her a look, and she knew the answer was: yes.

"Why aren't you playing tonight?" she asked.

Nick stiffened. "I'm kind of taking a break," he said noncommittally.

"A break?"

"From one of the guys."

"Why?" Sawyer asked, interested.

Nick narrowed his eyes. "Do you always interrogate people being nice to you?"

"Pretty much, yeah." Sawyer grinned.

Nick cocked his head, considering. Finally, he sighed. "I don't know," he said. "Dan's just been fixated on us spending a bunch of cash on this studio."

"To record?" Sawyer pressed.

Nick shrugged.

"Why don't you want to do it?"

"It seems like a cliché waste of money." He paused, and added, "I just don't see the problem with being in the here and the now. Playing live. That's what music is *supposed* to be—right?"

"Playing live?"

"Yeah. And community, I guess. To be honest, part of the reason a lot of these guys here seem happy to see me is because I've helped run things over the years—get people stage time, get people booked, recommend musicians when someone's short a drummer, that kind of stuff."

Sawyer's lips twisted into a satisfied smile.

"So, this is your thing," she asserted.

"Yeah. I guess you could say it's something I care about," Nick acknowledged.

"Aha! You *do* have passions."

"I do."

"You're human after all."

"An argument could be made to that effect."

Sawyer continued to smile in triumph. They locked eyes for a long moment, until Sawyer felt that unfamiliar flutter of intimidation again. She looked away, pretending to observe the garden.

"I read your poem," Nick said.

Sawyer's eyes flicked back to his face and went wide. Her brain silently traced how it must have happened—the link she sent during that oddly unguarded moment during their online chat. But there was more than that—there was Nick returning to it later, Nick clicking on her poem, Nick reading.

Her stomach did a somersault.

"It's good," Nick said, his voice low, somber . . . and earnest. "You're a good writer," he continued. "And I can see why that's *your* thing."

She tried to reply, but felt herself choking on each sentence that came to mind.

"Look, Sawyer," he said, seeing her struggle. "It's good to be *good* at something. You shouldn't be embarrassed or try to hide it."

"It's just that . . ." Sawyer struggled. "I mean, I've never . . ."

Each time she found a sentence it slipped away from her, like a wet bar of soap. Nick continued to wait patiently.

"You're the only one who's read it," Sawyer blurted out, finally.

He looked surprised.

"I mean . . . like, strangers have probably read it. It's a public website, after all," Sawyer said, finding herself babbling. "But you're the only one who's read it . . . who *I* know." She paused, then babbled to add, "Personally."

Sawyer willed herself to stop talking.

Nick was quiet a moment, thinking.

"I'm glad you told me about it," he said finally. "I'm glad I got to read it."

The blood rushed to her face. Her tongue felt thick again.

"Thank you," she managed to force out.

She coughed, and gathered herself.

"And . . . thank you for today, I guess."

"What do you mean, you 'guess'?" Nick teased.

Sawyer blushed again and laughed. "To be honest, I had a bad morning, and I came down here thinking we'd probably resume our debate, and I'd stick it to you. You know? Really tell you off."

"I see." Nick laughed. "Therapy by way of human punching bag. I've been told I bring that out in people."

"But . . ." Sawyer continued cautiously. "I have to admit: I'm having a good time. This afternoon took my mind off everything. I probably would have sat in my apartment stewing about it otherwise."

"What's been bugging you?" Nick asked.

Sawyer glanced at him. He sounded genuinely interested.

"Besides, you know . . ." he added.

"Oh, *besides* that?" she half joked, attempting to act blasé but feeling a pang at the unspoken mention of Charles and Kendra.

"Yeah, besides that."

"Well . . . this morning, I was feeling discouraged about work stuff."

"What happened at work?" Nick asked.

Sawyer sighed. "You remember me telling you about that unsolicited manuscript I pulled from the slush pile?" she asked.

She went on to tell him about Johanna's lack of acknowledgment, and about Preeti coming into the office and not having the faintest clue who she was.

"I can tell you what I think if you want," Nick said, once she'd finished her story.

"OK," Sawyer agreed with a hint of apprehension.

"I think it's up to you to ask for what you want," he said.

Sawyer wasn't offended, exactly, but she was surprised.

"Think about it," Nick insisted. "How many editorial assistants do you think Johanna has had over the years? Countless people in publishing wash out at the assistant level. They realize it's a lot of work. Maybe they don't have a knack for it, or worse, they don't have the passion. Or they simply move into a career field that pays more. It won't occur to her that you're in it for the long haul . . . unless you *make* it occur to her."

Sawyer mulled this over.

"Don't sit around waiting to be singled out for acknowledgment," Nick concluded. "Ask for what you want."

"You might be right . . ." Sawyer murmured.

"What? Could you say that again, a little louder?" Nick cupped his ear.

"You might be right," Sawyer repeated, rolling her eyes.

"Hmm, 'might be,'" Nick echoed. "I guess I'll have to settle for that."

"As good as it gets right now," Sawyer confirmed.

"Hey," Nick said. "For what it's worth, I think it's really cool that you pulled that manuscript out of the slush. And it's cool that you care about your job. Most people don't put themselves out there to do what they love; they settle for mediocrity and a paycheck."

"It's funny," Sawyer remarked. "I love my job so much I would work for free—"

"You work in entry-level publishing; we've already established that you *do* work for free," Nick interjected.

"Ha ha." Sawyer warned dryly, "That joke's getting old already."

"Sorry. Go on."

"But you're right; I need to remind people to take me seriously *because* I love my job—not in spite of it." She paused, then added, "Even in the bigger picture, too. Sometimes people act like working in publishing is a fun little hobby . . . compared to, say, working at Wexler Gibbons."

Nick nodded and rolled his eyes. "I get it. But it's not like Charles and Kendra are curing cancer. They're underlings, baby sharks, proofreading the paperwork for a merger between two huge companies who—let's face it—are probably just trying to get around violating antitrust monopoly laws."

Sawyer was surprised by Nick's nakedly open disdain. She shifted in her chair. It felt unfair to Charles to agree.

"I thought we weren't going to talk about them," she reminded Nick now.

"You're right," he agreed. "Scratch that last part."

The thump of drums began to pulse inside the club, and soon, the wail of a guitar began to spill into the little courtyard.

"It sounds like they've started," Nick said. "Ready to go back in?"

Sawyer nodded.

• • •

They stayed and watched Nick's friend's band. And then another band after that. And then another.

It was interesting, Sawyer thought. Bands starting out were like writers just starting out. The more novice they were, the more you could tell who their influences were, who they were trying to imitate. Pearl Jam. Nirvana. Stone Temple Pilots. Some that played that night were good, and others . . . not so much (for the bands that were bad, imitation only invited a painful comparison). Nick, who was usually full of opinions, listened without giving any. But Sawyer became convinced that she could make out subtle changes in Nick's expressions—tiny crinkles at the outside corners of his eyes when a talented group jammed in perfect time. A tightness near his mouth when a subpar lead guitarist launched into a melodramatic solo.

She was staring too much. A couple of times, much to Sawyer's embarrassment, Nick caught her studying these expressions. She retrained her focus on the stage.

People steadily drifted in. The club began to feel like a club, thrumming with bodies standing close together. Sawyer and Nick were eventually pressed close, just by virtue of the crowd's density and the room's small space. But it was different from the cozy intimacy Sawyer had felt at the Tenement Museum. All around them, people were dancing with abandon, spilling beer, and making out while trying not to lock piercings. When she and Nick touched it was an awkward, accidental jostling together. Sawyer was very aware of her legs, her hips, her arms, her elbows.

She couldn't help but notice, too, other girls in the crowd eyeing Nick. They gazed at him admiringly, occasionally pausing to glance at Sawyer. She knew they were trying to guess who she was—his date? His coworker? Hopefully someone completely platonic, like a cousin? One of the girls moved closer in the crowd, and managed to catch his gaze. A blond girl like Kendra, only with black roots and a nose piercing. She nodded in Nick's direction as if to say hello. Sawyer felt a surprising flicker of something inside her chest she didn't quite understand, something that felt vaguely territorial, which made no sense at all. She watched Nick's face closely for his reaction.

He nodded and gave a small smile in the girl's direction, but Sawyer thought she glimpsed the tightness around his mouth she'd seen earlier. He made no move to approach the girl, and Sawyer relaxed.

The band onstage wrapped their set. They took a bow, and another band quickly rearranged the stage to take over, plugging in different things, adjusting mic heights. Nick turned to look at her and grinned.

"Refill?" he asked, pointing at her empty pint glass.

She nodded, despite the fact that her head was already spinning.

He took her glass and headed to the bar. Sawyer watched him move through the crowd, shouldering his way near the blond girl, who was also watching Nick, with laser focus. When Nick passed without stopping, the blond girl turned to glare at Sawyer. She had the wrong idea, of course, but Sawyer couldn't suppress a tiny smile.

• • •

Another Sea Breeze and an hour or so later, a ska band clearly hoping to become the next Sublime had taken the stage. They weren't particularly good, but it didn't matter; the crowd had begun to hop along to the brassy, jazzy beats. Sawyer felt herself joining in like a fool, grinning from ear to ear, thoroughly tipsy.

By then it was packed, and she and Nick stood shoulder-to-shoulder. She could feel him watching her out of the corner of his eye as she did a silly little wiggle to the music. He shook his head, amused.

* * *

Sawyer was shocked when she noticed the time. In astonishingly quick succession, the afternoon had turned into evening, and evening into night. She felt a mild tingle of panic wondering if Charles had beaten her home for a change, and what he would think to find her not there.

They left the club. Nick walked her to Astor Place, where they stood beside a sculpture of a giant cube perched upright on one pointy corner, like a diamond.

Nick was quiet. He cleared his throat and shuffled his feet, seeming reluctant to call it a night.

"Thanks for coming out," he said.

"Yeah," Sawyer agreed. "I hope I didn't cramp your style."

"'Cramp my style'?"

Sawyer laughed. "I saw the girls in there, tossing their hair every time you crossed the room to the bar."

"I was crossing the room to the bar to get a drink for *you*."

"And I could feel them all looking at me, trying to guess who the hell I was to you."

"If they only knew," Nick joked.

Sawyer relented. "I guess that *is* a pretty weird story," she agreed. "Anyway. I just hope I wasn't a drag to have along."

Nick gave her a funny look.

"*I* asked *you* to come out, remember?" He paused, giving her a serious look. "I'm really happy that you did."

Her face felt warm, probably from the numerous sugary, vodka-laden Sea Breezes, she figured.

"And besides," Nick continued. "It's not like I'm really . . . *looking* . . . you know?"

Sawyer frowned for a moment, relaxed and tipsy enough to be confused. Then a light bulb clicked on.

"Oh! Right—of course," she agreed.

The indirect mention of Kendra hovered around them for a moment. Sawyer stared down at her feet. An awkward silence settled.

"Did you know this thing turns?" Nick asked Sawyer, breaking the silence. He gestured to the giant metal cube.

"It does not." Sawyer laughed.

"It does," Nick insisted. "It's a feature of the sculpture. I swear. If you push hard enough, it rotates. Look—you push on that side and I'll push on this side."

Sawyer wasn't sure she believed him. It seemed like a possible trick to show how gullible she was. But she moved to the far side of the cube and reached up to get a hold of one of the corners.

"OK, on the count of three," Nick said. "One . . . two . . . three!"

The cube didn't budge.

It felt like she was the only one pushing, but Nick was making straining noises.

Theatrical straining noises.

She stopped. "All right. I get it."

"I'm just kidding around," Nick admitted, laughing. "But I'll push for real now. I swear it turns!"

Sawyer glared at him as he laughed.

"C'mon—please. I promise."

"Fine." Sawyer pushed.

To Sawyer's utter surprise, the cube gave a soft metallic moan, and began to turn on its base. It was, indeed, turning—very slowly, but turning nonetheless.

A group of passing NYU students spotted Nick and Sawyer. They ran over and joined in, helping to push. The sculpture began to turn faster and faster. The NYU students—clearly also tipsy—hooted and hollered with laughter as the entire group of them ran in mad circles, turning the cube. Sawyer giggled, giddy. They were like children on a playground merry-go-round, all of them nearly tripping over their feet to keep up.

"WOOO-HOOOO!!!"

Finally, after a minute or two of furious spinning, the students splintered off.

"Peace out!" one of them called.

"See ya!" another shouted.

Sawyer and Nick slowed down, and gradually let the sculpture grind to a stop. They were panting, laughing.

"Told you it turned," Nick jeered.

"You *might* be right," Sawyer joked.

"Hmm, 'might be,'" Nick echoed for the second time that night. "I guess I'll have to settle for that."

"As good as it gets," Sawyer confirmed.

They had a regular comedy bit now.

He smiled, and walked her to the subway entrance.

• • •

Charles was on the sofa, watching the eleven-o'clock news when Sawyer arrived home.

In the scheme of things, this was not so late—not for two people still in their twenties living in Manhattan. But seeing Sawyer come in, Charles lifted the remote and muted the TV, waiting for some kind of explanation.

"Sorry," she said. "I should have called and left a message on the machine or something; I didn't picture you getting home first. You've been getting home so late, and I thought I was only going out for one drink."

Charles's brow furrowed.

"Who'd you go out to meet?"

Sawyer tensed, mute, thinking of what she could say. Uttering the name "Nick" seemed out of the question; the details that made up the truth were far too unwieldy.

(So, I started meeting up with your coworker's boyfriend because we wanted to compare notes as to whether or not you and your coworker are having an affair . . .)

"Oh . . . um, Kaylee wanted to vent about some work stuff," she said instead.

"Did you two have fun?"

"We did," Sawyer said, thinking back over the surprisingly good time she'd had hanging out with Nick. When she remembered she'd just told him "Kaylee," a new thought occurred to her: It had been a summer Friday. She'd had the afternoon off—that was an awfully long time to hang out for some after-work drinks. It seemed inevitable that Charles would ask about that.

But in the next breath, he switched off the TV, rose from the sofa, and stretched.

"Well, that's good," he replied, patting Sawyer on the shoulder. "It's good that you're starting to bond with some work friends."

Sawyer frowned. He sounded distracted and vague, like he'd already left the conversation behind him. He stretched again and let out a sigh.

"I'm beat, and I have to get up early and go in for a few hours tomorrow, after the gym."

"Again?" Sawyer asked. "You've had to work the last three weekends in a row."

"It won't always be like this," Charles said. "I know I sound like a broken record, but it's true. It's this case—if we get recognized for doing a good job, it will lead to bigger and better things."

There it was again: *we*.

Charles and Kendra.

Sawyer bristled. But Charles didn't notice. He leaned toward Sawyer and tenderly gave her a gentle peck on the cheek.

"Seriously—I'm so tired I'm gonna drop dead if I don't go to bed right now. Can you get the lights out here?"

Dressed in his boxers and undershirt, he sauntered off in the direction of their bedroom. Sawyer heard him flop onto the bed, not bothering to get under the sheets in the summer heat. A click sounded and the bedroom went dark.

She was reminded of her own exhaustion. One by one, Sawyer switched off the living room lamps. Then, instead of heading to the bedroom, she sank into the corner seat of the L-shaped sofa and sat there for several minutes. She blinked as her eyes adjusted to the dim blue light of the streetlamps outside, still buzzing from the whirlwind afternoon she'd had with Nick, and unsure what to think about anything anymore.

When she closed her eyes, she was suddenly turning that sculpture of a cube again in Astor Place, pushing with all her might and laughing, and spinning, spinning, spinning.

10.

SUNDAY, JULY 4

"All right, let me just ask and get it out of the way," Kathy warned. "When are you two having babies?"

Sawyer blinked dumbly at her future mother-in-law.

"Oh, don't look so surprised!" Kathy chastised, smiling. She patted at her perfectly pinned blond French twist with an absent-minded hand.

"Hey, Mom," Charles objected. "Mind if we get married first?"

"Of course, of course." Kathy waved him off. "But after the wedding, that'll be the only question the girls will be asking down at the club. And I can't wait to meet my future grandbabies!"

"Well, the future will have to wait a bit, Mom."

"How long is 'a bit'?"

Charles scowled in response.

Kathy nudged Sawyer with one shoulder and leaned in conspiratorially. "You know . . . if you started trying now, no one would be the wiser if you two were carrying around a little secret on the big day . . ."

Sawyer's eyes went wide, and Kathy misread the somewhat terrified expression on her future daughter-in-law's face.

"Oh!" Kathy said. "Did I stumble upon something by accident? Could it be? Are you two already . . . ?"

"Mom!" Charles outright scolded. "No. We're not pregnant!"

"Oh, but you'll be so happy when you *are*," Kathy cooed, insistent. "Because then the pressure is off, and all you have to do is pick out a christening gown and a boarding school—right, Ed?"

Charles's father, Edward, responded by flagging down the waitress.

"Another one of these?" He smiled politely at the waitress and pointed to his Bloody Mary. "Thank you."

They were having brunch at one of Charles's favorite spots on the Upper West Side, a restaurant that featured bottomless Mimosas and a glassed-in patio in the back. He'd long ago learned the key to his parents' happiness was a trendy brunch spot with an outdoor space that gave them the illusion they were still in Connecticut, coupled with an unceasing fount of booze.

Ed and Kathy were in town visiting for the Fourth of July weekend. Charles had miraculously taken a rare Friday afternoon off to join Sawyer in meeting his parents when they got off the train at Grand Central. Saturday had been spent making the rounds of the compulsory "cultural sites" in the city—mostly museums and restaurants that Kathy felt were an important rite of passage when it came to "being in New York." Now, Sunday morning, they'd happily tucked into brunch. Later that evening, they had plans to reconvene for their official celebration of the holiday; Charles had made reservations for a catered yacht party that promised to deliver great views of the fireworks over the East River.

Sawyer marveled silently at Kathy's words. *Christening gowns and boarding schools*. One thing Sawyer knew for certain: she and Kathy were two different species of creature. Kathy was always dressed to the nines, in what Sawyer thought of as country club chic, and talked about things like cotillions and "coming out" as a "deb." She lived for gossip and material pleasures, but somehow, she was never nasty about it.

In fact, despite how little they had in common, Sawyer genuinely adored her future mother-in-law. She was intrigued with the way that Kathy and Sawyer's own mother, Carol, were like completely opposite sides of the same maternal coin. Take books, for instance. Sawyer could always count on her mother to have read all the classics (major and minor, marginalized and newly discovered alike), and to offer a deep, highly academic critique of any long-ago-written book Sawyer wished to talk about . . . but Carol had no interest in the novels that topped the *New York Times* bestseller list. Kathy, on the other hand, devoured the latter with her Chardonnay-fueled, twice-monthly book club, and was only too happy to gossip with Sawyer about the characters as though they were every bit as real as the neighbors or someone she'd met down at the country club.

Kathy might let her eyes drift down to Sawyer's feet and say things like, *Oh my—we really need to go shoe shopping!* Or even blurt out in the middle of a meal, *Let me give you the card of the woman who cuts my hair. I think she could really help you!* But Kathy also said things like, *Working with writers to publish their novels! What a wonder! I brag to my friends about how smart you are; they all want to meet you.* It was impossible to dislike Kathy when she said things like that—things that Sawyer had all but given up on hoping her own mother might say.

Sawyer had come to realize that it was a question of focusing on different things; Kathy often focused on things that were considered more superficial, but beneath it all, her intentions were pure. Right now, Kathy might be yearning for a grandchild simply in order to pick out a Jacadi christening gown, or boast about nabbing a spot at Deerfield or Groton—or even simply so she might have a cute photo at the ready in her purse to show people and have them exclaim, *How is it possible? You're too young to be a grandmother!* But Sawyer knew if a baby were to actually arrive, Kathy would love it fiercely. For all her cloying, materialistic snobbery, her heart was genuinely warm.

"Don't think you're off the hook just because you dodged my question, Ed!" Kathy said now to her husband. "Tell Charles and Sawyer what *you* think."

"What *I* think?" Ed teased. "Or what *you* think I should think?"

Kathy sniffed. "I don't see the difference."

Sawyer honestly couldn't tell whether or not Kathy was joking. She glanced at Charles with a mixture of amusement and alarm, but, meeting Sawyer's eye, he only shrugged.

Ed sighed, carefully composing his answer.

"I think Charles and Sawyer have their hands full planning a wedding, not to mention just making ends meet in the city as a young couple," Ed said in a gentle tone. He patted Kathy's hand as if to offer her some of his share of patience. "And on top of that, Charles has been assigned to work on a big merger case—that has to be making things a little bit tricky for them just now."

"Actually, it *has*—"

"It's been totally fine—"

Sawyer and Charles responded at the same time, halting and locking eyes. Ed glanced between them, his forehead furrowed with an expression of concern.

"It's been fine," Sawyer said, readjusting her words to match Charles's. "It's just that . . . his hours have been crazy. I miss him."

"It's romantic, isn't it?" Kathy cooed, nudging Ed. "To be young again . . . never wanting to be apart and alone . . ."

Ed turned and gave Kathy a sweet, close-lipped smile of sympathy. But he seemed distracted, his mind still puzzling out the exchange between Charles and Sawyer.

Kathy brightened as a new thought occurred to her, and she turned back to Sawyer.

"You know when you *never* feel alone? When you become a mother."

Charles groaned. "Oh, God—Mom. Seriously!"

"But it's true!" Kathy intoned plaintively, as if to say, *Don't shoot the messenger!*

Charles laughed and reached for Sawyer's hand. He gave it a warm squeeze under the table.

"Let's talk about something else, why don't we?" he suggested.

Ed cleared his throat and brought up the short Warhol film they'd seen at the Guggenheim the day before.

As brunch carried on, Kathy managed to work in the subject of babies no fewer than four more times.

* * *

Once their brunch plates had been cleared and they'd all drunk their fill of Mimosas and Bloody Marys, Ed and Kathy went to use the restroom while Charles and Sawyer strolled to the front of the restaurant and waited outside on the sidewalk.

"Sorry about my mom and all that baby talk," Charles said, affecting a kind of overly polite, endearing sheepishness, like they were still on their first date, getting to know each other. "She means well," he added.

"Of course," Sawyer agreed. "Kathy's great. Always . . . very Kathy."

She hesitated.

"It's just . . . I don't know," Sawyer added. "Her whole thing about babies. It's kind of a moot point."

Charles frowned. "What do you mean? You don't want kids?"

"I do. Someday."

"Of course! That's what I meant," Charles rushed to agree. "We're on the same page. *Someday.* Not now!" He grinned and chuckled, relaxed. But after a moment's pause, he asked, "But 'moot point'? What did you mean by that?"

Sawyer swallowed. "I just mean . . . well, we're not in any risk of having one right now. You're never home."

Charles's shoulders slumped. He looked cranky—irritated, even. "C'mon—this *again*? You know this case—"

"I know," Sawyer replied, cutting him off. "I'm just saying . . . we don't spend time together anymore. Time we would need to spend if . . . if we were going to get pregnant."

"Sawyer . . ." Charles started in a low voice.

"I'm lonely, Charles."

"Part of this is just because Autumn's away in Japan. You probably wouldn't notice how busy I was if she were around this summer."

It was the opening of an argument.

"Still—" Sawyer started to say.

Charles opened his mouth to cut her off, but froze upon hearing the sound of a man clearing his throat.

They turned to see Charles's father, Ed, standing on the sidewalk, having emerged from the restaurant's entrance.

"Hey, Dad," Charles greeted his father. "Sawyer and I were just saying how nice it is today. Maybe instead of taking a cab back to the Plaza, it would be nice to walk through the park."

Ed stared at them, wordless, clearly troubled by what he'd just overheard.

"The park?" a feminine voice chimed in.

They all turned to see Kathy joining them, her lipstick freshly applied from her visit to the ladies' room.

"Ooo, that sounds like the perfect way to burn off that French toast I never should have ordered in the first place!"

* * *

Unfortunately, as lovely and as expensive as they were, Kathy's shoes were not made for walking the distance necessary to traverse the park from the Upper West Side to where the Plaza Hotel awaited on the park's southeast corner.

At the first hint that his wife's overpriced shoes had begun to pinch her feet, Ed flagged down two ornate horse-drawn hansom cabs that came clop-clop-clopping by.

After a quick negotiation, Sawyer found herself climbing up into the open car of a horse-drawn carriage.

"How about you two go in that one," Ed said to Kathy and Charles. "Sawyer and I will take this one, and we'll race you."

He winked. Ed had arranged for the drivers to take them on a pleasantly slow, scenic tour of the park before dropping them off in front of the Plaza.

Each carriage seated four, so hiring both carriages and splitting into two groups wasn't *exactly* necessary. Sawyer couldn't quite guess why Ed might want to ride with her, but the arrangement suited her just fine, and Charles and Kathy seemed equally happy with it. She settled into her seat—a series of well-worn, lumpy velvet cushions loosely positioned on a lacquered wooden bench—and peered over her shoulder to wave at Charles in the next carriage. The buggy rocked on its springy shocks as Ed climbed in and sat opposite Sawyer.

The driver gave a smart snap of the reins in the air, and the horse set off at a leisurely walking pace. As the carriage trundled along under the riotous green leaves of the park's lush summer canopy, Sawyer felt her brain slipping into a pensive reverie.

"How are things, Sawyer?"

Sawyer snapped to attention to see Ed smiling kindly at her. The horse and carriage was slowly ambling toward the little brick overlook by Bethesda Fountain. They had fallen out of reasonable earshot of the horse and carriage carrying Charles and Kathy.

"How are things, *really*?" Ed pressed.

"Oh," Sawyer said, flustered by his penetrating concern. "They're fine. I mean, they're great—Charles and I are so grateful for the wedding help." She paused, then added, "Kathy is a godsend when it comes to all the planning. She's amazing, truly."

"She is, she is," Ed agreed, but it sounded like there was something bigger gnawing at him. The carriage continued to trundle along. He sighed.

"Look," Ed said now, "I know it may seem like you and Charles have different priorities right now. Or maybe it seems like *his* priorities are out of whack, and are taking him away from your time together, as a couple."

Sawyer didn't say anything, taken off guard that Ed was getting this personal.

"Charles can be like his mom," Ed continued. "A bit materialistic, really."

Ed coughed, trying to hide a laugh at Sawyer's attempt to hide her reaction.

"But they're also the same because all they really want is reassurance that the people they love are going to have all the best things in life."

"They both have truly good hearts; I understand that," Sawyer said quietly.

"I believe you *do*," Ed replied. He held Sawyer in his gaze. "I believe you do."

A moment passed. He cleared his throat again.

"Charles has had to deal with some unexpected changes over the years," he said.

Sawyer frowned, unsure where this was going.

"Throughout Charles's entire childhood, we were . . . I don't know how else to put it, but 'well-to-do.' Kath and I both had a bit of family money, and I was running my own investment firm," Ed said. There was no bragging in his voice, and Sawyer understood immediately that there was far more to the story Ed was telling her now. "Charles and his younger brother came into a world where they were not only safe; they could have anything they ever wanted," Ed continued.

It sounded less like a point of pride and more like a confession, and in the next sentence, Sawyer understood why.

"But a few years back, I got caught up investing in a friend's company. It seemed—at the time—like the big one, the one you don't want to miss. All of our friends were investing in these amazing hedge funds and start-ups and making a killing. I thought I was being an old fuddy-duddy not to. I thought I should get with it, and not get left behind."

Ed paused, shook his head, and swallowed.

"Anyway," he continued. "In one fell swoop, it was all gone. I was a fool, driven by idiotic hubris. A more prudent person would have held something back. They wouldn't have left their son suddenly in shock and struggling to make tuition during the final semester of his senior year at Harvard."

A weary expression settled on Ed's face. He rubbed his forehead, pinching his thumb and index finger at the bridge between his eyes.

Sawyer's jaw had gone completely slack. "Charles?" she murmured. "He . . . ? I had no idea . . ."

Ed nodded. "More often than not, I'm too ashamed to really dwell on it, but I have to say, I'm proud of him—he finished his senior year, he put himself through law school. He figured it all out, clever boy."

Sawyer thought back over her relationship with Charles. It made more sense now—why she wasn't the only one with student loans, why together they'd perfected the art of slurping up Top Ramen in front of a Blockbuster movie, why they'd skipped skiing trips to Vermont with his friends, Charles rolling his eyes and suggestively saying he'd rather stay home (which she'd taken as a compliment).

"I'm sure you've wondered why—especially after moving here to New York—we haven't helped you more," Ed said.

Sawyer was quiet, thinking. *Had she wondered?*

"You don't owe us anything," Sawyer said to Ed now. "I don't expect it, and neither does Charles."

"You don't expect it," Ed confirmed, "because you're a good person. And Charles doesn't expect it because he knows there isn't much we *can* give. Kathy and I are living a different life now: one where our stake in the future is mainly rented and leased, one where we live on credit and a lot of illusions—illusions that make her happy."

Sawyer raised her eyes to meet Ed's, surprised anew.

"Kathy doesn't know you've lost your savings?" Sawyer asked.

Ed chuckled morosely and sighed, the weight of the conversation still upon him.

"It's hard to know for sure sometimes," he admitted. "But Kathy is a very smart woman—I'm sure you'd agree. I'd be surprised if she didn't know. But I think she is much happier to pretend. And, to be honest, maybe I am, too."

Wow, was all Sawyer's brain could silently comment.

"Listen," Ed said. "I see how you're looking at me now. And I didn't tell you this to shock you or scare you."

"Oh my God. Our wedding!" Sawyer gasped before she could stop herself. She clapped a hand over her mouth, then let it drop in her lap, numb with the realization. "The expenses, the deposits alone . . . !"

Ed shook his head and waved her concerns away.

"Please," he insisted. "Kathy wants those things. It's part of . . . of everything that matters to her."

"Oh, but to think of how much it's costing, given your situation," Sawyer protested. She glanced at him, deeply apologetic. "I didn't have any idea . . ."

"That was part of the point," Ed said.

Sawyer took this in.

"Sawyer, I'm just so grateful that you've been so accommodating and gracious in all of this."

"In all of what?" she asked, bewildered.

"Letting Kathy have so much of a say in the wedding planning. And . . . I sincerely hope you haven't felt rushed at all."

"What do you mean?" She frowned, suddenly overcome by a feeling of uncertainty again.

Ed sighed.

"They're each other's favorites, you know—Charles and Kathy," he said. "She's always wanted to be able to plan every detail of his wedding, and invite all her friends, bask in that sense of pride . . . And Charles . . . Charles wants his mother's happiness. When I came to him and told him that we still had enough in credit to cover the kind of wedding Kathy wanted, but that we might *not* have it in a few years' time . . . that might have nudged him along a little."

Ed read Sawyer's surprised and slightly horrified expression and hurried to add, "No, no, please don't take that to mean more than it does. Charles has *always* said that, from the moment he met you, there was never any doubt he wanted to marry you. So when I say 'nudge,' I only mean in terms of the timing—understand?"

Sawyer couldn't speak. She only blinked at Ed. She didn't know how to feel; her mind was busy revisiting the night of Charles's proposal, and the morning after, when he'd surprised her with his desire to set a date for the wedding within a year's time. She'd been so flattered by his eagerness to rush. Now, she felt her cheeks growing warm with embarrassment. She'd fooled herself into believing what she wanted to believe.

The horse and carriage continued to clop along, the buggy's rhythmic rocking like a boat drifting on a sloshing ocean. The driver had finally turned south again, toward the zoo and the little carnival of rides set up in Wollman Rink, and eventually the Plaza Hotel, where Ed and Kathy were staying.

"I'll be straight with you, Sawyer," Ed said. "Whatever Kathy wants, I will always try to give her."

He paused, then added, "And in his own way, I think that is what Charles is trying to do for you now."

Sawyer's frown deepened.

"I'm not saying Charles is in debt or is trying to keep up appearances like we are," Ed hurried to explain. "I'm saying he already has it in his head that, come hell or high water, he is *not* going to let it come to that. It's why he's putting in the long hours, and why he won't rest until he moves up at Wexler Gibbons. He's taking your time together and exchanging it for security, for a future together filled with security. And in some ways, maybe, that's because of my mistakes."

Ed paused one more time, looking sad.

"He doesn't know how precious time is yet. But that's not his fault. He's doing what he thinks is best . . . the only thing he knows how to do."

The horse and carriage was passing Wollman Rink, steadily moving through the dappled light of the trees. They would arrive at the Plaza soon.

"Why are you telling me this?" Sawyer asked.

"I just want you to understand him," Ed answered. "It's so important for the two of you to understand each other. It's obvious that his overtime is putting a strain on things. I don't want you to grow apart over this. He's doing it for your future. He's going about it all wrong, of course—but he's doing it for your future."

Sawyer stared at Ed. There was something powerfully urgent yet frail in his expression. His eyes were pale blue, his brow raised, his skin lined with long years of worry that Sawyer, being so young, knew she couldn't conceive of yet.

"I respect what you have to say," she said finally. "Thank you, Ed."

His eyes grew red and glassy. He reached for her hand and squeezed it, very briefly.

"You're my family, too, you know," he said.

Sawyer smiled. "I know," she replied. But the truth was, she'd only just now discovered it, as the words left her mouth. "I feel the same."

"Promise me one thing, Sawyer," Ed said, his voice pleading and his expression serious. "Promise me that, when Charles realizes it was a mistake to let all this time together get away . . . you'll be patient with him. You'll give him a chance to make it up to you."

Sawyer was quiet.

"Can you promise me that?" Ed prodded.

Sawyer took a breath. "I'll try."

* * *

A few minutes later, both horse-drawn buggies pulled up in front of the Plaza Hotel, one after the other. All four passengers—first Sawyer and Ed, then Charles and Kathy—climbed out as the carriages rocked and bounced under their weight. Ed reunited with his wife and gave no sign of the conversation he'd just had with Sawyer.

"Well!" Kathy exclaimed. "This has given me a stroke of genius! I knew we were missing *something* when it came to the wedding, and now I know what it is!"

Sawyer braced herself.

"We need to hire carriages for the wedding!" Kathy decided. "A wedding at the Plaza needs carriages, horses . . . how did I not think of this before? And just think—they'll add a charming touch to the photos!"

She glanced around the group of them.

"Won't they?" she demanded.

Charles and Ed smiled and nodded, silent but affable.

"Oh! I wonder if maybe they can do cushions to match our wedding party colors! Wouldn't that look super?"

Sawyer listened to Kathy prattle on, freshly aware of the fact that Kathy and Ed could not afford any of these things. Her stomach twisted and she felt a little sick.

"We'd better get back to the room, Kath, if we want to get a nap in before we have to start getting ready for dinner," Ed urged his wife.

"Oh, of course."

She leaned over and kissed Charles on the cheek, then Sawyer.

"Remember—the boat leaves at seven," Charles reminded them. "We'll swing by to pick you up around six."

"We'll be ready, sparklers in hand!" Kathy said, her eyes exuberant.

It was only a temporary goodbye, but Sawyer felt Ed squeeze her like he hadn't before.

"You're my family, too," he repeated, in a low voice only Sawyer could hear.

When he released her, he gazed at her, his eyes full of meaning. She nodded at him.

Then, with Kathy still blowing kisses over her shoulder, Ed and

Kathy walked arm in arm under the gilded awning, over the black-and-white checkerboard pavement, up the red-carpeted stairs, and through the brass revolving door . . . into the expensive hotel that had already been booked for Charles and Sawyer's wedding.

Charles turned to Sawyer.

"What did my dad talk to you about during the carriage ride?"

Sawyer wanted to tell him, but felt her throat thicken. She needed time—time to think through it all.

"Oh," Sawyer said reflexively. "You know. Small talk."

Charles looked unconvinced. "Are you sure?"

"Yep."

"It's just . . . I don't like not knowing."

Sawyer felt a rush of anger come over her, remembering everything Ed had just told her. "I don't either," she replied, her voice firm.

Charles paused for a minute. He studied her face, puzzled, but seemed to understand it was not the time to push her further. He took a deep breath, then pulled Sawyer toward him and folded her into his arms.

She felt his heart thudding in his chest, the intimate rhythm of his pulse as it always seemed to her—strong, steady, reassuring.

"I'm beat," he said. "Ready to head home and nap before we do this all over again?"

"Yeah," Sawyer replied.

They turned and headed in the direction of the nearest subway entrance, holding hands.

• • •

Their Fourth of July evening was a success; Kathy was tickled by the yacht, the food, the fireworks, and Ed was predictably tickled by Kathy's being tickled. Everyone went home with a champagne buzz, and the next morning, Ed and Kathy caught the train back up to Connecticut.

Charles and Sawyer saw them off, then came home and went straight back to bed, drowsily napping the rest of the day away as the summer sunshine streamed in through the windows. It was an afternoon of much-needed respite. But by the time the evening rolled around, Sawyer felt her mind drifting back to the carriage ride with Ed, and everything he had confessed to her.

Was she mad at Charles? She didn't think so. Or, at least, whenever she started to get angry about it, she could feel herself softening a little when she tried to picture what it must have been like for him to suddenly have the rug ripped out from under him right around the time his college tuition bills had come due. There was something to not wanting to repeat your parents' traumatic mistakes. The whole world over could relate to that.

It's so important for the two of you to understand each other, Ed had said.

Maybe her suspicions about Kendra had been one big rush to judgment.

And maybe if she went to Charles now, Sawyer thought, and let him know that Ed had brought her into the circle—that she knew about his family's financial struggles—they could open back up to each other like they used to. Maybe if she let Charles know that she understood now *why* he was working so hard to secure his future at Wexler Gibbons, she could also make a case for why there might be alternative choices that could still get them where they wanted to go in life, and allow them to spend a little more time together.

She smiled, buoyed by the thought that they could talk things through.

But when she entered the bedroom, she stopped short.

"Oh, hey," Charles greeted her as she entered, barely looking up.

"You're packing your gym bag," Sawyer observed stiffly.

"Yeah. It was great to see my parents this weekend, but I'm behind on everything."

"Including the gym," she observed.

"Yeah," he agreed. "The gym helps me stay sane."

Sawyer sat on the bed, pretending leisurely interest in watching him pack. Inwardly, she realized, she had an inexplicable urge to scream, just to get his attention. She felt something in her rib cage clench as she tamped down the urge.

She took a breath and changed the subject.

"I thought we might watch a movie together. *Ghost* is on NBC tonight."

"Hmm, sounds sappy," he said.

She could read the distraction in his face, his eyes moving around the gym bag. His mind elsewhere, contemplating some kind of calculation she wasn't privy to.

"I'd probably just nod off and annoy you with my snoring," he decided aloud. "But you can watch if you like. Mind keeping the volume down?" He put his gym bag on the floor by the door, then went to the bathroom, flipped on the light, and set about brushing his teeth.

Sawyer stared at him for a minute, dismayed.

Then she wandered back toward the living room and kitchen.

She turned on the computer—more out of habit than anything else. She felt like "talking" to someone. She began an email to Autumn, pouring her heart out. But after five minutes of typing, she deleted most of what she'd written. It felt like a violation to tell Autumn about Ed and Kathy's financial situation. And Sawyer wasn't ready to share her suspicions about Charles and Kendra with her best friend. She knew how protective Autumn could be; there was a good chance Sawyer's suspicions were wrong, and she wanted Autumn to genuinely *like* the man she planned to marry.

Instead, she found herself writing something totally unexpected—an email full of small talk, telling Autumn all about how she'd met up with Nick the other day, and how, to her surprise, she'd had a good time.

She clicked send, then logged off.

She wandered into the living room and, not really knowing what else to do, put on the movie she'd suggested to Charles.

It *was* sappy, of course.

And yet, as Sawyer watched Demi Moore ramble around an unrealistically enormous SoHo loft, haunted by the ghost of Patrick Swayze, there was something familiar about it: the idea that someone you loved could be so present in your life one day, and the next day steadily disappear into a series of small hauntings . . . your time together reduced to echoes of memory, the divide between the two of you evolving into different realms.

The movie ended with Patrick Swayze's spirit going into the light, Demi Moore sad but at peace. Sawyer raised the remote and clicked off the TV, then dropped her arm. She sat quietly for a moment. She could just make out the low buzz of Charles's snoring from the dark cavern of the bedroom.

11.

TUESDAY, JULY 6

"Sawyer?"

Sawyer looked up from her desk to see Johanna standing in the open doorway to her office.

"Did you put yourself on my calendar as my eleven o'clock by mistake?" Johanna asked, her lips pursed, her eyebrows drawn together in confusion.

"Yes. No! I mean, no," Sawyer replied, already babbling.

Johanna frowned.

"Well? Which is it?"

"Yes, I put myself on your calendar," Sawyer confirmed. "No, it's not a mistake."

Johanna's eyebrows shot sky-high.

"And the purpose of this meeting is?" she prompted.

Sawyer felt her shoulders hunch and her expression turn sheepish.

"I'd like to talk about how I'm doing, and ask for more responsibilities."

Johanna fixed Sawyer with a long look, as though deciding. She tapped her lacquered nails on the metal doorframe of her office, where they made an unnerving tick-tick-tick sound. Finally, Johanna sighed.

"All right," she said. "Come in and close the door."

Sawyer's heart gave a squeeze. She grabbed a pen and pad of paper and scrambled out of her seat. Kaylee looked on from the cubicle opposite Sawyer's, eyes wide with a mixture of awe and envy. She gave Sawyer a discreet thumbs-up.

Sawyer scampered into the office, closed the door, and took a seat.

"All right, shoot," Johanna ordered. "I've got things to do."

Sawyer swallowed and took a deep breath.

"I know editorial assistants come and go," she began. "A lot of them, uh—'wash out,' as some might put it. But . . . I wanted to make it clear that I intend to stay." She paused, and then added, "Well. What I mean is, I really want this—to work in publishing, that is. I'm committed."

Sawyer paused again. She felt winded; her tongue felt thick.

"'Committed'? You make it sound like a mental institution," Johanna joked, her delivery utterly flat and dry.

Sawyer laughed and blushed. Then she gathered herself, cleared her throat, and looked Johanna in the eyes again.

"I'm really . . ." She tried to find the best synonym. "Dedicated," she said finally. "I'm not going anywhere. Since being hired, I've worked hard and learned fast, and I'll go on working just as hard, if not harder."

Johanna pursed her lips but didn't speak. She regarded Sawyer from the side of her eyes. For a fleeting moment, Sawyer worried that, in her effort to be direct and bold, she had come off as overly combative.

"All right," was all Johanna said instead. "But what's the point of this meeting? What's your ask? Preferably in five hundred words or five minutes' time—whichever is shorter."

Sawyer drew a deep breath. *Don't lose your nerve now,* she chastised herself.

"I was wondering . . . especially when it comes to Preeti Chaudhari . . . if maybe I could sit in on author meetings and on author calls? I could keep quiet and take notes or something. I just . . . want to shadow you, I guess. If that's possible."

"You want to 'shadow' me."

It was a word that other senior editors at the publishing house used when they began inviting their editorial assistants and assistant editors along to lunches and important meetings, effectively grooming them to be the senior editors of tomorrow.

"Yes," Sawyer confirmed. "You know—like an apprentice might learn."

"I'm familiar with the concept," Johanna replied. She let out a sigh. "You *do* know that Kaylee was hired before you, though, don't you?"

"By three months," Sawyer pointed out, before she could stop herself. She cringed to hear the defensive notes creeping into her tone. "What I mean is . . . Kaylee knows I pulled Preeti's book from the slush. She understands how invested I am in this author in particular."

Sawyer had a flash of Kaylee giving her the thumbs-up just before Sawyer had walked into the office for this very meeting. It seemed possible that she and Kaylee could cheer each other on and *both* succeed, even buoy each other up. As it was, Sawyer and Kaylee already had a history of helping each other decode the tasks that Johanna hadn't taken the time to explain. They ultimately made each other more competent, like two students cramming for a test.

"I see," Johanna replied.

Johanna's tone was still flat; it was hard to tell if she was annoyed or impressed.

"Anything else?"

"No. That . . . that was what I wanted to talk to you about," Sawyer answered.

"Well, I'll give it a think and let you know what I decide is best with regard to our office's future dealings with Ms. Chaudhari. In the meantime, I'm sure your desk is full of plenty of things that need doing before the end of the day."

Sawyer understood: she was being dismissed.

"Thank you, Johanna," Sawyer said, getting up to go.

"Of course." There was a pause, then Johanna added distractedly, almost as an afterthought, "You know, usually the way it goes is an assistant waits for a senior editor to call a meeting like this—not the other way around."

Sawyer's hand was on the doorknob. She turned back and smiled awkwardly. "I just wanted you to know that I, uh . . . really want to be here."

Johanna raised her eyes from something she was looking at on her desk, regarded Sawyer, and pushed her lips into a tight smile.

"Well, good for you for being a go-getter," she said.

Sawyer grinned and thanked Johanna again. She let herself out and closed the office door—hoping that Johanna's last comment had been a compliment.

* * *

Sawyer was still mulling her meeting with Johanna later that evening when she arrived home to an empty apartment. It was hard to conclude whether the meeting had been an embarrassment or a victory. She couldn't believe she'd actually done it, but she was glad she'd been brave enough to make a case for herself.

Going through her usual routine, she hit her computer's power button and listened to the sound of the dial-up logging on as she blotted her face with a damp paper towel and chugged a glass of ice water.

"*WELCOME!*" the AOL voice greeted her. "*You've got mail!*"

She clicked, happy.

To: Adventures_of_Tom@aol.com
From: AutumnLeaves@hotmail.com

Wait—WHAT? Come again? *Who* is this new friend? I don't understand. He was RUDE to you at a party, but somehow you decided to go bar-hopping with him?

You didn't say what he looked like. Why do I get the feeling he's cute?

You better not be replacing me! Let Mister-Easy-On-The-Eyes know that the Official Best Friend position is already taken. He may be cute, but *I'm* the one who knows about the time freshman year when you tried to cut your own bangs, not to mention the water balloon fight in the quad when you laughed so hard you peed your pants a little, and tried to blame it on the balloons.

xo Autumn
p.s. Just kidding. A new friend is good. Glad you're getting out this summer after all. You deserve it!

Sawyer laughed and shook her head, then clicked to reply.

Nick's not your replacement, she promised. *But he turned out to be a pretty OK guy, actually.*

She typed in a few more details and clicked send, then sat there, re-reading her message and thinking.

She'd decided Nick *was* a pretty OK guy. Maybe more than OK. The truth was, she was feeling oddly let down that she hadn't heard from him since the Friday before last, when they'd hung out on the Lower East Side. Of course, it was only reasonable to assume he'd been busy over the Fourth of July—*she'd* been busy herself. Even if he'd invited her to hang out, she'd have had to awkwardly decline, explaining that Charles's parents were in town.

But still . . . the truth was, Sawyer felt like talking to Nick.

Her hands hovered over the keyboard.

Then, impulsively, she opened a new email and typed, *Dear Nick, I was thinking about you, and just thought I'd say hi . . .*

She stopped. Stared at it. Then hammered the delete key.

Her hands hovered again, and she typed, *Hi Nick, I'm guessing you're busy . . .*

She deleted it.

She typed, *Hey.*

She stared at the single word on the screen, the cursor blinking at her as though taunting her to figure out what should come next.

She sighed, irritated, and got up from her chair, did a lap of the tiny kitchen. She rummaged through the fridge and found a beer, popped it open, and took a swig from the neck of the bottle.

She sat back down and stared at the screen again, and at the single word she had managed to type. She reached for the beer and took another swig.

Then, like someone had waved a magic wand, a chime sounded and a box popped up in front of her email draft.

Nikolai70: Hey.

Sawyer almost choked on her beer. She managed to fight off a spit take, then gasped and smiled.

Adventures_of_Tom: Hey!

Adventures_of_Tom: You're psychic. I was just thinking about you

Nikolai70: I guessed

Adventures_of_Tom: What do you mean, "you guessed"?

Nikolai70: Seemed like the right amount of time for a check in

Sawyer fought back a little smile. Had he been somewhere, fighting off the urge to talk to her, too?

Adventures_of_Tom: Don't tell me you're one of those guys who has to wait a specific amount of time before checking back in with a female friend?

Nikolai70: That applies to girls you're dating. And I'm pretty sure you're referring to something you saw in the movie Swingers

Sawyer reread his response, somewhat chastened. *Reminder: this was not a romantic situation.*

Adventures_of_Tom: Sorry. You're right.

Nikolai70: But you've been on my mind. I thought I'd say hi.

Sawyer brightened.

She sat chewing her lip. For some reason, she didn't want to dance around things. She was gripped by a desire to be bold and totally frank for once. Her fingers tapped out the words, and—before she could change her mind—she hit enter.

Adventures_of_Tom: To be honest, you've been on my mind a lot. It wasn't just today.

There was a long pause on the other end. Sawyer wondered if she'd freaked him out.

Finally, a new message materialized in the chat box.

Nikolai70: You should have reached out.

Nikolai70: If you feel like talking to me, you should talk to me.

Sawyer smiled.

Adventures_of_Tom: Well, we're here now

Nikolai70: What's on your mind?

Adventures_of_Tom: I took your advice. I got brave and spoke to my boss about being committed to my job, and about wanting more responsibilities.

Nikolai70: Good for you. I think that's a solid move.

Adventures_of_Tom: Well, it was all because of your advice

Nikolai70: Nah. Any jackass can give you advice. You're the one who put it into action.

Adventures_of_Tom: I honestly couldn't read my boss's reaction. But I still feel like it was a good thing for me to do for myself, either way

Nikolai70: Absolutely. You can't sit around expecting others to know what you want if you don't tell them. And you can't sit around waiting to be acknowledged. That's the chick way. You have to ask for what you want and demand acknowledgment. That's the dude way.

Sawyer frowned, suddenly put off, irked.

Adventures_of_Tom: Why is this turning into a debate about gender stereotypes?

Nikolai70: There's no debate. I'm right.

Adventures_of_Tom: You sound like a chauvinist.

Nikolai70: Maybe. Maybe not. Maybe YOU sound like the chauvinist.

Adventures_of_Tom: How do you figure?

Nikolai70: I'm saying women don't always ask for what they're worth. And they should feel entitled to do so. They stand to gain.

Adventures_of_Tom: But you're calling that acting like a man

Nikolai70: Well in society today, it is perceived as "acting like a man"

Sawyer's frown deepened with her mounting irritation.

Adventures_of_Tom: I think we should change the subject.

Nikolai70: Alright, you got it

Nikolai70: What are you doing this Friday?

Adventures_of_Tom: Well

Adventures_of_Tom: That's another thing I was considering taking your advice on. Although, now I'm reluctant to keep giving you so much credit.

Nikolai70: Because I disagree with you about the differences between the sexes?

Adventures_of_Tom: Because you sound like a sexist.

Nikolai70: I thought we were going to change the subject

Adventures_of_Tom: You're right. We are.

Nikolai70: Let's get back to this Friday

Adventures_of_Tom: Yes. This Friday. I had an epiphany that I shouldn't just sit around all alone in my hot apartment. I should take advantage of summer Fridays and get out

Nikolai70: . . . a realization that was not inspired by me in any way.

Adventures_of_Tom: Nope. No credit

Adventures_of_Tom: ANYWAY

Nikolai70: Anyway . . .

Adventures_of_Tom: I made a list

Nikolai70: A list?

Adventures_of_Tom: Of stuff I'd like to do

Nikolai70: Cool! What's on your list?

Adventures_of_Tom: Well . . . I think you're probably going to laugh at me

Adventures_of_Tom: Especially because you grew up here

Adventures_of_Tom: Some of the stuff is touristy stuff. Well, maybe a lot of the stuff is touristy stuff. But it's all stuff I haven't done, and would like to

Nikolai70: C'mon. You brought it up. Just show me the list already. You wouldn't have brought it up if you didn't want to tell me about it.

Sawyer chewed her lip again. Finally, she opened a Word document she'd entitled "Summer Fridays." She copied the list she'd created, pasted it into their AIM chat, and tapped the enter key.

There was a pause, and Sawyer imagined Nick looking it over. Then a chime sounded, heralding a new message.

Nikolai70: I'm surprised Times Square and the Statue of Liberty aren't on here

Adventures_of_Tom: Times Square wasn't, but the Statue of Liberty actually was. But I looked up the price of tickets to take the tour that does Liberty Island plus Ellis Island. Ouch!

Nikolai70: You're right.

Adventures_of_Tom: Kinda pricey, and the tour is probably overrated, right?

Nikolai70: No, I mean you're right that this is some seriously touristy crap you've listed here

The irked feeling returned. She knew Nick was just being Nick. Still, it stung.

Nikolai70: A lot of this stuff is downright corny and embarrassing

Adventures_of_Tom: Well. Whatever. I'm sorry I showed you my list.

Nikolai70: I've pissed you off again, haven't I?

Adventures_of_Tom: No. It's fine. I should have expected it. Anyway, I should log off. I have to go

Nikolai70: You don't have to go. You're mad

Adventures_of_Tom: No, I really have to go do some work. Especially if I want to do some of this pathetically touristy crap this Friday.

Adventures_of_Tom: Catch you later

Nikolai70: OK. See ya, I guess

Sawyer stared at the screen, waiting, but she didn't know what she was waiting for. Finally, she logged off.

She sat for a minute, fighting off a wave of irritation and disappointment.

Then she logged back on.

She clicked to open a new email.

> To: AutumnLeaves@hotmail.com
> From: Adventures_of_Tom@aol.com
>
> p.s. Never mind what I said about that Nick guy. First impressions are always right; he's an ASS.

She clicked send, her cheeks still burning. After a few minutes, she logged out and turned the computer all the way off.

* * *

The next afternoon, when Sawyer's belated lunch hour rolled around, she carried a manuscript with her over to Greenacre Park to do a little work.

She lucked upon a café table pleasantly nestled in a shady spot near the waterfall. She unfolded a few paper napkins she'd pilfered from Starbucks and spread them on the tabletop (Johanna detested stains of any kind getting on manuscripts, even internal copies not destined for the authors), and set the manuscript on top (taking care to weigh down the loose pages with the stapler and a box of staples she'd borrowed from her work desk—she'd learned about the treachery of a sudden crosstown breeze the hard way). Then she laid out the contents of her bag lunch at a respectable distance off to the side, and got to work.

Ten minutes later, she had settled in. She was alternately snacking, reading, and scribbling notes when, from the corner of her eye, she glimpsed the figure of someone approaching. She looked up and instantly froze.

It was Nick.

He was dressed in a suit and tie, indicating he'd made the journey over from his own office. He smirked at the sight of Sawyer's shocked expression but didn't comment. Instead, he approached her table wordlessly, pulled out a chair, and casually sat down.

"What are you doing here?" Sawyer blurted, still blinking at him in total surprise.

"Looking for you," Nick replied with a shrug. "Well, maybe 'looking' makes it sound misleadingly laborious. Pretty sure I knew exactly where to find you."

"You remembered me telling you about this park . . ." Sawyer murmured to herself, dazed.

"Of course. I remember everything you tell me. It was a no-brainer. I left the office and came straight here."

Sawyer blinked at him, taken off guard.

"But . . . *why*?" she asked, confused.

Instead of answering, Nick casually craned his neck about, taking in the stone, the greenery, the café tables, the waterfall.

"I'll admit; you're right. This spot is pretty cool. I'd have never imagined anything like this existed in Midtown. 'An unexpected oasis,' just as you described it."

"But why are you here?" Sawyer repeated, still confused. She glanced at her watch. "Shouldn't you be at work?"

"Probably," Nick agreed with a shrug. "But I've got a few minutes."

He reached into one of her plastic baggies and helped himself to an apple slice. It made a crisp crunch as he bit into it. Sawyer only stared at him and watched as he continued to chew.

"You were definitely pissed at me when you logged off last night," he said. He reached for another apple slice and took a bite. "So I figured I'd come here in person in an effort to make things square between us."

"By . . . eating my lunch?" Sawyer questioned with raised eyebrows.

"No," Nick said. "By letting you know that I'm in."

"You're 'in'?"

"I'm on board with the plan."

"The plan?"

"Your list." He sucked in a burdensome breath and sighed. "*Someone's* gotta help you do it right. It may as well be me."

"I'm confused, Nick—what the hell are you saying?"

He smiled at this. Having finished the second apple slice, he reached for one of the still-folded paper napkins stacked under the weight of her Snapple and dabbed at the corners of his mouth. Then he stood, brushed his hands off, and straightened his suit.

"I'm saying: Meet me. This Friday. Three p.m. By Castle Clinton in Battery Park."

"Huh?"

"Friday. Three p.m. Castle Clinton. Battery Park," he repeated in staccato. "You can remember that. Don't make me write it down in an email."

With that, Nick turned to go.

Sawyer stared after his receding back, still dazed with surprise to have seen him in the first place.

"Three p.m.!" Nick shouted one last time over his shoulder as he walked away. "Be there!"

12.

FRIDAY, JULY 9

Sawyer sat on a bench facing the glittering harbor, her back to the round, rosy brick fort that was Castle Clinton. The air felt thick and smelled metallic—a little bit the way it had before the thunderstorm, only more intense, and there wasn't a cloud in the sky.

She'd only been to Battery Park once since moving to New York, on a cold winter day. She hadn't imagined how different Battery Park could be in summer, and it hadn't really occurred to her to go back for a second visit. It was so far from the Upper West Side, at the southernmost tip of Manhattan, an outer fringe even by downtown standards. Sometimes, subconsciously, Sawyer almost pictured New York falling off the map after Wall Street, like an old medieval belief about the ocean suddenly cascading off the edge of a flat Earth.

Now, as she observed the scene, she spotted joggers, couples strolling hand-in-hand, tourists and families, skateboarders and Rollerbladers, and what looked like stockbrokers yelling into their cellular phones. A group of delighted, squealing children took turns filling up paper cups and plastic bottles at a nearby water fountain and splashed one another, playing a makeshift game of tag. They chased one another, screamed, and ran away laughing, repeating the process until they were absolutely soaked, their shirts and shorts a heavy, soggy mess on their twiggy bodies. Sawyer smiled, remembering the fun of water balloon fights as a kid.

Somewhere even farther in the distance behind her—perhaps from one of the old historic churches bizarrely nestled among the modern skyscrapers—a clock tower bell sounded the hour. She counted the chimes out of habit.

Three o'clock.

Then, right on cue, she recognized a figure cutting toward her from the waterfront esplanade. He was dressed casually—as was she. They had turned back into the two twenty-somethings who had met up at the Watering Hole two Fridays ago.

She stood as Nick approached.

"Hey," she called in greeting.

He was carrying a backpack and what looked like a portable ice chest. They nodded hello.

"I had some errands to run," he said.

She couldn't tell if he was apologizing.

"You're not late," she said, just in case. "It's just now three o'clock, almost on the dot."

"Good," he said. "That works out perfect for my plan."

"Plan?" Sawyer echoed.

Nick turned on his heel. "Follow me," he called over his shoulder.

• • •

Sawyer tried to keep up with Nick's long, fast strides, peppering him with questions as he led the way back along the esplanade. Eventually, he headed to a big ferry terminal. Giant letters curving in a semi-arc above the exterior of the terminal read "*STATEN ISLAND*."

"We're going to Staten Island?" she asked, blinking in bewilderment.

"Yes and no," Nick answered.

"What does that mean?"

"It means we're traveling in that direction; I don't recommend getting off the boat there," he quipped.

Sawyer's brow furrowed, but he only smirked.

"C'mon," he said. "Hurry up! We want to get a nice seat in first class."

"First class?"

"That's a joke. But we do want to find a good spot on the ferry. Let's go."

Again, Nick led the way and Sawyer followed. He moved swiftly through the terminal and up the escalators, taking the already moving stairs two at a time. They joined a herd of people waiting in front of a set of closed doors for the ferry that had just arrived to finish deboarding its passengers. Then the doors opened, and Nick and Sawyer fell into step as the group shuffled forward to board.

"Don't we need tickets or something?" Sawyer asked, as they made their way onto the ship.

Nick laughed. "It's free." He looked at her and grinned. "Which makes it perfect for our purposes." They neared a stairway and he gestured to it. "Up here. We want the promenade deck, right side."

Sawyer followed him up a stairwell that smelled like diesel and spilled black coffee. They reached the top deck, a large fluorescent-lit room filled with rows and rows of orange plastic seats that somewhat resembled the ones on the subway. Nick veered right and pushed through a windowed metal door that led out onto a narrow open-air promenade. Orange benches lined the side of the ship, facing out to the water.

Nick walked out and then stopped in front of one of the benches. He dusted it off with a paper napkin, and flourished his arm.

Sawyer sat.

"What are we doing?" she asked.

"You said you wanted to visit Lady Liberty," he replied. "This is the way we locals wave hello to her, free of charge."

He sat down next to her. Sawyer stared at him as a shy smile spread over her face. She wasn't quite sure what to say.

"I'll even be your tour guide," Nick said. He wiggled his backpack off his shoulder, unzipped it, and reached inside to produce a large brown paper bag.

"What's that?"

"A sampling of the local cuisine to complement our tour." He opened the bag and tipped it in her direction to reveal a cardboard carrier containing several hot dogs with various toppings. "Gray's Papaya," he said.

"I've actually never had Gray's," Sawyer admitted.

Nick gave her a scornful look.

"Today we right that wrong," he said. "We'll commence meal service in just a moment." He raised a finger in the air. "Marvelous cruise director that I am, I came equipped with liquid refreshments as well."

He bent over and cracked open the cooler. Inside were several plastic cups with lids and straws, each filled with what appeared to be lemonade slushy. He lifted one of the cups out and handed it to Sawyer. He grinned and reached into the backpack again to produce one of those miniature bottles of vodka Sawyer had only ever encountered on airplanes and in hotel mini-fridges.

"To be added at your discretion," he said, handing her the mini-vodka. He showed her the inside of his backpack, where a few more tiny bottles clinked around in the front pouch. Sawyer suppressed a giggle. Then he reached into the cooler and grabbed a second slushy for himself.

Once their lemonade slushies were properly spiked, Nick knocked his plastic cup against hers.

"Cheers."

"Cheers."

The ferry gave a shudder and groan as it dislodged itself from the dock and prepared to depart. Sawyer watched the horizon and realized they'd begun to move. She stood and peered over the railing as the ferry navigated between the wooden pylons.

Nick came and stood beside her.

Together, they sipped their slushies and watched as the ferry pushed farther and farther into the bay. Eventually, the skyscraper-studded downtown tip of Manhattan receded, shrinking a little as the ferry left it behind.

Sawyer turned to look at Nick.

"This is definitely something new. Something I never guessed I'd be doing today."

"Wait until you try the dogs," Nick joked. "Actually, let's not wait. Not for nothing, but they don't call them 'cold dogs.' You hungry?"

Sawyer nodded and smiled. Nick retrieved two hot dogs and brought them over to the railing.

He held them out. "Mustard purist or the works?"

Sawyer thought for a second. "I'm not sure."

He grinned. "Here, start with this and we'll swap." He handed her the hot dog with mustard.

With the slushy gripped in one hand, Sawyer held the hot dog in the other and leaned her head sideways to take a bite. She hadn't had a hot dog in years, perhaps not since the days of running through sprinklers. She was surprised by how it all came back to her instantly—the softness of the bun, the saltiness of the meat, the tang of the mustard.

"It tastes like summer," she said, attempting to lick a stray dollop of mustard from the corner of her mouth.

Nick smiled. "It's almost like you're a poet or something."

They continued to eat, and the ferry continued to putter across the bay. In between bites, Nick pointed.

"So, here we have the famous Ellis Island," he said.

Sawyer squinted at the buildings—brick and stone, with two tall towers capped with domes framing the main facade.

"It kind of looks like an amusement park."

"Trust me—it *wasn't*," Nick retorted. "Some pretty serious stories of hardship and hope tied to that island."

Sawyer nodded. She thought back to the Tenement Museum they'd visited.

"Actually, those aren't the original buildings. There was a completely different set of original buildings—they were equally impressive . . . but they were made of wood. And. Well. You know . . ."

"Burned down in a fire?"

Nick nodded. "My mother said that always surprised her—all the houses made out of wood here, especially in the suburbs. She said growing up in the Soviet Union, it was all concrete and cinder blocks where she lived. Wooden houses were for old Russian fairy tales."

Sawyer reflected, mulling.

"Have you ever wanted to go there?"

"Sure. But growing up, I was always told that was impossible," he said. "At least for me and my mom, given her political history. But it's strange; there were times when I was super aware that she could never bring me back to where she came from, but other times I felt so completely that I *have* been there in my mind, I forget that I haven't, even now."

"Do you speak Russian?"

"Of course. My mom's English is perfectly fine, but we always wind up speaking in Russian together."

"Do you ever . . . dream in Russian?"

"I do."

Sawyer was quiet. She watched Nick's face, but he was staring out over the water, lost in thought.

"To you, those stories we heard at the Tenement Museum were interesting," Nick said, nodding in approval. "To me, those stories are . . . I don't know—*familiar*. I can feel the yearning in them; my mom's yearning to be here in America, mixed with her yearning for home."

Finally, he shook himself and turned to her.

"Here," he said, holding out half a hot dog and gesturing to the half a hot dog in her hand. "Swap."

They traded halves.

Sawyer struggled to wrangle the half hot dog she'd been given. In addition to mustard, "the works" included ketchup, onions, relish, and sauerkraut. As she bit into it, she received the same salt and tang, but now vinegar and sweetness also filled her mouth.

"And there, to the left of Ellis Island"—Nick pointed—"we're coming into prime view of Liberty Island. Before the French gifted us the Statue of Liberty, the island was home to a star-shaped fort whose pointed walls now make up the base. The fort was named—ironically enough—Fort Wood. No relation to the carbon-based building material."

"This is a good tour," Sawyer teased.

He narrowed his eyes at her playfully as though cautioning her not to insult the tour guide. "Hey—if I thought you'd allow me to swoop in and pay for us both to go on the Statue Cruise tour of Ellis Island and Liberty Island, I would have sprung for it."

"I wouldn't have let you pay," Sawyer conceded.

"That's what I thought. And here we are." He winked. "You said you wanted cheap, and you get what you pay for."

"I guess I'm a cheap date, then, because I'm having a good time."

Nick let his eyes linger on Sawyer's face for a long minute.

"I am, too."

The ferry was passing in front of Liberty Island now. Sawyer turned to look at the statue, taking it in.

"It's hard to imagine her not green. But she must have been," Sawyer said.

"Like a penny," Nick agreed. "She must have been a little bit blinding under certain angles of the sun before the oxidation set in."

Sawyer moved to take another bite of her hot dog, but "the works" were getting messier by the minute. As she bit into the dog, a mound of sauerkraut gave way, and a mixture of ketchup, mustard, and relish went sliding down her chin. She let out a muffled yelp. Nick laughed and dashed to his backpack to retrieve some napkins.

"Hang on!"

The next second he was at her side, still laughing, but valiantly saving her shirt by pressing a wad of napkins to her chin. Sawyer chuckled, embarrassed, as he wiped the condiments away.

"It got away from me."

"Why do you think I gave you the one with the works second?"

"So, you masterminded my humiliation."

"Hardly! I thought you could *practice* on the mustard-only one. There are levels of expertise when it comes to eating these, you know; you don't just go pro overnight."

Nick smoothed one last speckle of mustard off her chin with his bare thumb. He caught her gaze again. Sawyer suddenly felt self-conscious; she could feel herself grinning at him like a maniac, but couldn't help it. His eyes continued to linger.

But in the next second, they were startled by a rustle of feathers.

Nick instinctively hunched his shoulders against the flap of air and spun around. When he saw it was simply a gull, he nodded hello to it. The seagull only tilted his head, getting a better look at Nick with his flat, round, dinosaur eye.

Nick tore off a bit of hot dog bun and held it out.

The seagull tilted his eye this way and that way at the bread, then accepted the offering. For a seagull, the way he took the bread out of Nick's hand struck Sawyer as oddly polite.

"You made a friend." She laughed.

Nick tore off one last piece of bun, fed it to the gull, and then ate the last of his hot dog. The seagull tilted his head at them both, then perfunctorily flapped away.

"Alas, a fair-*feather* friend," Sawyer joked.

"Nah," Nick disagreed. "Did you see that look in his eye? The love was real."

She laughed again.

He pointed to her empty cup.

"Refill? Try another dog?"

* * *

When the ferry reached Staten Island, it docked in the terminal in St. George and the passengers disembarked.

But Sawyer and Nick simply stayed put. A ferry worker came around to usher people off the boat, but Nick only smiled and slapped the guy high five.

"Heyyyy, Carlo!" Nick greeted him.

"How's it hangin', Nick?"

"Good. You hungry?"

"Always."

Nick pulled one of the hot dogs out of the bag and Carlo accepted it with a smirk.

"You two stayin' on?" Carlo asked, ignoring the fact that it was his job to make them leave.

"We're, you know . . . sorta on a cruise to nowhere," Nick answered, nodding.

"All right," Carlo said, laughing. "*The Love Boat* it ain't, but you two enjoy the lido deck, eh?"

He left them alone and carried on, munching on the hot dog.

The ferry went back to Manhattan.

And back to Staten Island.

And back to Manhattan.

And back to Staten Island.

Sawyer lost count of the number of times they rode the ferry back and forth. By the second time she saw the Statue of Liberty, she'd started to feel a little buzz from both the lemonade slushy and the nonstop conversation that seemed to pour out of the two of them as the ferry puttered along. The afternoon slipped away steadily and quickly, and before she knew it, the sun sank low in the sky, lighting up several stray sprays of idling summer clouds with orange, red, and purple, making for a brilliant and vivid sunset.

"Just so you know," Nick said, nodding to the sunset. "Not every tour gets one of these for a finale."

They got up from the bench and stood side by side at the railing again, watching the sun slowly sink over New Jersey. Golden shimmers danced on the water like sequins on a dress. It was a surreal sunset. The kind of striking natural scene that had always left Sawyer, as a kid, scrambling for her little plastic Kodak camera—only to be disappointed when the prints came back, proving that there were some things that film simply can't capture.

It was also a romantic sunset.

Sawyer stole a glance at Nick, charmed. She felt a strange prickle of guilt, and settled her gaze on the middle distance over the water. Her thoughts turned back to Charles.

And then to Charles and Kendra.

"Maybe they're not having an affair," she said.

Nick turned and gazed at her.

Sawyer gave a shrug. "Maybe they're not."

Nick's eyes flicked back to the sunset. "If that would make you happy, I hope it turns out to be true."

Sawyer mulled for a moment.

"Do you ever think about just asking her, point-blank?"

Nick grunted. "I recommend that if you ask a question like that, just make sure you're really, truly ready to hear the answer."

Sawyer pictured herself point-blanking Charles, and him confirming that her worst suspicions were true. She winced.

When she glanced over at Nick and saw the expression on his face, she realized he didn't have to picture it.

"That happened to you," she said to Nick in a revelatory voice. "With someone before Kendra."

He nodded stiffly.

"Was it serious?"

"We lived together." He shrugged. "I had a ring. I hadn't given it to her yet, but I had a ring."

"*Wow—you?*" Sawyer uttered, before she could stop herself. The vodka had definitely loosened her tongue.

Nick raised an eyebrow at her.

"It's . . . just . . . at the Yale Club, you gave me such a hard time about being engaged."

He shrugged. "And now you know why. In my case, I would have been a fool to actually propose."

Sawyer was quiet again as she thought this over.

"And you found out there was someone else by simply asking her?"

Nick nodded again. "I'd been having this weird feeling. But there was no real reason for it; I thought I was just being nuts. I thought it would be an easy thing to put to bed, and then we could move on. We were making breakfast. I asked her if there was someone else, and she just looked at me and said yes."

He gave a bitter snort.

"It's funny, because I'd kind of pictured proposing to go more or less the same way. Breakfast. A simple question. A totally frank, wholehearted answer."

"Nick . . . I'm so sorry."

He shook his head. "Nah. It's not a sob story. I'm just saying, in my experience, if you ask that question, you have to be ready for the answer. Because there's not much to do after getting an answer like the one she gave me that day—except pack and move out."

"Do you really think that?" Sawyer asked, sincere. "Do you think there's really nothing to do but pack up and go? What if the person said they still loved you, and wanted to find a way to get through it, and work it out?"

Nick shook his head. "Not realistic," he decreed. "At least, not for dudes."

Sawyer sighed and rolled her eyes. "We're back to *that* again?"

"No. Let's skip the gender debate. I'll just say that's how it was for me. But who knows—it could be different for you."

Sawyer sensed that Nick had been vulnerable with her, and now she could feel his armor starting to go back up.

"Your second reason," she blurted with sudden realization.

"Beg pardon?"

"You said there were *two* reasons you'd wanted to meet up that day at the Yale Club. The second reason was that you felt I was a 'genuinely nice person.'"

"Pretty sure my assessment was accurate."

Sawyer gave him a sweet, close-lipped smile and shook her head at herself, wondering how she hadn't connected the dots sooner.

"*You* were a genuinely nice, engaged—well, *almost engaged*—person once," she said. "You initiated that meeting at the Yale Club because you don't want the same thing to happen to me that happened to you."

At this, Nick turned and looked at her again. His eyes were dark and penetrating.

After a beat, he shook it off and laughed.

"Don't be ridiculous," he said. "I was never a genuinely nice person."

"Ah," Sawyer replied, seeing he was intent on deflection. There was nothing to do but join in. "That's right. I see the flaw in my logic there."

They chuckled together. After a few seconds, Nick grew quiet. He looked almost sad.

His eyes dropped to her hand resting on the rail between them, and to her ring.

"Your situation is different from mine," he said quietly. "I wasn't being flip that day at the Yale Club. Your situation is harder, trickier. And . . . I feel for you on that."

He straightened up from where they were leaning over the railing, then cleared his throat.

"Look, there are plenty of reasons for me to be critical of the guy, and I don't really want to have an opinion about him, period. But I can tell you one thing," he said. "He'd be a fool to ever make someone like you feel second-best. I hope you know that's true."

Sawyer felt his eyes on her and met his gaze. It was a nice thing to say, the kind of generally nice thing you might say as a pep talk.

But Sawyer knew: Nick didn't do "generally nice," and he didn't do pep talks.

They stared at each other for a long moment, unblinking. His eyes moved to her mouth. Sawyer felt her pulse quicken and the warmth of her blood rushing to her cheeks. A chill ran down her spine. They were standing so close. She could feel his breath on her skin.

The air between them thickened . . .

Until an abrupt splatter of white paint broke the trance.

Sawyer blinked at Nick's shirt in surprise and realized it wasn't white paint at all.

"Oh no!" she cried, already fighting off a laugh.

"What the—?" Nick muttered, twisting and straining to see the full extent of where the seagull poop had landed on his shirt.

Sawyer couldn't help it; she was laughing uncontrollably. "I hope that wasn't your friend!"

"'Fair-feather friend,' indeed," Nick said, continuing to mutter obscenities.

By now the sunset was slowly extinguishing itself in a spectrum of light and dark purples, and the ferry was pulling back into Whitehall Terminal in Manhattan.

"All right, all right," Nick announced, calling it. "Tour's over."

He started packing up their makeshift picnic. Sawyer helped by rounding up and disposing of their trash. Out of the corner of her eye, she watched Nick making sporadic attempts to wipe his shirt clean with a napkin. He seemed genuinely grossed out. She'd noticed the T-shirt earlier. It looked well-worn to the point of being thin and soft, with Nirvana's band logo on the front and a concert date and location on the back—and likely irreplaceable.

"Hey. Do you like that shirt?" Sawyer asked innocently, as they made their way down the stairs of the ferry.

"I *did.*"

"I know how to get the stain out."

"Burn it?"

She rolled her eyes. "Don't be so dramatic. I'll show you how."

• • •

They trekked from Battery Park to Nick's apartment, which turned out to be an old brick walk-up in Alphabet City.

"What?" Nick prompted, catching the expression on Sawyer's face as he unlocked three different dead bolts on his front door.

She shrugged, a little embarrassed that he'd learned how to read her so well, then admitted, "For some reason, I didn't picture you living in a walk-up."

"What did you picture?"

"I don't know. You're a little like two different people. There's the guy who plays in a band and frequents the Watering Hole and Gray's Papaya . . . and then there's the junior advertising exec in the expensive suit I met that first night at the Wexler Gibbons dinner who refers to women as 'chicks' and belongs to the Yale Club."

She paused, then concluded, "I guess I pictured you living in a high-rise. One with a gym, and a doorman who you do that cool money-handshake with to tip, and who does you favors and calls you 'Nicky.'"

"I see." Nick nodded. "You were picturing 'slick bachelor.' But instead, you wound up with 'scary bachelor.'"

"No, I didn't mean—"

He waved her off, chuckling.

"No avuncular doorman or sad little gym that never gets used, but the roaches are on their best behavior, and I can promise you I have the dignity to never let the bathroom run out of toilet paper," he joked. "The ladies don't seem to like that." Then he pushed open the door, and gestured for her to step inside.

Once within, Nick threw his backpack and the cooler on the floor. He went to the bathroom to take off his shirt and wash his neck and chest. She heard him frantically scrubbing with a washcloth.

Sawyer stood awkwardly glancing around. The building itself was probably as old as the tenement they had toured a couple of weeks ago. The fixtures in Nick's apartment were impressively old—push-button light switches, a tall rectangular cabinet that no doubt had once contained an ironing board, and an enormous built-in bookcase that had likely housed a Murphy bed at one time. The space itself was reasonably large (not like the tiny apartments they'd seen in the Tenement Museum), but the layout was open in such a way that made it more like a giant studio than a one-bedroom.

Sawyer was impressed by how clean and cozy it was. Nick had artistic taste. The hardwood was covered in richly patterned loomed rugs in every shade of red, maroon, and burgundy. Vintage rock 'n' roll posters in black and white hung on the walls. Bob Dylan. Mick Jagger. The Doors. The sofa was covered and neatly tucked with a throw blanket with a pretty yet masculine Slavic flower design. A black leather Eames chair and matching ottoman were happily nestled into a corner beside the enormous built-in bookcase. Sawyer didn't see a television anywhere, but she did see a vintage record player and an enormous stereo flanked by two speakers.

The place was eclectic, bohemian; he'd managed to make the building's ancient fixtures look stylish and cool.

Nick emerged from the bathroom and ducked into the bedroom, a room that was uselessly divided from the rest of the apartment by two glass-paned French doors that would likely bump into furniture if anyone ever tried to close them.

In the kitchen, Sawyer spotted an old claw-foot tub.

"Wow!" she exclaimed, crossing the room to admire it. "I've always heard about old New York apartments having bathtubs in the kitchen, but I've never actually seen one."

"I know," Nick called from the bedroom. Sawyer could see a sliver of his shape from the kitchen as he hunted around for a new T-shirt. "People always think it's weird."

"I don't," Sawyer called back. "I think it's cool."

He came out wearing a fresh shirt and joined her next to the tub.

"People always ask if I actually take baths in there."

"And what do you say?"

"No, I don't take baths in my kitchen! That would be weird."

Sawyer slowly surveyed the books and candles on the ledges and shelves near the bathtub. Nick caught her taking stock, and they locked eyes. Sawyer smirked.

"And do you secretly take baths in your kitchen?"

"Of course. That tub is my favorite part of this place."

He lifted off the wooden board that turned the top of the tub into a makeshift countertop and reached for one of the taps.

"See?" he said. "Everything works. Hot. Cold. And the porcelain has even been refinished."

"The owner of the building refinished the porcelain?" She frowned, surprised. "I get why the tub's probably too expensive to remove, but I wouldn't think he would want tenants to actually use it."

"OK, well, maybe *I* sprung to have it refinished," Nick said. He laughed, sheepish. "Geez. I can't get *anything* by you."

Sawyer laughed. "Somehow . . . I feel like you're not really *trying* to get anything by me."

"You're right," Nick said. "With you, I'm just . . . not."

They caught each other's gaze again. Sawyer felt that same sudden uptick in her heartbeat that she had felt on the ferry. This time, her skin prickled hot and cold at the same time, and she felt a vein in her throat pulsing. She fidgeted and looked down at the floor, then caught sight of the shirt in Nick's hand.

"Your shirt!" she said, remembering. "We really only need two things to get the stain out. Liquid dish soap, and vinegar."

Nick rummaged around in his kitchen and produced a bottle of each.

"You really don't have to do that."

"Nah."

She set about scrubbing before he could stop her.

"It's easy—look! It's done." She gave the shirt one last serious scrub and rinsed it in the kitchen sink. She gently wrung it out. "Now it just needs to dry. And then you can run it with the rest of your laundry."

"And after I wash it twenty or thirty times, I'll be ready to wear it again," Nick joked.

"Hey," Sawyer warned. "In plenty of countries, being pooped on by a bird is considered good luck!"

"You're warning me not to . . . wash all of the 'luck' away?"

"No. Definitely wash it."

He laughed, then waited, sensing there was something she wanted to say.

"Today felt like a lucky day—poop or no poop," Sawyer admitted. "To me, at least."

Nick looked at her. "Me, too, I guess."

An awkward moment of silence settled between them.

A flickering worry unexpectedly popped into Sawyer's head: she didn't want the day to end. She felt Nick staring at her, reading her expression, and blushed.

He grinned. "There's a diner around the corner that serves the best egg creams and banana splits on the entire East Coast."

"What's an egg cream?" Sawyer asked.

"Ugh—are you kidding me? Now we're definitely going."

• • •

As Sawyer soon discovered, "egg creams" had nothing whatsoever to do with actual eggs.

She took a sip and wrinkled her nose at the unexpected carbonation.

"So, basically . . . it's a fizzy Yoo-hoo," she decided.

"OK, first of all: you say that like you're not impressed," Nick argued defensively. "And second of all: What do you expect? You ordered chocolate."

"You said chocolate is the best!"

"It *is* the best. Every soda jerk will tell you, chocolate is the best."

"*You're* a soda jerk," Sawyer joked, rolling her eyes. "This whole conversation is getting to be a soda circle-jerk."

Nick's eyes went wide with surprise at the unexpected crudeness. He laughed, mid-sip, and almost snorted soda out his nose.

When the banana split came, they devoured it before the ice cream had a chance to melt, their long-handled silver spoons flashing under the diner lights as they dueled, carving away greedy shovelfuls.

"Between the pastrami and the hot dogs and this . . . I have now gathered enough evidence to officially say: you and I both eat like a couple of animals," Sawyer observed, licking at a stray dollop of whipped cream in the corner of her mouth.

"Humans *are* animals," Nick pointed out.

"I suppose."

"It's a shame."

"Really? I wouldn't think you cared about manners."

"I don't," Nick confirmed. "I'm interested in the moment lasting longer when I'm having a good time."

Sawyer blinked at him. He shrugged.

So, he had read her mind, and he didn't want the day to end, either.

Her ears felt hot as she looked down shyly and spooned up another bite of sundae.

* * *

After leaving the diner, they took a leisurely walk together, meandering steadily west, so Sawyer could catch an uptown train.

She loved Greenwich Village at night, the old brownstones, the narrow streets, the people eating in the sidewalk cafés, the occasional fire escape lit up with a string of Christmas lights regardless of the season.

Eventually, they reached the subway entrance at Christopher Street. They stopped and turned to face each other.

"So."

"So."

Sawyer suddenly felt nervous, followed by a wave of embarrassment to find herself so jittery. She shoved it aside, and moved to hug him goodbye.

To her surprise, Nick jumped back.

"Are you sure you want to hug me?" he joked. "I got pooped on by a seagull today."

She shot him a squinty look for tricking her.

"Good point," she played along, and turned to go.

"Wait!"

She felt him grab her hand. She spun back and froze. His touch had sent a surprising tremor of electricity through her.

They looked at each other.

Nick's eyes went down to where he still had hold of her hand. He let it drop, as though it had made him nervous, too.

In the next second, he regained his cool attitude. "But you know . . . I *did* change my shirt," he continued the joke. "You're *probably* safe."

"I don't know . . ." Sawyer continued to play along. "Doesn't sound like much of a guarantee. But I guess I'll take my chances."

They exchanged a quick hug, now made less awkward by Nick's joking. Still . . . it was hard to ignore the way her heart sped up, the way her temples and neck felt the tingling chill of nervous perspiration.

"Thank you for today."

"Yeah . . . ditto," Nick replied.

"Ditto" reminded Sawyer of the line from *Ghost*. She laughed aloud.

"What?"

She shook her head. "Nothing."

"Well, then . . . see ya, I guess."

"Yeah. See ya. Thanks again," she said.

"Maybe we'll do it again sometime."

She smiled and turned to go down the subway stairs, a hot gust of air coming up from the tunnel and the sounds of train brakes squealing.

• • •

A few minutes later, Sawyer stood holding the metal pole on a 1 train as it rocked its way uptown.

As the 1 hurtled along, carrying Sawyer closer and closer to her stop, she closed her eyes and—for the briefest of moments—recalled the feeling of Nick reaching for her hand and enclosing it in his firm grasp . . . that strange jolt of electricity.

What was that?

She felt the ghost of it again and shivered, opening her eyes to see if anyone on the train was looking.

13.

WEDNESDAY, JULY 14

Sawyer had become so obsessed with logging into AOL and checking her inbox, she had forgotten to pay much attention to her regular mailbox.

Then, on the following Wednesday, she keyed open the tiny brass door of the mailbox in the antechamber of her apartment building to find something unexpected there.

An envelope. Slightly thick.

The self-addressed stamped envelope was both instantly familiar and alien to her at the same time. SASEs were standard practice when it came to sending out submissions to literary magazines. Sawyer had created this one on her home printer—feeding one of the security envelopes she'd bought in a value pack from Duane Reade through the printer's tray slot while praying that nothing jammed.

It was strange to print an envelope addressed to yourself. It reminded Sawyer of how, when she was a child, her father insisted that if she wrote to Santa, Santa would write back to her. Now, Sawyer pictured her father writing those letters, addressing them to their own house, and even taking the trouble to drop them at the post office, so Sawyer could have the joy of having them delivered by the mailman, and how he must have felt when he spotted their return. Her SASEs were a bit like that—a little jolt of recognition to see something you made coming back to you.

However, while her father's envelopes had brought charming albeit somewhat fictitious words from Santa, so far, Sawyer's SASEs had only brought tidings of rejection.

Submitting to a literary magazine via snail mail meant picking out one or two of your best short stories, or a handful of your best poems, writing a cover letter, enclosing a self-addressed stamped envelope, and popping the whole thing in the mail. Sawyer had mostly forgotten about the handful of submissions she'd sent off via snail mail. One had come back within a week. The rejection slip itself (*Thank you for thinking of us. Unfortunately, your submission was not right for the magazine at this time . . .*) actually appeared to have been typed multiple times on a single piece of printer paper, photocopied, and scissored into narrow strips. When Sawyer opened the envelope, she thought it was empty at first, until she felt inside and found that narrow little slip of paper, like a little piece of ticker tape, neatly folded in half. Well, she figured—at least they weren't killing more trees than they had to.

Another three SASEs had trickled back very slowly, all of them also very thin envelopes, but containing a full or at least a half sheet of paper. One even had a handwritten scrawl of blue ink: *We enjoyed reading your poems! Do please try us again!* Sawyer had been touched by the handwritten note . . . and even more touched by how happy it made her to be rejected so encouragingly. She'd all but forgotten about the "straggler" still out there. It was a long shot, anyway, and at some point, she figured no answer *was* an answer.

So, she was shocked when, that Wednesday evening, she reached into her small brass rectangle of a mailbox and pulled out her long-forgotten SASE. She was even more surprised when it felt like it wasn't so thin as to contain a single slip of paper. She looked at the return address (the address she had typed and printed herself) and flinched at the confirmation: *The Paris Review.*

Her heart leapt into her throat. She worshipped *The Paris Review.*

As she stared at the envelope (not fat exactly, but definitely much thicker than any of the others had been!), her mind raced through the possibilities. Maybe it was a mix-up. Maybe they'd returned her submission pages to her, although their submission protocol specifically said that was not their practice.

Sawyer only knew one thing for sure: she couldn't open the envelope there, in the cramped antechamber to her building where a neighbor (most likely Mrs. Kallenbach, who walked her incontinent beagle at least five times a day) was bound to pass by and ask Sawyer about the envelope she was clutching so tightly in her hand.

She took the envelope upstairs.

• • •

Once safely inside her apartment, Sawyer put the envelope on the desk in the kitchen and fired up the computer. She was tempted to email Autumn in Japan, but she knew she couldn't expect any kind of immediate response.

She needed to tell someone about the envelope *right now.*

She contemplated phoning Charles at his office. She might not catch him. And even if she did . . . where to start? She hadn't meant to keep her writing a secret; it had just sort of worked out that way.

The last time Sawyer had told Charles about her writing was back when they were in college. He'd humbly told her up front that he'd *never been smart enough to really get poetry.* So she'd given him a short story to read . . . and felt awful when he fell asleep, leaving most of it unread. This happened on a few successive nights, until she'd taken the story back. He never asked about it, and she let it drop.

She thought about this now.

And about Nick, and how he'd taken the trouble to find her previous poem on the internet and read it. There was really only one person in particular she was dying to tell about the envelope.

She hadn't spoken to Nick since they'd spent Friday riding the Staten Island Ferry. Since then, she'd found herself staring pensively at an empty AOL inbox, daring herself to email him and chickening out.

But now, staring at that envelope, she decided to simply roll the dice. She opened up Instant Messenger. The green dot indicated that he was currently online. Her heart skipped a beat.

Adventures_of_Tom: Hey

She hit enter and waited.

And waited.

And waited some more.

Finally, the computer beeped.

Nikolai70: Hey back

Nikolai70: Look who decided to take the initiative to be the first to say hello

Sawyer felt herself grinning from ear to ear.

She took a minute, trying to think of what she wanted to say, and where she wanted to start. But evidently, she'd taken a second too long—the computer beeped again.

Nikolai70: I'm happy to hear from you

Sawyer's smile widened to the point where it was almost maniacal.

Adventures_of_Tom: I've missed talking to you

Nikolai70: Ditto

Sawyer blushed, then felt ridiculous, then giggled, then felt more ridiculous, then chuckled harder.

Nikolai70: What's up & how've you been?

Her fingers flew over the keys, typing her response. She told him about the envelope she was looking at, and the fact that it was from *The Paris Review.*

Nikolai70: Wow. The Paris Review. That's big.

Nikolai70: Even us ad company guys know about that one.

Adventures_of_Tom: It could be a rejection.

Nikolai70: It could be. But it's not. You said the envelope feels thicker than one sheet of paper. I have a feeling. YOU have a feeling.

There was a pause as Sawyer stared at the envelope, realizing she'd failed to consider how her present plan could go wrong. Now she had an audience. The computer pinged with a new message.

Nikolai70: What are you waiting for? Rip that sucker open

He was right. There was no going back now. Sawyer took a breath, wiggled a finger under the sealed envelope flap, and ripped the envelope open.

Inside was a typed letter. Her eyes hungrily devoured the words. She read them twice, just to be sure.

Adventures_of_Tom: Nick . . . they want two of my poems! TWO

Nikolai70: That's great!!!

Adventures_of_Tom: TWO

Adventures_of_Tom: I can't believe it

Nikolai70: I can. We need to celebrate!

Sawyer was giddy. She read the letter again. There were other pages, too . . . a release form for her to sign and return, and an offer to pay fifty dollars for each of her poems. The grin on her face was so wide, her muscles actually ached.

Adventures_of_Tom: Yes! Let's do something this Friday

Adventures_of_Tom: Oh! I know! Coney Island is on my list. Let's celebrate by going to Coney Island!

Adventures_of_Tom: They're paying me 50 big ones for each poem, and I owe you a hot dog or two. We can eat hot dogs and ride the rides until we're literally sick with happiness

There was a pause when he didn't respond right away. Finally, the computer pinged.

Nikolai70: I would love to

Nikolai70: But

Adventures_of_Tom: But what?

Nikolai70: I have a gig this Friday.

Sawyer frowned. A gig actually sounded like fun; she'd give anything to hear Nick play. But . . . there was no invitation implied by his words. A peculiar feeling came over her.

Adventures_of_Tom: There's something else, too

Adventures_of_Tom: Isn't there?

Nikolai70: Yes.

Nikolai70: Kendra. She wants to hang out this Friday.

Sawyer blinked at the screen, dumbfounded for a reply. Her ears were ringing, and her fingers hovered over her keyboard, frozen.

Nick's words that day at the Yale Club about Kendra came floating back to Sawyer . . . he'd called her "spectacular," and "uncomplicated." *Any time I've taken a step back*, he'd said, *she's always made it worth my while to stick around*. Sawyer's stomach twisted.

She went to the fridge and poured herself a glass of cold wine.

She took a sip and sat back down.

Adventures_of_Tom: That's great. Have fun!

Nikolai70: Yeah. I guess

Nikolai70: We'll see. I should probably have a talk with her either way.

"A talk"? Sawyer wondered what this meant. But she reminded herself she had already gotten too involved, as evidenced by the present knots in her stomach.

Adventures_of_Tom: Hey, I've gotta run. I've got some stuff I've gotta go do.

Nikolai70: OK. Well, it was good to hear from you.

Nikolai70: Congrats on that Paris Review acceptance. That really is huge. I'm honored you looped me in. Someday, I'll be telling everyone "I knew her when . . ."

Adventures_of_Tom: Ha ha. I doubt it. But that's sweet.

Nikolai70: I mean it. You're

Sawyer waited.

Nikolai70: I'm trying to think of the right word. But all I can think of is "something else"

Adventures_of_Tom: Huh. That's sweet (I think?). Anyway, I really should go.

Nikolai70: OK. But let's celebrate soon?

Adventures_of_Tom: Sure. Talk to you later

She didn't wait for him to reply; she logged off.

* * *

The next day, Sawyer tried to hang on to her good feelings about having poems accepted by *The Paris Review* as long as she could. She carried the acceptance letter around in her bag and snuck a peek at it whenever she found herself feeling a little tired or discouraged about the workweek.

Or whenever she thought about Nick having plans on Friday.

That morning, Johanna surprised her by telling her to fetch a notepad and pen and follow her to the conference room, where she invited Sawyer to listen in on a scheduled call with Preeti Chaudhari to go over editorial notes.

"You said you wanted to shadow me," Johanna said to Sawyer in a dry monotone. "Just remember: shadows don't speak, so your role is to be a fly on the wall and take notes."

"Of course!" Sawyer eagerly agreed. "Thank you so much for including me, Johanna. I really am very passionate about this author's book, and I'm so grateful for the chance to learn."

"All right. No fawning. Let's see how we go. Remember—observe and take notes, only."

* * *

The hour-long call passed quickly. Johanna started by unpacking the thoughts in her editorial letter—the content of which was already intimately familiar to Sawyer, who had typed the final draft of the letter and mailed it, along with a marked-up draft of the manuscript, to Preeti.

Together, Johanna and Preeti discussed some of the changes that needed to be made, and different ideas of how they might be accomplished. It was especially interesting to hear Preeti talk about her original inspiration for the novel, and which things she wanted to keep, and why. Toward the end of the call, Johanna shifted the focus to talk about deadlines, publication season, and a preliminary discussion of the book's marketing tone. Preeti seemed humbly amenable and slightly awed. She laughed and admitted, "All of that part I totally leave in your expert hands, Johanna. Whatever I can do to help, I will, of course!"

What a strange thing it must be, Sawyer realized—to dedicate all that time to telling a particular story that seems to live solely inside you, and then hand it over to a publisher to be so formally introduced to the world as a "book" . . . and to have someone else decide the tone of that introduction, to boot.

As Johanna wrapped up the call, Sawyer felt a small inkling of confidence working its way into her bones. Something within her was rising like a balloon, growing increasingly certain with every passing day: *She could do this. She could be an editor someday.*

"Thank you again, Johanna."

"Type up those notes and make a copy for Kaylee," was all Johanna said.

"Oh, for sure. I'm on it!" Sawyer grinned.

• • •

Feeling like she'd had a productive workday, Sawyer went home that evening, her mood buoyed, despite the occasional thought that caused her mind to drift back to Nick.

When she arrived home, she was in for another shock: the sight of Charles in the kitchen, unpacking several bags of groceries.

"You're . . . home early!" Sawyer said, shocked. The time on the oven clock said 6:09 p.m. The summer evening's sunshine was still bright in the windows. "And . . . you brought home groceries?"

Charles grinned.

"Everything needed for . . . *spaghetti night*," he said.

He brandished an arm to a row of ingredients he'd neatly lined up along the counter.

Sawyer smiled, taken off guard. "Spaghetti night" was an old ritual they used to have, back when Charles was still in law school. Sawyer would spend all evening helping him cram for one of his exams—constitutional law, torts, civil procedure—and when they were just about ready to drop, they would take a break, put on an old Louis Armstrong album, and cook spaghetti Bolognese together.

The cheerful, nostalgic music and the busywork in the kitchen somehow always revitalized them. Charles, in particular, really got into all the chopping and the dicing. At one point, after seeing *Goodfellas*, Charles insisted on trying the kitchen trick with the garlic that Paul Sorvino does in the movie—the one where Sorvino slices the garlic with a razor blade, slicing it "so thin that it liquefies in the pan with just a little oil." Charles's garlic never fully liquefied, but it was heavenly nonetheless: paper-thin slices that turned as transparent as glass in the extra-virgin olive oil, releasing a heady aroma into the air that made your mouth instantly water.

"How long has it been since our last spaghetti night?" Charles asked.

"I . . . can't remember."

"So: *too* long, then. Go get some comfy clothes on," he said. "I'll put the music on and start prepping."

Sawyer hesitated, lingering for a moment. She glanced at the computer on the little desk in the kitchen, possessed by a brief longing to log on and check her email.

"What's up, slowpoke?" Charles prodded. "Something wrong?"

Sawyer shook herself. "No," she said. "I'll go get changed."

• • •

As Sawyer was changing out of her pencil skirt and blouse and into a comfy tank and pair of boxer shorts, she heard Louis Armstrong start to sing "La Vie en Rose" on the living room stereo speakers.

Back in the kitchen, she and Charles chopped and boiled and strained and simmered and prepared the spaghetti Bolognese like a well-olive-oiled machine. They had forgotten none of their old routine, and he had even bought some of the cheap Chianti they liked that came in a funny bottle encased in a straw basket that (as they had once been informed by a waiter) was called a *fiasco*. They sipped from two huge wineglasses as they cooked, the wine staining their lips and tongues a sickly purple.

The spaghetti came out perfect. Their teamwork was surprisingly still seamless, and Louis Armstrong's froggy crooning had lost none of its charm. But Sawyer couldn't help but feel she was floating outside her body, watching two strangers execute the motions to prepare a meal based on muscle memory alone.

* * *

When the food was ready, they sat down at the tiny kitchenette table squeezed between the computer desk and window. A tall glass votive with a picture of a Catholic saint on it that Sawyer had bought at the corner bodega flickered on the table between them. Charles refilled their wine with the straw Chianti bottle.

Their first few minutes of conversation were about how the food came out (good). Their next few minutes of conversation were about how Louis Armstrong was able to sing about sad things, yet put people in a happy mood (true then, true now). They politely asked each other how work was going (good, good).

A mutual silence settled between them as they continued eating.

"Hey," Charles said, breaking into a smile. "Remember the time we tried to do spaghetti night with that pressure cooker my aunt sent us for Christmas, back in our old apartment in Boston?"

Sawyer nodded and laughed. "I had to use a mop to get the red sauce off the ceiling. I'm pretty sure I never got it all; it was *everywhere*."

They laughed some more, and spent the rest of the dinner chuckling over old memories.

Later, as Sawyer washed the dishes and Charles dried, he planted affectionate kisses on her cheek in exchange for each dish she passed him. Eventually, she felt him sidle up behind her and nuzzle the back of her neck, planting little kisses there, too. Sawyer smiled at the warmth of his soft lips, but she found herself wondering at the return of the happy tide between them. Her thoughts eventually drifted back to how surprised she'd been to see Charles unpacking groceries in the kitchen in the first place . . . and then to his long hours, and Kendra.

She thought, too, about Nick and their online chat the day before. How he'd said he had plans with Kendra on Friday. It was only Thursday, but maybe Nick and Kendra were spending more time together in general. It was possible. Was Charles home now because Kendra was busy? Busy with *Nick*? Sawyer stiffened, bothered, though she could not be sure which part of the whole idea bothered her the most.

Meanwhile, Charles's kisses to the back of her neck had escalated. His hands began to run lightly over the curves of her hips and waist. Sawyer shook herself, then pushed the nagging thought of Kendra and Nick from her mind. She tugged the rubber gloves from her hands, threw them in the sink, and turned to face Charles, meeting his lips with her own.

They moved together in the direction of the bedroom and eventually to the bed. He lifted her tank over her head. She reached for his shirt in return. They kissed again and fell together on their sides—their routine move; they would kiss on their sides until it was silently decided between the two of them who would be on top. Sawyer was surprised by how familiar it all felt. It was as if they had picked up exactly where they had left off, the dry spell immediately forgotten.

Charles's torso twisted over hers and she understood he was moving to be on top. His kisses moved from her neck down her chest, his hands reached for the elastic waistband of the shorts she was still wearing, and—

"I KNOW," Sawyer suddenly blurted out, before she was fully cognizant of the words leaving her lips.

Charles froze, his lips parted, mid-kiss. He sat up, then sat back on his haunches, kneeling on the bed, no longer on top of her. He frowned. "Know what?" he asked.

Sawyer thought for a fleeting moment. She'd been thinking of Kendra, the gym, the restaurant receipt, but she surprised herself again by saying, "That day in Central Park, during the carriage ride . . . your father told me about their, um . . . financial troubles."

A dark shadow fell over Charles's face. He looked strange.

"Why would he do that," Charles finally said, when he spoke. It sounded like a thought, not a question, but Sawyer tried to answer it anyway.

"He was trying to help me understand why you've been working so hard, why you've been working such long hours to get your foot in the door at the firm," Sawyer ventured.

Charles didn't say anything.

"He felt it was important that you and I understand each other," Sawyer added softly. "I think he just wanted to let me in."

Charles remained silent. They were still on the bed together, but no longer touching. An unexpected palpable distance had opened up between them.

Sawyer pressed on.

"It did . . ." she started, but faltered, then gathered herself. "It *did* make me think about the timing of everything."

At this, Charles's spine straightened. "Timing?"

"Of our wedding," Sawyer replied. "I feel strange now, to think of the expense . . ."

"That's not why my father told you," Charles said. "He doesn't want you to worry about that."

"I know," Sawyer agreed, then paused. "And I know how important the wedding is to Kathy." She hesitated again. "But it also made me wonder if that's why our timeline has been so . . . you know, *accelerated*."

Charles frowned, studying her face. A sudden comprehension filled his features.

"I'd always planned to propose," he insisted.

Now, sensing that he needed to reassure her, he leaned forward on the bed and moved to draw Sawyer into his arms. He pulled her toward him, and they were lying together on their sides again, his arms around her.

"You were always the one for me," Charles said, gently stroking her hair as he hugged her to his chest.

It sounded sincere. Sawyer slipped her arms through his and hugged him back. Then, after a minute, she wiggled free just a little, looking to restart things. She began by kissing his neck.

But something had shifted.

Charles kissed her back, but his kisses had cooled. Eventually, he curled around her so that they were spooning. He held on to her carefully, but with an unfamiliar sense of tension in his arms. Several long minutes passed, and Sawyer wondered if Charles intended for them to eventually fall asleep like that.

His voice was strangely cold when he finally spoke.

"I'm sorry. My father shouldn't have told you anything about that stuff."

She realized: He was embarrassed and angry. He hadn't wanted to share with her about his parents' financial situation. She'd forced his hand.

She didn't know what to say. She threaded her arms through his, like drawing a coat tighter. They lay together in silence, both of them lost in thought, holding on to each other as if across a widening distance.

14.

FRIDAY, JULY 16

Sawyer woke up and realized it was Friday.

While "spaghetti night" hadn't quite ended the way either of them had anticipated, Charles seemed apologetic. He left the apartment that morning promising that he would try to get off work early and spend a summer Friday together.

We'll do something fun—you and me! he vowed.

As Sawyer walked to the subway that morning, she noticed: the weather was surprisingly pleasant. A thunderstorm had passed through the city in the middle of the night, and now the new day was crisp; sunny, but without a trace of humidity. She tried to take it as a sign. In a sense, order had been restored; Sawyer would be spending her Friday with Charles, and Nick would be spending his with Kendra. She couldn't have any complaints about any of that.

Could she?

At work, Johanna was in the office for the morning, with plans to leave for "Bridge" as soon as the afternoon rolled around. She seemed to be in an uncharacteristically upbeat, sociable mood, and demonstrated genuine delight when one of her oldest publishing friends spontaneously dropped in to see her.

Terry Stone was an important literary scout and a renowned master of publishing gossip. No matter the season or likelihood of precipitation, he was always dressed in fussy silk bow ties, a vintage Burberry umbrella hooked in the crook of his arm. And he always—*always*—knew everything about everyone in the publishing world.

To a certain extent, his talent for gossip suited his profession—which was, admittedly, a mystery to Sawyer at first. She knew what literary agents did, but she'd had to ask around to find out what a "literary scout" was. She'd learned that scouts advised foreign publishers and film studios when it came to which hot new book rights they ought to acquire. So, in essence, a scout's job was to know about *every* manuscript floating around the publishing world—and to know about it *first*.

As a seasoned scout, Terry always knew which books had been sold to which editors long before any deals were announced, and for exactly how much. By dint of his connections and cunning charm, he got his hands on manuscripts that publishing houses insisted they weren't officially sharing yet. But Terry's depth and breadth of gossip went far beyond this. He knew who'd been drunk at the London Book Fair, and who'd been drunker. He knew about interoffice affairs. He knew scandalous stories about editors who drank on the job and agents who did drugs in their offices. And all too often, he even knew who was slated to be hired and fired before the individuals themselves did.

For all these reasons, agents and editors were often skittish around him. One call from Terry Stone sent publishing assistants scrambling to ask their bosses what they should say—were they in to take his call? Most contrived to avoid him, but very carefully, in a way that would not cause offense.

But Johanna never avoided him. Instead, her door was always open to him; he was something of a coconspirator. They were old hat, having come up in publishing together. And secretly, Johanna delighted in Terry's endless supply of catty gossip. Or perhaps *not* so secretly, for Sawyer knew that Johanna made no apologies for her own cattiness. Sawyer had occasionally overheard her boss talking with Terry and knew that Johanna always came equipped with plenty of gossip of her own.

That Friday, Terry had breezed past the ground-floor security guys and the fifth-floor reception desk. He threw a perfunctory wave at Sawyer as he showed himself into Johanna's office. Only Terry could get away with that.

"Happy Friday, Mr. Stone," Sawyer greeted him as he passed her desk.

"Call me Terry," he said.

His tone indicated that he wasn't so much being friendly with her as he was saying *don't make me feel old.*

"Would you bring in a strong pot of that lovely loose-leaf Mariage Frères I brought Johanna last time?" he called over his shoulder as he knocked and opened Johanna's door without waiting for an answer. "Also, glasses and ice," he added. He slipped inside, leaving the door a crack open.

Sawyer could hear Johanna's muffled happy exclamation, *Terry! Dear! How are you?*

Sawyer got up to go make the tea Terry had requested, hoping to keep the two of them happy. Johanna's inclusion of Sawyer in Preeti's editorial call had boosted Sawyer's confidence. She imagined herself having old publishing friends someday who just let themselves into her office and dished all the gossip.

When the tea was ready and Sawyer had stocked the tray with everything Terry had requested, she made her way back to Johanna's office. She paused outside the cracked door, feeling the devilish impulse to listen in for a second or two.

So, that was little Eve Harrington, was it? Terry was saying. *She* does *seem awfully eager.*

Eager. And demanding; a prima donna, Johanna agreed. *Instead of negotiating with her, I decided to indulge her and see what she does with it. I just hope I haven't created a monster.*

Well, as long as she's willing to work hard—right? Terry replied.

Well, that's just it, Johanna said plaintively. *You saw how young she is, and would you believe? Already engaged!*

Really? I didn't think anybody got married right out of college these days. How archaic.

Exactly, Johanna agreed. *She gave her little song and dance about wanting to learn how to do my job and be just like me, but the wedding's this fall. What do you want to bet she'll ask for extra time off? And I'm sure it will only be a matter of months after that until she has babies or decides it's simply enough to stay home and be a lawyer's wife.*

She's marrying a lawyer? Terry asked.

Corporate law—Wexler Gibbons, as a matter of fact.

Terry laughed. *Two guesses whose career is "more important," and who stays home with the baby! Oh, Jo. She'll never stick. The things we have to put up with these days.*

Johanna sighed. *And in the meantime, I have to put up with her trying to claw her way up the ladder, of course.*

Stunned, Sawyer stood frozen outside the door. It felt like the blood had drained out of her body. She was still holding the tea tray, although her hands had gone numb. She felt a little dizzy and realized she was holding her breath. She forced herself to breathe. Then, after a few seconds, she forced herself to wrangle the tray into one arm and tap on the open door. The voices immediately ceased.

"Come in!" Johanna called.

Sawyer entered the office and set the tea tray down. She felt Terry's eyes on her. When she glanced at him, he was wearing a thoroughly entertained smirk.

"Anything else?" she asked Terry and Johanna, but to her own ears, her voice sounded like it had come from far away.

"No, thank you—if you've wrapped up everything else, you may leave for the day, in fact," Johanna said. "And let Kaylee know she may do the same. Happy summer Friday."

"Thanks. Happy Friday," Sawyer echoed back, and slipped out with the empty tray.

She dropped the tray in the kitchen, and went to her desk to pack up her things. Her head was spinning.

Sawyer knew Eve Harrington was the title character from the old black-and-white classic, *All About Eve*.

She understood perfectly well: it wasn't meant as a compliment.

• • •

Her eyes burned during the subway ride home—it reminded Sawyer of how it felt when she'd gotten hit in the face with a rubber kickball as a kid, the way her eyes had instantly stung and filled with water, even though she hadn't started crying yet.

She wished she didn't care whether her boss liked her or not.

She hadn't consciously recognized it, but since the day she'd been hired, Sawyer had been *dying* to win Johanna's approval. It was unnerving to realize how deeply this desire had built up in her. Somehow, Sawyer had been able to perceive all of Johanna's flaws—how elitist she was, how moody and ruthless, how lacking in warmth and humor and generosity—and yet Sawyer had still measured herself according to Johanna's opinion of her.

One thing had made itself clear: Sawyer wouldn't win with Johanna—she *couldn't* win. She understood now that no matter which path she took, Johanna would condemn her ambition or lack thereof, equally. To Johanna, there were really only two kinds of younger women in the world, and they were all versions of Eve Harrington—undeserving usurpers, or lazy nuisances.

* * *

Charles wasn't home yet when Sawyer keyed into the apartment. He'd said he was going to take a "real" summer Friday, but she knew that leaving the offices of Wexler Gibbons likely could still take a while.

She poured herself a cold glass of lemonade, turned on the computer, and checked her email.

Empty.

She opened a blank email and stared at it. She wanted to tell Nick about what had happened to her at work. But then she remembered again: he'd told her he'd be busy. For a fleeting moment, she wistfully tried to picture Nick—where he was, and what he was up to. Was he hanging out with Kendra?

She reminded herself it was none of her business, then deleted the blank email draft and made herself comfy on the couch with a book instead. Every year, she reread an old beat-up paperback copy of *The Heart Is a Lonely Hunter*, by Carson McCullers, purely for pleasure. She didn't want to think about Nick, and she also didn't want to think about work.

Forty-five minutes or so later, she heard footsteps in the outer hall, and Charles's key turning in the lock.

"Hey." She smiled up at him, genuinely happy to see him.

"Hey," he said, tossing his keys on the console table, loosening his tie, and slipping it over his head. "We don't have any plans tonight—right?"

"I mean . . . we said we'd hang out, but nothing specific."

"Good!" he said. "Because I have an idea." He walked into the bedroom, calling loudly enough so they could still talk between rooms. She heard the sounds of him taking his watch off, his belt unbuckling, and the squeak of the bedsprings as he sat to slip off his suit pants. "I was thinking we'd go hear this band play."

"Huh?" Sawyer called back, genuinely puzzled.

Charles came back into the living room, half-dressed. "You remember

Kendra? From that dinner we went to a while back, downtown, at Cipriani?"

Sawyer froze, eyes wide. "Sure," she said in a casual tone. "I remember her."

"Well, she invited us to go hear her boyfriend's band play tonight," Charles replied, seeming happy.

Sawyer frowned.

"In the East Village," he added. "Well, *way east*—Alphabet City, or whatever. It's probably pretty dive-y, but could be fun. Something different—right?"

He smiled and waited for her to react, his eyes cheerful. Sawyer blinked, still catching up.

"Uh, yeah," Sawyer said. "That would definitely be different."

"Does that mean you're up for it?" Charles pressed. "She actually invited us to join them for dinner first—sushi. You love sushi."

He waited.

Sawyer willed herself to speak. The words seemed stuck in her throat, trapped there by some sort of muscle she'd never felt constrict before. She cleared her throat.

"So . . . you want to go to sushi, and then to a club to hear Kendra's boyfriend's band play?"

"Yeah. It'll be fun. I swear."

"And she invited both of us?"

"Of course. I'm gonna grab a shower and get changed. You're game for a night out, right?"

Sawyer felt numb, mute; either answer—yes or no—seemed wrong.

"Don't worry, we have plenty of time," Charles said. "His band doesn't go on until nine. We're supposed to meet them at the sushi joint at seven."

Charles disappeared into the bathroom. The bath taps gave a shrill squeal as he turned on the shower.

Sawyer remained frozen on the couch, staring after him, still blinking in disbelief.

15.

Charles spent forever picking out jeans and a black button-up.

It was too dressy, and wrong for where they were going. Sawyer knew it was wrong for where they were going because she had already *been* to where they were going. She remembered how hot the club could get. She put on a spaghetti-strap tank, a skirt, her Docs. She pulled her hair up, off her neck, brushed her dark bangs down so they neatly skimmed her eyebrows, and applied a bit of dark eyeliner.

"That's what you're wearing?" Charles asked.

"Yep."

Charles insisted on a cab so they wouldn't get sweaty after having just showered. The driver didn't seem thrilled that they wanted him to take them from the Upper West Side to Alphabet City, traversing the whole of Manhattan diagonally, but he grumbled and put on the meter.

Sawyer simply sat quietly in the car, lost in her own thoughts.

The evening was bound to be bizarre to the point of awkward. It didn't seem possible that Charles or Kendra knew anything about the time she'd been spending with Nick. Was she supposed to pretend that Nick was essentially a stranger to her? She was also acutely aware of the fact that the invitation had come via Kendra; Nick himself had not invited them.

The last thing she wanted was to be an interloper, intruding on another couple's date night. On *Nick's* date night.

She fidgeted at the thought, uncomfortable in her seat. They had already crossed the park and now they were making record time to the opposite end of the city. Then, in what seemed like mere minutes later, they were abruptly there.

The sky was still light, but twilight was beginning to settle in. The exterior of the sushi restaurant sported peeling paint in baby pink and black. Alternating pink and green neon letters glowed over the entrance, spelling out *"AVENUE A."* It had the air of a dive, just as Charles had predicted, but a popular one. A large group of people milled around out front, waiting. The prospective patrons looked very "East Village"—with piercings and colorfully dyed hair, and the stringy bodies of dancers. They wore funky secondhand-shop clothing, the majority of which was purposely ripped or tied or safety-pinned to achieve a kind of sexy nonchalance.

"Kendra said they would meet us in front of the restaurant," Charles said, clearly a little uneasy and feeling out of place as he and Sawyer joined the milling group.

He turned and bummed a smoke and a light off of one of the kids waiting. It struck Sawyer as an obvious attempt to blend in better. The kid handed him a cigarette, but looked Charles over with a skeptical expression as Charles bent over the flame of the kid's lighter.

A few minutes later, Nick's tall shape and Kendra's blond hair appeared, rounding the corner of Seventh Street. Kendra spotted Charles and waved.

As soon as Sawyer glimpsed the expression on Nick's face, she knew: he was not happy. His jaw was clenched; his hands were shoved in his pockets. He glanced at Sawyer but did not make eye contact.

"This is Nick's neighborhood," Kendra said, after everyone had greeted one another.

I know, Sawyer thought silently. Then her stomach did a little flip and she felt her cheeks burning to recall: *she'd been to Nick's apartment*.

"He's a regular here and can get us a table quick," Kendra promised. She turned to Nick and tugged on his arm, and he led the way.

The restaurant was packed inside. And dark. Everything was painted black—the walls, floors, and ceilings. The light fixtures had been swapped out for UV black lights, giving everything an eerie, bluish-purple glow and making the whites of people's eyes and teeth look freakishly bright as they lifted succulent bites of sushi on chopsticks. A handful of giant goldfish swam lazily around in a big glass tank. Graffiti artwork in neon colors hung on the walls, and a live DJ spun from a booth crammed in beside the bar.

Near the service end of the bar, a middle-aged man in a porkpie hat sat on a stool reading a newspaper. Sawyer wondered how he could read in such low light, but he seemed to be doing just that, utterly unfazed. Nick made a hand gesture to get the man's attention, and Sawyer realized the guy must be the owner. He nodded to Nick, and—without exchanging a word—got up and pushed two tables together in a far corner of the restaurant. He pointed for the four of them to sit, nodded again at Nick, then walked away, cool and indifferent.

"You wouldn't think it, but the sushi's really good here," Kendra said over the DJ music pumping through the room.

"Why wouldn't you think it?" Nick asked, frowning.

"Well, you know . . ." Kendra said, her voice wheedling. "Because it's so *gritty*."

Nick looked annoyed by her answer, but Kendra draped her arms around him flirtatiously, giving him a cross between a hug and a squeeze. In fact, Kendra had been touching or hanging on Nick in some way ever since they'd appeared on the street. Now, she hung on him as she read the menu. The music continued to thump loudly.

Sawyer tried not to stare as Kendra reached a hand up to ruffle Nick's hair. But as she averted her eyes, Sawyer noticed Charles *was* staring. In fact, he seemed as though he couldn't stop staring. She saw his eyebrows knit together in consternation as Kendra's hand came to rest on Nick's knee under the table.

"Hey man, so we're going to get to hear your band play tonight, eh?" Charles shouted over the music to Nick.

Sawyer cringed. It was the style of speaking Charles often adopted when talking to a guy he didn't know. It struck Sawyer as phony, a combination of fake friendliness and a hostile caveman beating his chest.

"Looks like it." Nick's voice was flat.

"I thought you were a junior ad exec over on Madison Ave. or something," Charles continued.

"I am."

"Oh—I see. Weekend warrior. That's cool, man."

Sawyer's cringe deepened. She glanced at Charles, willing him to stop or at least change the subject, but he seemed utterly oblivious to her presence.

Nick didn't reply. His expression had turned to stone. Charles rattled on.

"Yeah. My best friend in high school was in a band and they were always playing out of someone's garage. They were pretty good, I think."

Sawyer shouted gently to Charles. "Hey . . ." She tried to redirect his attention to the menu. "Are you going to get a beer, or would you like to split some sake with me?"

"I'm just saying, it's cool to be musical," Charles insisted. "I wish *I* had a hobby."

At the word "hobby," Sawyer saw Nick bristle ever so slightly.

Kendra, on the other hand, had now turned her attention to Charles. She swatted him on the shoulder. "What are you talking about? You *are* musical! You have an amazing singing voice!"

Charles waved off the flattery, but the corners of his mouth curled, secretly pleased. "Nah. Karaoke doesn't count," he insisted.

Kendra turned to Nick and Sawyer. "He's downplaying it. Oh my

God, you gotta hear this guy sing 'Fly Me to the Moon'! I'm serious—he slays it! Gave me chills."

Sawyer jolted to attention.

"When did you go to karaoke?" she asked Charles, quietly enough so the others couldn't hear over the loud DJ music.

"It was just a quick work thing," Charles reassured her. "Everybody on our team went to blow off steam for a few minutes."

Charles patted her hand and turned back to Kendra.

Sawyer sat digesting this information, fuming.

Karaoke.

"Fly Me to the Moon."

Fly. Me. To. The. Fucking. Moon.

She felt someone watching her and looked up to find Nick studying her face, deep in thought. They locked eyes and he looked away.

But a second later, she caught him looking again. But this time, Nick's eyes had dropped to the table, to where Charles's hand lay upon Sawyer's. His jaw and temples flexed as if he was bothered. She felt her pulse speed up. She tried to gather herself and tune back in to the conversation.

"Karaoke hardly qualifies as a *real* hobby . . ." Charles was saying.

"That's OK. It's not like you'd have time for a 'real' hobby, anyway," Kendra pointed out with a laugh. "Not with this case!"

"You're right," Charles agreed. He withdrew his hand from Sawyer's and grinned. "I guess I don't."

Kendra addressed Sawyer. "It's nuts how much they're making us work."

"Seems like it," Sawyer agreed.

"Although, we *do* get a laugh in every so often," Kendra continued. "We've got a funny team. They're always coming up with new ways to prank one another."

At this, she brightened and turned to Charles.

"Oh my God, that prank they pulled on Doug!" she exclaimed in delight.

Now she touched Charles's arm much the same way she had squeezed Nick's. Charles's face picked up a hint of red, but he smiled and joined in Kendra's laughter.

"The poor bastard," Charles agreed. "That was epic."

Sawyer and Nick sat silently as Kendra and Charles continued to seize up with fresh waves of laughter. Finally, Kendra explained: Doug had made the mistake of telling them he had something called "globophobia"—an acute fear of balloons. They'd filled the men's room with balloons—really packed them in there like sardines.

"Both helium *and* regular balloons," Kendra said. "So they were all over the ceiling *and* the floor. Everywhere. Every stall. He couldn't even walk in without having to touch them all."

And as a particularly devilish coup de grâce, one of the guys had slipped a little bit of Ex-Lax into Doug's coffee.

"Oh, the poor bastard!" Charles repeated. "I felt so bad for him. The pure panic on his face! He looked like he was going to explode, one way or another."

He and Kendra broke up into more laughter.

Sawyer gave a strained smile, feeling a sense of revulsion; she hated these kinds of cruel pranks on other people. And besides her lack of enthusiasm for the story itself, she was distracted by Kendra's body language. Kendra had now shifted her full attention from Nick over to Charles, touching him playfully as they reminisced about the prank.

Sawyer was confused, until . . .

Suddenly, a light bulb blinked on. Sawyer recognized some primal trace of Kendra's behavior from high school, when some of the popular girls used to do the thing where they used one boy's attention to provoke the envy and attention of another.

She likes attention, Nick had said of Kendra, back at the Yale Club. *She needs a lot of it from guys.*

Sawyer couldn't tell if Kendra ultimately wanted Charles's or Nick's attention more.

When the sushi came, everything was fresh and delicious; the salmon and avocado were buttery, the red maguro tuna velvety, and the sushi rice sticky and sweet, with just a hint of rice vinegar. Sawyer's tongue tingled with the salt of the soy sauce and the sharpness of the wasabi that shot pleasantly up her nose. She sipped the floral, chilled sake out of a porcelain thimble of a cup that was faintly beaded with condensation from the muggy heat of the packed room.

The food made up for the group dynamic.

Charles and Kendra chattered away as if they were the only two people in the world. Sawyer managed to force an air of polite attentiveness. And Nick . . . Nick was so quiet, so sullen. She felt a strange sense of missing him, even though he was sitting right there, at the same table. The handful of times Sawyer and Nick had eaten a meal together, it had been a joke: how they both ate with such passionate gusto. But now he seemed to have lost his characteristic appetite.

Nick ate a few small pieces of sushi, then excused himself.

"I want to get there early to help get our stuff unloaded," he said in a quiet voice to Kendra.

Sawyer watched as Nick made his exit. He didn't look back at her, or anyone at the table. He stopped to shake hands with the owner, who was still sitting in the service section of the bar, reading a newspaper. Then he slipped through the restaurant's front door and disappeared.

When the waiter came over at the end of the meal, he didn't ask them if they wanted anything else. He only refilled their waters, glancing at his watch as he poured, as though impatient to turn the table over to a new set of paying customers.

"I guess we'll take the check," Charles said.

"Nick already took care of it," the waiter mumbled.

"What?" Charles said, shouting over the booming music the DJ was spinning.

The waiter repeated himself, and turned on his heel without further comment.

"He shouldn't have done that," Charles said. "I would've taken care of it."

"Get the next one." Kendra shrugged. She gave him a smile.

The next one? Sawyer didn't think she could handle another double date. And it was clear Nick hadn't wanted to see her and Charles tonight. How much stranger and more uncomfortable could the evening get?

• • •

The three of them finished up and wandered leisurely over to the club. By then, it was dark outside, but the summer weather had trapped the warmth of the day in the city. The brisk night air mingled pleasantly with the heat still emanating from the sidewalk.

When they got there, there was a guy collecting cover charges and checking IDs at the door. Sawyer watched as Kendra strolled to the head of the line and insisted they were on a list. Soon enough, they were inside.

A band was playing, but Sawyer saw that it was not Nick's. He had yet to go on.

"Drinks," Kendra decreed, once they crossed through the door. She led the way to the bar. "FYI, it's the kind of place where you should probably stick to beer or shots," she advised Charles, as they shouldered their way closer to the front of the bar line.

When it was their turn, the bartender looked up and recognized Sawyer.

"Hey!" Jake or Blake said. He grinned. "I've got grapefruit tonight—you want a Sea Breeze?"

Charles and Kendra slowly turned to Sawyer, confused.

"Uh . . . sure," Sawyer replied. She smiled. "That sounds great."

Jake or Blake proceeded to make an enormous pint glass full of Sea Breeze. He waved her off when she tried to put a twenty on the bar. He pointed to Charles and Kendra. They ordered beers.

"What was that about?" Charles asked Sawyer in a low voice, as they bumped and shuffled their way through the sea of bodies, away from the bar and closer to the stage.

"I don't know," Sawyer said. "I guess I look like the kind of girl who could use a good Sea Breeze."

"Do you even like Sea Breezes?"

"I do, actually. It's a good summer drink."

"Huh. OK," Charles said with a grunt. "I'm just saying, it was kinda ballsy of him to give you a drink on the house with your boyfriend standing right there."

"Maybe he thought you were with Kendra," Sawyer said.

"Hmm, maybe," he mused, oblivious to the barbed tone of her comment.

By then, they were following Kendra deeper into the club, over to the foot of the stage, carefully holding their drinks high over their heads as they made their way through the crowd of bodies.

They stood and listened as the band onstage wrapped up their last song, which sounded a little too derivative of Green Day.

Then, Nick's band took the stage.

They quickly set about readjusting and plugging in and unplugging things. Well, unplugging, mostly. It looked like the only thing getting plugged in was a keyboard; Sawyer realized most of their instruments were acoustic, with lots of guitars of different sizes, even what looked like a mandolin of some sort. One of Nick's bandmates carried on a French horn and a harmonica.

"What does Nick play?" Sawyer overheard Charles ask Kendra.

"Oh my God—*everything*," she replied. "He, like, plays every instrument under the sun."

"Wow," Charles said, but stiffly, as though he begrudged Nick the compliment.

"But I guess tonight he'll mainly play lead guitar?" Kendra said. "That's usually how it goes on gig nights."

"Why did he learn to play so many things?"

"I don't know," Kendra replied. "He just, like, got really into music when he was little. He always says 'the children of immigrants never do anything half-assed.'"

"He's an immigrant?" Charles asked, eyebrows raised.

Sawyer didn't like his tone; it was as if Charles had just discovered that Nick had a weakness, instead of a strength.

"His mom." Kendra nodded. "Russian. Or Soviet, or whatever."

Charles's eyes widened. "No kidding?"

He and Kendra kidded around, making jokes and talking with accents à la *Bullwinkle*'s Boris and Natasha.

Annoyed, Sawyer ignored them and trained her focus on Nick instead. She watched him moving around the stage, getting everything ready. His band tuned up for a couple of minutes. Sawyer felt her heart pounding, inexplicably nervous to hear him play.

Finally, Nick stepped up to the mic for their first song. Sawyer was immediately blown away. They were . . . whatever is utterly the opposite of a Green Day tribute band. Each musician was plainly very, very skilled. Their influences seemed older—retro, vintage—a hint of sixties folk mixed with the Rolling Stones, the Beatles . . . and a touch of Bob Dylan in the lyrics. Yet, they also had a sound all their own, one that was vintage with an updated edge, full of intelligently calculated compositions that still somehow cut loose with heart.

They finished their first song and played another, and another after that. Then, they launched into what was clearly a love song, a song about longing and desire. Sawyer was drawn in; it had such an urgent yet muted undertow to it.

Nick looked handsome, charismatically comfortable, and confident in his mastery of his surroundings. His voice was low but surprisingly melodious. Listening to him, it was like he was singing directly into her ear. Sawyer was riveted—so riveted that she felt self-conscious and embarrassed; it was as if, if someone were to look over at her, they'd be able to see a kind of naked intimacy on her face and in her eyes.

And she couldn't shake the feeling that Nick was looking at *her*, singing to *her*.

But wasn't that common? Sawyer was pretty sure she was just experiencing the phenomenon that informed the all-too-familiar lore of musicians and groupies, of women moved to throw their panties onto the stage.

And besides—she reminded herself—she was standing next to Kendra. If Nick was singing to anyone, it was Kendra.

Nevertheless, as the song finished, Nick's eyes flicked in their direction one last time, and Sawyer could have sworn he was looking at her with that intense gaze he had, the one she'd come to know during the time they'd spent together. She felt her throat constrict and a shiver trip lightly down the back of her neck.

It was time for the band to take a break.

Nick leaned close to the mic, thanked the audience, and promised they'd be back to play another set in ten minutes. He exited the stage. Sawyer wondered if he would come over to say hi, but someone came up to talk to him. Sawyer watched from across the room.

"I'm going to grab another drink while they're on break," Kendra said.

"I'll go with you," Charles agreed. He glanced back. "Sawyer?"

"I'm going to run to the ladies' room."

Charles nodded, already moving to follow Kendra through the crowd and over to the bar. Sawyer crossed the club in the direction of the hall that led to the bathrooms, then turned back to look for Nick. He had vanished.

She had a feeling she knew where she could find him.

• • •

Sawyer cracked the door marked "*DO NOT OPEN—ALARM WILL SOUND*" and slipped outside quickly, before anyone in the club could really take notice of her. She stepped into the familiar ramshackle courtyard where she'd sat with Nick only a few Fridays earlier.

The cool night air surprised her. The only light in the courtyard came from a few yellow squares of windows from a neighboring building. It took her eyes a minute to adjust after having stared at the bright, colorful stage lights for so long.

Finally, she saw him. Sitting in one of the plastic patio chairs they'd sat in during the sunset magic hour, that night they'd come to the club together to hear his friend play.

"Hey," she called softly.

Nick didn't answer. Sawyer felt her throat tighten with nerves.

She approached.

"Can I sit?" she asked.

He nodded at the chair opposite him.

Sawyer sat. As her eyes adjusted further to the darkness of the courtyard, she began to make out the features of his face. She wanted to talk to him the way they had the last time they'd sat together in the courtyard . . . or the way they'd talked aboard the ferry—or even just the way they talked to each other online.

But for the hundredth time that evening, Sawyer couldn't help but wonder if she and Charles had crashed Nick's night; she flashed to the way Kendra had been openly flirting with Charles right in front of Nick's face.

"Hey, I'm sorry, Nick . . ." she began, but faltered for a second. She regained herself. "I'm sorry we came out tonight. I can tell you weren't expecting us."

Nick didn't reply.

"I hope we didn't ruin your night," she said, feeling genuinely sorry. "When Charles brought it up, when he said Kendra had invited us . . . I should have found some way to say no, some way to talk him out of it. I didn't think it through, Nick."

He remained quiet.

"I didn't think," she repeated. "And, well, part of me got really excited by the idea that I might get to hear you play."

She paused, then added, "I *am* glad I got to hear you play. You're really talented. I'm sure you know that already. But I still want to tell you . . . I don't know . . . just how much it moved me to hear you, to watch you up there. You're *good*. Really good."

Nick remained quiet.

A sense of anguish gripped Sawyer. She wished he would say something—anything.

The club door abruptly banged open and a rectangle of light flooded the courtyard. One of Nick's bandmates poked his head out.

"Hey, Nick—we need to get back onstage for the next set."

"OK. Be right there," Nick replied, finally speaking.

The door banged shut, leaving them in the relative urban darkness again.

Sawyer made out the shape of Nick, standing up from the plastic chair to go. She jumped to her feet.

"Wait—Nick . . ." she said, gripped by the sense of anguish again. "I mean it—I *am* really sorry. And . . . well, I can see that Kendra is driving you crazy."

"Kendra?"

"Yes. You know—all that stuff with Charles. I think she's probably doing it to make you jealous. Again, I'm sorry. I hope we didn't ruin your night."

He started to speak, but his voice seemed to catch in his throat. Finally, he said, "I gotta go."

He turned to head back inside the club.

"Look, Nick—I can tell you're bothered," Sawyer insisted. "Please just let me apologize."

He froze and looked down at the ground. It was too dark for Sawyer to make out his expression, but he shook his head.

"Kendra isn't driving me crazy," he said in a low, quiet voice.

Sawyer frowned. "I don't understand."

"It's not Kendra. *She* isn't driving me crazy," he repeated.

"Nick—" she started to say, but in the next moment, he had taken a sudden step toward her. His arms pulled Sawyer's body against his own, urgently.

She was kissing him back, a split second before his lips even met hers. She realized they had already been rushing at each other for some time now, before they gave this feeling a physical shape. When she breathed in, she was filled with a sense of desire mingled with a sense of coming home.

Sawyer felt the kiss go all the way down to the marrow of her bones.

Then, he released her.

There was something intimidating in his movements, a kind of frustration or anger. He turned and stormed through the club door without another word.

She stood there, blinking after him in the dark, dizzy and stupefied.

What the hell had just happened?

* * *

Sawyer had no idea how long she stood there by herself in the courtyard, holding a surprised hand to her tingling lips, stunned by what had just happened, thinking. At least ten minutes must have passed by the time she finally gathered herself and went back inside the club.

Nick's band was already onstage, playing another song. Charles and Kendra had returned to their previous spots in the audience, standing near the foot of the stage. Sawyer made her way through the crowd, back over to them, and stood there, still in a daze. She felt Nick's eyes on her and knew he had been watching for her return. She dared herself to meet his gaze, and when she did, the tension between them caused the little hairs on the back of her neck to prickle.

After a while, the band finished the song they were playing, and a small pause ensued as Nick turned to each of his bandmates, conferring about what to play next. Finally, he leaned close to the microphone. "We're gonna play a little cover."

The crowd waited to hear what it would be.

"That's weird," Kendra said to Charles. "They never play cover songs."

The band began to play.

Sawyer immediately recognized "Sweet Thing." It sounded like Nick had written a special arrangement of it specifically to suit his band's instruments and musical style.

Which meant he'd been thinking about playing this cover for a while.

It was a gentle song: simple and sweet, true to its name.

This time, as Nick sang, Sawyer didn't just think he was looking at her; she *knew* he was looking at her. She knew in the marrow of her bones, that same unnerving place where she'd felt every second of their kiss. She tried to keep her composure as she listened, but Sawyer could feel something fluttering inside her chest and stomach every time she willed herself to look in Nick's direction onstage and meet his intense stare.

She suddenly felt a rush of self-consciousness, wondering if others were witnessing their exchange. She glanced at Kendra. She glanced at Charles. She looked to the stage and locked eyes with Nick again . . . and suddenly felt a rush of emotion that gave her a thoroughly disorienting wave of vertigo.

The entire night made no sense.

Or her entire life made no sense.

Or both.

"Charles," she begged softly. "I'm not feeling good."

"The Sea Breeze?"

"I don't know," she said. "I'm just . . . I feel dizzy. I need to go home."

Charles looked reluctant to leave. But after a few minutes of apologizing to Kendra and saying goodbye, he redeemed himself by helping Sawyer through the club and out the front door.

It took everything she had in her to resist looking back to where Nick stood playing and singing onstage.

* * *

It took a while to find a cab on the Alphabet avenues, but Charles managed to flag one down.

Soon, they were speeding back uptown, the cab driver's easy-jazz station playing on the speakers.

"Ugh—what a night, eh?" Charles said. "I'm sorry I didn't realize what I was getting us into. That club, having to listen to that guy's band . . . *Whine, whine, whine.* And not to sound like an old person, but my ears are still ringing. Maybe that's what got you dizzy and made you feel so unwell, you think?"

"I don't know," Sawyer lied.

She'd desperately wanted to leave the club, but now all she wanted was to tell the driver to stop, to turn around and go back . . . back to Nick.

She squirmed in her seat.

"Things getting worse?" Charles asked, his voice full of kind concern. "Is it your head? Or your stomach, too?"

At this, the cab driver threw a wary glance over his shoulder to where Sawyer sat in the back seat. She read his mind perfectly: *Don't even think about throwing up in my cab, lady.*

"I'm fine," she snapped, suddenly gripped by a wave of irritation—not directed at the driver, but rather, at Charles. "I just needed to get out of there; too many people."

Charles accepted this. He nodded and looked out the window at the lights shimmering on the surface of the otherwise unromantic East River, suddenly lost in his own thoughts.

"Yeah, I get it," he said. "Not our scene."

He sank deeper into his own thoughts, and almost seemed to forget Sawyer was there.

"I'll tell you one thing: that guy's all wrong for her. Kendra can do better. Way better."

Sawyer didn't reply.

Charles shook his head and repeated, "He's all wrong for her. What the hell is she thinking?" He was getting worked up.

Sawyer glared at Charles, but he was oblivious. She felt a sense of irritation building all around her; it buzzed around her like a cloud of gnats.

The problem was—she wanted to be *angrier* with Charles than she actually was. He deserved it—karaoke, "Fly Me to the Moon," the way he'd behaved with Kendra all night, the receipt . . .

"I just don't see why *this* is what you wanted to do today," she complained, spoiling for a fight. "I don't see why we couldn't have spent your first summer Friday off together, just the two of us."

This seemed to snap Charles out of his reverie. He turned from staring out the window, back to Sawyer, chastened. He reached for her hand.

"You're right," he agreed. "You're right; I'm sorry. We should have spent today together, just the two of us."

He squeezed her hand, and they rode the rest of the way home in silence.

Sawyer would have preferred the fight. She was terrified, because all the wisest parts of her knew what she was feeling toward Charles wasn't anger.

It was guilt.

16.

WEDNESDAY, JULY 21

For days, all Sawyer could think about was that kiss.

That kiss.

That. Kiss.

It was as if the memory of it lived in the cells of her body, volatile and touchy, like a bomb ready to go off. If Sawyer allowed herself to recall the kiss—to play it back in her head, remembering the hungry look in Nick's eyes just before he stepped toward her and the feeling of his mouth on hers—it set off full-body chills and left her cheeks flushed. Which, of course, was pretty undignified. She hadn't felt this confusing state of giddiness simultaneously mixed with mortification since she was a teenager.

She tried in earnest *not* to recall it.

That seemed safer.

There was still the grind of going to work, riding the subway, sitting at her desk in her cubicle. Most of the time, she could almost convince herself it hadn't happened. But then something would inevitably make her think of Nick, and the memory of the kiss would come rushing back at her, daring her to face the truth that—yes, it had really happened.

And, of course, the only other person who knew it had really happened was Nick.

She'd checked her email that Saturday that followed. And Sunday.

. . . And Monday.

. . . And Tuesday.

But he didn't write.

On Wednesday, Sawyer came home to her usual hot, stuffy apartment feeling confused and vulnerable, afraid to get her hopes up. She let the computer log on while she opened the windows and switched on a fan.

"WELCOME! You've got mail!"

Sawyer froze. It felt like her heart was suddenly in her throat. She rushed over to the computer and clicked on her inbox, to see . . . an email.

But from Autumn, not Nick.

She clicked on it.

To: Adventures_of_Tom@aol.com
From: AutumnLeaves@hotmail.com

Sorry I haven't checked email in a while! I told my friend Emiko I was dying to check out Tokyo and she and I took the Shinkansen train over the weekend! It was amazing. I took a thousand pics—I'll mail some to you as soon as I get the roll developed. We also met up with her brother, Hiro. He's studying to be a doctor in Tokyo and is suuuuuper cute.

Speaking of super cute men (although you haven't confirmed that)—I don't understand. You hated this Nick guy. Then you said he was "pretty OK." THEN you emailed to say never mind, he sucks?

Methinks there's more to this story . . .

Spill or else,
Autumn

Sawyer clicked on reply, but only sat there for a moment, staring at the screen. More than anything, she wanted to *talk* to her friend, not just send back an email.

She glanced at the time. 5:34 p.m. in New York meant . . . sometime in the morning in Japan? Before she'd left, Autumn had written down her phone number in Japan, along with dialing instructions, just "in case of emergencies." Sawyer already knew: the long-distance charges were exorbitant, but . . .

Before she knew it, she'd logged off the internet, and was dialing 011 and the country code for Japan, then listening to the jittering electronic sound of the foreign ringtone.

"*Moshi moshi?*" came a very groggy voice over the line.

"Autumn!"

"Sawyer?"

"Crap—you were sleeping, weren't you? What time is it?"

Autumn didn't answer right away. "Six . . . uh, something?" came the response eventually.

"I'm sorry! Never mind, never mind!"

"No, no—I need to get up soon anyway. It's good to hear your voice. What's on your mind?"

Sawyer bit her lip, feeling stupid.

"I don't know," she said finally. "I guess I can't figure this Nick guy out."

Autumn let out a laugh that crackled with morning congestion, then coughed. "I *KNEW* there was more to that story!" she gloated. "Tell me everything!"

Sawyer recounted the details of her time hanging out with Nick . . . but stopped short of telling Autumn about the kiss.

"Huh," Autumn said, after listening.

"'Huh'—what?"

"I don't know. I guess I thought you were going to tell me the story of some pompous jackass who was annoying you, and I was going to tease you, then give you some excellent pointers on how to annoy him back. But this Nick guy . . . it sounds like the two of you really connect. And if you like hanging out with him, then there's got to be something redeeming about him."

Sawyer was dying to tell Autumn about the night of Nick's concert, and the kiss . . . What had it meant? But Sawyer couldn't get the words to come out of her mouth.

"Either way," Autumn said now. "I'm glad you're making new friends. I worry sometimes."

Sawyer frowned. "What do you mean?"

"Just that, after you and Charles got together . . . I don't know. Your social circle got a little . . . closed off. You were always staying in—the two of you."

"We were saving money."

"Sure. I'm not criticizing. I just think a wider social network can be really supportive—and you deserve it!"

Later, after they hung up, Autumn's words gnawed at her. The stuff about her social circle growing smaller after she'd started dating Charles shocked her; she'd had no idea Autumn felt that way.

While she'd called Autumn to talk about Nick, it occurred to her now that she had a lot to figure out with Charles. Perhaps there had been things to figure out all along, things she hadn't noticed. Sawyer had always put faith in the steady forward momentum her relationship had—it had always been one foot in front of the other. Each step had made sense at the time.

It never occurred to her that from where Autumn stood on the outside looking in, the view might look different from her own.

* * *

Sawyer was still thinking about her conversation with Autumn when Charles came home later that evening.

She glanced at the time—9:21 p.m. They'd fallen back into their old schedule. Early mornings at the gym, long evenings at the office, work on weekends. He told her stories about some of the other teams working until 2 a.m.—making an indirect case for his situation, she thought, as if to imply, *We're lucky! We could have it worse!*

Sawyer wanted to be supportive—still. But she was definitely starting to wonder how it had gotten so normal to spend so much time apart . . . the summer before they were slated to get married.

Now, as he loosened his tie and slipped it over his head, he flopped down on the couch next to her with a deeply apologetic smile. She wondered—for a fleeting moment—if he could read her thoughts.

"Don't hate me . . ." he began to say.

Sawyer frowned, unsure where this was going.

"But . . ."

"But what?" she prompted. Her body tensed for a curveball in the form of a confession.

"But I have to go to Chicago, after all," he finally finished.

Sawyer blinked, surprised. She'd thought it was going to be something bigger. But still, Chicago . . . with his coworkers . . .

"It's just for two weeks coming up in August—to wrap up the case."

"And Kendra is going?"

"Of course," Charles answered, that peculiar note of forced casualness returning to his voice. "The whole team is."

Sawyer looked at him a long moment.

"Charles—what are we doing?"

"What do you mean?"

"I mean . . . we're supposed to be getting married . . . in *October* . . ." she said, lamely.

She wanted to get it all out in the open. She wanted to confront Charles about Kendra, and ask him to tell her the truth.

But something held her back.

It wasn't just the fact that Nick had kissed her. In that moment, it fully dawned on Sawyer: *she had kissed him back.*

Suddenly, she felt very small, and very lost—like she had no business interrogating Charles about Kendra when she'd been thinking of Nick all day.

"I don't understand. What's wrong with October?" Charles nudged, either pretending confusion, or genuinely confused. But Sawyer only stood there, tongue-tied, lost in thought.

The phone rang, making them both jump.

Charles answered, and Sawyer knew right away from his tone of voice, it was his mother.

"She wants to talk to us both on speaker," he said, pointing to the phone. He pushed the button to activate the speakerphone on the phone's base and set the receiver down in the cradle.

"Charles? Sawyer? Am I on?" came Kathy's voice through the tinny speaker.

"Hi, Kathy," Sawyer greeted her.

"Hello, my dear! Are you two sitting down? I have some news for you!"

Sawyer was on the couch, but Charles was standing.

"We're sitting," he lied. "What is it?"

"Well," Kathy began, her voice jittery with excitement. "You're never going to believe this, but I heard back from the *Times* about the wedding announcement I sent in, and they might be interested in doing a feature!"

Sawyer froze, suddenly dizzy, overwhelmed.

"They decide that kind of thing this early?" she asked. She was aware of the timid sound of her voice.

"Oh, honey," Kathy chided. "I sent yours in early, and made sure they had every single detail of note and every single contact number they might need! I would have killed myself if they'd passed on considering us for a feature due to too little lead time! By the way, tell your parents they might be getting a phone call; the *Times* really does check these things, you know."

"*The New York Times* might call my parents?" Sawyer repeated, unsure if she could believe what she was hearing.

"Oh, absolutely," Kathy insisted. "Oh! But one detail—they said the engagement photo I sent in was good, but not 'great.' Something about it being not as 'natural' as they would like it to be. If we're really serious about a feature, they would prefer an outdoor photo, maybe the two of you in Central Park . . ."

Sawyer stared, wide-eyed and in a total daze, at the plastic grill of the speakerphone as Kathy rambled on with instructions on how to take a "natural" engagement photograph that *The New York Times* simply couldn't resist blowing up to a full half-page size in their wedding section.

17.

THURSDAY, JULY 22

The next morning, Sawyer stirred to the rustlings of Charles getting up while it was still dark, and packing up his gym bag.

She felt strange that morning, withdrawn and a little down; after talking to Kathy on the phone, they'd never gotten a chance to circle back to the conversation about Chicago . . . or about other things. Now, as Charles soft-shoed around the bedroom, Sawyer rolled to face away from him, and accidentally fell back into a deep, dark sleep.

When she woke up later, she was jolted from a comatose state. She immediately realized she'd somehow overslept.

She was late for work.

She scrambled to shower and dress and tumbled out the door, running for the subway.

Usually, Sawyer beat Kaylee into the office by fifteen minutes, and beat Johanna into the office by at least an hour or two. As the "second assistant," she was unofficially expected to be the first person in. But as luck would have it that day, Sawyer wound up running for the elevator and shouting, "Hold it, *PLEASE*!"

A kind soul held the closing door, and as Sawyer slipped inside, she found herself in a crowd of bodies that included Kaylee . . . *and* an early-to-rise Johanna. The elevator smelled of coffee, newsprint, soap, and competing perfumes.

"Hey, Sawyer," Kaylee said, smiling sympathetically.

"Morning," Sawyer replied.

Johanna had not removed her sunglasses, but Sawyer was able to make out the shape of her eyes through the dark lenses. Her eyelids were partially lowered in a disapproving squint. She probably now assumed it was Sawyer's regular habit to arrive barely on time.

"Morning, Johanna," Sawyer said, immediately regretting her overly cheerful tone.

There was another woman in the elevator with them, also headed to their floor—a young, up-and-coming editor named Erin Michaels. Erin was older than Sawyer but still probably in her late twenties or very early thirties. She represented a kind of transitional make-it-or-break-it point in publishing; Erin didn't have an assistant yet (given that she had somewhat recently been one herself) but was already established enough for Sawyer to have admired the budding list of impressive authors and titles Erin had acquired over the past year.

Sawyer liked her, but didn't know her very well.

"Morning, Sawyer—I've actually been meaning to congratulate you," Erin greeted her, smiling.

Sawyer frowned, confused. "Congratulate me?"

"Yes." Erin nodded enthusiastically. "A good friend of mine works at *The Paris Review* . . . When we were out for drinks the other night, he mentioned that they'd accepted a poetry submission from someone who works here at the publishing house. I asked him who, and was excited to hear it was you—I didn't even know you wrote poetry; that's so great."

Sawyer's face had gone crimson, but she was grinning in spite of herself.

"Oh—thank you," she stammered.

"Of course," Erin said as the elevator dinged, announcing their floor. "I can't wait to read your poems, and congratulations again—it's an honor to have an accomplished writer among us."

Erin led the way off the elevator, dressed for summer in a casual linen sheath dress and matching linen jacket, somehow chic and practical, all at the same time. She smiled and nodded, then continued through the maze of open-plan cubicles, bound for the section designated for a neighboring imprint under the same overall publisher. Sawyer watched her go, feeling both flattered by Erin's compliment and a little overwhelmed. She hadn't really thought about telling anybody she worked with about her poems, much less pictured what it would be like to have her colleagues read one.

"*Tea*, Sawyer," Johanna reminded her, snapping her out of her reverie.

"Of course!" Sawyer said, shaking herself. "I'm on it."

She hurried across the office floor, threw her messenger bag on her desk, and headed directly to the kitchen to make Johanna's morning tea. Johanna disappeared into her office, but Sawyer was surprised when she felt Kaylee behind her, close on her heels.

"Hey."

"Hey," Sawyer volleyed back, filling an electric kettle with filtered water and standing on tiptoe to reach for a packet of English breakfast tea.

"God, that was awkward," Kaylee said. "But I don't think Erin meant to out you."

Sawyer frowned as she hunted for a teacup that would pass Johanna's standards of approval (*no mugs, and definitely no mugs with logos* was Johanna's rule . . .).

"What do you mean—'out' me?" Sawyer asked, confused.

Sawyer turned to look at her. Kaylee's eyes went wide.

"Oh . . ." she murmured. "You don't know . . ."

"Know what?"

Kaylee stared, wide-eyed, for another moment, then refocused her attention on Sawyer. "Can you grab a drink after work?" She darted a look in both directions, almost as though she was guilty of something. "Like, a quick drink?"

"Um, sure," Sawyer replied, caught off guard. "Is everything OK?"

Kaylee darted another furtive look, quickly left and right.

"Yeah. It just dawned on me that there are some things you might not know. And . . . well, we should do a drink and talk."

Kaylee pushed her hair behind her ears and smiled, then hurried back to her desk, leaving Sawyer to finish making Johanna's tea.

• • •

The day went by slowly after that. Sawyer couldn't help but wonder what Kaylee had meant—*oh, you don't know*—and what she wanted to tell Sawyer over drinks. Sawyer knew they would both wait until Johanna had left before leaving themselves. She would have to be patient.

Eventually, as the workday dragged to a close, Johanna emerged from her office and headed to the elevator, trailing a fresh spritz of perfume—the usual sign that she was done for the day. Once Sawyer and Kaylee were sure she wasn't coming back, they exchanged a look and quickly packed up their things.

Out on the streets of Midtown, Sawyer left it up to Kaylee to choose a place as they walked around. Sawyer understood: Kaylee was looking for a restaurant where Johanna was unlikely to ever set foot, in order to reduce the chances of running into her as close as possible to zero.

They passed a Houston's, and Kaylee finally stopped and doubled back.

"Here," she said.

They went inside and found a pair of empty seats at the bar.

The restaurant's ambience was difficult to pin down. A modernist Texas steak house, with iron sculptures, dark leather, and random splashes of black-and-white-spotted cowhide. The menu boasted "New American Cuisine" with steak and lobster prices. It was a confusing mixture of chic urban steak house and suburban chain restaurant, odd in the context of New York City.

Sawyer and Kaylee sat at the bar, and set about studying a menu that listed the restaurant's "signature cocktails." It was happy hour, which meant the overpriced sixteen-dollar cocktails were now eight dollars—still a little steep for Sawyer's everyday budget. She picked something that promised to have vodka and lime, and a splash of raspberry.

"I'll do the same," Kaylee agreed, after the bartender came to take their order.

She handed him the menu, which he accepted, but simply repositioned on the bar. He bustled off to make the drinks. Kaylee turned to Sawyer, her long strawberry-blond hair shining halolike under the bar's dark-and-bright spotlights.

"I feel bad," Kaylee started, "because you have that god-awful late lunch hour, so no one keeps you up-to-date when it comes to . . . well, the *grapevine*."

"The grapevine?"

"Yeah. Especially about Johanna."

"What about Johanna?"

"Well, for starters, let me just say: I think it's great that you write," Kaylee said. She grabbed Sawyer's hand and squeezed it for emphasis. "I think it's great that you're a *writer*."

Sawyer was touched. She smiled cautiously, not sure where this was going.

"But rumor has it, Johanna *hates* having writers for assistants. Evidently that's a thing with her. Usually, she refuses to hire them," Kaylee explained.

"Huh," Sawyer said, mulling this. *Great*, she thought. *Yet another reason for Johanna to dislike me.* She attempted a weak smile for Kaylee's sake. "But I've already been hired," she said with a small but cheerful shrug.

Kaylee made a pained face. "Well . . . that's the thing. When I first started, some of the other assistants told me a little bit about the girl before me—the one I replaced. I think her name was Christine, if I remember right. Anyway, everyone said she was really smart and organized and a hard worker . . . but it came out that she also liked to write. She was working on a short-story collection or a novel or something, and Johanna couldn't stand that about her."

Sawyer shook her head, confused. "What are you saying happened? Johanna fired her?"

"Well, yes and no," Kaylee replied. "The girl worked under Johanna for three years, and was due for a promotion. But I guess at some point she got into Yaddo, and asked for some time off to go. It was just going to be for two weeks in order to do a little work on her novel, and Johanna has always had the luxury of having two assistants anyway, but according to the girls who told me the story, that was the kiss of death for the girl's job. Johanna told the girl she could have the time off to go to Yaddo, but when she came back, Johanna basically made her life miserable, to the point of quitting. So, she didn't exactly *fire* her, but . . ."

"I see . . ." Sawyer replied, taking all this in. She chewed her lip, suddenly feeling more than a little doomed.

"I'm not saying that's what's going to happen to *you*," Kaylee insisted in an encouraging voice. "I . . . just . . . I thought you should know."

"I appreciate it, Kaye," Sawyer said. "I do."

"I feel bad. Like . . . I get all the gossip from the other assistants, and you don't . . ."

"That's not your fault, Kaye."

"Well, anyway, I wanted to pull you aside and give you the heads-up. It's good just to have a chance to talk outside the office sometimes. Let me get these drinks."

"You don't have to do that."

"Nah, I want to. And, Sawyer—whatever happens, I know you're doing a really good job for Johanna. I think you'll make an awesome editor someday."

Sawyer was moved by Kaylee's kindness.

She thanked her.

As they sat sipping their drinks, Sawyer could feel her brain whirring away, replaying this news about Johanna, and wondering what, if anything, she could do.

* * *

Back at her apartment a short while later, Sawyer sat in front of her computer, once again staring at an empty inbox.

The kiss was still on her mind, a swirl of confusion, longing, and guilt—all adding up to the conclusion that she should probably leave well enough alone. But she also sort of, just . . . *missed* Nick. Was that possible? She'd only seen him in person a total of six times—including the time they'd briefly met and he'd insulted her. And yet, somehow he'd become a sounding board for her.

Now, she wanted to tell him about how badly everything seemed to be going with her boss—the stuff about Johanna nicknaming her "Eve Harrington," and the warning Kaylee had just given her.

She wanted to talk to him . . . even just to hear one of his cocky opinions . . . she wouldn't even mind getting into a heated debate over his insistence on using the word "chick."

But then she remembered how he'd stormed off after kissing her, almost as if he was angry. And she recalled how she had suddenly left the club that night, when his band had been in the middle of playing a song—*her* song.

Maybe Nick didn't want to hear from her at all.

But she also recalled his words . . . *If you feel like talking to me, you should talk to me,* he'd written over chat. After staring at her empty inbox for a few more minutes, Sawyer finally made up her mind. She opened a blank email and, without salutation or preamble, tapped out:

To: Nikolai70@aol.com
From: Adventures_of_Tom@aol.com

You once said that if I felt like talking to you, I should talk to you. So here I am. I've been having some issues at work, and I've been wanting to talk to someone about them. Well—not "someone." You.

Sawyer hesitated, then added:

We don't have to talk about the . . . you know, the thing that happened last Friday. If you don't want to.

She paused one last time, gathering her courage, then added:

I just . . . I miss you. I've been thinking about you all week.

Before she could change her mind, she clicked send.

• • •

An hour later, she checked her email and saw that Nick had replied. She immediately clicked on his response.

To: Adventures_of_Tom@aol.com
From: Nikolai70@aol.com

Tomorrow's Friday. Meet me by the subway entrance at the south end of Union Square when you get off work. I'll be waiting.—N

Sawyer blinked at the terse email, reading and rereading the spare, toneless lines. She couldn't guess what he was feeling, or what was going through his mind.

But she did know one thing: she knew she was going to be at the south end of Union Square tomorrow afternoon.

18.

FRIDAY, JULY 23

It was hot and muggy when Sawyer left her office for the afternoon. The light in the city had taken on a slightly golden tint from the haze in the air.

Union Square was full of people enjoying their summer Fridays—everywhere Sawyer looked, she saw people lazing on benches, sipping iced coffees, talking to friends, reading books. Strollers and walkers and dogs. Fat pigeons strutting to peck at panini crumbs and flapping their wings in the puddles accumulating on the paving stones near the drinking fountains. Shoppers perusing the little farmers' market tucked into one corner of the park. Twenty-somethings sitting under the red-and-white umbrellas of Luna Park's seasonal open-air restaurant in the middle of Union Square, drinking pitchers of sangria and laughing.

As Sawyer made her way through the crowded park, she saw Nick exactly where he promised he'd be, waiting near the stairs that led down into the subway, at the south end of the park. He was clearly on the lookout, scanning people as they passed, but his back was turned to the direction of Sawyer's approach, so she had the advantage in spotting him first.

For a fleeting moment, the sight of him stopped her in her tracks. Her stomach did a flip and her limbs went numb, as if all the blood had rushed back to her heart, abandoning her extremities.

Then, he abruptly turned around—almost as if she had called his name—and saw her in return.

He also froze. People continued walking all around them as they stared at each other, a river of nonstop movement that was New York. Slowly, a smile spread over Nick's face, and Sawyer was relieved to realize: he was *happy* to see her.

Her legs and feet, which had felt weighted down and practically anchored to the sidewalk, became light again. She approached him shyly, also grinning.

"Hey," she said, when they drew within earshot of each other.

"Hey," he replied.

He nodded. She noticed: he did not move to greet her with a hug. She felt too timid to initiate one herself. An awkward beat passed.

"So, you ready?" Nick said. "Let's go."

Sawyer frowned. "Go where?"

"The N train," Nick replied, turning on his heel, clearly expecting her to follow.

Sawyer stumbled after him. "The N train?"

Nick nodded over his shoulder. "Coney Island's on your list. You said you wanted to go. So, here we go."

He galloped down the subway stairs and into the station. Sawyer hurried to keep up.

"And like all trips back in time to Brooklyn, our journey begins with a really long ride on the N train," he joked.

He offered her a coin. She accepted it, confused, and realized it was a subway token.

"I always wondered who still uses these," she joked. "I was sure they were all dead. Or, at least, in an old folks' home in Flushing playing pinochle."

He rolled his eyes and shook his head. "Tokens are old-school, classy. Hard currency. None of that flimsy yellow-school-bus-colored-plastic nonsense."

"My MetroCard pulls its weight," she said, pretending indignance. "It also makes an excellent bookmark."

Nick looked at her from the sides of his eyes. "I bet you've lost a lot of MetroCards that way."

She laughed and relented with a nod. "Whenever I clean out my bookshelves and the stack on my nightstand, I'm always finding one with a couple of dollars on it here, another one with a couple of dollars there."

Five minutes later, they were on a Brooklyn-bound N train. The car itself was typical of the line, with hard plastic bucket seats in various shades of cafeteria orange. They found a pair together and sat down. When the train jerked forward, it was all Sawyer could do to stop her shoulder from brushing against his; her whole body was wired with an acute awareness that they had yet to touch since the night of the kiss.

She fidgeted, wondering if either of them was going to have the nerve to bring it up.

"By the way, I'm sorry," she said. "About the way I . . . uh . . . left the club the other night."

Her mind replayed a flash of Nick onstage, singing.

And how she'd abruptly left.

Nick shrugged off her apology. "It was time to go home with your fiancé," he said, but his tone was a little strange. "I get it."

"But . . . I—" Sawyer struggled to find the right words.

"We don't need to talk about it," Nick cut her off in a conclusive tone.

There was a long, awkward pause. Then, finally he spoke again.

"So . . ." Nick said. "Lay it on me."

Sawyer looked at him, wide-eyed, faintly alarmed. Nick chuckled.

"I mean, about your work woes."

"Oh," she said. "That."

"What's been going on?"

Sawyer proceeded to tell Nick everything to do with her drama at work. Terry Stone. Johanna calling her "Eve Harrington" behind her back. Erin Michaels congratulating her about *The Paris Review* when they were in the elevator. Kaylee taking her out for a drink and relaying all the gossip about how much Johanna hated having aspiring writers for assistants.

Nick listened intently, nodding thoughtfully, periodically asking questions for clarity.

"So?" Sawyer nudged, once she'd finished unloading every detail she thought might be relevant.

Nick shook his head.

"You don't want to know what I think."

"C'mon—why would I spend the past seven stops telling you about all this if I didn't want to know what you think?"

"Well," Nick said, taking a deep breath and giving Sawyer a grave look. "I think when it comes to your boss, Johanna, you're basically screwed."

"Well, don't sugarcoat it, by all means!"

"You said you wanted to know what I thought," Nick reminded her.

"OK," Sawyer agreed. "But what can I do?"

"Nothing," Nick replied, matter-of-fact.

Sawyer gave him a look.

He shook his head, doubling down. "I can tell you're still operating under the belief that there's something you can do to make this woman happy. In fact—you seem *addicted* to the belief that there is something you can do to make this woman happy. But I can tell you right now: there's nothing you can do, except cut bait."

"Cut bait?"

"Yeah. It's a fishing expression."

"I *know* it's a fishing expression," Sawyer replied, indignant. "But what are you saying . . . I should quit?"

"Quit publishing, no," Nick answered. "But quit working for Johanna, hell yes."

Sawyer hadn't even considered this. She started to protest, but her mouth only opened and closed soundlessly, like a fish.

"I know, I know," Nick clucked. "You probably haven't even considered that. But it's the only way." He paused, then added, "What about that editor on the elevator?"

"Erin Michaels?"

"Yeah—her. She sounds like she might be young, but she's someone who you genuinely admire."

"I do, but . . ."

"And her congratulations to you sounded sincere."

"I mean, I think it was—"

"It sounds like she's the kind of person who thinks being a writer is a good thing. She sees the value in it, and doesn't see it as being in conflict with becoming an editor."

"Maybe," Sawyer conceded. "But it's not like I can just pick and choose my boss. I can't ask to work for her instead of Johanna or anything like that. That's not how it works. And if I went around trying to finagle some kind of transfer . . . well, besides pissing Johanna off, I'd probably land Erin on Johanna's shit list. And Erin might be encouraging, but she doesn't want to go around offending other editors with bad interoffice etiquette. No one does."

Nick shrugged.

"Well—what do I know? I'd just say don't rule it out. Here's my final two cents: it's better to study under someone lower on the totem pole who actually wants to teach you something, than it is to study under the highest-up person who doesn't want to teach you anything at all."

Sawyer looked at him from the sides of her eyes.

"That's some pretty deep wisdom," she joked.

"I have my moments."

"A few . . . here and there," she agreed, teasing. Then she sighed. "And you might even be right."

"*Might* be."

They continued to talk as the train hurtled them jerkily toward the end of Brooklyn.

On two occasions, they stood up to offer their seats to other riders. Once, to a pair of elderly women, one of whom hobbled onto the train with the help of a cane. And a second time when an exhausted-looking woman wrangling three very squirmy children under the age of five got on the train and glanced around helplessly.

Sawyer liked how seamless these transitions were, that she and Nick didn't need words in order to agree upon giving up their seats. They both just immediately stood, offering their seats to people who needed them more, with a quick tap on the stranger's shoulder and a welcoming nod, then continuing their conversation as they grabbed the overhead rail. She liked how Nick's thoughtfulness was automatic, with no showiness about it.

Finally, almost a full hour after they got on the train in Union Square, they reached the end of the line. By then, the tracks had gone from underground to elevated and the buildings around them had become increasingly squat, with only a few housing high-rises. The passengers all around them were clearly bound for the shore, carrying coolers and beach bags, and smelling of tropical-scented sunscreen. The conductor came on the muffled loudspeakers and announced that this was the final stop, that the train would be turning around, and that all passengers were advised to get off the train.

Bing-bong! The train doors opened.

"That's our cue," Nick said. "Let the adventure begin."

They shuffled along with the crowd, down the stairs and out of the station onto what looked like a broad city avenue. Sawyer was surprised by how urban it was; beaches in Oregon were cold, wild, rugged affairs.

Nick pointed out a few things as they made their way along the avenue, presumably headed to the waterfront (Sawyer couldn't see the water yet; she was all turned around).

"The very first Nathan's," he said, pointing to a large building with a giant cartoon hot dog and Nathan's signature vintage green-and-white signage. To the side of the building was an enormous patio filled with people sitting at picnic benches, eating hot dogs and lobster rolls. "But they charge twice as much here as they do in the city."

He continued to lead the way. They stopped to pay homage to the Coney Art Walls—a series of murals, giddy with color—then made their way through an open-air fairway, the carneys all calling to them to try their hands at various carnival games.

Nick waved off a man trying to heckle them into a ring toss.

"Maybe later."

Under his breath, to Sawyer, he confided, "I'm sure you know already, but there's rarely anything 'fair' about the games on a 'fairway' . . ." He smiled. "Still. I have a few favorites I like to lose at. How 'bout you? You have a favorite carnival game you like to lose at?"

"I don't want to toot my own horn, but I'm not half-bad at the one where you throw darts at balloons," Sawyer admitted.

Nick raised his eyebrows. "A secret sharpshooter," he commented.

"I won my one and only childhood goldfish that way," Sawyer added, grinning.

"What did you name him?"

Sawyer cringed and blushed. "Moby," she answered.

Nick's face squirmed. "'Moby' . . . as in, *Moby Dick*?"

"Go ahead. I know you want to laugh."

"Would I laugh at you?" he said with a mock air of incredulity.

"Pretty sure you already have," Sawyer said. "Anyway, you called it when we first met; my family is big on American classics. Or at least my mom is. Maybe my dad would have named him Hamlet."

"Ah, yes—an existential goldfish, always brooding about death," Nick joked. "'A man may fish with the worm that hath eat of a king, and eat of the fish that hath fed of that worm,'" Nick recited.

This time it was Sawyer's turn to raise her eyebrows in amused surprise. Nick shrugged.

"It was the fishiest line I could think of in *Hamlet*," he said. "The only other fish references in Shakespeare that I can remember are mainly about Caliban. Something about being half man, half fish. Which reminds me—there's a freak show here, of course."

Sawyer wrinkled her nose. "Those have always struck me as mean-spirited."

Nick nodded. "I figured. Even the name, 'freak show,' seems too derisive for your blood."

"What does that mean?"

"Nothing. You're just . . . *nice*."

"There's that word again. Don't make me beat it out of you."

Nick laughed. He continued to lead the way past Tilt-A-Whirls and bumper cars and roller coasters, until the fairway let out to a vintage wooden boardwalk, and Sawyer finally set eyes on the beach. A smile spread over her face to see it. *The ocean!*

The water itself was still a considerable distance away—the wooden boardwalk was broad and wide, and the sand leading down to the water stretched for a couple hundred feet before finally reaching the white-capped breakers rolling in on the steel-blue Atlantic. The summer sun had not let up, and the air above the sand shimmered in oily-looking, mirage-like waves. But, unlike in the city, the heat was tempered slightly by a pleasant sea breeze, Sawyer noted. Everything was sticky and hot—but not terrible.

"Where are we going?" she asked, as Nick continued on.

"Thought we'd walk to the end of the pier," he answered, pointing to a long wooden pier that jutted perpendicular to the boardwalk, out over the water. "You can get the lay of the land, and decide what you'd like to do first."

"*I'm* supposed to decide?"

"Of course. It's *your* summer Friday list," he reminded her. "I just have two stipulations. One: you pick whatever you want. And two: you let me treat you today."

Sawyer shook her head.

"C'mon, Sawyer," Nick said. "Choose what you want, and don't say sorry, for once in your life. I promise you it's not that hard."

"But it's your summer Friday, too," she countered. "Real New Yorkers take their summer Fridays pretty seriously. Wouldn't want you to waste yours."

"Well, even if you pick ten things I hate, I'd still be doing exactly what I want with my Friday," Nick replied.

Sawyer felt an extra flush of warmth in her cheeks.

"Because I get to hang out with you," he added, matter-of-fact. It should have sounded like a line. Instead it sounded frank, like the earnest truth.

The warmth in her cheeks bloomed down her neck, to her chest. She glanced away, hoping Nick wouldn't notice.

"I'm where I want to be," he confirmed, and they walked on.

When they reached the end of the pier, they turned and stood at the railing, looking back at the shore. A tall red metal structure dominated the scene. It looked a little like an extremely tall radio tower, except it fanned out at the top, like a giant mushroom.

"That's the old parachute jump," Nick said, following Sawyer's gaze.

"Parachute jump?"

"Yeah. Paratroopers in the army used to train by jumping off towers like that one. But when the World's Fair came to New York in the 1930s, they decided to build one that catered to fairgoers, as a ride."

Sawyer stared at the tower and tried to picture white parachutes falling from the top, like blossoms falling from a tree.

"That must have been pretty cool," she said.

"Cool," Nick agreed. "But too expensive to continue running the ride, and too expensive to tear down or move. So now that weird red tower has basically become the architectural feature that defines Coney Island. Like, if they had to print something on a souvenir keychain, that'd be it."

"That red tower is to Coney Island what the Empire State Building is to New York?"

"Pretty much."

"Huh," Sawyer mused.

They continued to study the view as Nick pointed out Coney Island's many features and attractions.

"So—what do you want to do?"

Sawyer thought for a minute and decided to be honest. "All that talk about Moby Dick makes me want to start with the aquarium," she conceded.

"The aquarium it is," Nick agreed.

• • •

They spent the next hour wandering around the eerie blue ambient lighting of the aquarium tanks, gravitating toward whatever caught their attention.

"You know what I loved about aquariums as a kid?" Sawyer said rhetorically. "It's like . . . when you get to a part of the aquarium that's super dark, and you have so many fish tanks all around you—especially the really giant ones with huge walls of glass—it's like for a second you feel like you're in the fishes' world, and *you're* the one visiting . . . the one in a tank."

Nick looked at her. Sawyer laughed.

"That makes it sound like I want to live in a fish tank."

"No," Nick said. "I get it. Especially as a kid. It's that same fantasy of being able to get in a spaceship and visit aliens."

"Yes! Exactly. It's weird. There shouldn't be anything primal about it, but it feels primal."

"Unless it *is* primal, and all of us humans were originally put here by an alien-fish species, and all we want to do is go back and visit."

Sawyer laughed.

"You think I'm kidding," Nick complained. "But what if 'evolved from the primordial ooze' is just code for 'brought here from another planet by an alien-fish species'?"

"And I thought *I* was the one with all the weird ideas," Sawyer replied.

"Nope. If one thing's for sure, it's that we're total weirdos, *both* of us."

• • •

They decided the aquarium made them hungry, and returned to the bright sunshine and unrelenting heat of the boardwalk in search of food.

"I *would* recommend we get lobster rolls, but seafood feels a little obscene after the aquarium," Nick commented.

"Agreed."

They wound up getting corn dogs and slushies from Ruby's and found a table just outside the entrance with a view of it all—the boardwalk, the beach, and the water. For a beach, Coney Island was distinctly urban, with a touch of eccentric. As they sat people watching, they witnessed a drug deal, a woman wearing what looked like a hot-pink wedding dress, and an old man covered in green face paint and tinfoil. The last was the most surreal. Besides the green paint and tinfoil, music blared from some unseen speaker under the tinfoil, and he was on roller skates.

"See?" Nick teased Sawyer. "Now, there's a guy who plainly remembers our alien-fish ancestors. He's overdue for a visit home."

Sawyer resisted the urge to laugh. She put a hand to her forehead and eyes and let out a soft chuckle in spite of herself.

• • •

When the sweet-and-salty corn dogs had been reduced to just wooden sticks crusted with charred batter at the base, and the cherry syrup in the slushies had stained their lips an unnatural shade of red, they went in search of a few carnival games on the fairway.

They both lost miserably, but laughed so hard Sawyer felt tears squeezing from the outer cracks of her eyes.

"Well, look at it this way," Nick said. "Now we won't have to carry around one of those giant stuffed animals like some sort of cliché in a movie."

"Yeah," Sawyer agreed, but thought, *That's a romance cliché.*

Her mind drifted back to the kiss. She glanced at his lips. She started to sweat and looked away.

They decided to ride the Wonder Wheel—Coney Island's famously enormous vintage Ferris wheel. Sawyer figured it would be a peaceful ride, a nice view at the top, possibly they'd catch a cool sea breeze from higher up. While waiting in line, she'd seen that some of the Ferris wheel cars moved—sliding back and forth on tracks within the wheel itself, in a vague *Z* pattern. Probably some engineer's idea to jazz up the otherwise rather staid ride; an interesting nuance, but it didn't strike Sawyer as anything to be intimidated by.

But the first time their car zipped forward, she wasn't really expecting it, and the feeling of it dropping and swinging forward had her reaching for Nick out of pure instinct. He allowed her to grab him. Then, finding herself in his arms, she freaked out and just as instantly jerked away in polite reflex.

It all happened in seconds: jump, grab, clutch, flinch, release, jump back.

He'd laughed when she'd clutched at him, then abruptly stopped laughing when she recoiled.

The truth was, she hadn't reacted to his body so much as she had reacted to the effect that his body had on *her* body. The magnetism she'd felt in touching him had scared her. It forced her to be honest with herself: she hadn't just been thinking about that kiss all week; she'd been wanting more . . . she'd been wanting *him.*

After the awkward moment, the two of them sat quietly, making strained small talk, not touching for the rest of the ride.

When they got to the bottom and found themselves back on solid ground, Nick asked, "So . . . anything else you want to do in Coney Island, or are you getting tired and ready to call it a day?"

They'd been there for a few hours, but the summer sun was still high in the sky as though it had no plans for setting anytime soon. The idea of the day ending—her day *with Nick* ending—filled Sawyer with a sense of desperate protest.

"But we came to the beach," she said. "And we haven't walked on the beach at all yet."

"You want to walk on the beach?"

"Of course," she insisted. She scanned the shore. "Maybe over there," she said, pointing. "Where it's less crowded. We can walk in the surf, and I can say I dipped my toes in the Atlantic Ocean today."

Nick gave a slow smile. "All right. Let's take a walk."

• • •

They walked along the boardwalk to the stretch of less crowded beach that Sawyer had pointed out, then kicked off their shoes and picked their way through the hot sand toward the water.

When they neared the surf, they inched closer and closer to it, tempting the waves, until one surged a tad more powerfully than the others and rushed over their feet. Sawyer gave an appreciative hoot.

"Oh, that is brisk!"

"Yeah," Nick agreed. "It'll get a little warmer around August, but you know . . . we're still in New York, not Florida."

"I *like* it," Sawyer said. "A swim in this would be refreshing!"

"I guess I should have told you to bring a swimsuit," Nick replied. "I didn't think of that."

"That's OK," Sawyer said. "I'm pretty happy with today, just as it is."

They continued to walk, leaving footprints in the sand. As Sawyer stepped, a fresh wave washed over her toes.

"In fact . . . I personally felt a little . . . I don't know—*panicked*? I guess?—right after we got off the Wonder Wheel," she admitted. "When you suggested we call it a day."

"You just seemed uncomfortable," Nick answered.

She understood he was referring to how she'd sprung away from him in the car of the Ferris wheel.

"I wanted to give you an out, in case you wanted one," he said.

"I *don't* want one," Sawyer insisted. "I'm having a good time." She paused, and dug deep for some courage. "I don't want the day to end, because I like being around you, and I don't want that to end, most of all."

They'd been walking leisurely along the surf. But at this, Nick drew up short, stopped, and turned to look at her.

Sawyer froze. Her heart was hammering again.

He studied her face.

"Then it's mutual," he said quietly, almost as if stating the conclusion to himself.

They'd stopped abruptly, with Sawyer almost bumping into him. Now they stood face-to-face, unexpectedly close.

She was self-consciously aware of a tension building between them again, growing steadily thicker, exhilarating and unbearable at the same time. They moved incrementally closer and closer, until . . .

SPLAT.

Sawyer stared wide-eyed at Nick's shirt, frozen by total disbelief. The white stain was almost identical to the one that had splattered his T-shirt on the Staten Island Ferry. Nick looked down, his brow furrowed.

"What the—"

Sawyer clapped her hands to her mouth, fighting back laughter.

"NO. WAY." Nick looked accusingly up at the sky, deeply offended. "No fucking way did this happen *twice*!"

Sawyer gave up; she stopped fighting to keep her composure and broke into unbridled laughter.

"If that really *is* a sign of good luck . . . you've got to be the luckiest person I know!" she said.

"Gee, thanks," Nick retorted. "I think I'd be fine being a little *less* lucky." He gave up looking for the rogue seagull and set about stripping off his shirt.

"What are you doing?" Sawyer asked, suddenly nervous, taken off guard by Nick's shirtless body.

"Washing this off," Nick said. "Just so happens, there's an ocean conveniently right here."

He tossed his shoes onto a dry spot of sand and moved farther into the surf, then stooped over to submerge his shirt in the break of the waves. Sawyer put her own shoes next to his shoes, along with her bag, and waded in to stand next to him.

"I think you have to scrub it," she advised. "Do you want me to do it?"

"No," Nick snapped. "Thanks for getting it out last time. But I don't want to be the guy whose pooped-on shirts you're always cleaning."

Sawyer laughed until Nick couldn't help but laugh a little, too.

"What the hell did you do to the seagulls in a past life?" she teased.

"Wish I knew."

"You're clearly a marked man in their book."

"Literally," Nick grunted, having little success in getting the stain completely out.

"Here—seriously, let me."

"No. I said: hands off!"

For a minute they played tug-of-war with the shirt, then something went confusingly wrong. Sawyer stumbled; Nick tried to catch her. At the same time, a wave rolled in, and they wound up toppling into the water.

This time Nick was the one to give a loud hoot about the temperature.

They'd been completely dunked, head to toe, hair and all.

They struggled to get to their feet as another wave sloshed lazily to the shore, and started laughing again until they were both hysterical.

"Screw it," Nick said, now laughing so hard his eyes were barely open. "There's only one thing left to do now," he said.

"What's that?"

He threw his T-shirt onto the sand where they had stashed their shoes. It landed with a wet splat.

"You said you wanted to go for a swim," he said.

Sawyer grinned.

Instead of getting out of the water, they turned and swam farther in, laughing and splashing each other playfully as they went.

* * *

Once they got a little more distance from the surf, they got away from the break of the waves, and away from the brownish silt the waves kicked up in their wake. It was even colder than it had been in the shallows, but once the shock wore off, the water was cool and refreshing. And salty. Sawyer noticed: the Atlantic seemed far saltier than the Pacific. It felt a little easier to float. She'd never gone swimming in a dress before; she could feel the loose skirt of her sundress blooming around her, but her legs were mostly unfettered.

She and Nick swam in little half-moons around each other, daring each other to go farther and farther out. Every once in a while, they surged toward each other and gave a little joking splash.

Finally, at one point, when Sawyer surged toward Nick and splashed him, he caught her arms and pulled her toward him.

She was surprised when her body instinctively relaxed into it. She felt his arms circle her waist and her own arms hook onto his shoulders and neck. They bobbed together for a couple of minutes, like a pair of buoys.

Sawyer felt her skin tighten with goose bumps, but not so much from the temperature of the water as from the strange electricity she felt. Away from the break of the surf, the waves were gentle. She could feel the warmth of the sun on her face. The smell of funnel cake from the boardwalk drifted to her nose in wafts. It smelled so good and the goose bumps felt so good and the water was so cool and Nick's touch was so warm, it all made her feel a little dizzy. What an unexpected, slightly absurd paradise she had wandered into. She licked her lips, tasting the salt, and waited for Nick to kiss her.

But in the next moment, Nick released her and swam away.

* * *

When they got out of the water, they returned to the spot where they'd dropped their things and sat on the sand, having brought along no towel to speak of. Nick's T-shirt was almost dry, but hardly clean, caked in a dark sand that was more like mud.

As they sat warming themselves under the sun, their bodies encrusted in salt and sand, they began to contemplate the folly of their ways.

"Riding the train back to Manhattan like this is going to be . . ." Sawyer started to say, pausing to think of the right word.

"Dirty, disgusting, and beyond uncomfortable," Nick provided.

"Yeah," Sawyer agreed. "*THAT.*"

She paused, and ran her fingers through her hair, where they caught in a tangle. Her dark hair had turned surprisingly wavy after the salt water.

"Not to mention, it's a really looooong ride," she added. "You know . . . you *might* say, we really didn't think this through."

She laughed, but Nick only grunted, lost in thought.

“Huh.”

He was quiet for a moment.

“Well, I think I know of a solution,” he said. “But I’m not sure what you’ll think of it.”

Sawyer looked at him. His face was so serious. She laughed.

“Try me,” she said.

19.

It was about a fifteen-minute walk along the boardwalk from Coney Island to Brighton Beach. The restaurants began to change from hot dog stands and seafood shacks to Russian restaurants that appeared—at least from the outside—to strike a cross in tone between hotel banquet rooms and nightclubs.

Sawyer had begun to quietly freak out about meeting Nick's mom.

"Are you sure she won't mind?" Sawyer asked nervously. "She isn't expecting us. Maybe she's resting and doesn't want company around."

"She'll be glad to see us," Nick insisted.

"We're bringing a complete mess of soggy sand right to her doorstep." Sawyer continued to fret.

"We'll shower. We'll wash our clothes. We'll say hi to my mom—who I've been meaning to visit anyway. We'll make sure to clean up after ourselves."

"But . . ."

"But what?"

"I don't know." Sawyer squirmed. "I just . . . feel bad."

"You feel bad about everything," Nick quipped. "You're too nice."

Sawyer frowned. Nick noticed her expression and chuckled.

"Look, it's part of your charm. But it's OK to avail yourself of others every so often."

Sawyer repressed a dubious sigh.

Eventually, after passing several Russian restaurants clustered together in a row, they turned and left the boardwalk. Nick continued to lead the way deeper into Brighton Beach proper, past Russian bookstores and butchers and convenience stores and even a Duane Reade bearing the Cyrillic letters "аптека." It was like entering a different nation, but without a passport.

Finally, Nick turned onto a street mostly lined with the kind of brick-and-siding two-story row houses that characterized most of Queens and outer Brooklyn. The majority sported little metal awnings over the front porch. The yards in front of them were mostly paved over with concrete or gravel. A few houses sported gaudy touches, with ornate wrought iron fences or front doors that boasted cut-glass windows.

Nick drew up short on the sidewalk outside one of the houses.

"This is it," he said.

No ornate wrought iron or stained-glass door. It was clean and cheerful in its simplicity, with brick that looked like it had been power-washed and regrouted, and white siding that looked like it had been freshly painted. To the right of the house was a narrow driveway and what looked like a beat-up old Mercedes-Benz from the 1970s.

"C'mon," Nick urged, taking the stoop two stairs at a time.

What am I doing here? Sawyer thought to herself. If someone had asked her earlier this morning, *Hey, what are you doing after work?*, never in a million years would she have been able to guess it would be this. Any of it, really.

Nick knocked and shouted something in Russian. A faint response came back from within. He produced a key, unlocked the door, and let himself in, waving for Sawyer to follow. She obeyed, still feeling timid.

Once inside, Sawyer looked around. The main living room was clean, the walls were Spartan and white, but the room was dominated by otherwise weighty things: a thick Oriental rug; a big, bulky maroon sofa set; and a heavy, round, ornately carved wooden coffee table. A couple of very green spider plants hung from a pair of 1970s-style macrame hanging planters on either side of the bigger of the two sofas. And in the middle of the sofa sat a diminutive older woman, her hair dark as a raven's wing, a cannula tube connecting her nose to a low-hissing oxygen tank. She put the newspaper she'd been reading aside and smiled.

Sawyer's mind flashed back: *I know someone with respiratory problems*, Nick had said about not smoking, that night they first met.

Nick's mother didn't get up from the sofa, but threw her arms wide to Nick. He perched next to her and gave her a hug and a kiss, then pointed to Sawyer and said something that sounded vaguely like *Eto moya podruga*, followed by something she *did* recognize: "Sawyer."

His mother looked at Sawyer and without missing a beat proclaimed, "*Welcome!*"

Sawyer started to say a formal hello, but Nick's mother waved her off. "Lena, Lena!" she corrected. "You are friend of my son—call me Lena."

Nick switched to English, and explained about what had happened at the beach, their need for showers, and to use the washer and dryer.

Lena clapped her hands and laughed.

"So then," she said to Sawyer. "You are also just like my son!"

"I'm sorry?"

"You are just like my son," Lena repeated. "When he was small boy, he would see water, he would jump in with all clothes on. I had to make sure if I take him anywhere near water, he has swimming shorts on, or else he jump in, doesn't matter what he is wearing!" Lena laughed, thoroughly amused. "All these years, and nothing changes," she said, very pleased by this idea.

Sawyer had no clue how to respond, and wound up simply laughing along with Lena.

Lena grabbed her arm. "He love swimming," she insisted.

"I love swimming, too," Sawyer agreed.

Lena smiled. "Swimming is great pleasure of life."

"Yes," Sawyer agreed. "It is."

• • •

Nick showed Sawyer to a bathroom and brought her a fresh, fluffy towel. He offered her a few items of clothing.

"A T-shirt," he said, looking a little sheepish. "And a pair of boxer shorts. To wear while I run our clothes through the washer and dryer."

She accepted the towel and the T-shirt and shorts, then closed the bathroom door and slipped out of her sundress and underthings, wrapped herself in the towel, and cracked the door open enough to hand her wet garments out to him.

"Thank you . . . for doing all this . . ." she managed to say.

Their hands touched briefly in the exchange.

The door closed.

• • •

When Sawyer emerged from the shower, she wrapped herself in the fluffy towel, then put on the T-shirt and boxers . . . which were obviously from a stash of clothing that Nick kept at his mother's house. She knew he'd picked them because of the summer heat. But they were so light as to make her feel almost naked. There was also a strange and unexpected thrill in having Nick's clothes so close to her.

Sawyer thought about this for a moment, shivered, and then shook herself back to reality.

• • •

Nick took a quick turn in the shower, and the next thing Sawyer knew, the three of them were sitting around Nick's mother's kitchen table, drinking from a pitcher of iced tea that had been soaking in a copious mixture of sugar, lemons, and cherries.

"I have some potato salad!" Lena said, a finger in the air as though she'd just had an idea. "Are you hungry?" she asked Nick. "Will you eat?" she asked Sawyer.

"I . . . uh . . . sure . . ." Sawyer said. Even after the corn dogs and slushies, the impromptu swim and the walk and the shower had made her strangely hungry again.

"I'll get it," Nick said, putting a gentle hand on his mother's arm to stop her from getting up. Lena was still tethered to the oxygen tank, which rode along in a wheeled basket of sorts wherever she went, but seemed a cumbersome anchor nonetheless.

Nick pulled a big glass bowl out of the fridge and peeled off the plastic wrap covering it.

"When did you make this?" he asked his mother, as though surprised.

"This morning," she answered. "I don't know why I made it—and made so much. Maybe I knew you would come. Maybe I am psychic."

Nick laughed. "I wouldn't put it past you."

He pulled out three plates from a cupboard. They were white but very thin, and painted with tiny delicate pink roses. He put a scoop of potato salad on each plate, then passed them around the kitchen table and set down three forks.

Sawyer accepted her plate and fork and took a bite. A mix of cubed potatoes, carrots, onions, hard-boiled eggs, pickles, and salty ham, tossed in a healthy coating of mayonnaise and sour cream, and infused with a surprisingly heavy amount of dill. It was heartier, sweeter, saltier, and creamier than the usual potato salad that Sawyer's own mother had always thrown together for picnics and PTA meetings.

"Do you like it?" Lena asked, eagerly watching Sawyer's face as she chewed her first bite.

"Very much," Sawyer replied.

"It's *Russian* potato salad," Lena emphasized. "*Salat Olivier!* Good for holidays." She nodded and chuckled. "Here we have potato salad for summer . . . but in Russia we have *salat Olivier* on New Year's Eve."

Lena grinned, the apples of her cheeks showing her high cheekbones. She was such a petite woman—small boned, birdlike. Sawyer could see now that the glossy black hue of her hair was likely the result of dye, but it was tastefully done, as was the cut of her bob. And although age and her poor health had put a few lines around Lena's, she and Nick shared the same bright, clear blue eyes.

"Well, this is delicious anytime," Sawyer said, taking another bite of the potato salad. "I like the dill."

Nick laughed. "Don't you know?" he teased. "That's the way to make any dish 'Russian'—stir in a bunch of sour cream and mayonnaise, and throw in a ton of dill."

"That's not true!" Lena protested. But she laughed, clearly not offended. "OK," she said, wheezing a little into the cannula, "is maybe a little true."

They all chuckled and tucked into the potato salad. After a few bites, though, Lena laid down her fork and reached for Sawyer's hand. She gave Sawyer's left hand a gentle pat where it rested on the table.

"You are the first girl Nico has brought home," she said. "And his face . . . his face is so happy."

Sawyer looked at Lena, blushing with a bit of shock, and dreading having to let the woman know she'd gotten the wrong impression.

"Oh . . ." she said awkwardly, trying to find the words. "I'm . . . I'm not his girlfriend," she explained.

Lena's face fell.

"But—he does have a girlfriend," Sawyer added quickly, unwilling to disappoint Lena. "Yes," Sawyer continued. "Nick's girlfriend is a very pretty blond woman, named Kendra. She is very nice . . . very . . . pretty . . ."

Sawyer quickly ran out of things to say about Kendra.

Nick cleared his throat.

"Actually, Kendra and I broke up," he said, correcting Sawyer.

She looked at him, surprised by this nugget of news, and more surprised that he hadn't thought to mention it all day, until now.

"What?" Sawyer uttered, blinking at him, and feeling more than a little disoriented.

"Yeah," Nick said to her. "I have no plans to see her again."

"Oh . . ." Sawyer murmured. "Nick . . . I'm sorry. I didn't know."

Sawyer became aware that during this entire exchange, Lena had been looking between their faces, her eyes flicking to Nick, then Sawyer, then back to Nick.

Lena smiled to herself as if she had just decoded a secret. But then . . . her hand was still resting on top of Sawyer's. She glanced down now, as if suddenly aware of something she'd been touching.

Lena lifted her hand and observed Sawyer's ring. She let her eyes linger there, frowning, not saying anything. Then she appeared to gather herself. She put on a smile again.

"Well, it is nice to have you here," Lena said kindly.

"Thank you—really," Sawyer replied, smiling back, suddenly nervous again.

Lena nodded, smiled warmly, then turned her attention to take a tiny bite of the potato salad. She glanced up briefly, and shot a slight look of concern in her son's direction.

• • •

After they'd eaten, Nick buzzed about, fixing a few things around the house: a light bulb that needed changing, a towel rod that had come a little loose in the bathroom, locating a TV remote that had gone missing, and resetting a TV menu of options that had somehow gotten tangled in commands. He took care to hunt down and vacuum up any sand he and

Sawyer may have tracked into the house, then exchanged a few words in Russian with his mother.

He turned to Sawyer. By then, they had redressed in their clothes, clean and crisp from the dryer.

"Ready to go?"

"Oh, sure," Sawyer agreed. "Actually, if you want to spend more time with your mother, you can just point me in the direction of the train."

"Cut it out," Nick scolded. "I'm not letting you ride the train back alone. And besides, we're not taking the train. I'm driving us."

"Driving us?"

"Yeah. It's late, and that's a really long ride."

Sawyer laughed nervously. "And your mom doesn't mind you borrowing her car?"

"Of course not!" Lena piped up. "Anyway, the car belongs to Nico."

"I bought the car for *you*, Ma," Nick reminded her. "It's yours."

Lena turned to look at Sawyer and shrugged. "We only use it to go to doctor, and always Nico drives. I never drive it."

"Well, my point is," Nick said, "it belongs to her, but she says we can borrow it. We'll use it to drive back to Manhattan tonight, and then tomorrow I'll drive back out to return it to her."

Lena grinned at both of them. "Is good for me—I get double blessing of double visit from my son," she said, happily signing off.

"So, ready to go?" Nick repeated.

They said goodbye to Lena, who hugged them both. Sawyer was a little awkward, taking extra care to make sure she didn't disturb the woman's cannula or oxygen tank, and feeling the delicate weight of Lena in her arms.

They made their exit. Nick waited to hear his mother turn the dead bolt before going around the side of the house where the dilapidated Mercedes was parked.

"I bought this off one of my mother's friends in the neighborhood. I'm pretty sure the guy used to be in the Russian mob. It runs just fine but stinks of diesel. My mom always says that's the smell of the Old Country. That, and Russian cigarettes—which, according to her, smell like perfume and are so strong they can kill non-Russians with two inhales."

They got in and pulled the doors shut. Nick started the engine, then worked the clutch and gears, putting the car in reverse to back out. The car was old in an oddly comfortable way—the seats dipped low on their springs, the sunroof sported the kind of tinted glass that had been popular in the seventies, and there was a very lived-in smell that resembled the smell of the sand at the beach.

"She's why you don't smoke," Sawyer said, as Nick steered the car through the streets of Brighton Beach. "That thing you said about knowing someone with respiratory problems—you meant her."

"Yeah."

"Was it from smoking?"

Nick shook his head. "She *did* use to smoke, and I don't think smoking helped, that's for sure. But the issues with her lungs came from her work as a chemist."

"What . . . happened? If you don't mind me asking."

"No. You can ask," Nick said. But his body language definitely stiffened. "I'll try to give you the abridged version of the whole thing."

Sawyer humbly waited.

"My mom was a research chemist. She was assigned by the government to work in Kremlyov, one of the so-called 'closed towns' a couple hundred miles outside Moscow, where everyone who lives in the town basically works for the lab. Many important chemists worked there, but there weren't a lot of freedoms.

"One day, she found out she was pregnant. She told no one. Instead, she put in an application for special permission to attend an academic conference in Belgium. She says she was surprised when she got approved—she felt that someone had made a clerical error, or else God had intervened.

"She went. Once in Belgium, she made contact with the American embassy. They were sympathetic to her story . . . and interested in the fact that she was a high-ranking Soviet chemist who wanted to defect.

"When the plane that was supposed to take her back to Moscow began to board, she was already on a plane bound for America."

Nick paused, redoubling his concentration on the road. By then, they'd joined the Belt Parkway and they'd run into traffic.

"What about . . ." Sawyer ventured, but trailed off.

"My dad?" said Nick.

"Yes."

"My mom says she was genuinely in love with the man who was my father—a fellow chemist—but that their affair was on-again, off-again, and he was deeply patriotic. And very proud. He never would have come with her, and she believed he might have even stopped her. Anyway, for all of those reasons, she never told him about the baby. About me."

"Wow," Sawyer said, solemn. "That's got to be hard, Nick," she added softly.

Nick shrugged. "It is what it is," he said, his voice flat. "I admire my mom for her courage. And I'm happy I grew up in America, free to be a wannabe-musician-turned-junior-ad-exec." He glanced at her. "The American Dream," he joked.

"What did your mom do when she got to America?"

"Well, given her background, they wanted her to come work for the big lab in Brookhaven."

"That's . . . Long Island?" Sawyer asked, still getting used to New York's geography.

"Yep. By Stony Brook University. The lab is by far the area's biggest employer. She really liked it at first; said it was different from the town where she'd worked in Russia, more relaxed and open. And to tell the truth, I really liked growing up in Stony Brook. It's got a kind of small-town charm to it that I miss. That whole area is old-school Long

Island—lots of colonials, churches with little white steeples, a quaint little Main Street in Port Jefferson, an old stone lighthouse . . . oh, and going to Cedar Beach in the summer to swim, of course."

"Or—according to your mom—taking an impromptu swim anytime of the year," Sawyer teased.

"Yeah, or that," Nick agreed affably. He smiled at Sawyer. "To be honest: my mom rarely tried to stop me."

"She seems big on joy. Especially for her son."

"She is."

Sawyer tried to piece everything together. "Stony Brook, huh? For some reason . . . I thought you grew up in the city. Or, well—in Brighton Beach."

"We moved there when I was thirteen. So . . . it's home, too. But in a different way."

"Why did you move?"

Nick stiffened again. "Well, I guess that's the not-so-great part," he said. "My mom was working at the lab in Brookhaven when she started having respiratory issues. She went to the doctor, and after a whole bunch of tests to try to determine a diagnosis, they believed her lungs had been damaged by exposure from working in the lab. Brookhaven kind of freaked out, insisting her exposure wasn't from their lab and must have come from her time in the lab in Kremlyov—which, who knows, maybe it did. Either way, the whole thing made my mom a pariah to them. They gave her severance, sent her packing, distanced themselves from her. So my mom was faced with starting over, with lungs that were starting to fail her, and trying to keep up with health insurance premiums that the lab was no longer covering."

He paused. Sawyer could see his clenched jaw in profile. He took a breath.

"Anyway, I think there was a time there when my mom's personal American Dream turned into a nightmare."

Sawyer was quiet, taking this all in. The pieces of Nick she'd been steadily gathering were all falling into place now. The reasons he'd worked so hard to get into an Ivy League school and attend on scholarship. The reason he worked in advertising even though he seemed to disdain it a little. The reason he held down a nine-to-five despite the fact that he was a talented musician. The reason he lived in a walk-up in Alphabet City with a bathtub in the kitchen, instead of blowing a bunch of rent on a doorman building in order to keep up with his colleagues at work.

"It was weird," Nick mused now. "Because it kind of happened in reverse order. Growing up, I felt like I was an all-American kid . . . then, at thirteen, I was suddenly very aware of the fact that I was the son of an immigrant, and what that meant."

"I'm sorry," Sawyer said.

Nick's jaw clenched again and he shook his head. "Don't be," he insisted. "I'm not. It was one of the most important lessons life has ever taught me."

Sawyer fell quiet, respectfully contemplating his words. Nick continued to navigate the Belt Parkway, upshifting and downshifting as the traffic lurched forward, stop-and-go-style. Finally, the Verrazzano Bridge came into view, the flow started to pick back up, and they began cruising slowly but steadily along.

The sun had begun to set in the west, and the sunset was putting on yet another spectacular summer show. Driving along the water's edge, with the brilliant colors dancing in the sky, was surreal and unexpectedly beautiful.

"Wow. It's like we're literally driving off into the sunset," Sawyer joked.

She expected Nick to laugh, but he glanced at her with a mixed expression she couldn't quite read, then turned his eyes back to the road.

An awkward moment passed.

Sawyer cleared her throat.

"When did you break up with Kendra?"

"That night at the club."

"Oh."

"I'd wanted to talk to her in private sooner than that," Nick said. "But I never was able to get her alone."

"And then she invited Charles and me out to sushi and to hear you play."

"Yes."

Sawyer fell quiet again, thinking. She still wasn't sure whose attention Kendra had wanted most that night, Nick's or Charles's. She found her brain turning its focus in an unexpected direction.

"So, I guess now that you're single again, the girls at the club will be happy."

Nick looked at her. He didn't deny it.

"How will you vet them?" Sawyer teased. "By applying more of your 'math'? Only, with an extra emphasis on hotness?"

"C'mon," Nick said. "I'm not that bad."

"Yeah, but something tells me you're not that good, either."

Sawyer laughed, but again, Nick refrained.

He was quiet for a long moment.

"I think I've made it pretty clear what I want, Sawyer," he said finally, in a low, steady voice.

Sawyer felt a jolt go through her, shocked. She wanted to say something in return, but found herself tongue-tied.

"But I've said it before . . . I know your situation is far more complicated than mine," Nick said.

They fell back into silence. When he went to shift gears, his hand grazed the side of her leg. It didn't seem purposeful, but . . . Sawyer felt her heart pounding again, an excruciating battering beat under her ribs, the whooshing of her pulse filling her ears. The car had grown warm and muggy, despite the air-conditioning. The sunroof was adding a kind of greenhouse effect, and their intense conversation had somehow only magnified it further.

Nick seemed to read Sawyer's thoughts.

"Here," he said, pressing a button to open the sunroof, then another to drop the windows.

A rush of fresh air instantly filled the car. Sawyer's long dark hair—still damp from the shower—began to blow and twirl in the wind.

They continued to drive, passing the Verrazzano and winding along the Belt Parkway as it turned parallel to the setting sun. Sawyer was reminded of the sunset they'd witnessed on the Staten Island Ferry—also a crazy riot of blazing orange and vibrant purples. Then they reached the tunnel and dipped underground . . . eventually popping up again near Battery Park and making their way over to the West Side Highway.

• • •

When they drew closer to Sawyer's neighborhood, she gave Nick lefts and rights to get them to her Upper West Side walk-up.

It was a relatively quiet street, sandwiched between two otherwise busy avenues. Nick was able to pull over in front of Sawyer's building and idle. The proximity to her apartment had a strange effect on her; she dreaded leaving Nick, but being so close to her own home—the home she shared with Charles—made her feel peculiar and jumpy.

Nick seemed to read this in her body language.

"Earlier, on the pier, you said you wanted me to do what I wanted with my summer Fridays," he said. "But the same goes for you, Sawyer—you should do what *you* want . . . with your summer Fridays, and with your life."

Sawyer was quiet.

"That's just my opinion," Nick said.

Sawyer nodded.

She lingered.

"I should go find a place to put the car for the night," Nick said.

"Oh. Of course. OK," Sawyer said in a rush, awkward. "Well, thank you for today. And tell your mom thanks, too."

"My pleasure. And I will."

Sawyer reached for the door handle and hopped out quickly, almost as if the seat had burned her. She swung the door shut, waved, and ran up the steps of her apartment building's stoop.

Nick waited until she had gotten the door open, then drove away.

• • •

The TV was on and Charles was sitting on the couch when Sawyer keyed into the front door. Sawyer froze, surprised. It wasn't quite nine o'clock. She hadn't expected Charles to beat her home.

Actually, she hadn't expected anything either way, really—the truth was, she hadn't thought about Charles the entire day.

"Hey," he said now, aiming the remote with a raised arm to mute the TV and turning toward her. "Where were you?"

His tone was friendly enough. More curious than accusatory.

Sawyer didn't answer right away. She dropped her keys in the dish on the little hall table and started slipping off her shoes. What could she possibly say?

"Did your coworker—what's her name? Kelsey? Kaitlin?—want to hang out again?"

Sawyer opened her mouth to reply . . . but then realized: she didn't want to lie.

"Kaylee," she corrected Charles. "But no—she didn't ask me to hang out."

"Oh. Who were you hanging out with?"

Suddenly, Sawyer felt overcome by a surge of guilt. But as swiftly as the guilt came rushing in, it transformed into something else. She was suddenly irritable and angry.

"Most nights, you come home later than this," she pointed out, "and I don't drill you about where you were or who you were with."

Charles blinked, looking utterly stupefied by the combative turn the conversation had taken.

"I've been working long hours because of this case. You know that."

Sawyer stared at him, critical. He seemed so earnest. She sighed.

"We haven't even talked about Chicago," she pointed out.

"What about Chicago?" Charles said, a defensive note creeping into his own voice now.

"Two weeks," Sawyer said.

"Two weeks is not *that* long."

"Two weeks with—"

She was interrupted when the phone rang. Sawyer glared at it in disbelief, still full of outrage.

"It's probably my mom again, with some wedding stuff," Charles said.

Sawyer knew he was right.

"Charles," she said, before he could reach for the phone. "Would we still be getting married if we weren't always saved by the bell?"

He frowned. "What do you mean?"

"Would we still be getting married, if Kathy didn't always interrupt us with nonstop wedding planning . . . and we actually got to *finish* one of our conversations?"

"Of course," Charles insisted. Then he stiffened, as though offended. "What kind of question is that?"

He hurried to grab the phone before the answering machine picked it up.

Sawyer listened to Charles murmuring replies of "That's great" and "Thanks, Mom" and "We appreciate it" into the receiver, as Kathy no doubt delivered more wonderful news about their impending nuptials in October.

20.

TUESDAY, JULY 27

Someone was standing in front of Sawyer's desk, waiting.

She looked up.

"Oh! Erin! Hello," Sawyer stammered, surprised by the sudden appearance of her distinguished visitor. "Were you looking for Johanna?"

Erin smiled. "No. I was looking for you," she said. "I was wondering if you have lunch plans today."

"Uh . . . *me*?" Sawyer's brain spun. "I don't . . . but I usually don't go to lunch until one thirty."

Erin didn't reply right away. Sawyer felt her awkward urge to babble kick in.

"Johanna leaves around noon, Kaylee goes from twelve thirty to one thirty . . . and then I go at one thirty to two thirty . . . and most days I usually just bring a bag lunch to Greenacre Park—do you know it? It's really pretty. Anyway, yeah . . . those are my plans . . . which is to say I have no plans, I guess . . ."

She felt Erin smiling patiently at her.

"I know Greenacre Park," she said, when she finally spoke. "Would it be all right if I joined you today?"

"Oh! Uh—yeah, of course," Sawyer replied. "I, um, sure!"

"Perfect. Let's meet downstairs at one thirty."

"OK! Uh . . . great!"

Sawyer willed her mouth to close before she could launch into another stream of babble.

Erin smiled and turned to go. "See you then!"

Sawyer watched her walk away, flattered, but also dazed and wondering why the hell Erin Michaels would want to take a late lunch hour just to hang out with her.

* * *

When Sawyer got off the elevator and stepped into the lobby a few minutes after one thirty, she found Erin waiting there for her, as promised. Erin held up a bakery bag.

"I don't want to step on the toes of your bag lunch, but since I was at that little French bakery around the corner picking up a to-go sandwich, I thought I'd also pick up a couple of pastries to share—if you're game."

Sawyer grinned. "Who says no to dessert?"

"No one you should ever trust," Erin agreed.

They walked over to Greenacre Park, and found a little table and two chairs not far from the waterfall. By then it was 1:40 p.m., and they had the park mostly to themselves.

"So, is this what you do every day?" Erin asked.

"Pretty much," said Sawyer. "I mean, when the weather's decent."

"But always alone?"

"Well, everyone usually goes earlier . . . But it's not so bad. I actually get a lot of reading done. I've even edited manuscripts here, and I think being in the park is better for concentration than being at home, or at my desk with the phone ringing."

"So, you spend your lunch hour doing work for Johanna?" Erin asked.

"Well—you know. Just the editorial stuff, which is kind of the fun part, anyway—right?"

Erin nodded. "Yes. Definitely." She paused, then added, "I heard you pulled Preeti Chaudhari's manuscript out of the slush pile."

Sawyer tried and failed to suppress a proud grin. She nodded. "I loved that manuscript. I was reading it and just felt like, *Oh my God, I can't believe this is so good*. I'm definitely a believer in the slush pile now."

"Yes," Erin agreed. "But it wasn't Johanna who told me you were the one who discovered it. I heard about that from the other assistants."

"Oh . . ." Sawyer said, disappointed but not surprised. "Well, Johanna is so busy. And anyway, she arranged for the actual deal, introducing Preeti to Celine and whatnot."

"Hmm," Erin said, in a tone that suggested she was unconvinced.

Sawyer wondered where this—the lunch, the conversation, all of it—was going. Erin laid down her sandwich and dabbed at her mouth with a napkin. She cleared her throat.

"Mainly, Sawyer, I wanted to take a minute to chat with you today, and to apologize."

"Apologize?" Sawyer repeated, utterly confounded.

"About bringing up your *Paris Review* poems in the elevator," Erin explained. "I didn't know Johanna harbored such a grudge against having assistants who have writerly aspirations. Again, some of the other assistants tipped me off—but only after I'd congratulated you in the elevator, I'm afraid. I hope I didn't let the cat out of the bag in any way that might affect you negatively."

"Oh . . ." Sawyer said, caught off guard. "That's . . . nice of you. Thank you. I'm sure . . . I'm sure it'll be fine," she stammered.

Erin sighed and resumed eating her sandwich. Between bites, she shyly said, "Well, there's something else—just a general announcement I'll be making soon. It's not about Johanna; it's just about me."

Sawyer sat wide-eyed, waiting.

"I've accepted a position at Knopf. So I'll be moving over to Random House at the end of the month."

"Oh . . . oh . . . oh!" Sawyer stammered. "Wow. Um, congratulations, I mean!"

"Thank you."

"But you'll be missed! You started building such a great list of authors, and in such a short time!"

"Well, that's kind of you to say, Sawyer."

"It's so true!" Sawyer insisted. "I know we haven't socialized much, but I've been following your list; you're my inspiration."

Sawyer halted, realizing that as *Johanna's* assistant, she was probably expected to look up to Johanna most of all, not Erin.

Erin smiled kindly.

"I'll be sad to say goodbye to everyone, but I'm also excited about the move. And part of what I wanted to say to you today is that my door will always be open to you, Sawyer. It's a shame Johanna doesn't like writers, because I believe the two pursuits lend themselves to each other. I think you're going to make an exceptional editor someday."

Sawyer was genuinely touched. And surprised. It was the kind of encouragement Sawyer had been starving to hear from Johanna.

"Now," Erin said, as though getting down to business. "Sandwiches are gone. Carrot sticks are gone. Apple slices are gone. I'd say we've done a very dutiful job of it." She paused and smiled. "Time for some dessert?"

Sawyer watched as Erin reached into the bag she'd brought and produced two of the most perfect French pastries Sawyer had ever seen. One was some kind of hazelnut chocolate ganache, and the other was lemon and red currant. Erin produced two plastic forks and two plastic knives and set about slicing each of the pastries in half.

"Cheers," Erin said, tapping plastic forks with Sawyer and grinning.

"Cheers," Sawyer agreed.

They each took a bite of the first one. Then, each took a bite of the second one.

Sawyer made a face, allowing her eyes to roll back in her head.

"OK," she joked. "Official verdict: great taste in books and authors . . . *and* in French pastries!"

Erin laughed, and together they gobbled the rest of the sugary delicacies down, chatting, chewing, happy.

• • •

When Sawyer got home that evening, she went immediately to the computer and logged on, before even bothering to step out of her shoes.

Adventures_of_Tom: Hey. You there?

Sawyer waited a minute, and took the time to kick off her shoes and wiggle out of her skirt and blouse, then poured herself a glass of ice water and gulped it down. Finally, her computer pinged.

Nikolai70: Hey

Adventures_of_Tom: Good! You're online

Nikolai70: Indeed I am

Adventures_of_Tom: Are you busy?

Nikolai70: Nah. I've just been sitting around waiting for this gorgeous brunette weirdo with a nerdy literary name to reach out and contact me

Adventures_of_Tom: What are the odds? I just so happen to be a brunette weirdo with a nerdy literary name

Nikolai70: You don't say . . . but it doesn't go unnoticed how you edited out the gorgeous part. Learn to take a compliment.

Adventures_of_Tom: I'm actually writing to give YOU a compliment

Nikolai70: I'm listening

Adventures_of_Tom: Well, I think it's a compliment—basically, I'm writing to tell you that you were right about something.

Nikolai70: What was I right about? (Not that I doubt my correctness on said matter)

Adventures_of_Tom: That editor—the one I told you about from the elevator, who said the nice things about my poems being published in The Paris Review

Nikolai70: What about her?

Adventures_of_Tom: We ate lunch together today. She's moving to Knopf. She said her door was "always open to me"

Nikolai70: See? What are you waiting for. Go work for her

Adventures_of_Tom: Well, it's not THAT simple. But . . . yeah . . . I think you were onto something

Nikolai70: Of course I was. I know everything

Sawyer snorted and rolled her eyes, but smiled. She paused to take a long sip of the ice water. It had been a sweaty subway ride, and she'd practically bolted up the stairs of her apartment building. Now she was finally starting to cool down. She could feel the beads of sweat on her skin slowly transforming to a light film of salt.

Adventures_of_Tom: Hot today. Makes me miss swimming

Nikolai70: Me too

Adventures_of_Tom: According to your mom—you always miss it

Nikolai70: Well. If it ain't broke . . .

Adventures_of_Tom: Anyway, thanks again for a fun day

Nikolai70: I meant it when I said my pleasure

Sawyer paused again, flattered.

But after a minute . . . she became aware of the instant effect a single flattering word from Nick had on her. A flicker of self-consciousness crept in.

She hadn't really asked him, point-blank, *why* he'd broken up with Kendra.

She had a flash of Nick at the Yale Club, praising Kendra for being "uncomplicated"—and that was basically code for sex without strings, wasn't it?

She had a flash of the girls at the club, flipping their hair, trying to catch Nick's eye. Sawyer knew well enough to know those girls had been around before Kendra and were fated to be around long after.

What exactly did he *do* on all those days between their Fridays together?

She felt an inkling of paranoia creep in that she was being naive to think Nick honestly cared about their time together as much as she did.

She drained the rest of the ice water in her glass and went to the fridge. This time, she poured herself a glass of wine, and cut it with seltzer to make a homemade wine spritzer. She sat back down in front of the computer.

Adventures_of_Tom: Am I really the first girl you've brought to your mom's house, like your mom said?

Nikolai70: My mom said so, didn't she?

Adventures_of_Tom: Yeah, but that's like, hyperbole. Right? It can't be totally true

Adventures_of_Tom: Can it?

Nikolai70: What are you getting at, Sawyer?

Adventures_of_Tom: It just seems like you've probably had a lot of female friends

Sawyer waited, but Nick did not reply. She took another sip and continued typing.

Adventures_of_Tom: What about the girl you lived with—the one you almost proposed to? Didn't you bring her to your mom's house?

Nikolai70: No.

Adventures_of_Tom: You didn't? Why not?

Nikolai70: NO. Stop.

Adventures_of_Tom: Stop what?

Nikolai70: I don't want to answer all these questions over the internet like this.

Nikolai70: To be honest, I really hate messaging with you

Sawyer blinked, surprised.

Adventures_of_Tom: You hate messaging with me?

Nikolai70: Yes

Adventures_of_Tom: Nick . . . I love logging on, finding you online, and trading messages.

Nikolai70: Of course you like it. You're a writer. But for me, it's tiring. I do it because it's all I've got. Until Fridays, when I get to actually see you.

Sawyer didn't reply right away. She knew she was probably missing the point, but she was hung up on the fact that she'd grown to *love* talking to him online, and he . . . "hated" it?

Nikolai70: Look, all I'm saying is that if you're going to ask me these kinds of questions, this is a conversation we should have on the phone at least.

Nikolai70: Send me your phone number. I'll call you.

Sawyer put her hands over the keyboard again, intending to type her phone number. But she surprised herself when she paused, full of a new and unfamiliar hesitation.

Nikolai70: Sawyer? You there?

Nikolai70: Send your number, or you can call mine—212-555-0374.

Again, Sawyer hesitated. She could feel Nick waiting for her, but for some reason she was paralyzed.

After a long pause, the screen blinked with a new message from Nick.

Nikolai70: OK. It's fine. Forget it.

Adventures_of_Tom: Nick—wait. I'm just thinking.

Nikolai70: I know. I think I understand what's going on here.

Adventures_of_Tom: What

Nikolai70: You don't want us to start talking on the phone, because you're worried I might call when he's around.

Charles. Nick meant Charles.

And he wasn't wrong.

As soon as Nick had brought up talking on the phone, Sawyer's mind had gone straight back to the night she'd come home from Coney Island.

The night she hadn't been able to answer Charles's question: *Where were you?*

Something about Nick's offer to talk on the phone had scared her.

The screen blinked with another new message.

Nikolai70: I'm right. I know I'm right.

Adventures_of_Tom: Nick—hang on

Nikolai70: It's fine, Sawyer.

Nikolai70: But I've gotta go. This is taking it out of me.

Adventures_of_Tom: Wait—you're logging off?

Nikolai70: Yes. I'm tired

Adventures_of_Tom: Wait

Nikolai70: Sorry. I'll catch you later.

AOL User Nikolai70 has gone offline

Sawyer stared at the screen—this time in utter dismay. It felt like Nick had just slammed a door in her face.

She couldn't decide if she was mad, sad, or sorry.

She logged off, and sat and thought things over for a very long time—long enough for the summer sunlight to dim in the windows, and dusk to fall.

Finally, once she had made up her mind, she returned to sit in front of the computer and logged back in again.

She did not open AOL Instant Messenger.

Instead, she checked the weather forecast. Unfortunately, a big rainstorm was predicted for Friday. Almost everything on the list she'd sent to Nick revolved around doing something outdoors.

She'd have to come up with something else. Sitting on the computer desk was an old copy of *New York* magazine. Sawyer picked it up and idly flipped through a few glossy pages . . . until something caught her eye. She folded the magazine covers together, and read closely about the little-known historical spot in the city that was becoming newly trendy.

She came up with a plan, and clicked to open a new email draft.

To: Nikolai70@aol.com
From: Adventures_of_Tom@aol.com

Dear Nick—

You're right. I was weird about getting on the phone. I'm sorry.

I'd like to apologize in person.

I'm inviting you to meet me this Friday, at 1:30pm, by the clock in the main hall inside Grand Central. And if you can, dress up just a little—no jeans.

Forgive the email invite—you're under no obligation to write back. (I know you said you find this mode of communication tiring. Personally, I've never enjoyed checking my inbox so much as I have since I've met you, but I get it, I hear what you're saying.)

And if you don't show up, I guess that's a kind of reply, too, and I'll understand.

Still hoping I'll see you, though—

Sawyer

Sawyer looked the email over, reread it twice, and clicked send. It was her turn to plan a Friday.

21.

FRIDAY, JULY 30

When Sawyer woke up on Friday morning, it wasn't raining, but clouds sat thick and heavy over the sky, like a dark gray lid.

The weather stayed that way all day, giving the workday a strange, hourless feeling. Morning and noon looked the same, according to the gloom of the window. The only real mark of time came when Johanna finally left the office for the day.

Sawyer and Kaylee turned to each other and smiled, then promptly packed up. Sawyer went down the hall to the ladies' room and spruced up her hair and makeup. When she emerged, Kaylee was waiting by the elevator.

"Whoa." Kaylee whistled. "I noticed you were kind of dressed up today—hot date?"

Sawyer blushed. "Nah. Just meeting up with a friend."

"I'm only teasing." Kaylee winked. "Although, dressed like that, your fiancé *should* take you out, before some tall, mysterious stranger comes along and sweeps you off your feet!"

Sawyer flinched and stared.

"Did I say something wrong?" Kaylee asked, innocent.

"No, no—you're fine."

* * *

The clock in Grand Central's main hall turned out to be a less ideal meeting point than Sawyer had hoped.

It was, in essence, a clock sitting atop an information booth. Sawyer had never used the information booth before, so she'd never really noticed its function. She noticed now, however, as she tried to figure out how to stand near it and not be in the way of New Yorkers doing their thing.

And it wasn't so much the information booth as it was the sheer volume of people who crisscrossed the Main Concourse. It felt like the entire world was streaming toward her, and veering away, which was unnerving. The clouds had held steady and rainless during her walk to Grand Central, but just as she'd stepped inside, lightning flashed and a crack of thunder sounded. It was almost like a tarp that had been holding too much water finally ripped open. The sky unleashed a downpour so prodigious, Sawyer could actually hear it as she continued farther inside the busy train station. Even now, as she stood waiting by the clock, she could see raindrops spattering against the gray panes of the three giant gilded windows, streaming down in little rivers. As large and cavernous as it was, the hall began to fill up with humidity and the scent of wet leather as people tracked in watery footprints from the pavement outside.

She glanced at the clock—an ornate golden globe from 1913, with four glowing faces. According to the clock, it was a few minutes after one thirty.

She fidgeted. She was wearing a very slim dark navy sheath dress. It was a dress she'd only worn once or twice before, but she'd always felt good in it; it was one of her dresses that seemed to invite Audrey Hepburn comparisons. In the bathroom at work, she'd slyly converted it from office wear to something a bit more suited to going out, subtracting her cardigan, putting her hair up, and adding earrings and heels.

But now she just felt overdressed and silly.

She wondered, briefly, if Nick might not come after all.

The way he'd logged off during their last chat was more or less like he'd hung up on her. And given that she was the one who'd refused to get on the phone after firing off a bunch of personal questions about his love life . . . she didn't blame him for being fed up.

She stood and waited, scanning the faces coming toward her, inexplicably nervous to see the one face she was hoping to see. The hall echoed with hurried footsteps, the hard heels of shoes like stones clacking together in a riverbed. She took a deep breath, and looked up to admire the ceiling. The ceiling was one of her favorite parts of Grand Central. It was painted a turquoise-ish Tiffany blue and embellished with golden constellations, the stars gathered into whimsical illustrations of Orion, Taurus, Pegasus—as on a vintage celestial map. Sawyer rarely had a chance to stop and simply look up; New York had instilled a kind of peer pressure in her to always avoid looking like a tourist. But now she tipped her head back and stared, gazing at the stars.

And then, after gazing upward for a few minutes, when she looked down again . . . there he was: *Nick*.

Her throat tightened instantly to see him. He was headed straight toward her across the echoing marble hall, shaking an umbrella and tying it shut. For a moment, Sawyer was overcome by how attractive she found him; it was as if she had forgotten the handsome lines of his face and was now suddenly reminded. He wore a nice suit, and it even looked like he'd gotten a haircut since she'd seen him last.

She couldn't read his expression, but at least she knew one thing: he hadn't stood her up.

He stopped short in front of Sawyer. "Well, well. You clean up nice." His tone was gruff, almost begrudging, but in a way that suggested he felt true admiration.

Sawyer blushed. "I was starting to doubt that you were going to come."

"You should know better by now."

She smiled but he remained stoic. She glanced down at her feet.

"Listen," Sawyer said, "I'm really sorry about—"

"It's OK." Nick waved a hand to stop her. "I get it."

He paused, and shrugged.

"The way we met in the first place," he said. "You know, the reason we started communicating to begin with . . ."

He meant Charles and Kendra.

". . . makes things pretty awkward." He paused and shrugged. "That's not your fault, Sawyer," he finished.

Sawyer mulled this and nodded. "I'm still sorry."

"Don't be sorry. But cut me some slack, too," Nick said. He took a breath, then looked at her with a steady, unflinching gaze. "Trading online messages with you frustrates me because I would prefer to talk to you face-to-face. I hate it because I want *more* of you, Sawyer—not less."

Sawyer felt her blood rushing to her face. Her ears were instantly hot.

Nick read her reaction. He took the pressure off by changing the subject.

"So! What are we here to do today?" he asked. "I know your summer Friday bucket list by heart, and 'get dressed up and stand around in the middle of Grand Central' was never on it."

Sawyer composed herself and nodded. "It wasn't. But I was thinking, because of the rain . . . have you been to the Campbell Apartment?"

"Ah," Nick said in a revelatory way. "I've heard about that place, but I haven't been."

Sawyer smiled. According to the *New York* magazine article, the Campbell Apartment was a "secret" apartment inside Grand Central, originally owned by railroad financier John W. Campbell back in the 1920s. Campbell hadn't really lived in the apartment, per se; he'd wanted a stately office that was centrally located smack-dab in the middle of it all, and a place for him and his wife to entertain guests. The space had fallen into disrepair in the 1950s . . . until recently, when the novelty apartment had been turned into a bar.

"It's tucked in somewhere here in the station, right?"

"Yes," she replied. She pulled out a handwritten note with info she'd copied out of the magazine. "Supposedly if we go down the corridor in the southwest wing, we should find a little elevator there with a plaque next to it that says 'The Campbell Apartment.'"

"What are we waiting for?"

* * *

After a short walk through the terminal halls, they found the elevator. It was a somewhat old-fashioned one, with art deco touches and a three-paneled door that looked a little like windowpanes.

"After you," Nick said, and Sawyer stepped inside.

Once off the elevator, they saw another plaque for the Campbell Apartment, and a carpeted staircase bathed in a rose-colored spotlight. Sawyer's heels wobbled on the carpet as they made their way up the stairs.

Despite the photograph Sawyer had glimpsed in the magazine, nothing could have prepared her for the unusual bar at the top of the stairs. It was like a medieval great hall, with gothic arched windows, stone walls, and a heavy, ornately painted, dark-wood-beamed ceiling. As they walked in, Sawyer realized the wood-paneled wall behind them had a small balcony level above it, built in a fashion that reminded her of a choir loft in a Gothic church. On the opposite wall was a massive fireplace with a giant stone hood, modeled in the fashion of a French château. The bar ran along the right side of the room, and behind it was a spectacular multipaned window of leaded glass.

"Wow," Sawyer uttered. "God, my parents would *love* this."

"The professors?" Nick smirked and nodded. "I'll bet."

A beautiful, sophisticated-looking hostess approached them, and asked them in an incongruently childish voice whether they were looking for a table or the bar. They opted for the bar and perched on a pair of high stools with curved backs.

"Do you think they know how to make a Sea Breeze in this joint?" Nick joked.

"We can find out," Sawyer suggested.

"Nah—pretty sure it wouldn't hold a candle to Vic's."

Sawyer smiled. "Yes. Vic's are probably the best in the city. And then Jake's surely take the prize for runner-up—seeing as how they come in a giant pint glass and all."

"Jake? Oh! Blake. At the club," Nick said.

Well, now she knew. "It was loud in there," Sawyer said, and they both laughed.

By then the bartender had approached them and was ready to take their order.

Sawyer gestured in Nick's direction.

"Anything the gentleman wants," she said. "My treat."

Nick raised his eyebrows, amused, but shook his head. "It's more fun when you choose," he insisted.

Sawyer thought for a few seconds, then turned to the bartender.

"Champagne?" she said. "And maybe—if you have them—in Gatsby glasses?"

The bartender gave her a wry smile. "'Gatsby glasses'?" he repeated.

"Those glasses that are wide but shallow," Sawyer explained, feeling stupider by the minute.

"A coupe," the bartender diagnosed. "But I like 'Gatsby glass' better—that's what I'll call it from now on, old sport." He winked, then turned to pour the drinks.

She couldn't tell if the bartender was making fun of her or flirting with her. She surreptitiously put the back of her left hand to her cheeks, one at a time, feeling each one for warmth and imagining how red her face must be.

Nick smirked. "Do you have to charm *everyone* we meet?" he teased.

"Hardly."

"Gimme a break," Nick said. "*Old sport.*"

He rolled his eyes, and Sawyer laughed.

"But hey—if it winds up getting us free drinks, I won't complain," he concluded.

The bartender returned with two coupes of chilled champagne. "Cheers," he said, with another wink at Sawyer.

Nick raised his glass once the bartender had gone. "To Jay."

"Jay?" Sawyer echoed, quizzically.

"Gatsby, of course."

"Oh—hah."

"I should be making fun of you for naming a goldfish 'Moby' and a champagne glass 'Gatsby.'"

"And you're . . . *not*?" Sawyer challenged.

"No," Nick said. "Actually, I'm . . . I don't know. Enjoying the details that make you, you."

He held his glass out for Sawyer to clink, and gazed at her with that unnervingly intense stare. Suddenly, Sawyer was jittery, self-conscious, overtaken by nerves. She moved to clink his glass with her own but her hand was trembling, and the wide brim of the "Gatsby glass" betrayed her. Before she knew it, she'd accidentally spilled a good quarter of her glass right over Nick's lap.

With instant, catlike reflexes, Nick jumped off the stool, setting down his own glass.

"*Hoooo boy!*" he quietly exclaimed. "Refreshingly cold, but not in the most refreshing spot . . ." he joked.

Sawyer, meanwhile, scrabbled for bar napkins, mortified. She handed them to Nick, who blotted his suit pants as they laughed. Her hands continued to tremble; she tried to hide them.

"I'm sorry. You . . . make me nervous."

Nick looked at her. "*I* make *you* nervous?"

Sawyer cast her eyes down, unable to return his gaze. She focused all her energy on trying to rein in the trembling she could still feel in her stomach, her hands, her eyelids. "Yeah," she insisted. "You know that. It's pretty obvious. I . . . get nervous when I'm around you."

When she looked up again, Nick was quiet, but there was an expression on his face she couldn't quite read—it was like a mixture of sympathy and delight and satisfaction all at once. On some instinctive level, she understood she'd just given him something, and now he was taking a brief moment to savor it.

"You're *enjoying* this," she said, narrowing her eyes at him and calling him out.

Nick shrugged. He sat back down. "It's nice to know I have an effect," he said.

Sawyer rolled her eyes. "I'm sure you have 'an effect' on lots of girls."

"We're back to that again?" Nick challenged her.

"Well, it's true."

Nick looked her full in the face. "It's nice to know I have an effect on *you*," he repeated firmly.

Sawyer blushed again.

She looked down at her glass and took a sip. The bubbles tickled her nose, and the champagne greeted her tongue with a peppery dance, crisp and dry as a green apple.

Nick fell quiet, mulling something.

"Champagne coupe for your thoughts?" Sawyer teased.

Nick snapped out of his reverie. He cleared his throat.

"It's just that . . . I can tell you don't believe me when I say things like that."

Sawyer attempted to pass the insecurity off with a casual, jokey air. "I don't know . . . I heard a rumor that good-looking musicians get laid."

He looked at her.

"No?"

He shrugged. "It's been known to happen, I guess."

"I just have to remind myself that other people don't take things as seriously as I do. You probably say these things to a lot of girls."

"I *don't* say 'these things' to a lot of girls," he retorted in a low voice.

"I'm not trying to offend you."

"I'd hate to see you *trying*."

Sawyer tried to put it into words a little better. "You said what you liked about Kendra was that she was uncomplicated. I'm . . . not."

"I *did* like Kendra because she was uncomplicated," he admitted.

He paused.

"But with you . . ." Nick continued. "I'm different with you. It's like everything is backward."

Her heart fluttered. Sawyer glanced up from her drink. They locked eyes.

"With you, I'm putting it all out on the table," Nick said. "And the ironic part is, I can tell you don't believe me."

He stared at her, unabashed, his eyes hungry. She felt the heat rise in her cheeks again.

"It's a way for you to deflect," Nick concluded.

"Deflect from what?" she asked.

"Having to acknowledge what I want, and telling me what *you* want."

Sawyer stared back at him. *Was* he saying what she thought he was saying? Her heart was pounding; she could feel her pulse in her neck, and her throat was tight again.

But before Sawyer could speak, the bartender approached them, carrying a bottle of champagne.

"Thought I'd top up your Gatsby glasses."

He refilled their coupes and winked at Sawyer again.

"On the house," the bartender said, and turned to go again.

Nick eased the moment with a grin.

"See?" he said. "I told you—as long as it winds up getting us free drinks."

Sawyer pretended to shoot him the stink eye. They broke up into a mutual chuckle.

"How is your mother?" Sawyer ventured.

Nick gazed at her, then gave a gentle smile.

"She's good," he said. "She really liked you. I could tell." He paused, then added, "Which means, of course: now I'm going to have to put up with her asking questions about you every time I visit."

Sawyer smiled. "I liked her, too."

Nick's expression turned serious. "You really are the first girl I've ever brought there, to her house," he said. "And it's not because my mom wouldn't welcome them; it's me. Girlfriends—even friends, sometimes—I don't let a lot of people in."

Again, that intense gaze. Sawyer flashed back to the kiss in the courtyard of the club. She was overcome with a surge of wanting that terrified her, and that she was afraid to let him see. She tried to come up with something to say, and felt her brain and mouth wrestling between saying too much and saying too little.

Nick noticed her squirming.

"What's the latest with your work stuff?" he asked, changing the subject.

Sawyer told him.

They talked it over and ordered another glass, and talked some more.

"What's next?" Nick asked, once they'd closed out their tab. "You got anything else planned?"

Sawyer smiled, feeling the effects of the champagne. She felt light as a feather, and "floaty," as she liked to call it. Her fingertips tingled in a pleasant way.

"Well . . ." she said. "I mean, I don't know how impressive it is, but . . . there *is* something else, right here in Grand Central. I read about it once, but I've never checked it out."

"All right. Lead the way."

• • •

Nick followed Sawyer as they left the Campbell Apartment, retraced their steps down to the Main Concourse, and then went farther down, to the lower level.

Finally, she stopped in the brick-and-marble Romanesque archways just outside Grand Central's old Oyster Bar. She turned.

"We're here," she said with a grin.

"The Oyster Bar?"

"No. *Here.* Right here."

"What's right here?" Nick asked. He sounded sincere.

"You ever hear of the 'Whispering Gallery'?"

Nick frowned and gave Sawyer a funny look.

"You haven't!" she exclaimed. "Hey—something about New York that I knew first."

"Well, don't gloat," Nick admonished. "Tell me what the deal is already."

Sawyer took a breath. "Maybe I've oversold it here, I don't know," she said, losing confidence. "But this section of the hallway is called the Whispering Gallery. It's supposed to be an acoustical phenomenon. Evidently, if two people stand in opposite corners of this archway and speak into the corners of the arch, they can hear each other loud and clear, as if they're standing right next to each other."

"Ah," Nick said, looking intrigued. He studied the archway, craning his neck to look at the shape. "I guess that makes sense, engineering-wise," he said. He looked back at Sawyer and smiled. "Sounds pretty cool. Shall we try it out?"

Sawyer nodded, and they moved to opposite corners of the archway, diagonally from each other.

"I don't know if it works. We might just wind up looking like two weirdos, talking to the walls!" she called over her shoulder to Nick.

Nick laughed. "You're not a real New Yorker until you've done something really weird in public and not given a shit who sees you," he called back.

"OK, let's try it?" Sawyer called.

He nodded and they each turned to face their corner wall of the archway. In a quiet, low voice, Sawyer said, *"Hey, can you hear me?"* She inched her face in, closer and closer to the wall, and tried again, until finally she heard Nick:

"Yup."

"Oh, good! It works?"

"It works."

"Hmm, OK, then—go ahead," Sawyer whispered.

"Go ahead, what?"

"Tell me a secret."

"A secret . . ." There was a long pause as Nick ruminated. "When we were in Coney Island, I was hoping we'd fall into the water all along," he said. "After you mentioned swimming, that's all I wanted to do."

"That's not a secret!" Sawyer admonished, raising her voice. She dropped it back down low. "Your mom basically said that was your MO."

"OK, then—you tell *me* a secret," Nick challenged in return.

Sawyer bit her lip and thought for a long minute. She knew what she wanted to say, but she didn't know if she had the real courage to say it.

"Fine," she whispered, finally. "I'll tell you the secret of what I want."

She waited again, gathering one final burst of nerve.

"I can't stop thinking about you, Nick. All I want is to kiss you again."

With that, Sawyer froze. She could feel that Nick had already turned away from the corner of the arch and was facing *her*. Very slowly, with her heart pounding in her ears, she turned around to face him in return.

They locked eyes and stared at each other from across the space of the archway. Commuters passed between them, simply going about their business.

As they stared at each other, it felt as though a million unspoken thoughts and emotions were exchanged. Sawyer remained frozen, but her heart was still pounding, her whole body tensed, waiting.

Then, all at once, he began to stride toward her with purpose. She stepped toward him in return. When they reached each other, their bodies instantly intertwined, the surge of desire suddenly erasing the last traces of awkwardness between them. The next thing Sawyer knew, they were kissing, their mouths melding together, the smooth muscles of lips and tongues moving together in a language beyond words, the aftertaste of champagne mingling between them.

A kiss.

A damn good kiss.

New Yorkers—being New Yorkers—walked past them with seldom more than a second look, stepping around the two young people locked in passionate embrace with indifference, and hurrying on to their urgent and infinitely varied destinations.

22.

As Nick turned the key to unlock his apartment door, Sawyer stood behind him in the hall, fidgeting, incredibly nervous. All the confidence and determination she'd felt during their kiss at Grand Central had left her again, evaporating into the humid air as her nerves steadily returned.

After their kiss, Nick had turned incredibly calm. In fact, he'd looked happy. He'd asked if Sawyer was hungry, then suggested they check out Grand Central's market, where they could pick up some things to go. He'd reached for her hand to hold as they strolled through the market hall. She was surprised; she hadn't pictured him being a hand-holder. Or really, a big fan of any of those little mundane, cutesy things that couples did. But there he was, smiling, holding her hand in his.

They'd picked out a few things—an artisanal loaf of *pain de campagne*, a couple of different kinds of cheese, some prosciutto and smoked almonds, a bottle of red wine, two little gourmet pots of tiramisu.

Nick had flagged down a cab, and held the umbrella so Sawyer never got wet. The next thing she knew, the cab was racing down to the East Village and into the Alphabet avenues, the rain crackling on the windows and the wipers flailing wildly to keep up . . . and now they were suddenly here, standing in front of Nick's door.

He pushed the door open and hurried ahead inside to turn on some lights as Sawyer timidly stepped over the threshold. It was still daytime, but the sky was dark and the rain was still coming down in a steady downpour, making it feel like night. As Nick switched on a few lamps, the room instantly took on a cozy ambience. The rain had cooled things down a little, but the air both inside and outside was still warm, humid, thick as soup, with a kind of languid energy about it. Nick opened a couple of windows in an attempt to achieve a little air circulation. The room filled with the scent of rain on trees and brick and concrete.

"Here," Nick said, doubling back and taking the market bags from Sawyer's hands. He gestured for her to come farther inside. "What's wrong?" he asked, reading her face. "You look spooked."

He brought the bags over to the kitchen area and set them down on the butcher block, then waited for her to reply.

Sawyer searched within herself, trying to identify the source of her feeling and put a name to it. It felt different to be in Nick's apartment this time. Things had changed. They'd kissed—twice, now. Their kiss in Grand Central was a hungry kiss, full of desire. In other words, Sawyer was here as something different than just Nick's friend, and she damn well knew it.

"It's just . . . I don't know how this works. I don't know if I'll disappoint you." She paused, struggling to find the right words. "I don't know how to be like anyone but myself."

Nick raised an eyebrow and stared at her for a long minute. "Well," he said. "I guess it's a lucky thing I don't want you to be like anyone but yourself."

He crossed the room. She thought he was going to kiss her again, but he took her hands and led her over to the sofa, then took off her wet shoes and put them back by the door. Her heart sped up and she'd been a little scared when she'd thought he was coming to kiss her, yet she found she was disappointed when he didn't.

"Look," Nick said, returning to the kitchen area and unpacking the things they'd picked up at the market. "I don't know how 'it works' any more than you do."

"But . . ." Sawyer struggled. "You've done this a million times—" she started to say, then stopped.

Nick looked at her. "No. I haven't," he said, deadly serious. "This is something new."

Sawyer blinked at him, and they did that thing that was fast becoming commonplace between them—exchanging words with their eyes. Finally, Nick finished pulling out the cork in the bottle of wine and poured two glasses.

"Can you put a little faith in that?" Nick asked.

"Yes," Sawyer answered. "I can."

"OK. Good," Nick said. "Now, if sitting still and relaxing isn't your thing, you can always come help me." He picked up one of the two wineglasses and held it out, a gesture for her to come take it. Sawyer got up and came over beside him at the butcher block.

"You can either cut the bread or the cheese."

Sawyer fought the urge to laugh but wound up snorting.

"Did you . . . just . . . ask me . . . *if I wanted to cut the cheese*?" she said, still chortling.

Nick smirked and shook his head in amusement.

She unwrapped the bread, and he handed her a long, flat bread knife.

"Yeah. That's how we single-guy musicians do it," Nick said sarcastically. "Bring the ladies home, pour them a little wine, and ask them if they'd like to cut the cheese . . ."

They laughed. The tension relaxed. They stood side by side, busy preparing the food. Nick nudged her with his body, then bent over to give her a small kiss on the side of her cheek by her ear. Again, she was surprised at the tenderness of the gesture, just as she had been by the way he'd held her hand back at the market.

Together, they assembled a nice little makeshift cheeseboard. Nick carried it to the coffee table, along with the tiramisu and some spoons. Sawyer followed, carrying their wine. He put a record on the record player, and the Monkees started singing "I'm a Believer" in cheerful, easygoing voices. They sat cross-legged on the floor and started picking at the food.

"I used to watch reruns of the Monkees' TV show as a kid," Sawyer confessed. "My mom said I was weirdly into it. It came on around dinnertime and she had to peel me away from it." She paused, then added, "For the life of me, I can't remember the plot of a single episode now."

Nick laughed. "Did they have plots, really?"

Sawyer nodded. "I think the Monkees usually helped people. They were like goofy benevolent superheroes, but without any actual powers that went beyond being goofy and making music."

"When you put it like that, that's shockingly relatable," Nick joked.

Sawyer rolled her eyes at him.

"Although, I probably lean more toward Machiavellian than benevolent," Nick qualified, roguish.

"Hah. You can't fool me, Nick," Sawyer replied. "I've already gotten a peek behind the curtain."

"Oh yeah?"

"Yup. Packing a picnic for the ferry ride, always giving up your seat on the train, the way you look out for your mom . . ." Sawyer started to rattle off the list. "I hate to give you the bad news, Nick, but sometimes, you can be downright *thoughtful*."

He laughed and shook his head as though Sawyer's accusation was foundationless—but she could see: he was glowing again, secretly happy that Sawyer knew him well enough to call him out as a good guy.

Nick had stacked several records on the record player, and it had an automatic changer. They continued to talk and laugh as the player cycled through all kinds of great old classics—Frankie Valli and the Four Seasons singing "Can't Take My Eyes Off You," Etta James singing "At Last," the Shirelles singing "Will You Love Me Tomorrow."

After a while, they stopped snacking and moved up to the couch, still talking, occasionally reaching for their glasses and taking a sip of wine.

"This music . . ." Sawyer shook her head, commenting on the selections as the next record dropped onto the turntable and Elvis started singing "Can't Help Falling in Love."

"What about it?"

"Well . . . let's just say, I can't believe you had the nerve to call my summer Friday bucket list *corny*."

"I never said I didn't *like* corny," Nick countered. "You stormed out of that online chat before I got to say I actually liked the list, and that I wanted very badly to do everything on it with you." He paused and looked at her. "You tend to do that."

"Do what?"

"Avoid the part where people tell you all the things they like . . . especially the part where people tell you all the things they like about *you*."

The familiar heat returned to Sawyer's face. They were sitting close together at two angles on the couch, their knees almost touching. She was so completely aware of her body, and aware of an aching within it.

Nick seemed to be experiencing something similar. His eyes ran over her face and his mouth twitched, almost as if in annoyance. "Sawyer—you drive me nuts."

"That doesn't sound like something to like," she joked.

He shook his head.

"It's not a question of 'liking' it. It's more than that." Nick moved toward her with an expression of determination. "It turns out I'm addicted to the way that *you* in particular drive me nuts," he said.

In the next instant, Nick was kissing her, and she was kissing him back. His body moved as though to encircle her, and her own body responded by twisting closer. Somehow they slid seamlessly from sitting to horizontal. She wanted to be beneath him and on top of him at the same time; they moved so fluidly together it was oddly like swimming. They drank each other in; deep, passionate kisses, and then coming up for air.

Nick took her over to the bed, then slowed things down. He continued to kiss her, but more slowly. They began peeling items of clothing off of each other. Sawyer felt like she must be high; she was absolutely enthralled by every detail of his body, by the feel of touching him, by the scent of his skin. Even more than that, she could feel him taking in every detail of her body with a kind of reverence. She felt worshipped—*carefully worshipped*—and the sensation had a disorienting, dizzying effect.

As they grew increasingly naked, she felt an inkling of self-consciousness creep in, the noise of feedback, of the outside world. Her brain asked her if she was really ready to commit to what they were about to do.

But then, to her surprise, Nick slowed things down even more, and stopped. They were down to their underwear. Sawyer felt a brief moment of relief for the pause . . . followed by a terrible panic that something had gone wrong, or that she had disappointed him in some way.

"You . . . you stopped."

"We don't have to rush," Nick said.

They were lying on top of his bed. Sawyer was aware of her naked body, dressed now in only a very small pair of underpants, her dress in a crumpled ball on the floor, along with her bra. And aware of Nick, too, down to only his boxers. His skin and her skin still together, touching, warm and clammy at the same time.

"I just . . . sort of figured . . . that . . ."

"What?" Nick asked.

"That when you bring girls home, it's for a purpose."

A slight flicker of irritation passed over Nick's face.

"You gotta stop with that. This is our own thing . . . something that's just ours."

Sawyer was surprised by the sentiment, and the vehemence behind it. She wondered if what he suggested was even possible. She opened her mouth to speak, but then closed it.

She snuggled in closer to Nick, aware of her naked breasts pressing up against him, aware of the thin fabric of her underwear, aware of their cooling skin growing sticky. She felt her ear seal to Nick's chest and she lay still a moment to listen, hearing his heartbeat as clearly as though she had a stethoscope. His heart was a drum, fierce and stubborn.

* * *

They passed a couple of hours like that, making out like a couple of horny teenagers, then slowing things down and resting, then doing it all over again. In theory, Sawyer had always thought a couple of hours of anything—even making out—was bound to get old . . . but she was surprised by how utterly absorbing it was, how constantly new it felt each time they touched.

She was also shocked by how badly her body had begun to want him inside her. Each time Nick backed off and they tried to cool down, it felt like torture. A very new and unexpected torture.

"You say I drive *you* nuts . . . but you're driving *me* nuts," Sawyer admitted as they lay in each other's arms.

"Good," Nick said. "It's only fair that we should be even on that score."

She pretended to punch him in the arm but he caught her wrist and they sank back into a kiss.

* * *

It grew dark outside.

Soon after, it was not only dark, but late.

Sawyer glimpsed the time on the clock on Nick's nightstand and flinched. Her "real life" came rushing back to her. If Charles came home and she wasn't there, he would worry.

The thought of Charles twisted her stomach; a deep shame gripped her whole body.

She was surprised by the suddenly messy, incongruent state of her life—the idea that it felt right to be with Nick, yet it felt wrong *not* to go home to Charles. Both things couldn't possibly be true; the contradiction made her feel sick, dishonest. Was she someone who was now having an affair? Her brain silently answered her: *Yes, you are.*

"What is it?" Nick asked, sensing the tension in her body, the shift in her mood.

"I didn't realize how late it is," Sawyer said. "I should go."

Now, Nick stiffened. He lay quiet for a long minute.

"You mean go home," he said in a low voice.

"Yes," Sawyer answered soberly.

"Home to the Upper West Side," Nick said warily. He did not say *to Charles*. But the unspoken name hung in the air.

After another long pause he said, "Stay. Stay here with me."

"I can't," Sawyer said quietly.

"And if we'd had sex . . . you'd still have to go home," Nick said—it came out sounding like a cross between a statement and a question.

Sawyer could feel: his whole body had taken on a new and unfriendly tension.

"I didn't . . ." Sawyer stammered. "I didn't know today was going to happen," she tried to explain. "That we would wind up like this."

"You regret it," Nick said. His voice had turned fully cold and flat.

"No!" Sawyer protested. "That's not what I meant. I just . . . I didn't plan for this—any of this."

"It's OK," Nick replied.

"Nick . . . are you mad at me?"

"Of course not. How can I be?" Nick said, but his tone was unconvincing.

He untangled his limbs from Sawyer's and got up from the bed, rummaging around the floor to collect their clothes. He politely handed Sawyer her dress and bra, and began redressing himself.

"I have my mom's car," he said as he dressed. "I'll drive you across town."

"I can take the train."

He shook his head. "You're right; it got pretty late. And . . . I don't know . . . it feels wrong. Let me drive you."

* * *

Once she'd dressed and put herself back together, they left Nick's apartment and Sawyer followed him over to a tiny parking lot crammed into an alley.

"Tino!" Nick greeted the parking lot attendant. They shook hands, and it was clear that Nick had some kind of regular deal with the guy.

The old Mercedes was already like a familiar friend. Sawyer climbed in and sank into the deep bucket seat as Nick worked the stick shift and wove in and out of traffic like a true New York driver. Just as last time, Sawyer felt hyperaware of his hand moving so close to her knee as he shifted. It astounded her that she could still feel the nervous excitement of being so innocently near him . . . after the way they'd spent the last few hours.

But Nick seemed a world away. He'd been friendly with the parking attendant, but now Sawyer realized that had been a facade. The second they'd driven off the lot, he'd retreated into himself. And even though he'd promised her that he wasn't mad, Sawyer was certain that he wasn't happy anymore—not the way he had been earlier.

When they arrived on her street, he seemed to read her anxiousness about being in the car with him, so close to the home she shared with Charles. He stopped a cautious distance away, pulling up to the curb a few doors down from her building. He didn't move to kiss her, and she didn't move to kiss him.

She realized they were acting exactly like two people with something to hide.

She wondered if they'd made a mistake in crossing a line they couldn't uncross. She wanted to ask if they'd spend another Friday together—or just feel the reassurance of their usual light, funny, heartfelt banter—but when she looked over at him, he was still looking straight ahead, staring out the window, his jaw clenching the way it had that night she and Charles had joined him and Kendra at the club, and she thought better of asking him.

The car idled. He did not turn off the engine. She thanked him and waited for a minute. He wished her good night. Finally, she slipped out of the car and watched as he drove away.

* * *

Once Nick was gone, Sawyer stood on the curb, gathering herself.

The rain had stopped. The sidewalks smelled clean. The trees were still dripping big, splattery drops. Some landed directly on Sawyer's head, a heavy tap, tap, tap. But she hardly noticed; she was picturing going upstairs. Charles waiting for her on the sofa, muting the TV, and asking her the dreaded question, *Where were you?*

She was unwilling to lie, but uncertain exactly *what* to say. Or how to say it.

She stood there on the sidewalk for a long moment.

Finally, she gathered herself and forced herself up the stoop, through the brownstone's outer door, then the inner door. Up three flights of stairs.

When she reached her front door, she paused again.

She produced her house key, took a breath, and slid the teeth into the dead bolt—ready to be asked where she'd been, ready to give an answer.

But as the door swung open, Sawyer immediately saw: the apartment was dark.

No one was home.

23.

Sawyer was at a loss for what to do. She turned on all the lights in the apartment, then sat down on the couch with the TV off, just waiting. In the past, watching the clock and waiting for Charles to arrive home had irritated her. But now, having come from Nick's apartment, and having been driven home in Nick's car, Sawyer felt too guilty to be annoyed.

So she simply sat and waited, all her emotions on hold, like an out-of-body experience.

When Charles finally came home, she heard him fumbling with his key at the door. She went to open it for him, and he surprised her by stumbling clumsily into the room. He was smiling and his face was pink. It took her a moment to recognize: he was drunk.

He was also clutching a cellophane-wrapped bouquet of assorted flowers that she recognized as having come from the bodega around the corner. Charles saw her looking at the flowers. He grinned and held them out to her.

"For you," he said triumphantly.

"What's going on, Charles?"

He waited for her to accept the bouquet, then sighed and heaved himself onto the couch in an exhausted manner, still wearing his suit from work. The knot of the tie was loosened and pulled down to about where his sternum was.

"Well, I figured you were probably pretty mad when you never showed up at the karaoke joint," he explained, the corners of his voice blurry. "And I figured flowers never hurt."

Sawyer frowned down at the bouquet in her hands, shaking her head in confusion.

"I don't understand—what are you talking about?"

"I told you," Charles insisted. "We went to karaoke, a bunch of us from work. We were trying to cheer Kendra up, because I guess she broke up with that asshole musician boyfriend of hers . . ."

He paused and blinked up at Sawyer from the couch, looking oddly earnest.

"But I know how uneasy you've been feeling lately about my long hours, and I didn't want to piss you off. So I called to invite you—*if you can't beat 'em, join 'em*, right? Kendra's idea, actually. She's really cool; she says if you hung out more, you'd probably become good friends . . ."

(Sawyer very much doubted this, but bit her tongue.)

"Anyway," Charles rambled on, "I called and left a big long message on the machine. But . . . since you never showed up, I figured I better come home."

He peered at her again with equal parts hyperfocus and drunkenness, his eyes wide, his pupils dilating from the effort of sincerity.

"You scared me the other day," he confessed. "That thing you said about 'would we still be getting married if we actually got to finish one of our conversations' or whatever."

He blinked slowly, his eyes twitching ever so slightly from side to side. Sawyer could see that, for him, the room was probably spinning. He gave a slovenly sigh and frowned down at a small stain on his dress shirt.

"I know it seems like I'm always working and we're not spending any time together. And whenever we do talk, it's all about my mom's plans for the wedding . . . but . . . Sawyer, I love you. I'm trying my best here. All of this is for our future."

He glanced up again, trying one last time to focus on her face.

"Do you understand?" he asked.

Slowly—and mostly because she had no idea what else to do; Charles was clearly wasted—Sawyer nodded.

"Good . . ." He sighed, and let his eyes close as he lay back. All the tension began to leave his body as he slumped farther and farther into the couch cushions. "You gotta understand about Chicago," he mumbled, turning drowsy. "This case . . . opportunity of a lifetime . . ."

His head dropped to one side and he passed out, into what was sure to be a deep, drunken sleep.

Sawyer gazed at him for a moment. Then, she crossed the room to the answering machine and pushed the play button. Charles's voice blared through the speaker, a little garbled by the background noise of the karaoke bar (she could hear a man yodeling Cher's "If I Could Turn Back Time" in falsetto to a rowdy crowd, it seemed), but intelligible nonetheless. It was just as he said: he'd called to invite Sawyer to join them, leaving the address and promising she'd have some fun if she decided to come out.

Now, Charles lay snoring on the couch, oblivious to the sound of his own voice as the message wrapped up and the answering machine concluded with a piercing *BEEP*. Sawyer watched him sleeping for a moment, his face slack, his expression innocent, a blank slate.

She knelt next to the couch and carefully unlaced his shoes and slid them off, then lifted his tie over his head and covered him up with a blanket. He stirred but did not wake, hugging a couch pillow closer and rolling onto his side.

She sighed, and went into the bedroom to sleep alone, confused by the mixture of annoyance and guilt she simultaneously felt for Charles, and the rest of her mind swimming with memories of her day with Nick, which already felt like something she had experienced in a dream.

* * *

The next morning was Saturday.

Sawyer woke up from a shockingly deep, sound state of sleep to see the midmorning sunshine already streaming in the windows. In the living room, the couch was vacant, the blanket folded and the throw pillows neatly arranged. In the kitchen, she found a note from Charles on the counter, along with a bag of bagels whose procurement she must have totally slept through. She picked up the note.

> *Gotta work a few hours today, and wanted to hit the gym to sweat out some of this alcohol before I have to be at the office. I'm so glad we talked last night, and that you are being so understanding about this crazy case and we're on the same page. I'm a lucky guy! Thought I'd pick up some bagels for my future bride.*
>
> *Love,*
> *Your Future Husband*

Sawyer blinked at the note, absorbing the fact that—from Charles's point of view—they'd "talked last night." She was surprised he even remembered coming home, much less the brief exchange they'd had before he passed out snoring.

But one thing was becoming steadily clearer and clearer to Sawyer: that brief conversation was probably as much as Charles ever wanted to talk about things. And her simple nod to his question, *Do you understand?*, had satisfied his conclusion that they were "on the same page"—no further input from Sawyer needed. It certainly didn't bode well;

the more Charles mentioned "their future" in passing, the more Sawyer became convinced that she and Charles were not picturing the *same* future.

But now, Sawyer found herself preoccupied by what she considered a matter of greater concern: the fact that she could not stop thinking about Nick.

Her brain began involuntarily replaying Friday in her head. It was too intense to think about directly—it was like staring into the sun. It came back to her in snippets. A flash of the hungry look in Nick's eyes. Of his naked body. Of his hands on her. The torture of wanting him so badly.

A shiver ran in a tight ripple down her flesh.

In some ways, she was caught in a state of suspended disbelief; the reality of what had actually happened between her and Nick caused a kind of overstimulation. She felt simultaneously euphoric and mortified, like there was a charge of dangerous electricity trapped in her body, with nowhere to ground out.

That Saturday, as Sawyer made herself a cup of hot coffee, she glanced across the kitchen to where the computer sat, already feeling like a teenage girl staring at the phone on the morning after a date.

She gave in, powered on the computer, and logged in to AOL. While she half expected it, she nonetheless felt a rush of unfamiliar intimidation when the automated voice announced "*You've got mail!*"

> To: Adventures_of_Tom@aol.com
> From: Nikolai70@aol.com
>
> Hey—I hope things are going well this morning. I'd love to check in. I'll be online today if you'd like to ping me.—N

Sawyer opened up AOL Instant Messenger, and spotted the green dot next to Nikolai70.

Adventures_of_Tom: Hey

She waited. Before too long, the window on the screen blinked with a reply.

Nikolai70: Hey—I'm here. How are you doing?

Adventures_of_Tom: I'm OK. You?

Nikolai70: Good

Adventures_of_Tom: That's good. I couldn't figure out how you felt yesterday

Nikolai70: Ha ha, really? I thought it was pretty obvious

Nikolai70: Yesterday was amazing.

Adventures_of_Tom: It was for me, too. But afterwards . . . I don't know. You got so quiet in the car when you drove me back. Almost like you were mad.

Nikolai70: I wasn't mad.

There was a long pause. She thought maybe Nick was formulating further explanation, and took a sip of her coffee as she waited.

Nikolai70: How were things when you got upstairs?

Adventures_of_Tom: What do you mean?

Nikolai70: Did he ask you where you were?

She realized he meant Charles. She stared at the screen. Nick could be simply asking out of kindness and concern. Or jealousy. It thrilled her a little to think Nick might feel any of the three for her. It scared her a little, too. Sawyer hovered her hands over the keys, thinking of how to respond. Finally, she typed:

> Adventures_of_Tom: He didn't ask

Nick didn't reply right away. She felt the need to elaborate.

> Adventures_of_Tom: He wasn't home when I got home. He came home later. Very drunk. I guess they went to karaoke again.
>
> Nikolai70: So you didn't need to tell him anything about where you were last night.
>
> Adventures_of_Tom: No
>
> Nikolai70: Will you?
>
> Adventures_of_Tom: I don't know

Another pause. Sawyer sensed he was dissatisfied, but she wasn't sure what to make of it. She waited.

> Nikolai70: Can I ask you a question?
>
> Adventures_of_Tom: Of course.
>
> Nikolai70: All this time you're spending with me—could it be there's a purpose behind it?

Adventures_of_Tom: What do you mean?

Adventures_of_Tom: I really value this—our summer Fridays hanging out, I mean.

Nikolai70: Me too

Nikolai70: But is there a purpose for you?

Adventures_of_Tom: I don't get what you mean

Nikolai70: Are you trying to get revenge on Charles? Because he's always working late

Nikolai70: Because he's always working late with Kendra

Adventures_of_Tom: No.

Adventures_of_Tom: I'm not hanging out with you to get revenge.

Nikolai70: Do you still plan to marry him?

Sawyer thought for a moment. She had a flash of canceling the wedding, and winced, overwhelmed. After a long hesitation, she began typing . . . then deleted it all . . . then tried typing again.

Adventures_of_Tom: I don't know.

Sawyer waited again, but got the sense that Nick had nothing to say in reply. She understood it was complicated. She wished she could explain better. Her fingers settled over the keyboard again, nervously tapping out her thoughts.

Adventures_of_Tom: I have to talk to him, and in order to do that, we both have to be in the same room for longer than two minutes.

Adventures_of_Tom: It's like you said—complicated. All the things that have been set into motion that have to be called off. Families . . . disappointment. Moving out.

Nikolai70: But people do it all the time.

Adventures_of_Tom: I know.

Adventures_of_Tom: I need to figure it out.

Sawyer paused and waited again for him to reply. A minute went by. Then another. She began to wonder if he was mad . . . or even if he'd maybe gotten disconnected. But then, finally, the screen blinked with a new message.

Nikolai70: Look, Sawyer, this time together has been really special to me. YOU are special to me.

Adventures_of_Tom: You, too—ditto

Nikolai70: You're the first thing I think of when I wake up in the morning. And you're the last thing I think of before I go to sleep.

Sawyer reread his last lines with a feeling that went beyond flattered, overcome with a surge of mutual desire. Nick was the first thing she thought about when she woke up, and the last thing she thought about before falling asleep. She moved to type as much, but before she could finish a thought, the screen blinked with a new message.

Nikolai70: But I have to be honest with myself

Nikolai70: I'm not interested in the feeling of being so utterly happy to spend time together only to send you home to someone else.

Sawyer felt abashed. She tried to think of what to say.

Adventures_of_Tom: You didn't send me "home" to him

Adventures_of_Tom: It's not like that

Another long pause from Nick.

Nikolai70: Sawyer, the way it felt to drop you off . . . I'm not interested in that feeling, and I'm not looking to repeat it.

This time it was Sawyer who paused, sobered by his message. She had a flash of seeing it through Nick's eyes, and she didn't like what she saw.

Adventures_of_Tom: Nick, what are you saying? Do you want to talk about it next Friday?

Nick didn't reply right away. Then, finally—

Nikolai70: I don't think we should meet next Friday.

Sawyer's stomach dropped. She stared at the screen with a mixture of disbelief and devastation.

Adventures_of_Tom: You don't want to do something this Friday?

Nikolai70: I don't.

Adventures_of_Tom: I wasn't expecting you to say that.

The screen went wavy for a brief moment. Sawyer realized her eyes had involuntarily teared up. She felt a sense of wounded anger trickling into her body—all the more torturous because she suspected she wasn't wholly entitled to it.

Adventures_of_Tom: Of course. Your math.

Nikolai70: My math?

Adventures_of_Tom: That thing you said at the Yale Club. About how you like to stick to your "math." I just realized, I'm probably not very good in terms of your math.

There was a long pause.

Nikolai70: I don't know what you want me to say.

Nikolai70: I can't argue with that.

Another long pause.

Adventures_of_Tom: Where does that leave us?

Nikolai70: I don't know how we got here

Nikolai70: In this, I mean.

Nikolai70: But the point is, I'm fully here, and I'm not sure you are.

Adventures_of_Tom: What does that mean?

Nikolai70: Maybe we cool it. And then down the road, you give me a call when things change.

Sawyer's heart dropped into her stomach. She felt cold.

Nikolai70: It makes the most sense.

Adventures_of_Tom: Mathematically speaking.

Nikolai70: Look, I gotta go.

Adventures_of_Tom: OK. I understand.

Adventures_of_Tom: Goodbye I guess.

Nikolai70: See you later.

"See you later"? Sawyer logged off quickly, before another word could be said.

She shut the computer all the way down, as if their exchange could somehow emerge from it and hurt her further if she left the computer on.

She moved to the living room, where she sat on the floor in the corner of the room.

She was still reeling—not from a lack of understanding the logic, but from the pure emotional gut punch of it all.

She knew he'd been expecting a clearer answer regarding Charles. She'd been brutally honest about not knowing what she wanted.

And he'd been brutally honest about knowing what he didn't want.

24.

To: AutumnLeaves@hotmail.com
From: Adventures_of_Tom@aol.com

Dear Autumn,

I have a confession. I haven't been totally keeping you up-to-date. Life is kind of a mess here in New York, actually.

Charles's mother is planning this amazing wedding that no one can really afford. Meanwhile, Charles and I have been inexplicably turning into strangers. You used to joke in college that Charles and I were joined at the hip, but now it's been so long since we've seen them, I'm not sure if we would even recognize each other's hips! (Joking . . . but not really joking.)

At first, it was easy to chalk it all up to the fact that Charles had to put in overtime hours on this big case at work . . .

but then it seemed like there was more to it than that, and now we've reached a point where I honestly believe he is actively avoiding me. He comes home so late now, I'm usually already asleep in bed—and then he sleeps on the couch because he "doesn't want to disturb me." And then he leaves for the gym super early, often before I'm even awake. He communicates with me via notes (and sometimes bagels, which I appreciate, but that's neither here nor there). I think he is worried that if we spent more than 2 minutes in the same room together, we'll get into some kind of argument and call off the wedding.

Which means we shouldn't be getting married, right? Except neither of us knows where to begin, calling it off. I'll admit, I've been wondering for a while now, if Charles really wants to marry me . . . or if he just doesn't want to deal with what it would be to *not* marry me.

And there's more. That guy, Nick. I've been spending my Fridays with him. And . . . I don't know. When I'm around him, I feel like myself. I feel like my *old* self—that kind of whimsical, arty book nerd I was back when you and I first met freshman year—and somehow, I feel that old me connected to *future* me, the writer and editor and adult version of me I want to become. I think Nick has a way of bringing people's truest selves out. Or maybe just me.

He's pretty special. I mean, don't get me wrong—he's also cocky and opinionated and so blunt sometimes he's downright *rude*. I guess you can tell I kind of like him.

But of course, I've gone and messed that up, too, with my disaster zone of a life. He doesn't want to hang out anymore. I don't blame him.

But I'm going to miss him this Friday.

And probably all the Fridays.

And of course I miss you, too.
Sawyer

• • •

When Friday rolled around, Sawyer got off work a little after noon and decided to walk over to Bryant Park. She'd passed by it before but never really stopped to visit it on purpose.

It was green and leafy, full of café tables and gravel—a curious hint of Paris, smack in the middle of Manhattan. Sawyer watched children ride the ornate carousel with its green-and-white-striped circus top and listened to the squealing laughter of their happy voices.

She wandered over to the entrance of the New York Public Library, walked the marble staircases, and peeked into the famous Rose Main Reading Room, with its long wooden tables and brass lamps, its dark wooden coffered ceilings inset with neoclassical murals of a cloudy sky at sunset. She gazed at all the people studying, reading, scribbling notes . . . and wondered if some of them were writing poems, or even a novel that might one day cross her desk at a publishing house.

After a while, she walked back outside, where the summer sunshine temporarily blinded her as she reemerged. She crossed back through Bryant Park and stood around for a while, watching the old men playing chess. The group she was watching was a loud, boisterous bunch, all of them with heavy mustaches, shouting in what sounded like Greek. It was hard not to dwell on how much more fun everything would be if she were spending the day with Nick. Nick would have tried to join the chess players, finding a way to charm the grumpy old men. Or he would have roped Sawyer into a game; something she would never dare to do on her own.

They would have laughed. Traded inside jokes. Strolled the park and sat in the dappled, leafy shade. Nick would have caught her gaze and held it in that intense, knowing manner. She would have shivered despite the sticky summer heat, wishing for his mouth on hers again.

Now, Sawyer stood watching the chess players from a distant remove, and felt an emptiness widening within her. It was still early—not even quite four o'clock. But it was also no use. Without Nick, the earlier magic of summer Fridays now eluded her. It almost felt like a physical thing leaving her body, like wind abandoning a sail, leaving it slack in a dead calm. The heat of the day suddenly felt oppressive, and she felt a new sense of weariness.

It wasn't as if there was anything or anyone waiting for her back home, but she turned, and headed for the subway.

• • •

Sawyer was alone for the rest of Friday evening, as well as most of Saturday.

But on Sunday, Charles was booked on a 6:20 p.m. flight to Chicago out of JFK. The trip was actually a little more than two weeks—sixteen days; out on a Sunday and back on a Tuesday, not the following Tuesday, but the one after.

That morning—to Sawyer's surprise—he slept in and skipped the gym.

He was full of affectionate cuddles that morning, but his touch felt confusingly both familiar and alien to her, like being kissed by a brother.

The ground had shifted between them. Sawyer knew: it was time for them to talk.

As if reading her mind, he pecked her chastely on the forehead and got out of bed, intent on a shower.

"Hey," he said, "I was hoping we could keep things really low-key and simple today, you know—before I have to pack and head to the airport. Chicago's a big deal. It would do me a world of good to take it easy. Maybe even no wedding-plan talk today, no nothing—just a nice, homey day like we used to have all the time back in Boston."

Sawyer looked at him. She bit her lip, reluctant.

"Could we do that?" he nudged, with a hint of gentle pleading.

"Sure," she relented, finally.

He smiled, then disappeared into the bathroom. She heard the all-too-familiar sound of the taps squealing and the shower water sputtering to life.

Later, they ate deliciously greasy breakfast sandwiches from the deli next to the bodega, then tidied the apartment together. It was almost strange, Sawyer thought, to spend time together again, doing all those mundane little everyday things.

Around two o'clock, Charles started packing his bags. He spent the better part of an hour adding and subtracting things, angling his suits still on their hangers into a garment bag, rolling undershirts and boxers into tight tubes that he later packed into his gym bag like sardines, and occasionally asking Sawyer her opinion about matters like exactly how many pairs of socks a person could need for two weeks in an office environment.

"I'm sure you'll get some time away from the office," Sawyer said. "A night off, here and there."

"Doubtful," Charles said, shaking his head. "Pretty sure I'll be sleeping in these suits. I hope the hotel has dry-cleaning drop-off."

Sawyer smiled sympathetically and turned her attention back to balancing their checkbook. Something caught her eye as she looked over their monthly bank statement. She frowned.

"Charles," she said, alarmed. "This can't be right. There's two thousand missing from our savings."

Charles looked up from his packing with a serious expression but didn't say anything.

"We should call the bank," Sawyer said. "Oh—but it's Sunday . . . What do we do? What if it's been . . . I don't know, stolen or something?"

"It wasn't stolen," he said.

She blinked at him.

"My mom was racking up so many charges for our wedding, her credit card was getting full," he explained. "I felt bad. I wired some money to clear a little space on her Visa. It seemed like the least we could do."

"That was the money we were saving to eventually take a honeymoon someday," Sawyer murmured, surprised.

"Yeah, but we weren't actually planning to go for at least a year or two. I can earn it back; by then I'll have probably gotten a raise. Maybe I'll even get one from this case. And it's not like we'd be able to take the time off for at least another year, anyway."

Sawyer simply stared at him.

"My folks are paying for *everything,* Sawyer," Charles added. "It seemed like the least we could do," he repeated.

"I don't have a problem with that part," Sawyer said softly, steadily comprehending that they were on two very, very different pages. "You know I've always felt funny about them paying for the wedding."

"Look, you can't say anything. My dad doesn't know. And my mom thinks the payment came from him. I doubt they'll compare notes. Everyone believes what they need to believe, and everyone's happy. I'm just trying to help out, be a good son, et cetera."

"That's not the part I have a problem with," Sawyer reiterated. "It's more the . . . disconnect. We've been disconnected in a lot of ways. It's not just this."

He paused for a moment, closing his eyes and pressing his lips together like he was suddenly angry and trying to keep calm. After a moment, he let out an irascible sigh.

"I *knew* if we talked before I left for my trip, we'd find something to argue about," he said, his voice full of accusation.

Sawyer was silent a moment, taking this in.

"Charles . . . we really need to sit down and talk."

At this, a look of fear passed over his face briefly, and his anger gave way to something much softer.

"Please," he said, the combative tone in his voice gone. "This case is huge for me. I'm not saying you can't have your feelings and we won't talk eventually, but I can't have the rug ripped out from under my feet right now. I need your support to focus and get this done."

Sawyer stood blinking at him dumbly, taken off guard by the look of fear she'd glimpsed, the sincere pleading in his voice. She felt sympathetic to how hard he'd worked and how critical the case was; a part of her understood that if their talk led to calling off the wedding, his Chicago trip would be full of calls to and from his parents, an unfathomable weight on his shoulders over all the wedding deposits they were unlikely to get back. He would be, in effect, sabotaged.

"Can we at least table this conversation? My car is supposed to be here to pick me up in like ten minutes, and I can't miss this flight. This is too important to tackle in passing like this, when we really can't get into it."

Sawyer took a deep inhale and let it out, feeling some of the weight on her own shoulders, too.

"OK," she agreed reluctantly.

* * *

Ten minutes later, the car came to pick up Charles, exactly on time.

Two minutes after that, Sawyer stood in the empty apartment, staring at the pile of ties and belts still strewn on the bed, the rejects Charles had left behind.

Alone for two weeks.

She checked her email. Her inbox was empty.

• • •

Several hours later, when Sawyer was getting ready for bed, Charles called to tell her he'd gotten into Chicago and checked into his room.

"You know, we should look into getting one of those cards that give you airline miles," he told Sawyer. "Kendra has one and she was able to use miles to bump us up to first class. A total lifesaver—there was a crying baby back in coach. Screamed its head off all the way from JFK to O'Hare."

Sawyer was quiet. She didn't bother to remind him that they were both paying off student loans and the last thing they needed was another credit card.

"Anyway, we got here in one piece and I'm in my room now," he continued. "Getting ready to call it a day. Room 213, if you need to get a hold of me. Not that I'll probably be here in the room much—it's seriously looking like it's gonna be round the clock."

"Do you have the number there, in case of an emergency?" Sawyer asked.

"Where? The office, you mean? Gosh, I don't know off the top of my head, but I'll double-check and let you know. Anyway, I should turn in for the night. I wanna get up early and hit the hotel gym . . . we'll see if I manage it, ha ha. At least I've got the one-hour time difference on my side . . ."

They said good night and hung up.

Afterward, Sawyer lay in bed for a long time, studying the cracks in the ceiling. It was an old brownstone and the plaster bubbled a little in places from water damage. If you stared long enough, you could find shapes and faces. A language of hidden things, only they weren't really hidden if you thought about it; they had always been hidden in plain sight.

* * *

The next morning was Monday.

Normally, Sawyer loved her job. Passing through the revolving door of the publishing house still gave her a tiny thrill—to think she actually worked there, doing something she enjoyed.

But that week, her heart wasn't in anything. Sawyer rode the subway to work and home, read manuscripts, and lay in bed at night staring at the ceiling.

Making matters worse, the week was marked by an extreme and relentless heat wave that only grew hotter and hotter with each passing day. The heat wave was headline news, and there was no getting away from it. People foolhardy enough to insist on their morning jog around the reservoir in Central Park were fainting and being carted off by paramedics. The asphalt on the city streets felt sticky, sucking at the soles of shoes as though the tar itself was melting. The underground subway stations baked with a ruthless steamy heat, utterly unbearable, leaving riders dripping in their own sweat, the air thick with body odor.

For Sawyer, the only relief came during the air-conditioned hours she spent in the office. She started getting in earlier and earlier, and leaving later and later.

* * *

On Thursday, Sawyer arrived at her office at 6:03 a.m., already sweating from the terrible heat.

Around 10 a.m., she noticed a kind of buzz going around their open-plan floor of cubicles. Evidently, everyone was excited about a giant vanilla orange-blossom cake in the break room, the description of which intrigued Sawyer . . . until she learned that it had been procured in celebration of Erin Michaels's last day at the publishing house.

At the appointed hour—three o'clock—the office gathered together and presented Erin with a banner that read *"GOOD LUCK!!! WE'LL MISS YOU!!!"* and a greeting card that was signed by their core group. In the break room, they cut the cake and turned on some music (curiously, reggae), then invited everyone on the floor to come join in.

Sawyer definitely planned to stop in, but the phone kept ringing. When she finally found a free moment, she stood up to head over but was surprised to see Erin standing beside her desk, holding a paper plate of cake in one hand and a small slip of paper in the other.

"I just wanted to say goodbye," Erin said with a kind smile. "And I wanted you to have my contact info."

She held out a Post-it. Sawyer gratefully accepted.

"I don't have business cards yet, of course," Erin said with a happy laugh. "But they tell me that this will be my new email address." She leaned over and pointed to the address scrawled on the Post-it. "If you need anything, or just want to chat, I'd love to keep in touch."

"Really?" Sawyer said, before she could stop herself. She was bowled over with flattery.

"Absolutely! It's been such a pleasure. I think you're going to be a great editor someday, Sawyer."

With that, Erin nodded and waved. She headed back in the direction of the break room, pausing to say goodbye to others, smiling and swaying to faint sounds of Bob Marley still drifting out from the break room as she delivered the occasional bite of cake to her lips via a plastic fork.

Sawyer watched her go, feeling both sad and hopeful at the same time.

* * *

That evening, Sawyer came home to her apartment in a hot, humid fog of utter defeat. There was nothing she wanted to do. She hadn't written anything in at least a week. She was acutely aware that the following day was a summer Friday, and that she had no plans.

It was too hot to do anything on her list, anyway. The heat wave was expected to hit a peak spike tomorrow. Sawyer couldn't imagine it getting even hotter; it was already intolerable. Maybe when she got off work tomorrow, she could go hide in the cool, air-conditioned dark of a movie theater, she thought. She caught herself involuntarily imagining meeting Nick for a movie . . . that magical teenage feeling of simultaneously being entranced by the silver screen, yet aching for the person sitting next to you in the dark. Aware now that her mind had entered the realm of blatant fantasy, she silently scolded herself to get a grip.

As she tried to think of what else she could do, she absent-mindedly turned on her computer and logged on to the internet. She no longer had any expectation of finding a message waiting in her inbox, but the ritual of checking her email was like a phantom limb of sorts.

She was genuinely shocked when her eyes skimmed the screen and spotted Nikolai70@aol.com. Her heart gave a forceful thump, then skipped a beat. The subject of the email was, simply, "TOMORROW."

Sawyer's finger clicked, lightning fast.

To: Adventures_of_Tom@aol.com
From: Nikolai70@aol.com

OK. I give.

I can't stand the thought of you stuck home alone on a summer Friday sweltering in this God-awful heat wave.

Unacceptable. So, I propose to pick you up at your place at 1pm tomorrow. Bring a bathing suit.

I still meant what I said the other day, but the bottom line is, a Friday with you is highly preferable to a Friday without you. I'll take what I can get.

—Nick

Sawyer read the email at least five times.

Her dread of the heat wave's peak had instantly vanished; tomorrow could not come soon enough.

25.

FRIDAY, AUGUST 13

At the exact stroke of noon, Sawyer hurried to turn off her computer and grab her bag. She didn't even wait to confirm that Johanna had left the office for the day or not. She felt Kaylee blinking after her in surprise as she made a mad dash for the elevator.

"Take it easy! It's too hot to be moving that fast!"

Kaylee wasn't wrong. The heat wave was reaching its terrible, brutal peak.

The subway ride home was positively disgusting. Sawyer didn't care; she felt a smile curling the corners of her mouth in spite of it all. Her happy grin was so obvious it even appeared to annoy the other subway riders, who frowned at her as though she must be crazy or completely stupid to be smiling in the middle of such hot misery.

Once at her apartment, Sawyer stood under the cold spigot of the shower for a few minutes, then toweled off and put on a bathing suit under a T-shirt and jean skirt. She stuffed a fresh change of clothes in her bag and went downstairs to wait on her stoop.

Despite the heat, the sweat beading on her skin prickled like ice, and she tried to hide a shiver.

Sawyer was nervous.

When she spotted the tinted windows of the beat-up old Mercedes turning onto her street from the end of the block, her heart leapt to her throat, then dropped to her stomach. Nick pulled to the curb. The car's sunroof and all its windows were wide open and classic rock drifted into the air. From where he sat at the steering wheel, he leaned toward the open window, caught her eyes, and smiled in a way that was strangely yet deeply familiar to her.

Recalling a vivid flash of their semi-naked bodies together, Sawyer felt a rush of sudden shyness. She stood from where she'd been sitting on the stoop, wondering how she should greet him . . . debating whether or not she should touch him.

Before she had made up her mind, Nick put the car in park, jumped out, and hurried around to the sidewalk and opened the door for her.

"Ready?"

"Where are we going?" Sawyer asked, as she sank into the passenger seat and tucked her feet in for Nick to swing the door shut.

"You'll see." He grinned into the open window. He went around and got into the driver's seat.

"The Hamptons?"

"Nope."

"Jersey Shore?" she guessed again.

He shook his head. "Nope."

"Hmm, and here I thought you were tipping your hand with the instructions to bring a bathing suit," she said instead.

"Oh, rest assured, we'll put the bathing suits to use," Nick teasingly replied. He pointed at the air-conditioning vents in the car's dash. "Technically, the AC works, but it's pretty weak. So we gotta do it the old-fashioned way: keep the windows rolled down, and drive like a bat out of hell."

And with that, Nick was true to his word—dropping his foot heavy on the gas and zipping through traffic, keeping a steady flow of wind whipping in through the open windows. It wasn't "cool," exactly, but it did the trick, drying the sweat on their brows before it had much of a chance to form.

Sawyer pretended to be afraid of his driving, making roller-coaster faces as he accelerated and braked and maneuvered in and out of traffic, but her constant laughter gave her away. Nick rolled his eyes and shifted into a higher gear as the road opened up.

When the bit had run its course, Sawyer leaned forward and turned up the radio, then leaned her head back on the headrest, closing her eyes and feeling the wind on her face. There was an atmosphere of lighthearted freedom in the car—the kind of thing she hadn't felt since the days of driving around with a carful of friends in high school, windows down, yodeling along to the radio.

When she opened her eyes after a minute of simply enjoying the sensation of the car, the music, and the wind, Nick was looking at her instead of the road.

"Safety first," she teased.

He shrugged. "Just thinking of all the times I stared at you, thinking about how beautiful you are, but didn't say it aloud."

He said it so matter-of-fact, it didn't even come off as flattery . . . which somehow had the effect of magnifying the power of the compliment. Sawyer had no idea what to say in response. He had a way of speaking frankly when complimenting her that knocked her off-balance, leaving her totally tongue-tied.

He drove on, and they left the city behind them. They were driving north, she realized, zipping along parallel to the Hudson River, until eventually Nick turned off the expressway. He turned onto one main road, then another, then began winding along a series of smaller back roads.

"Where *are* we going?" she insisted.

"I said, you'll see."

The roads got smaller and smaller. The woods got thicker and thicker. The houses began to look less suburban, more like cabins, and steadily grew fewer and farther in between.

Finally, Nick turned down what looked like a private, narrow one-way road. Leaves fluttered down from the canopy of trees overhead, stirred by the breeze of the car; a few fluttered in through the sunroof. Sawyer caught one in her hand and smiled at it. The road dipped down, and then she glimpsed a dark, glimmering body of water.

The road sloped even more steeply, turned to dirt, and ended at the water's edge. Nick pulled off to the side and parked.

"Here we are."

Sawyer got out to take a look.

It was a lake. Small in circumference, but its dark, sparkling water suggested that it was quite deep. It was also very hidden and private; the woods were thick on all sides, growing right to the water's edge, and Sawyer could only make out five or so cabins in the vicinity. The scent of crushed leaves and hot country dust hung in the air. Nick led the way along the path that hugged the lake's perimeter to a small, weathered dock piled with a couple of kayaks and little Sunfish sailboats, their otherwise colorful plastic and fiberglass hulls bleached pale by the sun.

At the end of the dock, Nick turned and pointed back to one of the few cabins along the shore.

"I used to come here as a kid, with a friend. His mom only had eyes for Long Island and the beach, but his dad loved going fishing in the woods. He built that little shack of a cabin over there. He used to take us here to fish for trout. The cabin isn't much, so it was a little like camping, and not having a dad, I guess I thought it was pretty cool."

Sawyer listened, watching the surface of the lake make golden reflections on Nick's face as he talked, trying to picture him as a little boy excited to learn how to bait a hook, reel in a line.

"Anyway," Nick said, turning back to the edge of the dock and looking down. "It's tiny as far as lakes go, but the water here is always super clear and cold, and there's never a crowd." He smiled and gestured around them, and it was true—there wasn't another person anywhere in sight.

Nick's smile spread into a grin. He kicked off his flip-flops and stripped off his T-shirt. Glimpsing his bare skin, Sawyer automatically blushed. She did her best not to stare—or at least pretend not to stare.

They locked eyes. Sawyer blinked. Nick laughed. He let out a war whoop and got a running start. The next thing Sawyer knew, Nick launched himself into the air and dropped into the water, cannonball-style.

Sawyer choked back a surprised squeal as the splash doused her lower half where she stood.

"C'mon in!" Nick taunted, once he surfaced. "Don't just stand there! This is what we came to do!"

The truth was, the splash had felt good against the heat, but Sawyer pretended to glare at him.

"Fine!"

She kicked off her sandals, lifted her shirt over her head, and wiggled out of her jean skirt. She was down to her black bikini. She tucked her dark hair behind her ears and debated between easing into the water from the dock or diving and feeling the sudden shock of cold. She could feel Nick watching her. She glanced over to where his head bobbed in the water and felt a rush of flattery to see the look in his eyes, both hungry and admiring. It made Sawyer feel less crazy for her own intense desire, the way she felt when she looked at Nick.

She made up her mind quickly.

Light on her toes, she jumped and tipped her fingertips over her head, slipping into the water with hardly a splash. Underwater, she swam to Nick and gave a playful yank on his swim trunks, before surfacing next to him.

"Whoa!" she heard him shout as she rose from the water. "Look out! There's a mermaid in these waters intent on undressing me." He laughed, struggling to pull up his shorts while continuing to tread water.

"Can't blame her," Sawyer replied.

Nick looked at her with a devilish twinkle in his eye.

"Race you to the other side," Sawyer challenged. She turned in the water and set off in a speedy crawl stroke. After a moment, she felt Nick swimming alongside her, racing. She smiled as she swam, and picked up the pace.

It was a tie as they reached the opposite side of the lake. Laughing and panting, they swam to a large granite boulder that was submerged about a foot below the water's surface and lounged on it, listening to the lake slosh against the shore. The sun warmed their faces and shoulders as the water lapped cool and refreshing over their lower halves.

"This is pretty great," Sawyer admitted.

She looked at Nick, studying the way the water beaded on his eyelashes.

"Thank you," she said. "Thank you for bringing me here."

He looked at her with an expression she didn't recognize; it almost struck her as shy. "I don't know about you, but . . . this is my idea of happiness."

She smiled. They were sitting side by side on the boulder, their hips and legs almost touching. Sawyer studied his face. She noticed a tiny leaf that must have been floating in the water now stuck to his cheek near his jaw. She leaned over and moved her hand to gently wipe it away. Nick looked surprised, but calmly held her gaze, allowing the touch.

Sawyer was burning with the urge to kiss him. It was almost torture—like someone slowly putting all their weight onto your toes until you screamed uncle. She thought about acting on the impulse, but wasn't sure anymore where they stood.

Nick finally broke their gaze and looked away, back across the lake.

"All right," Sawyer said, in a cheerful voice. She was worried her desire to kiss him was so obvious that maybe she'd unnerved him. "Now to get back to the other side." She smiled, stood on the boulder, and dove back in.

Nick followed.

This time, he seemed determined to beat her. Spurred on by a second wind and the feeling of being in close competition, they swam faster and faster, until they were both kicking and paddling frantically, with everything they had. Nick reached the dock first, by just a stroke or two. He hauled himself out, and lay panting on the weathered wood. Sawyer followed suit.

They lay there, side by side, flat on their stomachs, exhausted, dripping wet, their cheeks pressed against the unsealed, splintery wooden boards of the dock, letting the water evaporate from their skin. They made two wet stains on the dry wood in the shape of their bodies. Their rib cages rose and fell like accordions as they tried to catch their breath. They were face-to-face, noses almost touching.

Once their breathing slowed and the mood grew calm and still, Sawyer reached a hand out and traced a scar on Nick's back. "Where did you get this?"

"Real story or fictional story to impress you?"

"Hmm," Sawyer said, deciding. "I'm naturally curious about the quality of the fictional story."

"Cage diving with sharks," Nick said.

Sawyer gave a grunt of laughter.

He dropped his voice to a confidential level. "Old playground injury."

He sat up and pointed to a small scar on her leg.

"Now. How did you get that?" he asked.

Sawyer smirked. They continued to play the game, making up stories about their scars, and then slipping in the real explanations under their breath at the end.

How about that one?

Freak accident at an archery competition.

(Tripped while hiking in the woods.)

Finger completely sliced off by the blade of an ice skate during a seriously badass ice hockey fight; had to be sewn back on.

(Finger stuck when a friend rolled up the car window too fast; minor damage.)

Donated a kidney to an orphan.

(Had appendix out.)

Alien abduction, during which they performed multiple experiments to try to explain my genius IQ and universal sexual appeal.

(Surgery on a broken clavicle from a skateboarding accident.)

"Hmm," Sawyer said, to Nick's last story. "As an editor, I'd say that one strains credulity a bit."

"What? That aliens would be trying to measure my enormous sex appeal?"

"No, that part checks out," Sawyer said.

Nick gave her a shocked, offended look. "Wait—then you don't believe in aliens?"

"Well . . . actually . . . maybe I do a little bit. Kind of."

"'Kind of'?"

"I mean, I think it's arrogant of us to assume that—given how big the universe is—we're, like, the *only* form of life," Sawyer explained. "But I also think—given how big the universe is—the odds are pretty slim that we're going to ever cross paths."

"Tell that to the aliens who picked me up in their ride last Friday," Nick joked.

Sawyer gave a sad grimace. "Ah. So that's what you were doing last Friday," she said.

The smile faded from Nick's face. "Last Friday . . ." he said, turning serious. "All I could do was try to avoid thinking about how much I missed you." He paused, then said, "But I failed."

"All I did was think about how much I missed you, too," Sawyer said. "I even wondered if you could feel me thinking about you."

"I did."

They looked at each other for a long moment.

Finally, Sawyer shifted and broke the gaze. She glanced at the kayaks on the dock, then pointed to one of the Sunfish.

"Is that a sailboat?" she asked idly.

Nick looked to where she was pointing. "Yup. Do you sail?"

"Never been."

"Never?"

"Nope."

Nick frowned, lost in thought for a moment. Then he stood and moved to flip the Sunfish over and check the foldable mast and sail.

"Well, it's not exactly a majestic vessel for your maiden voyage, but they actually use these small hobby boats to teach people the basics," he said.

"Wait—Nick! What are you doing? Whose boat is that?"

He shrugged. "We'll put it back when we're done."

Sawyer squirmed. They were already swimming in a lake on private land with no public beach. Commandeering property felt like a step too far; she'd never been the kind of teenager who was cool with trespassing.

"Wait—wait—" she continued to protest, but Nick had already eased the boat into the water.

"Look," he said. "This thing clearly hasn't been used in forever; if nothing else, we're washing off the dust for them."

He gestured for her to step into the boat, holding out a hand to steady her. The whole boat wasn't much bigger than a large surfboard. Nick sat on top of the hull with his feet in the square-shaped cockpit in the middle, and Sawyer settled opposite him. He started hoisting the sail up.

"Lucky for us, the wind's picked up a little," he remarked.

It was true. The sun was still blazing down, hot as ever, but a pleasant breeze had begun to stir. Sawyer knew that the peak of the heat wave was predicted to break later that evening.

"We might actually be able to get her to scoot along pretty good," Nick decreed. He angled the boom and sail until he was able to catch the wind. "And . . . off we go!"

They sailed across the lake a couple of times. Nick showed Sawyer how to "tack," cutting a kind of zigzag path forward while keeping the sail full on one side, and then the other.

He had Sawyer try manning the boom and the rudder. She was a little clumsy at it at first, losing the wind a few times, but after a while she got the hang of it. On her third crossing, she was able to make decent time across the lake.

"It seems you're a quick learner," Nick observed. "You'll be kicking my ass in no time. I'll try to pretend I'm not totally threatened by that."

Soon, he was itching to captain the boat again, and Sawyer switched with him.

"Let's see how fast we can get her to go," Nick said. "There are people who actually race these tiny things."

He caught the breeze and angled the little Sunfish hard, getting the tiny boat to sail along with everything she had in her. At one point, the Sunfish was hung over so hard they both had to lean off to one side—until finally the boat capsized and they went tumbling into the water.

Sawyer came up laughing.

"You did that on *purpose*!" she shouted.

"I take the Fifth," Nick joked.

He swam closer to her as she continued to laugh, then put one hand on the capsized Sunfish in order to stay afloat, and put the other arm around Sawyer's waist, pulling her to him in the water and kissing her.

Sawyer felt her spirit soar.

"Couldn't help it," Nick said softly, once their lips broke contact.

She kissed him back.

They floated like that for a few moments, kissing as Nick held on to the sailboat's buoyant hull. Their bodies slowly intertwined underwater; Sawyer wrapped her legs around him and felt him against her.

Again, her acute aching for him surprised her.

Finally, Nick released her, and swam to tow the Sunfish to the dock. Once there, he pulled himself up onto the bottom side of the hull, gripped the edge, and used his weight to flip the capsized boat upright again. Sawyer swam over and got out of the water to help him drag the Sunfish back onto the dock.

Nick folded the mast down and rolled up the sail, then flipped the boat back in place where they'd found it.

"OK, so we *briefly* borrowed it," Sawyer said, reassuring herself and remembering Nick's words earlier, when he'd promised *we'll put it back when we're done.*

"Exactly," Nick said. "See?"

They looked at each other, two benevolent coconspirators, and grinned.

• • •

At first, Nick was happy and light when they finally climbed back into the car and he started up the motor. The kiss had unsealed something between them; their physicality had palpably shifted. As he drove, Nick put his hand on Sawyer's knee, taking it away only to shift gears. It was something no one had done since her high school boyfriend. She'd assumed that, as an adult, she'd find it corny. But instead, each time Nick's hand touched her knee she felt a genuine thrill.

Once, she reached for his hand, took it in her own, and lifted his hand to her lips and kissed it.

Another time, as Nick stopped for a light before getting on the expressway, he leaned over and kissed her—a good, long kiss. She didn't want it to end, disappointed when he broke away to drive again.

The heat wave had already started to let up a little when they left the lake, and the breeze had begun to pick up even more than when they'd gone sailing. They'd managed to while away the entire afternoon and evening; the sun was sinking low in the sky as they followed the Hudson River back toward the city, and a few clouds had gathered on the horizon. Sawyer understood: the real break in the heat would come when the rain did.

"Wow," she said, gazing at the colorful sky. "Another good one. Every time we're together, we get the best sunsets."

Sawyer knew there were plenty of scientific reasons for this. Summer. Longer days. Seasonal thunderstorms. The fact that, in going on all these outings, she and Nick were in better locations to witness the sunset, period. But it felt like luck, like magic.

Nick studied the sky briefly and nodded.

Something in his demeanor had slowly shifted over the course of their drive. His light, happy mood had faded. His hand no longer rested on Sawyer's leg, and over the last few miles in particular, Nick had grown quiet. She looked at him now and understood that he had begun to withdraw into himself. The city loomed into view in the distance.

As Nick took an exit off the Henry Hudson Parkway, Sawyer began to comprehend: he was driving her home.

"Are you hungry?" she asked. "We could . . . um, get some dinner together."

As the words left her mouth, she remembered that they weren't really dressed to eat out in a restaurant . . . their clothes still a bit damp, their bathing suits and flip-flops not exactly Manhattan-restaurant-ready.

"We could pick up some takeout and eat it at your place," she suggested.

Nick turned to gaze at her.

"I think if we do that, we both know what will happen," he said quietly.

It wasn't what Sawyer had been getting at—at least, not consciously—but Nick was right, of course. She didn't know what to say.

"I'm just . . . not ready to stop hanging out with you," Sawyer said.

"Neither am I," Nick agreed, his voice low and sober. "But if I have to drop you off later . . . I'd rather just drop you off now. I told you: that's not an experience I'm looking to repeat."

Sawyer fell quiet.

Nick continued to drive until he reached her street. He pulled over a few doors away from her apartment. He didn't make a move to kiss her.

Sawyer understood that she was supposed to get out of the car, but she couldn't move.

"I want to take you home with me, Sawyer. You know I do," Nick said. He let a long pause settle in the car. "I'm waiting for you to know what you want. I'll wait as long as I can stand it, and I'll be honest about when I can't anymore."

Sawyer understood. She felt the urge to reply . . . but couldn't find the right words. Her words were all caught somewhere in the translation process between feelings and thoughts. Everything she could possibly think to say seemed wrong.

Nick wished her good night.

She was out of time.

Finally, with the heavy feeling still permeating every limb, Sawyer reached for the car door handle and let herself out.

The sound of Nick driving away made her heart sink even lower.

• • •

Once upstairs, Sawyer turned on the lights in her apartment and took a shower, washing away the smells of the lake—a perfume of moss and leaves and fish. She scrubbed her skin until it was pink, and stood under the blast of the shower spigot for a long time.

Afterward, she wrapped herself up in a bathrobe and huddled cross-legged on the sofa, sipping a glass of ice water. It was still hot, despite the fact that she'd opened all the windows in the apartment.

She willed herself to stop thinking about Nick, but couldn't seem to manage it. Her brain kept racing back to him. The sunshine on the lake's surface making golden reflections on his face. His laugh right before the little Sunfish capsized. The look in his eyes when he pulled Sawyer close in the water and kissed her.

She pictured what he might be doing now, in his own apartment.

Whether or not he couldn't stop thinking of Sawyer, the way she couldn't stop thinking of him.

I'm waiting for you to know what you want, Nick had said.

She closed her eyes for a long moment.

Then, she opened them again.

Sawyer knew what she wanted.

Once her mind was made up, her body sprang into action, every motion hurried, her pulse pumping with adrenaline. She threw on some clothes and didn't even bother with drying her hair.

The next thing she knew, she was outside on the street, flagging down a cab.

And soon after that, sitting in the back of the taxi, watching the city fly by the windows as the driver gunned the motor of the Crown Vic, hurtling down the streets of Manhattan toward the East Village until at last they lurched to a final stop. She was a tumble of movements: shoving cash in a wad through the hinged chute in the Plexiglas divider, shouting thanks at the driver, running to the now familiar stoop, and ringing the buzzer like a maniac, hoping to be let upstairs.

When Nick opened his apartment door, he looked startled by her sudden knock . . . but not surprised to see her. He stared at her for a moment. He didn't speak, and neither did she, but she felt him reading what was there in her eyes.

He pulled her inside, into his arms, and kicked the door shut behind them.

26.

At first, things moved furiously fast.

They were already kissing and yanking each other's shirts over each other's heads when the door slammed shut. There was a kind of tripping, grapevine step they did—like a drunken waltz, almost, swinging wildly toward one piece of furniture, then another—as they continued to kiss and unbutton and unzip, making their stumbling way across the apartment, to Nick's bed.

But then, when they reached the same place where they'd left off last—nearly naked, down to the thin fabric of underwear—Nick slowed down. But this time was different, and Sawyer understood. She searched his face, then slowed her own kisses, slowed her own urgency, and matched her breathing to his. They peeled off those final layers slowly, and kissed and touched and tasted each other's bodies all over, with intense care.

When Sawyer finally felt Nick inside her, she gave a small gasp, but she never broke away from his gaze. He seemed to thrill at her gasp; his expression struck her as faintly yet delightedly smug—as though he had just gotten the last word.

But Sawyer knew the night was still young, they had many hours ahead of them, and he had most certainly not gotten the *last* word. She kissed him deeply and rolled on top, taking her turn at making *him* gasp.

* * *

Later, they lay tangled in each other, still intertwined.

"You'll stay?" Nick asked.

"Wait—that's it? We're done?" Sawyer teased.

He laughed softly. But Sawyer could feel he wanted a real answer.

"Charles is in Chicago," she said finally, not wanting to hide anything. "He left last Sunday."

"Ah," Nick said, with the slightest touch of cynicism.

"What?"

"So I have you *on loan*."

"No," Sawyer insisted. "I'm here."

He didn't respond.

A lingering doubt passed through her brain.

"I mean . . . unless a loan is all you want," she added.

He frowned, and squirmed to get a look at her face where it was tucked under his chin. "What's that supposed to mean?"

"I don't know . . ." she murmured. "I just don't want to assume anything about what kind of, um . . . relationship you want this to be. Maybe 'relationship' isn't even the right word."

"Ah," Nick said. "More of that 'musicians just wanna get laid' dogma, I see."

He was making fun of her, but there was a touch of bitterness.

She shifted, embarrassed, and shrugged. "I mean, there's a lot of ground between friends, and hooking up, and . . . you know."

"A commitment?"

Her mind suddenly flashed to Johanna, sneering as she said, *'Committed'? You make it sound like a mental institution.*

"Huh," Sawyer said, musing on the memory. "That word *does* sound rather institutional and ominous, now that I think about it."

Nick laughed. "Sure. OK. I grant you that."

Then, after a moment, he turned more serious.

"But I've been pretty clear, I think," he said. He paused and added, "I don't want you just on loan."

Sawyer smiled quietly to herself, happy.

But in the next few seconds, her mind moved beyond Nick's bed, Nick's room . . . and back to Charles. She closed her eyes for a moment and saw a flash of Charles's face, felt a pang of the heartbreak for the past they'd shared together.

A long list unfurled in her brain—conversations that needed to be had, wedding arrangements that had to be canceled, the dividing of their things, the awkward tango of moving out.

It was likely to be messy. Not the kind of thing a guy like Nick would sign up for willingly. She recalled again what he had said at the Yale Club, when he'd laid out his rational approach to love and relationships with an air of cynical detachment that had downright stunned her.

"But, Nick . . . what about the math?"

"The math?"

"You know—the math. Weighing the risks involved in maintaining a boyfriend role in relation to me."

Nick laughed a little.

"You said it yourself; I'm a bad bet in terms of your math," she insisted.

"Sawyer," he replied, "if I'd been applying my 'math' with you, we wouldn't have ever gotten here in the first place."

"What does that mean?" Sawyer asked with an innocent frown.

He twisted so they were looking at each other again. "I keep trying to tell you. This is something new. Something different. When it comes to you . . . all the math in the world goes right out the window."

He pulled her close and tipped her chin to kiss her.

* * *

Sawyer spent the entire weekend at Nick's.

She didn't go home, not once, not even to get a change of clothes. She showered at Nick's place (at one point, together—although this arrangement took the focus off of getting clean somewhat, not to mention all but ignored water conservation). He found clothes for her to borrow ("Huh," he remarked admiringly, upon loaning her a Stones T-shirt, "and people always say Mick Jagger can't get any sexier . . ."). He gifted her a toothbrush from Duane Reade, and propped it in the cup in the bathroom next to his own, the handles crisscrossed, the two brush heads facing each other as if in collegial conversation.

When they were hungry, they ordered in. Time became strange and elastic; in one regard, the weekend flew by, yet each moment felt full, as though it contained a lifetime. Neither had any desire to do much outside the apartment itself; there was nothing they would rather be doing than touching each other and soaking up the euphoria that came from simply being near each other.

They left the apartment exactly once, and took a meandering walk together. At Second Avenue and Third Street, they stopped in front of a large glass window belonging to a piercing and tattoo parlor. Inside the red-painted room, two girls who looked like possible NYU students were getting their noses pierced, while a glimpse of a room farther back showed an artist working on a young man's back tattoo, the needle's loud buzz faintly discernible through the glass window.

They meandered on, and took a walk through Washington Square Park, pausing to listen to a group of street musicians jamming with drums and a harmonica, then settling in to sit on the steps leading down into the park's big circular fountain to people watch. Skateboarders whizzed recklessly around them, the wheels making heavy grinding sounds over the paving stones, while small children played in the fountain's base as though it was one big urban paddling pool. A boom box competed with the street musicians, adding to the cacophony of boisterous noise.

Nick watched Sawyer watching the children splash one another, and grinned.

"How hot are you?" he cajoled.

"Not *that* hot." She shook her head, reading his mind.

"OK. So we just run through the middle—just once, real fast," Nick suggested.

"That water's disgusting." Sawyer laughed.

"C'mon!" Nick said. "On hot days like this, I've always stared at this fountain but never gone in."

She gave him a wary look from the sides of her eyes, but already she was beginning to cave. There was pretty much nothing she could resist doing with Nick.

He fished in his pocket and pulled out a coin.

It was a subway token.

"Heads, I run in first. Tails, you run in first."

"You can't bet on a subway token," Sawyer complained.

"Why not? This coin is worth more than most—a dollar fifty, not to mention an invaluable ride anywhere you want to go in our great city's five boroughs."

"You really oughta work for the MTA."

"Heads, I run in first," he repeated. "Tails, you run in first."

"What about the side for not running in at all?"

"Sorry—we've run out of sides. Just the two," Nick said.

"And . . . exactly which is which?"

"'New York City Transit Authority' is heads," he said. "Duh. And 'Good for One Fare' is tails."

She smirked at him and rolled her eyes, then nodded for him to go ahead.

"Here we go."

He flipped it, caught it, and slapped it onto the back of his left hand.

"Tails."

"No way," Sawyer complained. She reached for the coin. "Is that thing broken?"

"Go on," he urged, gesturing to the spurting water at the middle of the fountain's base.

Sawyer pretended to give him a murderous stare. He laughed and waved her on.

She stood up and smoothed down the oversize T-shirt she'd turned into a "dress" by cinching one of Nick's work ties artistically around the waist.

"At least I'm wearing *your* clothes," she pointed out. She glanced at the T-shirt. "And thank God this is black."

She took a deep breath, then dashed nimbly down the remaining fountain stairs and through the middle of the fountain itself. She heard Nick laughing behind her as she shielded her face and squealed "*Sorry! Sorry! Coming through!*" to the children playing in the shallows.

When she reached the other side, she came back around on dry ground to where he stood, still laughing. She'd tried to run fast enough to avoid getting soaked, but her bangs were wet and plastered to her forehead, and water dripped off her hair onto her shoulders.

"Your turn," she said.

"Are you kidding me?" he teased. "Who runs through a fountain in New York City? Do you know the kinds of pathogens and microbes that are probably in there?"

Sawyer gave him another murderous stare. This time she did not have to pretend.

"I'm kidding," Nick reassured her. "That's one thing you can count on, actually," he said. "I don't go back on my word."

He handed her the token he'd flipped. "Here. You earned this."

She shook her head. "That thing already took me on one ride today, thank you."

"I'll let you in on a little secret . . . coins don't decide anything. *People* do," he said. "Some part of you was dying to run in that fountain."

"Yeah, yeah. A bigger part of me is dying for *you* to run in that fountain."

He gave a Cheshire grin and tossed her the token, which she caught purely out of reflex. Sawyer rolled her eyes at him, but with a smile. She watched as he turned and ran into the fountain. When he got to the center, he stopped and stepped up onto the elevated circle in the middle, right in the center of the spurting jets of water, letting them drench him.

"Satisfied?" he shouted up to her.

She waited a long minute before responding.

"OK," she shouted back. "Satisfied."

By then the summer sun was directly overhead, beating down on the city without mercy. They were both dry by the time they made it back to Nick's place, but they took another shower together, anyway.

• • •

By Sunday night, Sawyer had to face the truth: she had to return to her apartment before the start of the workweek.

Complicating matters was the fact that she had completely neglected the pile of manuscripts she'd promised Johanna she would read as part of the "increased responsibilities" she'd requested. She would have to play catch-up every night after work for the first few days of the week . . . and then use the second half of the weekday evenings to get ahead if she wanted to spend the following weekend at Nick's again.

She explained the situation to him.

"All right," he agreed. "Until next weekend. We've still got summer Fridays to kick things off."

"Thank God for summer Fridays," Sawyer said, already looking forward. Then she gave a slight frown as a new thought crossed her mind. "We're running out of them."

It was true. There were only two more left before Labor Day, when the publishing and advertising worlds of New York would go back to their regular workday schedules.

"You know, originally I was dreading this summer, stuck in the city," Sawyer said. "Now it feels like it went too fast."

"We'll figure it out," Nick said. "Together."

27.

She came home expecting a ton of messages on the answering machine from Charles—perhaps some of them angry, demanding to know why she hadn't been home all weekend.

She was surprised to find only two messages from Charles, both brief, with breezy lead-ins like, *Hey! Guess you're out running errands or taking a walk*... And there was something else Sawyer noticed, a particular note of relief in his voice, like he was glad to have missed her and gotten the machine.

They were deadlocked, it seemed, in some kind of unspoken pact of avoidance. She wasn't quite sure how to feel about it.

She went to the computer and turned it on out of habit, then checked her inbox and found that Autumn had finally replied to her email.

> To: Adventures_of_Tom@aol.com
> From: AutumnLeaves@hotmail.com
>
> SAWYER!!!
>
> I am SO SORRY—I went out of town on another little side trip and couldn't get to the internet café for, like, a WEEK! I had no idea things were like this for you.

That sounds like more than cold feet. It sounds like you are honestly thinking about calling off the wedding—do I have that correct? I can only imagine the weight on your shoulders right now. No matter what, Sawyer, I love you and you are amazing!

Speaking of. This Nick guy has turned up with lousy timing. And "cocky" is a hard sell. But . . . it's hard as your best friend to hear you say he makes you feel like the best parts of "old you" and the most optimistic parts of "future you" . . . and not like the guy.

It's what every girl wants for her best friend. And I love Charles, but I never heard you say he made you feel that way.

Did Nick really say he doesn't want to hang out anymore? I find it really hard to believe that he could resist, given any kind of a choice. My money's on: He can't, if he has any kind of taste and sense.

Anyway, I tried to call you but I kept getting your machine and I didn't want to waste minutes on my phone cards leaving a message, and now I'm out of phone cards (I'll try to get more). But I'm desperate to know that you're OK. Please write.

Love you buckets,
Autumn

Sawyer reread Autumn's words, smiled, and clicked reply.

When Sawyer finally clicked send and looked up from the keyboard again, an entire hour had passed.

She regarded the clock, thinking. Charles had left the message earlier that day, a little after noon. It was 10:47 p.m. now, which meant it was 9:47 p.m. in Chicago.

She picked up the phone and dialed his hotel, then pressed the extension for the switchboard.

"Good evening, room number of the guest you wish to contact, please?" the operator's voice came over the line, when Sawyer finally pushed enough buttons to navigate the menu and get a person.

"Two thirteen," Sawyer spoke into the phone.

"Thank you!"

She heard a click. Then the line began to ring.

It rang.

And rang.

Finally, there was another click, and a different cheerful operator.

"Your guest appears to be unavailable—would you like to leave a message?"

"No . . . that's OK," Sawyer replied. "I'll try again later. Thank you."

"Have a pleasant evening."

Sawyer hung up, and set about preparing her things for Monday morning. A heavy shadow of anxiety followed her around the apartment. Despite being utterly exhausted, she dug a manuscript out of her bag at random and started reading, figuring the only way to catch up . . . was to catch up.

The manuscript wasn't half bad, although Sawyer already knew Johanna's taste well enough to know she would pass. As she read, she jotted down notes on a pad for the eventual reader's report she would type up and turn in.

After a couple of hours, she decided to try to call Charles again.

"Good evening, room number of the guest you wish to contact, please?"

"Hi. Two thirteen, please."

"Thank you!"

Click.

The line began to ring.

And ring.

And ring.

"Your guest appears to be unavailable—would you like to leave a message?"

Sawyer blinked, this time genuinely surprised. She looked at the time. It was after midnight in Chicago. On a Sunday.

"Ma'am? Would you care to leave a message?"

"No," she said finally. "No, thank you."

• • •

She woke up early on Monday, went to the office early, intent on making up for the time she'd lost over the weekend, reading, making notes on manuscripts, and checking over all the other spreadsheets and reports she'd promised to update.

To her relief, Johanna came in very late that Monday, when it was nearly already noon.

"Rumor has it, Johanna has started seeing that famous journalist, Martin Wolf," Kaylee confided in a low voice.

Sawyer took this in, nodding coolly. But inside, she was slightly shocked to realize that, in a bizarre and unexpected twist, it was entirely possible that she and Johanna had lived similar weekends.

For now, she merely hoped it would buy her more time to catch up on her work. Falling behind and having Johanna express her dissatisfaction with Sawyer (which, in some ways, might ironically bring Johanna another kind of satisfaction altogether) was not something Sawyer wanted to endure.

* * *

On Tuesday evening, Sawyer was home, still picking away at her backlog of work by reading yet another manuscript, when the phone rang.

For a moment, she thought it might be Charles calling from Chicago. Then, the more likely guess materialized, floating up like a cue card in her brain: *Kathy.*

She felt a gut-wrenching pang of guilt.

"Sawyer!" Kathy sang her name in greeting. "I spent the day with Charles's cousins, and we had the bridesmaid dresses fitted. Oh, I think they look just super, and Elizabeth and Kimberly agree! I took plenty of photos for you to see." Kathy paused very briefly for air, then asked, "Do you have a fax? Can I fax them to you?"

"Oh," Sawyer said. "Um, a fax? We don't, like, have one at home here or anything . . ."

"How about at work? Can I send them there?"

Sawyer pictured the look on Johanna's face (and in particular, the tight mouth and narrowed eyes that signaled utter disapproval) as color photos of Charles's cousins, Elizabeth and Kimberly, slowly unfurled from the office fax machine next to Johanna's office. Knowing Kathy, there were sure to be at least a dozen photos, if not more.

"I don't think that would work either, Kathy," Sawyer replied gently. "Would it be possible to just attach them to an email?"

"An email?" Kathy repeated. "How do you do that? Ed printed them out for me. I have the photos themselves right here."

"Hmm, well, if he printed them for you, then it sounds like you might have taken them with a digital camera?" Sawyer tried to help by conjecturing. "So if you can just upload the memory card, then you can send the photos by email . . ."

"Ooo, that sounds complicated. Hold on, Sawyer. Ed? *ED?*"

As Sawyer listened, she heard Kathy talking with Charles's father in the background (*Is this a digital camera, Ed? Can we just send the photos over email?*).

The next thing Sawyer knew, Kathy had put Ed on the line.

"Hi—Sawyer?"

"Hi, Ed. I'm here."

"I'm going to upload these photos for Kathy and send them to you. Do you have a moment? What's your email address?"

She gave him her AOL address.

"'Adventures of Tom'? Oh, I get it! Ha! How clever." Ed laughed.

They chatted for a few minutes as he turned on their home computer.

"How are you doing these days, kiddo?"

"I'm . . . OK," Sawyer replied.

It made her both happy and sad to hear Ed's voice. She genuinely liked him.

"I know Charles is in Chicago. You must be ready for him to come home to you!"

"Yes," Sawyer agreed lamely.

"I'm sure that big case will wrap up soon," Ed reassured her. "And then you'll have him back, just like normal. Well—not normal! I guess you'll be married!"

The conversation was making Sawyer a little queasy.

"Well, I'd better free up the line so we can log on," Ed reminded her.

"Of course."

"It was lovely hearing your voice—it's always lovely hearing your voice, Sawyer."

"You, too, Ed."

"Oh, hey—Kathy wants to say a few words before we hang up. Hold on . . ."

There was a muffled ruckus as Ed handed the phone back over to his wife.

"Sawyer?" came Kathy's voice over the phone.

"I'm here."

"I can't wait for you to see the photos. I guess your friend Autumn still needs to get her maid-of-honor dress? I know she wants hers to be different, but we'd love it if she could match somewhat! Can you send these photos on to her? And don't forget—we have the second-to-last fitting for your own dress next month in September. And your bridal shower! I can't wait to come to town and host it all; I'm so looking forward! Oh, honey, we are so happy you're going to be a part of the family soon! It feels like you already are."

Sawyer tried to reply, but her throat had suddenly thickened with emotion. She tried to clear it.

"Thank you, Kathy," she said, when she was finally able to speak. "You and Ed . . . mean a lot to me."

It was true, which only made her throat tighten up again, and her heart feel like a washcloth being wrung dry.

"OK, Ed tells me I have to get off the phone if we're going to send those pictures. Look for them in your email, and tell me what you think! OK. Love you, talk to you soon!"

After Sawyer hung up, she checked her email. Thirty minutes later, the email from Ed and Kathy came through. She clicked on it, and stared at the photos for several minutes, lost in thought. She mentally calculated the days until the wedding, and was gripped by a wave of vertigo. She logged off the internet to free up the phone line and tried Charles's hotel room again.

There was no answer.

28.

FRIDAY, AUGUST 20

The phone call with Kathy and Ed had literally made Sawyer sick to her stomach; she couldn't eat. She couldn't sleep, either. The weight of what she had yet to do—call off the wedding and smash their hearts to pieces—was crushing her.

She thought about emailing Nick that she couldn't make it that Friday. Several times over the course of that week, Sawyer sat staring at a blank email message, ordering herself to write to Nick that she couldn't make it.

The message—despite her best efforts—remained blank, unsent.

After a while, she considered modifying the plan. If she was going to cancel their Friday together, it would be better to explain to Nick in person.

But when Sawyer saw Nick a few minutes after noon on that Friday, sitting at her favorite table near the waterfall in Greenacre Park, it was like the sun breaking through an ominous storm cloud, lighting the way. She felt her body warm and loosen up, her chest grow lighter.

He was sitting, waiting for her with a couple of hot dogs and a big grin. In that second, she knew she wasn't willing to spend a second of that weekend without him.

"I thought I'd be blatantly obvious with the symbolism of what I *really* want to give you," Nick joked, handing her one of the hot dogs.

She snorted with laughter, accepted the hot dog, and raised an eyebrow—first at the frank, then at him.

"Well, that makes me want to hurry up back to your place," she teased. "How fast can we eat these?"

Nick looked at her, dead serious. "I don't know, but I'm ready to give the world champion hot dog eaters in Coney Island a run for their money."

They wolfed down the hot dogs and raced to Nick's. Once there, they didn't quite make it to the bed and wound up having sex on the floor.

Afterward, they lay on the rug, exhausted, naked despite the bright afternoon sunshine streaming in the windows. They talked, until they were kissing again. Finally they moved to the bed, and discovered each other all over again, this time more slowly and deliberately.

Time took on that strange, elastic quality again, where the moments stretched long and short at the same time. After a while, the light began to wane in the windows with the first hints of evening dusk.

"When I'm with you, it's almost like another dimension," Sawyer observed in a murmur, her body entwined with Nick's. She heard her own words aloud and felt a self-conscious twinge. "That sounds like some kind of cheesy cliché, I know," she said.

"No," Nick disagreed. "I think I know what you mean. Things feel different to me, too. The light, the time, the hours in the day."

Sawyer smiled, relieved to know the experience was shared in some way.

"Actually, I've been thinking about this," she admitted. "I think maybe New York exists on multiple planes." She paused, and added, "It's like I was living in an entirely different New York until this summer . . . with you."

Nick pulled her closer against him, then craned his neck to give her a kiss. She kissed him back, then laid her ear against his chest, listening to the even inhale and exhale of his lungs. She felt strangely light, and also like she was slowly falling through the bed, through the floor, through the planet.

She dozed off for a brief spell.

• • •

A short while later, Sawyer awoke to the sound of water rushing through a tap. As she stirred in the bed, she realized that Nick was gone. The windows were fully dark, glowing only with the incandescence of the streetlamps outside, and streaked with rain. The heat had broken, giving way to the cool relief of a summer storm. She lifted her head and looked in the direction of the sound.

The claw-foot tub in the kitchen.

Nick was filling it, and lighting candles.

She got up and crossed the room, gazing wide-eyed at the candlelit scene.

"First time you were here, you were so curious about it," Nick said.

"I've never taken a bath in the middle of a kitchen before."

He stepped in, and held his arms out to help her follow him in. "C'mon," he urged.

Sawyer stepped up carefully into the tub. They faced each other, like a dare, and eased their bodies into the warm, sudsy water, then leaned back against opposite ends. Nick had added some kind of oil; the water felt silky and smelled like lavender and cedar. At first, Sawyer gazed at Nick across from her, the planes of his face catching the flickering candlelight. She felt his hand on her leg under the water, surprised that even after everything they'd done that afternoon, his simplest touch still managed to give her a little thrill. She breathed in the scented oils and took in the scene around them, surveying the details more closely.

"The romance level here is pretty impressive."

"Good. That's what I was aiming for," Nick said.

She gave him a coy, suspicious look.

"What?" he demanded, wary.

"Don't kill me . . ."

"What is it?"

"Have you hosted many ladies in this tub?" she asked. "Do they all get . . . you know . . . ?" She gestured to the candles and the scented oils.

"Only the really special ones."

"Ah. So this is your 'move.'"

"This old bathtub is my favorite secret in this apartment," Nick said. "I already told you that. But as far as secrets go, I've never shared it with anyone."

"Wait—you're saying you've never taken a bath with anyone else in this tub?"

"Nope. You're the first," he answered. "This is 'my move' with *you*—the one and only you." He shook his head. "I've never had to work so hard to impress someone as I have with you."

Sawyer frowned, puzzled.

"What?" Nick said, reading her face.

"I guess sometimes I wonder . . . why me?"

He shrugged. "You're someone to impress."

"Not sure you felt that way the night we met," she retorted. "I'm pretty sure you mocked my name, then hauled ass to the bar, desperate for a fresh glass of whiskey."

"Scotch," Nick corrected. "And I *did* think you were someone to impress. You're the kind of girl I never bother to ask out, because I figure a girl like you is way out of my league," he explained. "And of course, the cherry on top is that girls like you always end up with guys like Charles, who's even less in your league."

The mention of Charles made her unsettled, nervous. She was silent for a moment.

"Anyway, I wasn't exactly in a good mood the night we met," Nick said.

He paused, then proceeded to paint the picture from his own perspective.

"There was my girlfriend: flirting with her jackass coworker. And sitting next to her coworker, there was this beautiful, intelligent, kind-hearted girl trying to salvage the situation by being cheerful and making friendly small talk. I was rude because the whole thing sucked, from top to bottom: canceling a gig to attend a stuffy corporate dinner for a company I don't even work for, Kendra, Charles . . . and the fact that a girl like you would put up with a jerk like that."

Sawyer was surprised. She would have never been able to guess he'd felt that way.

"And clearly you stayed on my mind," Nick said. "Because I jumped through a few hoops to get your email address and send you an apology."

"Did you . . . like me, um, *this way* . . . then?" she asked, baffled.

"Well, I thought you were attractive, but I wasn't hitting on you with that apology, if that's what you're asking," Nick replied. "I really did just feel like I owed you an apology. But then . . . you started being all cute and charming over the internet . . . and then I guess the stuff with Kendra and Charles just got to me; you didn't deserve that."

"It's strange, isn't it," she mused. "We came together because we thought they might be having an affair, and now, we're the ones . . . well, *here*." She glanced between their naked bodies in the bathtub.

"I still say they're having an affair," Nick said.

Sawyer looked at him. He shrugged.

"Not to be a guy about it, but if it's like you say, and there's nothing going on at home . . . well . . ." Nick shrugged again.

Sawyer wondered if she'd ever know the truth. But it felt different to wonder now—less personal, or at a slight remove, almost like she was wondering about a friend's life instead of her own.

"So, you admit: you invited me to meet you at the Yale Club because you wanted to protect me from the same thing that once happened to *you*, in the past . . ." Sawyer said, remembering her revelation on the ferry.

"Yeah, but by then I could tell some part of me was already trying to impress you, too. I'd read your poem and couldn't stop thinking about it. And I subconsciously did all the things I usually do when I'm trying to wow a girl—nice suit, rooftop drinks at the Yale Club—only, you impressed *me* when it was obvious that you weren't into any of that. That day we spent on the Lower East Side—the Watering Hole, the Tenement Museum, Katz's, listening to my friend's band at the club—that day, I knew it was already too late. And each time I've seen you since, I've only wanted more."

Sawyer sat there, absorbing all this, surprised by how everything had totally realigned itself. That first evening they'd met, Nick had come off so cocky and rude . . . she'd been *sure* he disdained her. It was a shock to think that he'd noticed her—*really* noticed her—right from the start. It was a shock to hear him say she was the kind of girl he felt was out of his league, when she'd felt the reverse was true. And it was a shock the way he spoke so frankly now, as they sat naked in the tub facing each other, unmasking his initial behavior—the way he'd mocked her name, his dry cynicism, and his aloof demeanor—for what it was: the defense mechanisms of a person who, in the end, cared a great deal. And cared a great deal about her, especially.

She scooted toward him in the bathtub and gave him a sincere, lingering kiss.

Nick smiled.

He kissed her back, until eventually they were doing much more than kissing, and the lukewarm water was lapping over the edge of the tub, falling to the floor in tiny splashing waterfalls.

* * *

Once the heat broke and the rain passed, the weather turned tauntingly perfect.

It was sunny, but the air was dry and cool, tempered by a gentle breeze from the western direction, over the Hudson. The streets smelled clean. People walked around rosy-cheeked but sweat-free. Everyone was bright-eyed and in a good mood, a rarity in New York.

The problem with the spell of perfect weather was that it was *so* perfect, it was impossible for Nick and Sawyer to stay indoors for the entire weekend.

By Sunday afternoon, they finally gave in, and made up their minds to venture out, setting their sights on Central Park and packing up a picnic blanket. On their way, they stopped at Gristedes and filled up a couple of grocery bags with snacks. When they got to the park, they walked around for a bit first, showing each other their favorite spots.

Nick loved the echoing arcade tunnel under Bethesda Terrace, with its arches and antique tiled ceilings lit up with white carnival light bulbs.

"The perfect spot to do a clandestine drug deal," Sawyer joked about the tunnel.

"Or play the violin," Nick replied, nodding to the violinist taking advantage of the acoustics.

Sawyer smiled. It *was* a beautiful spot, actually. A play of light and shadow mingled with a play of sound and echo. Inside the darkness of the tunnel, its belle epoque arches framed the Bethesda Fountain with its winged angel behind them, and the lake beyond. They continued through the tunnel and up the stairs to one of Central Park's classic wide paths lined with enormous trees, their leaves forming a lush canopy.

"Now I'll show you my favorite place in the park," Sawyer said, pointing off to the right.

She led the way along a few smaller paths that wound around a couple of small hills, then reached a clearing and a paved road. Disco music pumped from a boom box hooked up to an amp. A low wire fence roped off an irregular oval shape, and roller skaters whizzed in circles, pumping their legs in time to the music, spinning and swirling and dancing. Nick laughed.

"Interesting!" he commented. "I never would have guessed. Skater's Circle is your favorite spot in the park?"

"I love it," Sawyer admitted. "Roller skates . . . the campy music . . . Everybody's so happy in this little corner of the park."

"Have you ever joined in?"

Sawyer shyly shook her head.

"I don't even own a pair of roller skates," she said.

"You can always get skates," Nick said. "Easy. But maybe you don't even need 'em to join in and have a good time."

Sawyer thought about it for a minute and shrugged.

Nick pointed to a grassy slope beside the makeshift roller rink.

"Partial shade," he said. "Perfect. Let's go."

They staked out a spot and laid down their blanket, then unpacked the picnic they'd cobbled together. Strawberries, carrot sticks, apple slices, barbecue-flavor chips, cheese and crackers, a deli tub of gourmet mac and cheese, a couple of cans of Limonata, plus a slice of very fancy-looking quiche from a French bakery they passed on the Upper East Side as they made their way from the subway to the park.

They grazed on the food for a while, watching the roller skaters, then sprawled out on the blanket.

Sawyer stared at the skaters, mesmerized. Nick stared at Sawyer staring.

"You really love watching those skaters."

"I do," Sawyer admitted. "They're so *free*. There's something in the air all around them. Like, a general good mood."

"Could be a contact high from all the weed in the air," Nick joked cynically.

Sawyer laughed. She looked at him and shrugged. "Anyway, I love it. Just sitting nearby, listening to their music . . . you kinda feel like part of the party." She paused, and added, "It's funny because the other thing I love to do in the park is kind of opposite—very solitary."

"And that is?"

"Sit and read and get lost in a good book."

"Of course," Nick grunted and smiled.

He asked Sawyer how things were going at work, and she caught him up to speed.

"It sounds to me like you're dying to follow Erin over to Knopf," Nick commented. "So why not go for it?"

Sawyer sat up. She fidgeted, thinking, and pulled at the grass next to the blanket.

"I don't know," she said.

Nick laughed. "Look, Sawyer—it's pretty simple. If you want to do something, you should do it."

"Oh yeah?" Sawyer teased.

Nick shrugged. "There's nothing stopping you."

Sawyer mulled this for a moment. The music faded out and a new song came on as the DJ started playing "If You Feel Like Dancin'" by Kool & the Gang. She took it as a sign.

"Know what? You're right."

She stood up from the blanket and brushed herself off.

"Where are you going?" Nick asked.

"To do what I want to do," Sawyer replied, her lips twisting into a secretive smile.

Nick watched with incredulity as she strode off in the direction of the makeshift roller rink. She picked her way around the perimeter until she found a break in the fencing and squeezed in. With a quick look to her left and right to make sure she could cross, Sawyer scampered to the middle of the rink, where the DJ worked the boom box and amp.

She shouted hello to the DJ and gave him a high five in greeting, then began dancing.

There was no truly graceful way to boogie down to Kool & the Gang wearing flat shoes when everyone else was whizzing around you wearing roller skates, but Sawyer didn't care. She started dancing tentatively at first, but soon enough, she was dancing with total abandon. There was a good chance she looked like a dork, but she didn't care; she was really feeling the music now. She closed her eyes and tossed her hair.

When she opened her eyes again, they went straight to where Nick sat on the picnic blanket. He was laughing and shaking his head at her . . . but she could see deep affection in his expression, too, a kind of adoration. No one had ever looked at her this way; her stomach did a tiny flip as she caught Nick's gaze and exchanged a knowing look.

A song or two later, she'd danced herself into a state of exhaustion. She returned to the picnic blanket, sweaty but buzzing with her newfound feeling of freedom.

"Oof, dancing is hard work!"

"It is when you do it like you were doing."

Sawyer plopped down, flat on her back on the picnic blanket, and stared up at the pattern of tree leaves against the sky, steadily slowing her breath and letting her sweat cool her. She felt Nick studying her where she lay.

"What?" she asked cheerfully.

"You know . . ." he began. "You don't need my advice, by the way. You have it in you to do whatever you want. Half the time, I'm telling you what you already know—I'm just repeating the thoughts and feelings I hear you saying back to you, basically."

Sawyer looked at him and smiled.

"I know," she said.

"I just wanted to make that clear."

Sawyer nodded.

He reclined on the blanket near her, and she scooted closer and slightly perpendicular, using his stomach and chest as a pillow. Nick seemed to relax, happy. He ran his fingers idly through her hair. Then he reached for her hand. It was her left. He played absently with her hand, feeling each of her fingers in turn, but paused when he reached her ring finger. She could feel him tense, and saw him looking down at her engagement ring warily, lost in thought. Then, he took a breath, as though changing the subject.

"I was thinking I really want to go somewhere together," he said.

"Somewhere?"

"Out of the city. For the weekend. A real weekend getaway, before the summer's over," he said. "Doesn't have to be far. I'd really love to take you around Stony Brook, and show you where I grew up. And go to Cedar Beach and go swimming together."

Sawyer smiled, imagining it. "That sounds really cool," she agreed.

"I was thinking next weekend. Leave on Friday since we still have summer Fridays. I can pick you up around one, one thirty."

Sawyer involuntarily froze. Her brain ticked through the details. Next weekend, Charles would be home from Chicago . . . *What the hell would that be like?* Her brain tried to imagine even further: If she and Nick went away for the weekend . . . then what? What would come next, after that?

Nick sat up. She felt him frowning at her, and she understood that he had glimpsed the hesitation written on her face.

"Damn it, Sawyer, I don't know what to do sometimes."

"What do you mean?"

"It's just . . . I've never had to chase a woman so hard. Or wonder so much. To be honest . . . it feels a little like I'm the chick in the relationship."

Sawyer quelled the urge to launch into a gender debate about what it meant to be "the chick in the relationship." Nick was telling her something about himself; she understood that much.

"The way I feel about you, Nick . . . I've never felt this way about anybody," she said quietly. "I want this. I want you."

He gazed at her, steadily studying her face.

"Then, you'll come next weekend?"

"I want to. I'll . . . try to figure it out."

His eyes dropped to the ring on her left hand again.

"I forget sometimes," he said, tipping his chin in the direction of her ring. "You still haven't taken the leap with me. Not really."

She was uncomfortable. She slid the ring off her finger and held it in her palm, staring at it thoughtfully. She'd forgotten she was wearing it. At the same time, to say it meant nothing to her would be a lie.

"I owe him a conversation," she said, still staring at the ring. Her voice was hushed but certain.

Nick was quiet for a long moment.

"You're a nice person," he said finally.

It didn't sound like a compliment. But it also carried the weight of acceptance.

She realized she would feel strange putting the ring back on in front of Nick. She reached for her bag, and tucked it safely into one of the zippered pockets within.

Nick watched her with an expression she couldn't quite place. Hope. Or cynicism. Or both. When it came to Nick, she realized, the two often sprang from the same deep well within his heart.

29.

Charles was originally scheduled to fly back from Chicago to New York on Tuesday. But when Sawyer arrived home on Sunday evening, there was another message from him on the answering machine, apologizing and explaining that wrapping up the case was taking even longer than expected, and Tuesday's return had now been pushed back to Thursday evening.

"I know I sound like a broken record, but I'll make it up to you," his recorded voice promised as it blared through the answering machine's speaker. "Actually, I have a big surprise for you. I'm pretty sure you're going to be blown away by it. Seriously. Can't wait to see you Thursday! Love you, be back before you know it!"

The message ended.

Sawyer chewed her lip, anxious, frustrated. She made no move to phone him in his hotel room; she already knew he wouldn't pick up. He was busy with the case. Or busy with Kendra.

They really needed to talk. A two-day delay might as well be an eternity.

She felt a surge of anger . . . and deep guilt.

With nowhere else to point it, she directed her anger at Wexler

Gibbons. She was sick of hearing the name, sick of the faceless corporate entity having so much influence over the circumstances of her life.

• • •

On Monday, Sawyer's busy weekends finally caught up with her at work, when Johanna called Sawyer into her office.

"I've noticed you're a little behind on those readers' reports you were eager to take charge of," Johanna remarked. "I hope the workload is not too much for you?"

"No," Sawyer insisted. "I did get a little behind, but I'm almost all the way caught up again. It's not too much for me, and I'm really happy to be doing it."

"I've also noticed," Johanna continued, unmoved by Sawyer's sincere enthusiasm, "that you tend to turn your reports in toward the end of the week."

Sawyer didn't know what to say to this.

"I hope you're not using office hours to do the reading. In general—and while it may seem like quite a lot to ask—reading is something that takes place in *addition* to our regular hours in the office. You understand that, right?"

Sawyer blinked. She did know that it was "expected" in the publishing industry to do a lot of reading outside of paid office hours, but she'd never had anyone spell it out so plainly to her face, and with such imperious implication.

"Yes . . ." she stammered, when she found her voice. "I understand that."

"Good," Johanna said, sucking in a deep breath and letting it out as though relieved. "Well, anyway. I simply wanted to check in and make sure the workload isn't too much for you."

"Thank you. It's not."

"Good. Publishing is hard work if you really want to keep up with it. But by the same token, reading books is what we would all be doing for fun, anyway, right?"

"Absolutely."

"Your fiancé probably works longer hours than we do, when it comes down to it."

"Beg pardon?"

"Doesn't your fiancé work at Wexler Gibbons? Now, there's a company that likes to squeeze every last ounce of dedication out of its employees—as I'm sure you're becoming aware."

Sawyer froze. She wasn't sure who she disliked more in that moment, Johanna or the whole of Wexler Gibbons.

"Sure," Sawyer finally forced herself to agree.

Johanna shrugged and turned her attention to some papers on her desk.

"Wexler Gibbons . . ." she repeated, with a contemplative sigh. "With a company like that, eventually, you'll find you have to make room in your career in order to support his," she concluded, not bothering to raise her gaze to meet Sawyer's. "So much of the time, that's the way it goes."

Sawyer had no idea what to say to this. Everything that sprang to the tip of her tongue was fundamentally inappropriate.

"Thanks, Johanna," she managed, and left.

Back at her desk, Sawyer sat still for several minutes, trying to put a name to her emotions. After a while, she realized she was stewing in a kind of quiet rage.

• • •

After saying goodbye in the park, Sawyer didn't hear from Nick on Monday. But after getting home from work on Tuesday, she knew him well enough to know he would be waiting for her online that evening.

She opened Instant Messenger and clicked on Nikolai70.

Adventures_of_Tom: Hey, you there?

His reply came almost immediately.

Nikolai70: Hey

Nikolai70: How'd it go with Charles?

Adventures_of_Tom: Well

Adventures_of_Tom: The case is taking longer. His return flight was pushed back

Adventures_of_Tom: He's getting back on Thursday now

There was a long pause.

Sawyer waited.

Nikolai70: So you haven't talked

Adventures_of_Tom: No.

Another long pause.

Nikolai70: I booked a place for us to stay this weekend.

Nikolai70: Do you still want to go?

Adventures_of_Tom: I want to

Adventures_of_Tom: I guess I just thought I had more time to talk to Charles, and see how that was going to go.

Nikolai70: And now . . . ?

Adventures_of_Tom: Now I don't know

Yet another long pause—longer than the first two combined. Sawyer started to type, then deleted it all.

Then she tried to type again, but deleted that, too.

Nikolai70: When did you find out his trip had been extended and his flight had been pushed back to Thursday?

Adventures_of_Tom: He left a message

Adventures_of_Tom: On Sunday

Another long pause. Sawyer could sense Nick absorbing the details and reacting, withdrawing back into his shell, and there was little she could do to stop it. Again, she felt compelled to explain, but everything she typed felt wrong, and she deleted it before hitting enter.

Finally, the screen blinked with a new message from Nick.

Nikolai70: Look, Sawyer, I don't want to make things more complicated than they already are for you

Nikolai70: I want to see you next weekend, and I've booked everything for us to get away.

Nikolai70: But you know all this messaging is not my thing. And the not knowing where you stand is too hard.

Nikolai70: Send me a message on Thursday if you still want to go.

Nikolai70: OK?

Adventures_of_Tom: But if I don't know until Thursday . . . will you lose money on stuff you've booked?

Nikolai70: Screw the money. That part's not important

Nikolai70: What's important is that you come if you want to come

Nikolai70: Or you don't, if you don't want to.

Nikolai70: Don't worry about the rest of it.

Adventures_of_Tom: Nick, I do really want to go

Adventures_of_Tom: I'm just trying to figure all this stuff out

Nikolai70: I know. Just let me know where you are by Thursday, OK?

Nikolai70: If I don't hear from you, I'll take that as your answer. And I'll understand.

Nikolai70: I gotta go. This messaging stuff always drains me, and I have some things to take care of.

Adventures_of_Tom: OK. Talk to you soon?

Nikolai70: Shoot me a message on Thursday

Adventures_of_Tom: OK, I will

AOL User Nikolai70 has gone offline

Sawyer stared at the screen. She scrolled up, back through their exchange, and reread it, as though looking for an answer to a question that wasn't quite settled in her mind. Then she realized: the part that was absent was something she'd wanted to say, but hadn't.

• • •

On Wednesday, Sawyer logged on again. She looked for Nick, although she already knew she wouldn't find him online; he'd wait and look for her message on Thursday, just as he'd said.

Somehow, over the course of the summer, Nick had become the sole person Sawyer wanted to talk to when she was troubled—the ironic twist being that now, the thing she most wanted to talk about was *him*.

Sawyer thought for a moment, then picked up the phone and dialed. It rang a few times, then clicked as someone finally answered.

"Moshi moshi?"

"Did I wake you again?"

"Nope—already up! Eating some *natto* for breakfast."

"What's that?"

"I doubt we have enough time or money for the long-distance bill in order to adequately explain what's that."

"Fair."

"What's up?"

"Well, seeing as how it's tomorrow there, and you know all about what's going to happen in the future . . ."

Sawyer explained the situation, all about Nick's invitation to go away for the weekend, and the timing of Charles coming home from Chicago . . . her total fear of calling off the wedding.

"You already know what I'm going to say," Autumn responded, after listening. "But it sounds like you need to hear me say it." She paused, then took a breath. "Of course you need to follow your heart on this one. There will be fallout. But there will be longer-term fallout if you're not true to yourself—you *know* this!"

Sawyer was quiet, absorbing.

"Look," Autumn continued. "Whatever you decide, I'll be there when the day comes in October . . . whether it's to walk down the aisle with you, or meet your new boyfriend and help you mail back the entire contents of your registry."

"Thanks, Autumn."

"Although, keep in mind that no one can *prove it* if a stray toaster or waffle iron were to go missing . . ."

Eventually, they hung up, Sawyer already dreading the imminent phone bill. It was worth it; talking to Autumn had buoyed her, the way only a call with a true friend could.

She sat thinking of whom else she might call for additional fortification. After a moment, she picked up the phone again and dialed.

"Hello?"

Sawyer smiled with relief to hear her mother's voice, suddenly feeling like a child again.

"You've got cold feet," her mother diagnosed, after Sawyer hinted she was considering canceling the wedding. "That happens to everyone! I know you: you'll be fine when the day comes."

Sawyer was silent, surprised. Her mother had always seemed to be opposed to Sawyer getting married so young; Sawyer realized she'd been counting on Carol to affirm her own doubts about October.

"I don't know, Mom," Sawyer said. "I don't know if it's just cold feet."

"Well, you can't back out now," her mother said, but in a light, joking tone. "Did I tell you? I got a call from someone at *The New York Times* about your wedding announcement . . . I was so surprised! But how fun. I suppose some of that is Kathy's doing . . ."

"Yes," Sawyer said, feeling her body go slack.

"I don't give her enough credit," Carol admitted now. "She's doing so much to make your special day great. I'll make sure I thank her properly when I see her next month for your shower."

Sawyer closed her eyes and listened to her mother talk. The lightness she'd felt after talking to Autumn steadily evaporated. She felt herself sinking again under that now familiar mountain of pressure and guilt.

• • •

Charles finally made it back to New York on Thursday, but his flight was delayed twice, and he didn't wind up getting all the way home to the apartment until sometime after 10 p.m.

He came in smelling like travel—stale coffee, hotel soap, chlorine-scented bath towels, and cigarette smoke. There was a chaotic, whirlwind energy about him that Sawyer hadn't expected; his presence immediately filled and took over the room.

He put his bags down in the tiny alcove of the entry hall and hugged Sawyer immediately, then reached into his inside jacket pocket and produced a glossy envelope of some sort.

"I promised you a surprise," he reminded her, and gestured to the couch.

She followed him and sat in the crook of the *L* in the couch, while he settled into one of the sides. He grinned, still holding the envelope, then slapped it down on the coffee table and slid it in her direction.

"Go on," he said. "Open it."

Sawyer glanced at him, her brow furrowed in puzzlement, and reached for the envelope. The outside of the envelope had the name of an airline on it, and inside, she found two round-trip tickets to Bermuda. The tickets were dated for the end of October.

"I was wrong," Charles said. "And I'm sorry. I shouldn't have given away the honeymoon money we'd been saving up without asking you. I was wrong and I wanted to make it up to you."

"I don't understand." Sawyer shook her head. "You booked us on a trip to Bermuda?"

"A honeymoon trip," Charles confirmed. "I also booked us into a resort—all expenses included."

He was excited, happy, triumphant.

She was confused.

"But I thought you put the money toward your mom's Visa bill . . . we don't have anything else . . . not to cover something like this . . ."

"Well, my parents and I talked, and moved some things around. My mom and dad actually suggested Bermuda—that's where they went on their honeymoon."

Sawyer stared at him, bug-eyed.

"What?" he nudged.

"I can't believe you did that."

"Aren't you happy?"

"No."

Now it was Charles's turn to look surprised. "Are you kidding? I can't tell if you're joking."

Sawyer was quiet. Charles shifted on the couch cushions, newly agitated.

"They're nonrefundable, and it was a lot of money. I can't believe you're not happy. You wanted a honeymoon. Now we don't have to wait another year or two."

"We've got bigger problems," she reminded him. "Problems we haven't even had a chance to sit down and talk about . . ."

He looked pained, but the surprise was gone from his face. "I know," he said. "Somehow things fell apart a little. But we can fix that. We've been spending too much time apart, so the solution seems simple: we spend some time together. I'll pay more attention, now that the case is nearly wrapped up."

She bit her lip and shook her head.

"But, Charles, there's so much more to it, too. All this time we've been spending apart . . . is also time we've been spending with . . . well, *other* people—"

"Look, I know it's been a shitty summer for us," he continued, cutting her off. "I know I let my job get in the way and things between us kind of snowballed. Looking back, I think I expected you to be impressed by how hard I was working . . . but I could see that you were annoyed instead. And then *I* was annoyed that *you* were annoyed—vicious cycle!

"It stressed me out to feel like I was constantly letting you down! And then, the humiliation to find out that you know about my parents' financial troubles. I admit that I reacted by doubling down and working even harder . . . avoiding things.

"But, Sawyer . . . I just want *so bad* to make it to this wedding. I can't imagine what it would do to my parents if we don't. They *love* you—you are already a member of the family.

"Going to Chicago and being apart put things into perspective for me. And I wish now, after this trip, that I could just take it back—all of it. This whole summer."

He paused and stared at her earnestly.

"Wouldn't you want to take this summer back if we could?"

She still couldn't tell if anything had happened with Kendra—in Chicago, or anywhere else. But she thought about the summer—*her* summer, with Nick.

"No," she said. "I wouldn't take it back."

Charles didn't reply right away. He looked at her for a long time with a serious, heavy expression. He looked defeated, beaten down.

"It's late," he said, when he finally spoke. "I'm exhausted."

He stood up from the couch to go, then stopped, and turned back around. He took a breath to speak, but nothing came out. He cleared his throat, and tried again.

"You know, I'm not an idiot," he said, finally.

She was silent for a moment, unsure what he meant by the comment. She thought of the evening she'd come home from Coney Island, her hair still damp from the shower at Nick's mother's house, smelling like a strange shampoo. She thought of the messages Charles had left on the answering machine while he was in Chicago . . . because she wasn't home to take his call.

"I know you're not an idiot," she agreed quietly.

"When it comes to us, I'm just trying to picture calling everything off," he said. "And . . . it's a lot, Sawyer. I would hope we could at least sleep on it."

He picked up his bags and carried them from the entry hall into the bedroom.

Sawyer remained on the couch, unmoving for a long time.

Eventually, she glanced across the room, to the kitchen, and to where the computer sat on the small desk, the screen black, filled only with the dim, hazy reflection of the amber-tinted streetlights outside the kitchen window. She hadn't had a chance to turn it on. Or to send a single message.

She got up from the couch and crossed from the living room to the kitchen, then stood in front of the computer. Her whole body was dying to turn it on, check her email. She knew Nick was somewhere on the other end, waiting.

She reached a hand to push the power button, but stopped when she pictured herself writing the email, an email she didn't feel she *could* write. What could she possibly say? She dropped her arm.

She glanced at the time. 12:07 a.m.

It was already Friday.

* * *

Somehow, Sawyer not only slept, but overslept.

She woke up with a jolt, filled with panic, adrenaline pumping in her veins, giving her a horrible clammy sensation all over. The panic had followed her out of a dream, into real life, and she could identify enough of it to understand that it had to do with being late for something, or missing something. But she couldn't discern whether it was a fear of being late for work, or else . . . the fact that she had not emailed Nick.

The bed next to her was empty. She rose in a haze of confusion, and found a doughnut—a maple bar from the deli on the corner—in the kitchen, along with a note.

> *I didn't want to wake you. I gotta shake off some of this travel stress by hitting the gym, but I promise I will get off work early today and take a real summer Friday and we can spend some time together and finish our talk and hopefully you'll hear me out.*
>
> *Love,*
> *Charles*

Sawyer read the note twice. After all that, Charles had gone right back to his old tricks. She began to realize that, if she stayed with Charles, she'd be in for a lifetime of notes, of him bailing whenever there was a difficult conversation to be had.

She stood there, still holding the note, but she wasn't really thinking about Charles. The panicked feeling she'd woken up with hadn't left her, and she realized it had everything to do with the fact that it was *Friday.* She was late for work. But most of all: *it was Friday, and she had not emailed Nick.*

She looked at the computer again.

She thought for a minute, realizing she'd have to do several things at once if she wanted to make it to work on time. She sprang into action. First, she pushed the power button on the computer. As the machine started up, she raced around, changing into a dress and flats and brushing her hair. She clicked to log in to AOL and brushed her teeth as the computer connected to the dial-up. Then, once online, she sat down at the computer desk and took a deep breath. She clicked on the icon to start a new email.

But then, as soon as she settled her fingers over the keys, she froze, stymied again.

She couldn't think of what to say.

The clock's ticking grew steadily louder as she sat unmoving, staring at the screen.

Finally, she rubbed her eyes and sighed in frustration.

She checked the time. She'd already taken too long. Now, she was sure to be late to the office. She turned the computer off, defeated, then gathered up her things to head out the door.

But as she slid her messenger bag over her shoulder, something dropped to the floor with a small metallic clatter. She looked down and froze, recognizing it immediately.

A subway token.

The subway token Nick had given her as a joke, that day by the fountain in Washington Square Park.

She knelt down and picked it up, staring at it, lost in thought. She remembered the smirk on his face and the sound of his voice, right before he'd tossed her the token. *I'll let you in on a little secret . . . coins don't decide anything,* Nick had said. *People do.*

Suddenly, Sawyer's heart was pounding, a fresh flood of adrenaline filling her veins. But this time, her panicked urgency was laced with excitement. She dropped her messenger bag on the kitchen floor and turned the computer back on, then sat. Her hands were shaking. This time, she typed fast. Her fingers fumbled at the keys; she had to keep deleting typos and retyping. But the message finally poured out of her.

> To: Nikolai70@aol.com
> From: Adventures_of_Tom@aol.com
>
> Dear Nick,
>
> I'm sorry I didn't send this sooner, and I understand if it's too late—or if you're angry and I've blown it and missed my chance—but I'll be ready and waiting outside with my bags packed at 2pm this afternoon if you'll come pick me up.
>
> I know what I want.
>
> I want to take the leap with you. Am I too late?
>
> Love,
> Sawyer

She reread the email just once, her eyes catching on the closing salutation, "Love."

As she clicked send, she felt that word in particular go, like releasing a bird, and she felt a sense of freedom spreading throughout her own body. It was the thing that had been missing, the thing that had been building up inside her, trapped, and sending it to Nick hadn't made her feel vulnerable at all; in fact, it had given her a curious sense of strength.

* * *

Once at the office, Sawyer's newfound sense of strength immediately began to dissipate. She was still full of energy, but excitement had steadily been converted into nail-biting suspense.

Nick might not even check his email before 2 p.m.

He might have spent Thursday feeling angry.

What should she do if he didn't write back?

To top it all off, there was little way to check her personal email at work. Johanna was atypically present and social. She'd left her office door open, and the way the cubicles were angled, Johanna had a direct eyeline to Sawyer's monitor screen. Even if Sawyer *could* figure out how to log in to AOL from her work computer, Johanna might see.

That morning was the longest of Sawyer's life. She'd had zero coffee, yet her brain was practically buzzing against her skull. She tried to organize the different ways the afternoon might play out in her mind. She'd told Nick she'd be ready and waiting at 2 p.m. Charles had promised to leave work at noon, and she hoped the window of time would give her a chance to talk to him in person, as opposed to leaving a note. She had no idea how Charles might react.

Either way, Sawyer was resolute.

* * *

Finally, at noon, Johanna donned her ritual Hermès and left, and Sawyer was free to go. She raced home, even running to catch the train with an air of desperation, as if the extra five minutes to wait for the next one meant death.

When she arrived at her building, she awkwardly blew past Mrs. Kallenbach and her beagle in the lobby, shouting an apology over her shoulder.

Sawyer made it upstairs and burst into her apartment, throwing her bag and keys on the floor. She ran straight for the computer, sticky with sweat, out of breath.

She logged on and waited impatiently through the static and squelch of the dial-up connecting, then clicked on her inbox.

There it was: a reply from Nick.

> To: Adventures_of_Tom@aol.com
> From: Nikolai70@aol.com
>
> Sawyer—
>
> To answer your question: It *IS* too late.
>
> For me, that is. I guess I've fallen. Pretty hard.
>
> I wanted to be pissed when you didn't get back to me last night. But all I felt was empty. So unless you have a way for me to travel back in time (which evidently involves a DeLorean and some technology that I'm pretty sure is fictional) and un-fall for you, I'm stuck.
>
> I will be there at 2pm to pick you up.
>
> Ditto,
> Nick

Sawyer read it twice. Her heart gave a squeeze and her chest felt tight, like her lungs had filled with too much air.

She let it sink in.

It wasn't too late.

She'd said she'd be ready at 2 p.m.—she needed to pack her things. She logged off and got up from the computer, then scrambled around the apartment, throwing together a weekend bag. Questions began to trickle into her brain as she sorted out what to bring. It dimly occurred to her that she didn't have a single thing in her life figured out beyond the weekend. She pushed these thoughts away. The first step in jumping off a cliff was jumping off a cliff.

Once her bags were all packed, she set them by the front door. She took a quick shower, changed her clothes, and tried to cool down by simply sitting on the sofa and taking a few deep breaths.

It was a quarter past one o'clock; Charles should be home any minute. She tried to come up with what she would say, and steeled herself for his reaction.

She got up from the sofa and paced the room.

She sat back down, and tried a few more deep breaths.

Any minute now, Charles would walk in that door. They would talk. She took another deep breath—

She jumped at the shrill ring of the telephone.

Sawyer stared at the phone itself for a minute, blinking dumbly at it like it was some kind of uninvited guest. The ring was so unexpected, and so unfamiliar sounding for some reason. There was a panicked wailing to the ring Sawyer had never noticed before. It rang several times before she was able to gather her wits and reach for it.

When she finally picked up the receiver, everything that had been turned upside down in her life was turned upside down once more.

30.

"Sawyer? Sawyer?" Kathy's voice rushed at her over the phone line. "Oh, thank heavens, honey, is that you?"

Kathy sounded odd; her voice warbled in a way that made Sawyer's stomach turn.

"I've been trying to call Charles at his office, but they told me he already left, so he must be on his way home to you . . ." She trailed off. There was a small choking sound.

"Kathy—what's wrong? What's going on?" Sawyer asked.

She heard Kathy make the choking sound again.

"Kathy, I'm here. Just take a breath and tell me when you're ready," Sawyer urged gently, but already her own heart was pounding and she could feel a cold tickle of sweat on her face and neck.

"It's his father . . ." Kathy finally got out.

Ed had suffered a heart attack and gone into massive cardiac arrest.

"I did all the things," Kathy half stated, half sobbed. "All the things they always tell you to do. I called 911, I did the rescue breathing, I got an ambulance, I got him to the hospital . . . but . . ."

"But what? But what?" Sawyer stammered, her limbs strangely light and bloodless, her jaw gone slack.

Kathy finally delivered the bottom line: It wasn't enough. The doctors had confirmed it. His heart had stopped working for too long.

"I thought because he's breathing, he'd be OK, but they say it's only the ventilator doing everything . . . he's not OK . . . they're saying he'll never be OK . . . he'll never wake up . . . they're telling me we'll have to decide about the ventilator . . ."

"Oh, Kathy," Sawyer said, barely able to push the words out, her throat was so tight.

Kathy proceeded to give Sawyer all the hospital information and a phone number for Charles to call when he got home.

"They promised he can dial that number and they'll page me," Kathy said. "I have to go . . . They just came up to me here at the nurses' desk and they're telling me I need to talk to someone and sign something. But I need to talk to Charles—you understand?" she said, letting out a muffled sob. "Oh, please—you understand. Can you tell him, Sawyer? Can you tell him to call me?"

Kathy sounded so small and young, like a lost child. Sawyer felt her own heart straining and wrenching in reaction.

"I understand, Kathy," Sawyer reassured her. "We'll get him on the line for you. I'm so sorry. I'm so, so sorry."

The line went dead.

Sawyer stood there for a moment, still holding the phone to her ear, listening to the dial tone, utterly numb.

• • •

Eventually the phone began to bleat with a busy signal and Sawyer put the receiver back into the phone's cradle.

The apartment suddenly felt empty. And quiet—*too quiet*. Sawyer crossed the room in a daze and sat back down on the sofa, thinking. She let her gaze move around the space, not really seeing anything until her eyes landed on her suitcases, packed and waiting by the door.

She flinched, remembering everything that had come before Kathy's phone call.

Then, just as abruptly, she heard Charles's key in the door.

He came in carrying the mail. He looked up and smiled to see Sawyer sitting on the sofa.

"All right! Let the summer Friday begin!" he said cheerfully, tossing the mail on a console table and setting down his messenger bag.

"Charles . . ." Sawyer said. Speaking was difficult; her chest was like a vacuum; her lungs felt empty, airless. "Something's happened."

31.

Charles stayed on the phone for a long time with Kathy.

Sawyer sat on the sofa, listening.

Something was hurting her, needling her, sharp and uncomfortable. She understood the pain was emotional, not physical. But it *felt* physical. Her heart was like a piece of paper, ripping into two halves.

I've been thinking, she'd told Nick. *I think maybe New York exists on multiple planes.*

She pictured Nick coming to pick her up.

She pictured Charles going to the hospital alone. Holding his sobbing mother as they signed paperwork, standing next to Ed's bed as the hospital workers somberly unhooked him from the machines.

She thought about that day in the park, Ed's trust in telling her their family troubles, his concern for his son's fear of making the same mistakes, his concern for his wife, wanting her to have everything she ever wanted, and his concern for Sawyer's happiness.

You're my family, too, you know, Ed had said.

She pictured Charles going to the hospital alone, until she really couldn't.

I guess it's a lucky thing I don't want you to be like anyone but yourself, Nick had said.

She glanced at the clock and saw that it was already five minutes to two o'clock.

Sawyer knew what she had to do.

She went to the bathroom and splashed some water on her face, then went to the bedroom and retrieved something from off the top of the dresser; she would need her ring to see Kathy. Then she quietly let herself out of the apartment, went downstairs, and sat on the stoop to wait.

It was hard not to think nostalgically about the last time she'd sat on the stoop waiting for Nick—the day of the lake.

She already felt the hole in her heart, despite the fact that he hadn't even pulled up yet.

• • •

Moments later, at two o'clock almost on the dot, the familiar shape of the old Mercedes-Benz appeared, turning onto the far end of the street. Music floated out the open windows as Nick pulled to the curb.

He emerged from the car with a wide grin spread on his face.

Sawyer was touched by the grin—by how sincere and hopeful and innocent it was. Not a grin you saw often on an adult, let alone on someone as sharp and cynical as Nick. For a fleeting second, Sawyer felt moved by the thought that what they'd had together had been very rare and utterly *real.*

But as he came around the driver's side of the car to the curb, the smile vanished, and Nick froze.

His eyes looked around the stoop for some sign of her bags, then searched her face for an answer. His eyes fell to her hand, the glint of her ring. Neither of them spoke a word, but Sawyer could see: he comprehended it all—everything.

She wasn't coming.

Nick studied her a moment. He raised his eyebrows.

Sawyer gave a small, terse, apologetic shake of her head. She felt her throat tighten and tears welling up in her eyes, hot, burning with salt.

She'd never seen him look so crushed. It felt unnatural, like she was seeing something she shouldn't see. The pain and betrayal in his expression was like a knife twisting in Sawyer's heart. She wanted to tell him her reasons why . . . and she already knew they didn't really matter. As he stood there, she watched as his wounded expression slowly hardened into something else.

He leveled his gaze to meet hers squarely, pursed his lips, and gave a single nod of acknowledgment.

Then he turned to get back in the car.

After that, Nick didn't make eye contact with her as he pulled away. The music was loud and he dropped his foot on the gas. In the next second, he'd whipped the Mercedes-Benz around the opposite corner of the street and vanished.

Sawyer stared after him. There was nothing to see. Only the empty street.

Something broke inside her. Her muscles gave way, her face crumpled, and she slumped onto the stone stairs of the stoop. She cried for a minute, her body racked with sobs, that tight feeling in her lungs and throat so acute she gasped for air and thought she might get sick on the stoop.

But in the next moment, Sawyer forced her feelings back down to the pit of her stomach. She panted until she could catch her breath, and forced herself to pull it back together.

When she was finally calm again, she breathed evenly until she could stand up from the stoop again. She smoothed down her skirt and hair, then wiped the tearstains from her face and composed herself.

Then, she turned to go back upstairs and give everything she could to help Charles through the death of his father, a man she had promised to love like family.

New York City

• • •

2001

32.

"Sawyer?"

Sawyer snaps to attention, and glances up to focus on the person standing in front of her desk. Her boss, Fiona, peers back at her with an expression of gentle concern, but with a friendly smile.

Sawyer realizes she's been doing it again: staring vacantly at a blank email message, trying to think of how to write what she wants to write, and failing.

She hurries to click the *X* and close the browser window, embarrassed. It's more of a reflex than anything else; Fiona is not the type to care whether or not Sawyer sends a personal email during work hours. Fiona doesn't care when the work gets done, only that it gets done, and gets done well.

"Sorry," Sawyer says. "What's up?"

"I was just talking to you about the launch space," Fiona says. She asks if Sawyer would like to leave early for the day and go check out the venue the marketing department wants to use for an upcoming book launch for one of the imprint's lead fall titles.

"It's an art gallery in SoHo," Fiona informs her, handing her a card with the address.

"Ha—clever," Sawyer agrees. The novel itself revolves around a set of eccentric characters in the New York art world.

"Is it *too* clever?" Fiona asks. "I don't think we want it to come off as parody or camp."

"No," Sawyer says. "Marketing must like the space for a reason, right?"

Fiona sighs. "They do. I think I'm always just more comfortable in a bookstore."

Sawyer laughs at this. "Makes sense. That's how we wound up here in the first place."

"Fair," Fiona agrees, also laughing.

"But I don't know," she adds after a minute, biting her lip. "I'm also worried it's too far downtown, and the tone is still wrong, considering . . ."

Sawyer understands.

"Everyone keeps saying the best way to support the city is to bring life back to the streets and businesses," Sawyer reminds her. "I think there's probably a lot of truth in that."

"You're right," Fiona replies. She smiles. "Do you want to go look at the space and tell me what you think? You don't have to, but I would love a second opinion, and I really value yours."

"Sure," Sawyer agrees happily. Fiona is always sincere with her praise.

"It's Friday, so if you want, maybe you can head over around lunchtime, and then just take off for the day?" Fiona suggests.

"OK—thanks," Sawyer says. "Will do."

• • •

She thinks about calling Autumn and asking her to meet up to check out the gallery together. Autumn's year in Japan led to an internship with a New York–based Japanese fashion designer; Autumn knows about all things arty in New York, and would be an excellent judge of the gallery space.

But Sawyer knows that Autumn's job has been extra stressful since the city made the solemn decision to cancel Fashion Week in the wake of the attacks. She doesn't want to bother her.

She imagines inviting Kaylee to go check it out—they've kept in touch. Ironically, they email each other more now than they did while working at the same company—oftentimes to compare notes and talk publishing gossip. But Sawyer already knows that Kaylee is still trapped under the watchful eye of Johanna, who would never allow her to slip out in the middle of the workday.

And so, a couple of hours later, when lunchtime rolls around, Sawyer grabs a quick hot dog from a vendor along the wall at the south end of Central Park before heading down to the gallery.

It's October.

The month of October still sometimes makes her think of her wedding. She'd pictured golden light, lukewarm temperatures, a placid breeze. But October wears many faces, of course. Today, it's overcast and there's a noticeable chill in the air. Leaves are already falling from the trees near the park. They clutter the sidewalks and gutters, dry and papery, crunching into powder underfoot. On the city streets, T-shirts have been replaced by sweaters and jackets.

Sawyer understands: in life, there are major events, and there are minor events.

Personal heartbreak, she knows, is a minor, rather unimportant event. Inconsequential compared to bigger, more permanent events, like a death in the family. And even more consequential compared to bigger events that affect people in greater numbers: A war. A famine. A terrorist attack. Compared to those things, personal heartbreak is hardly the end of the world.

Still, Sawyer can't help but think about the two girls who'd sat at the opposite end of her bench in the park a couple of weeks earlier, and about the conversation she'd overheard.

The attacks put things in perspective for him, the girl had told her friend about the ex who had gotten back in touch. *Made him think about what's important.*

Sawyer recognized some quality in the girl's voice as she continued to explain to her friend.

She'd said, *The thing is, I was thinking of him, too, when it happened. Wanting to know he was OK. And wanting to talk to him again, I guess.*

Later, Sawyer realized the quality she'd recognized in the girl's voice was a sincere and palpable longing, and the reason she recognized it was because she'd experienced the same thing.

She'd thought of Nick.

Two whole summers had passed since she'd seen him last. But when she stood watching the news coverage of the attacks, her mouth open in shocked disbelief, all Sawyer could think about was Nick.

And since then, the urge to connect with Nick has not gone away. She catches herself thinking about him, composing apologies to him in her head, even imagining the conversations they might have, the jokes he might make. But when she sits down to write to him, she also sees that look on his face, the day he'd come to pick her up, only to drive away alone. The crushed look, of total betrayal and disappointment.

I guess it says something if you were both thinking of each other, the friend had replied to the girl on the park bench.

She has no reason to believe Nick is thinking of her.

It has been two years.

Now, she finishes her hot dog and walks to the subway. The address on the card says "Prince Street," so she figures she'll take the N train over and down to SoHo.

She's a little bit nervous.

A friend who lives downtown told her that at Ground Zero, workers are still digging; the sounds of excavators and backhoes growl around the clock.

Sawyer agrees with what she said to Fiona: they shouldn't abandon these parts of the city. In the beginning, it was important to make way for the emergency workers, but now, a month later, it is important to bring life back to the downtown neighborhoods, little by little.

And yet, it still feels sacrilegious in some ways. The gravity of what has happened has left its mark. It's all around them, challenging them to be callous enough to go on living.

As Sawyer stands in the station waiting for the train, she stares at the "Missing" posters. When the train comes, they flutter violently in the whoosh and suction of the wind like a flock of panicked birds. A flurry of black-and-white bits: bright eyes and smiling teeth and bold-print letters *PLEASE* and *MISSING* and *CALL*.

When Sawyer steps onto the train, there are more posters inside. These aren't new; after September 11th, they seemed to pop up overnight, all over the city. Taped to streetlamps, to the trunks of trees. And here, now, taped to the tiled walls of the subway station, and on the train itself, taped to the windows, and over the Plexiglas panel that shields the MTA map.

The train slides into motion, and Sawyer steadies herself by grabbing the overhead rail, still staring at the posters. The most unusual thing about the posters is the fact that it is October, and they are *still here*—that they are still everywhere in New York. They always just appear, more of them daily, despite the fact that Sawyer has yet to witness someone in the act of taping them up.

Sawyer gazes at the individuals in the snapshots, holding babies, hugging dogs, wearing paper party hats, sipping rum drinks while on vacation in the Bahamas.

LAST SEEN HEADED TO WORK AT AON CORP, WTC 2, 8AM, SEPTEMBER 11

LAST SEEN OUT TO DINNER WITH FRIENDS, ELAINE'S, 9PM, SEPTEMBER 10

LAST SEEN LEAVING 242 E 75TH STREET AROUND 7:30AM, SEPTEMBER 11

It pains her to read these lines.

Hope is a wild thing, Sawyer thinks; with enough love, it will attach itself to the slimmest of chances, and hold on tight.

Sawyer can't help staring at them. All those faces. The faces of people someone, somewhere is longing to see, but more than likely already knows they never will. She feels the anguish of those who miss them, people who will never be the same.

The train reaches Fourteenth Street, slides to a stop at the station, opens and shuts its doors, then slides onward.

Still staring at the "Missing" posters, Sawyer feels a strange prickling at the back of her neck and turns. For a second, her heart stops.

And there—at the opposite end of the subway car—she sees an actual ghost, staring back at her.

33.

It's not a great day to go to Coney Island.

Even if September 11th hadn't left the city in a state of somber mourning, it wouldn't be an ideal time to go to Coney Island. It's October. The weather has turned. Everything will be shuttered, the boardwalk a ghost town.

Nick knows all this.

But he can't stop thinking about her. There are times when her memory is muted—a soft fuzz in the back of his brain, someone he used to know, something that once happened. And there are other times, when she blazes bright in the forefront of his mind, and provokes various different emotions, depending on the mood he's in.

On the days when he finds himself missing her, he goes for walks. He wanders, and goes to places they used to go. Sometimes, the magic of the memory is still there. Other times, the place looks smaller and more ordinary than it ever did before . . . and he tells himself: *This disappointment is good, the magic was never real, this is how you let go of her.*

He doesn't miss her all the time.

He doesn't think of her all the time, or even all that often.

But when the planes hit the towers, he immediately thought of her. Almost with a sense of panic—where was she, and was she OK? The idea that she could be anywhere near downtown didn't make rational sense, but he found himself stirred by an almost animalistic impulse to run and find her.

It was then that he realized: when your home is attacked, you suddenly have a very clear picture of what—*and who*—your home is to you.

It doesn't seem possible that she should still feel like home to him. But she does. He'd bought every edition of *The Paris Review* until he found the one with her poems. There was a line that haunted him—something about "a sense of you fills the void . . ."

> *like that time I found my misplaced house key*
> *in your mouth*

There are times when Nick feels like he can actually taste the metallic flavor of that key in his own mouth. A taste like iron, a taste like blood. A taste like home; the idea that memories taste like pennies.

It's not a great day to go to Coney Island, but Nick is going. He'll walk the boardwalk where they walked together, and along the sandy shore.

He waits for the N train patiently. There is a cellist playing on the platform, the first busker he's seen since the attacks. He pulls a twenty from his wallet and leaves it in the case.

The train pulls into the station. The doors burst open. People emerge. He waits for them to go their way, and steps on.

The fresh air will be good for him. The attacks had left everyone at home, glued to the television . . . and then afraid to go out during the weeks that followed. Guilty and afraid to talk and drink and laugh again. Or even enjoy a walk.

Perhaps he'll feel closer to her . . . or perhaps he'll feel she's moved even further away from him and is gone for good. Either would be a relief.

The train jerks forward, slows, then steadily builds up momentum. He is standing by the door, facing the windows. As the train zips forward, the windows darken and transform into a mirror. He sees his own face, the geometric shape of his features. Reflexively, he looks away.

His eyes stare into the train car, as reflected in the blackened window . . . and then he sees another familiar face, not his own.

He turns, and stares. He wears no expression on his face, beyond that of disbelief.

There she is, holding the overhead railing, studying the "Missing" posters with a furrowed, earnest brow: *Sawyer.*

He stares, still unwilling to believe she's real.

But it's her. It's her face. It's the compassion in her expression—a compassion he knows so well.

As though feeling his eyes on her, she turns, and looks in his direction.

They lock eyes.

The train continues to hurtle along, clacking and rattling, and sometimes screeching along the occasional bends of the track.

Nick feels a hole open up in time, and feels himself falling. He sees Sawyer, but he also sees her standing next to him, smiling and leaning on the railing of the Staten Island Ferry, the wind playing with her hair. He sees her sitting at his mother's kitchen table with wet hair, eating potato salad. He sees her diving into the lake and breaking through the surface, splashing and laughing. He sees her naked in his bed. He sees her kissing him in the claw-foot tub in the kitchen of his apartment. He sees her dancing with the roller skaters in Central Park, looking beautiful and throwing her arms and hips around with abandon, and bursting into embarrassed laughter as she sees him watching her.

Nick sees all this, and he can't look away.

And neither does Sawyer.

The train stops. The doors fly open. People get off and other people get on.

The train lurches forward again.

Neither of them has moved an inch. And neither of them has blinked.

Finally, Nick sees the trail of tears glistening on her cheeks, and he makes up his mind. As he steps toward her, she steps toward him.

People on the train are looking at them funny, staring. Nick doesn't care.

He feels something slick and warm turning cold on his face and reaches a hand to his cheek to discover, with surprise, that his own skin is wet with tears.

They meet in the middle of the train, and he folds her in his arms. It feels like coming home.

34.

"Where are you going?" Sawyer asks softly, speaking into Nick's shirt.

She doesn't want to let him go; doesn't plan to until she has to.

Nick is quiet for a moment, then gives what sounds like a cross between an embarrassed grunt and a laugh.

"Coney Island."

Sawyer stiffens with a mixture of bewilderment and amusement.

"Coney Island?" she repeats, almost in the same tone she used to use to tease him.

"Yep," Nick says, finally releasing her.

"Why are you going to Coney Island?"

"Honest?" Nick says, suddenly and very openly letting down his defenses. "I was going because I've been thinking about you."

"I've been thinking about you, too," Sawyer says.

Nick doesn't reply. The train stops at another station—Sawyer has already missed Prince Street. She doesn't care. She'll go to the gallery over the weekend; it can wait.

"So," she says. "Coney Island."

Nick wipes his eyes and reclaims his usual stoicism.

"Want to come?"

Sawyer gives him a silly smile, like she can't decide which of them is crazy. Finally, she twists her lips to one side and shrugs.

"Why not?" she says. "After all—you know what today is?"

"What?"

"*Friday*," she answers.

Nick looks at her with a bittersweet smile. His eyes grow slightly glassy again, but she can see he has made up his mind not to let another tear slip.

She grabs his hand and squeezes it.

"I'm in," she says.

At some point, they ride under the damage of Ground Zero, or at least very near it. Sawyer shifts uncomfortably. She doesn't want to think about it; she wonders if she's just being oversensitive and melodramatic, but just as she gets lost in this self-scolding thought, Nick grabs her hand, and she knows: he understands, and he feels the same. His touch brings her focus back to another moment.

He asks about Sawyer's work, and she proudly tells him Erin gave her a lead on an opening over at Random House, which she was bold enough to follow up on. She reports to a senior editor she really looks up to—Fiona—and often has lunch with Erin. She was recently allowed to acquire her first book, whereupon Fiona officially promoted her to assistant editor.

"'Assistant editor,'" Nick repeats appreciatively. "Sounds like you're moving up pretty fast."

"Maybe, maybe not." Sawyer shrugs. "But the big thing is: I don't sit around worrying about whether my boss hates me anymore. You can't imagine how liberating that is," Sawyer says, laughing.

"You're right; I can't," Nick says, still true to his own character. "Because I would never worry about something like that."

"Of course not," Sawyer says. She rolls her eyes. "But we can't all be *you*." She pauses reflectively for a moment, then says, "It's nice, though—

for a change—to ask myself who *I* like . . . who *I* want to work for . . . who *I* want to look up to."

Nick smirks. "It's like I always said it was, Sawyer . . . *you're* the one to impress. I'm glad you finally think so, too."

• • •

At last, they reach the end of the line, and the N train comes to a stop at Coney Island.

Sawyer is shocked by how empty the streets are. The parking lot full of picnic benches outside Nathan's is utterly empty, save for a handful of strutting pigeons, and a man bundled into a sleeping bag on a bench in one far corner.

They reach the boardwalk. Its wooden planks are gray and pale as whale bones, and mostly devoid of people. Only a few of the restaurants and snack shops are open, the workers within mostly cleaning and idly listening to a local radio station to keep from getting too bored.

Nick points across the boardwalk, to one of the benches facing out to the water.

"Sit for a while?" he asks.

"You mean—you don't want to go swimming?" Sawyer jokes.

"Please don't dare me," Nick replies. "I haven't changed *that* much."

Sawyer laughs and follows him over to the bench. They sit.

It's a long stretch of sand between the boardwalk and the water's edge, but they stare into the distance at the waves, which make a pleasant sound as they lazily roll onto the shore. Without the summer sun, the water is a flinty gray.

Sawyer shivers a little.

"Here," Nick says, starting to take off his coat.

"No, no," Sawyer refuses, insistent. "But . . ." She scoots closer.

He understands, letting her scoot so they are close enough to just touch.

They sit like that for a while, both of them at peace, staring at the water, breathing in time with the waves.

"I hope you're still writing," Nick says.

Sawyer smiles. "I have a book of poems coming out this fall," she replies shyly.

"A book? Wow," Nick says. "That's incredible, Sawyer."

"It's a small literary press," she says. "I was pretty excited to get the news they had accepted my collection. I was counting the days. But I guess I haven't thought about it much since everything that happened."

Nick shakes his head. "This is when people need poetry the most," he says.

"I guess you're right," Sawyer agrees.

"I'm always right."

They exchange a smirk.

Sawyer asks him about his music.

"I'm finally putting a little money into it," he says. "You know . . . recording things."

"That's great," Sawyer says, enthusiastic.

"I know I was kinda cynical about shelling out for studios and recording time before. It seemed like getting your hopes up to be crushed. But after that summer . . . I guess something changed." He pauses and then adds, "I decided it's OK to care about things."

They fall back into silence for a few moments.

"You know," Sawyer finally ventures. "I still think of you on summer Fridays. I'll wake up and realize what day it is, and part of me still wishes I were spending it with you."

Nick turns his head to look at her and she meets his gaze with a long look of her own, just as they used to do.

"Me, too," he says finally.

They look back to the water.

"That day . . ." Sawyer begins, and finally explains why she didn't go away with him that day he came to pick her up, how her heart was breaking but she had a clear idea of why she couldn't go, what had happened, and why it changed everything in the blink of an eye.

His jaw clenches. She can see a flicker of anger in his eye as she talks. She almost stops at one point—it is clear that part of it is still raw. She feels like she is inflicting the hurt on him all over again.

"I figured it was something like that," Nick says, when she's done explaining. He pauses, then adds, "I was still mad for a long time afterward, of course."

Sawyer nods, understanding.

She doesn't state the obvious—that she feels a piece of Nick in all of it: the way she's taken charge of her career, the pride she takes in her writing . . . even the decision she ultimately made that day.

She feels him looking at her now. She sees he is looking specifically at her hands, and her bare ring finger.

"No ring," Nick says.

"No. No ring."

He nods, his jaw clenching again. "You were always way too good for him, anyway."

"I don't know about that," she says, thinking back over the summer she spent mostly with Nick, a man who was *not* her fiancé.

"I do," Nick disagrees. "I remember the night we went to sushi, the night of my gig. The way he looked at Kendra. All I could think was what a jackass he was to not know what he had."

In the days following Ed's passing, Sawyer had remained by Charles's side—as a friend. When they finally officially called off the wedding, it had come as a relief to them both, and they'd sat down and had a longer, more open talk than they'd ever had while engaged. Charles had admitted that something *had* happened with Kendra. He skirted around the word "affair," but it was clear that their involvement had been sexual.

By then, all Sawyer could feel was relief—relief to know her paranoia wasn't unfounded. In all other ways, she felt strangely serene. She nodded and listened sympathetically, letting Charles explain about how he wasn't seeing Kendra anymore, but how at the time she was the only one who could truly understand the pressure he'd been under with the case.

Holding Charles's hand through his father's death had reminded Sawyer of the days when they'd made a good, steady team in college, and how deeply she cared for Charles . . . but also how this was not the same thing as love, or lifelong passion. They both understood this now, and were happier for it.

Kathy slowly accepted it in her own time. Sawyer knew she would always have a special place in Kathy's heart—because Sawyer had known and loved Ed—but likewise understood when she gradually, gracefully, began to hear from Kathy less and less often.

"You didn't deserve that," Nick says now.

She knows he means Charles and Kendra. She shrugs.

"Maybe," she agrees. "But I went and fell deeply and irredeemably in love with someone else."

Nick turns his head to regard her, and they lock eyes again for a long, intense moment. She can tell the words mean something to him. She wonders if they mean something to him *now*.

The bitter flicker of anger she'd seen in his face while she'd explained what happened the day he came to pick her up had been revealing. She had thought about contacting Nick—*a million times!*—after she and Charles had called things off properly. She'd danced on a knife-edge: whether it was braver of her to reach out to him, or if it would have been rubbing salt in the wound . . . too little, too late. An intrusion. An offense.

Or perhaps she was simply being a coward, afraid of what the devastation that total rejection from Nick might do to her.

The flicker of anger—tiny as it was—suggests that she was right to fear she'd wounded Nick too deeply that day on the stoop; he'd carried that anger a long time. But recent events have softened people, and she wonders if perhaps it has softened his anger enough to open a door again, even just a crack.

She opens her mouth to raise the question, not really sure how to word it, but before she can speak, the moment is interrupted by a digital ringing. Nick leans away from her to reach into his pocket. He produces a cell phone.

When he answers the call, Sawyer can hear the friendly softness in his voice, and realizes he's talking to a woman. He explains that he went to Coney Island, and on his way, ran into an old friend.

"No, I haven't forgotten about our date," he says. "I just . . . I don't know, felt like going to Coney Island. But I haven't forgotten. I'll be there soon."

He turns away from where Sawyer sits on the bench.

"OK . . . Yeah . . . Love you," he says quietly into the phone. "See you soon."

When he hangs up, he sees Sawyer looking at him.

She smiles at him, a genuine, heartfelt smile, but also a little bittersweet.

He holds up the cell phone and points at it.

"I guess nowadays we all have one of these obnoxious things," he says.

"Yes," she agrees. She'd resisted for a bit, too, but finally got a cell phone about a year ago.

"Sorry for the interruption. I had to get that."

"I understand."

He remains sitting on the bench, but she can feel: he is restless now. He'd rather be somewhere else.

"It sounds like you need to get going," she says.

"Oh." He glances again at the phone still in his hand, like he'd already forgotten he was holding it. "Yeah. I guess I do."

A few seconds of silence pass.

"Want me to walk you back to the train?"

She shakes her head. "Nah. I think I'd like to sit here for a bit longer. It was a long ride to get out here. I'm not ready to go back yet."

"Well, then . . ."

He gets up. She rises politely. They stand from the bench and face each other.

"I guess . . ." Nick starts to say, carefully trying to find the words. "I guess this is goodbye."

She nods. "This is much better than our last one. I'm still sorry about that."

She catches one last glimpse of the flicker of anger, but sees him push it away.

"I'm glad we got a do-over," he agrees.

They look at each other. She isn't sure if she should hug him. After the phone call, she suddenly feels sheepish. He smiles at her, a sad smile. She can feel her eyes getting glassy.

"Hey. Something's missing," Sawyer says.

"Missing?"

"Like, from our encounter. Something's missing."

Nick doesn't reply, unsure what she's thinking of.

"Hey—I know what it is."

"What?"

"Seagull poop."

He laughs. "I guess that means no luck today."

She shakes her head. "You don't believe in luck. Remember? You called seagullshit on that theory."

They laugh together.

"Well . . . I'm glad we ran into each other," Nick says.

"Yeah," Sawyer agrees.

Neither of them moves to hug or embrace in any way. It's almost as if they are afraid to touch again . . . of what it would make them feel, or what it might make them feel they've lost.

"OK, bye."

"Bye."

Nick starts to walk away, then pauses, and turns back.

"Hey," he calls.

Sawyer turns to look.

"It *was* luck," Nick insists. "I *was* lucky. Lucky to have had that time with you, even if I couldn't keep you."

Sawyer gazes at him. Finally, she smiles.

"Ditto," she says.

He grins one last time, and goes.

She watches him start to walk away, but feels her eyes watering up, until the image of him walking away dances a bit. She turns back around before a tear spills over, grabbing her cheek with a cold hand. She sits back down on the bench, alone.

35.

It's cold and unpleasant.

She is shivering, but she is intent on staying there until she can't stand it, memorizing the gray of the sky and the sand, the rough squall of the waves. Coney Island was such a bright, colorful place when she and Nick visited it two summers ago, in the full heat of July. But the derelict, abandoned version of it that is all around her now suits her mood better.

She feels strangely stunned, like she just got everything she wanted, and somehow walked away empty-handed.

She knows she should be grateful. Things went as well as could be expected. She got to apologize. They got to say their goodbyes in a dignified way.

The flicker of anger she'd seen ripple through his features when they talked about their previous goodbye was to be expected. *More* than expected, in fact. It could have been so much more than a flicker. Nick was truly gracious about it.

And the fact that he'd taken a phone call on his cell, that he ran off to go meet someone . . . she isn't entitled to any reaction at all to that.

But still.

A murky disappointment sinks into her brain. A sensation of hollowness, an emptiness she has not felt before.

She stares at the steely horizon of the Atlantic, listening to the frantic white noise of the waves tumbling the gray sand, feeling bereft, adrift.

Time passes. Her fingers become so cold she can't feel them. She should get up and make her way back to the train. There is probably a car waiting with open doors in the station and she can at least sit inside it and attempt to warm up while she waits.

But another fifteen minutes pass, and she still hasn't moved.

Part of her feels like if she gets up and leaves, she is agreeing to forget about her summer Fridays with Nick, that she is acquiescing to let them become just another memory of middling importance in the grander scheme of things.

She sits, and continues to study the distant waves.

Then, unexpectedly, she hears a noise.

Something is beeping. The cell phone in her bag. She pulls it out and flips it open.

"1 message" the screen says, with the outline figure of an envelope.

It's a text.

No one she knows sends texts.

She clicks the button to read it.

> For the record, I still prefer face-to-face, but I'll resort to this if I have to.

Sawyer frowns. She feels stunned again, but a different kind of stunned.

After a moment or two, a slow smile breaks over her face. She works the buttons to text back a reply.

> S: Hey! How do you have my number?
>
> N: I have my ways.
>
> N: I tracked it down a while back.

S: But you never used it.

N: I'm using it now.

Her brow furrows as she processes the information. She wants to ask more questions, but this would be tedious; Nick has already given her the most important answer. He tracked her number down a while back.

S: I see. And what are you using it for?

N: To tell you I was right

S: About what? (this time)

N: That after meeting you, my mom would ask about you every time I saw her.

The phone call he had taken. She revisits it in her head. He hadn't spoken in Russian. It occurs to her that he *wanted* her to have the impression he might be talking to someone else. A flood of relief surges into her heart.

S: Aha . . . So that wasn't just some chick on the phone

N: A wise person once told me you shouldn't call them "chicks"

S: Are you saying I'm right???

N: You might be right.

S: "Might be"? I guess I'll have to settle for that.

N: As good as it gets.

Sawyer feels her lips curling in a happy smirk, giddy to sink back into their old routine. But at the same time, an inkling of sweet despondence sets in. She isn't ready for this exchange to end again.

S: You're at your mom's now?

N: I had a date to visit her

S: Tell her I say hi.

N: Tell her yourself.

Sawyer freezes, wanting to be sure she is reading things right.

N: It's Friday. What are you up to?

As she thinks of how to respond, she glimpses a familiar figure: the old man covered in green face paint and tinfoil that she and Nick saw during her first visit to Coney Island. He roller-skates past her, music blaring from his battery-operated boom box. *Now, there's a guy who plainly remembers our alien-fish ancestors*, Nick had said at the time. *He's overdue for a visit home.*

Sawyer grins, impatient to share news of the sighting.

But before she can work the keys, her phone beeps with a new text.

N: Don't make me get the chimp in a tuxedo on the case.

A bark of laughter escapes her lips, but softens into a tender sob.

S: No one says no to a chimp in a tuxedo, I hear

N: It's true

Sawyer stands, and pulls her bag onto her shoulder. Tears are falling from her eyes again, but now the tears are different; they are tears of happiness, the tears of someone who has been on a long odyssey, and is finally walking the last steps that will take her home.

She taps in one more message, and clicks send.

S: I'm coming.

N: I'll meet you halfway.

Acknowledgments

I feel profoundly lucky to have worked on this book with the amazingly positive, sharp, and absolutely lovely Maya Ziv. I am grateful also for the welcome extended by John Parsley, whose astute insight made me feel confident that *Summer Fridays* would be in excellent hands with Dutton. My thanks to Lexy Cassola for additional shepherding; to Caroline Payne, Sarah Thegeby, Stephanie Cooper, and Amanda Walker for the magical work that is marketing and publicity; to Jillian Fata for championing foreign rights; and humble thanks to Christine Ball and everyone at Dutton in general. I am also grateful for the work of Vi-An Nguyen and Enya Todd with regard to cover design, and Eileen Chetti for copyediting.

My thanks to Liz Parker of Verve, who is the reason I landed at Dutton, and my thanks to Noah Ballard, who is the reason I landed at Verve. Agents make it all happen.

My immense gratitude to the early readers of this manuscript, and friends who have offered encouragement (not to mention a wellspring of sanity) in my life as a writer.

Jayme Marigza-Yeo, you are the most supportive and wise friend any living creature can ever have.

Thank you to Autumn Roe, who brings actual rainbows with her wherever she goes, even in the middle of a snowy winter in Central Park.

Kenny "Freakin" Fragas, I'm so lucky to have your creative take on all things! Throwback thanks to those long-ago days you read my early work on the Muni.

A huge thank-you to Maegan L. Johnson, lover of love stories, who offered great feedback and much encouragement to try something new in attempting this novel. Go Valley Vikings!

Julia Masnik, Sawyer's favorite author being McCullers is an homage to you. You are the wind beneath my pterodactyl wings. Thank you for always letting me hit you up for your opinion.

My thanks to Fil Lorenz, aka selmerguy, for your detail-oriented feedback and charming rapport with seagulls. Stay classy.

I'm so grateful for Amy Poeppel, who read an early draft and offered a ton of support, from blurbs to introductions to just generally being a marvelous, witty, and warm fellow author.

Thank you to Brendan Jones, for all the days when we read multiple drafts of each other's work and kept good company. And for the Oggsford days. B-Dawg and J-Dawg forever; I won't forget.

Olga Zilberbourg, thank you for your generous, thoughtful read, and for the Russian language edit!

Thank you to Elizabeth Romanski for not only being a friend, but also being the beautiful voice of many of my audiobooks.

Many thanks to Melissa Rindell for reading lots of drafts of lots of things over the years, and for sharing her work in return.

And, of course, thank you to my family, and in particular, Arthur and Sharon.

About the Author

Suzanne Rindell is the author of four novels: *The Other Typist*, which has been translated into twenty languages, *Three-Martini Lunch*, *Eagle & Crane*, and *The Two Mrs. Carlyles*.